UP AGAINST IT

UP AGAINST IT

M. J. LOCKE

A TOM DOHERTY ASSOCIATES BOOK

NEW YORK

This is a work of fiction. All of the characters, organizations, and events portrayed in this novel are either products of the author's imagination or are used fictitiously.

UP AGAINST IT

Title spread art courtesy of NASA / JPL-Caltech / University of Arizona

Edited by Patrick Nielsen Hayden

A Tor Book
Published by Tom Doherty Associates, LLC
175 Fifth Avenue
New York, NY 10010

www.tor-forge.com

Tor® is a registered trademark of Tom Doherty Associates, LLC.

Library of Congress Cataloging-in-Publication Data

Locke, M. J.
    Up against it / M. J. Locke.—1st ed.
        p. cm.
    "A Tom Doherty Associates book."
    ISBN 978-0-7653-1515-1
    1. Life on other planets—Fiction.   I. Title.
    PS3612.O249U7 2011
    813'.6—dc22

                                    2010036538

First Edition: March 2011

Printed in the United States of America

0   9   8   7   6   5   4   3   2   1

FOR LENELLE CITTADIN

There isn't room for eccentricity in an asteroid community. When you are not working your freezing, grimy ass off out on a mining stroid—or in the refinery—or snatching a bite of vat-grown chow or a few hours' sleep (or if you are lucky, some sweaty, low-gee booty), you are crawling around the habitat machinery, scraping knees and knuckles, replacing broken parts and plugging leaks. Because that is what keeps you alive.

Everyone thought things would change when they brought the bugs Up, a few decades back. But they are not the magic medicine everyone thought they would be.

Make no mistake; without them, the population beyond lunar orbit would be a tiny fraction of what it is today. Bugs build and maintain the primary structures, create food and clean air and water from the raw materials we provide.

But they can't do everything, nor be everywhere. Fact is, they are sensitive to temperature and pressure changes, they eat a lot of fuel, and they are *ass* to program properly. Keeping them primed and ready to do what you need takes a small army.

The short version? You want to live, Upside; you work very hard, all the time, and you play by the rules. Don't waste time, don't waste resources, and *especially* don't mess with the bugs.

—From *Downsider Upside,* Lesley Marcus Vaughn (New York, 2389)

UP AGAINST IT

1

So here they all were, Geoff and his three best buddies, way too early one Tuesday morning, in the spinning habitat city of Zekeston that lay buried a kilometer below asteroid 25 Phocaea's rocky surface: about to mess with the bugs.

Geoff and Amaya stood in the shadows near the university plaza. Kamal crouched behind a low wall on the mezzanine overhead. Kam's job was to call the op and film it. Ian sat blogging about rocketbikes at a nearby coffee kiosk on the edge of the plaza, eating a pastry and keeping an eye out for any city or university cops that might show up.

Geoff checked his heads-up. The timing had to be just right. A few seconds off in one direction and eight months' effort would be wasted. A few seconds off in the other and they would all go to jail. His heart was pounding harder than it ever did when he was out in the Big Empty, racing his rocketbike.

His fear wasn't of getting caught. No; what scared him was that in two minutes the whole solar system would know whether it would all pay off. All those hours of isolation; the sneaking around behind their parents' and teachers' backs; the endless succession of foul smells, burns, and stains that had ruined their clothing and scarred their hands—the risks he'd pressured his buddies to take, to help him do this—if this didn't work, he'd look like a fool.

Nearby, a handful of drowsy, puffy-eyed university students slumped on plaza benches. Class scrolls lay inert, half-furled in their laps, blinking unnoted. Pastries and bulbs of coffee or tea cooled beside them on the benches. The air was chilly and still, as always. Birds and ground squirrels— refugees from Kukuyoshi, the habitat's arboretum—snatched crumbs at their feet.

The fountain that dominated the plaza's center was called El Dorado. It was a tumble of rhombic, trapezoidal, and rectangular gold and platinum blocks jutting up at various angles in a metallic bloom. As usual, the fountain was turned off, though the toroidal pool at its base contained brackish liquid with bits of debris floating in it. The sour smell of spent assembly fluid wafted across to Geoff and Amaya in their hiding place. It seemed really noticeable to him, but no one in the plaza seemed bothered by it.

Kam radioed them. "A minute-fifteen before the cameras go live. We need to move now. Amaya, Geoff—you set?"

He and Amaya exchanged a glance, nodded to each other. "Set."

Kam's voice whispered the countdown. "Ten seconds . . . five . . . two, one. Amaya, go!"

Amaya strode into the plaza, not glancing up at Kam's shadowed spot, nor over at Ian. Kam said in his ear, ". . . two, one. Geoff, go!"

Geoff crossed the plaza, about six paces behind Amaya and to the left. He might as well have been invisible. Amaya had dressed up in Downsider chic: bustier, translucent beaded overshirt, short-shorts, lace-up sandals; makeup, hair, neon animated tattoos that ran the length of her exposed flesh; the works.

She transected the plaza, headed away from the fountain, pulling the college students' gazes along in her wake. Geoff reached the fountain. He tossed the packet of triggering proteins he held into the dirty water. Then he headed for the coffee shop. No one seemed to notice; everyone's gaze was on Amaya as she strode breezily away.

Geoff sat down next to Ian at a small table near the plaza. His heart beat so hard it hurt. He tried to catch his breath and as nonchalantly as he could, turned to look.

Some guy had fallen in step with Amaya, trying to chat her up.

"Shit!" Geoff started upright, but Ian grabbed his wrist.

"Relax, doof. We're chill."

Geoff forced himself back down. Ian was right. Amaya shed the college student—smiling with a shrug, turning to walk backward as she made a reply, then spinning again to continue at a swift, casual pace—without even breaking stride. She exited the plaza.

Geoff checked his waveface again. The blackout had just ended—the "Stroider"-cams were now live. It was close. He couldn't tell whether she had been on-scene or not when the cameras came on.

"Stroiders" was a reality-broadcast back to Earth. Up to two billion Downsiders tuned in to see what the good people of Zekeston were up to at any given moment. The "Stroider"-cams made it hard to be sneaky. But there were always ways to get around the cams. You just had to put your mind to it.

Sneaky? They had been downright paranoid.

Geoff had done the bug programming. That was how it had all started. In Honors Programmable Matter last semester—the only class he'd ever done truly well in; the only one he cared about—he learned that assemblers were made from complex silica-based molecules.

You manipulated assemblers by washing them with certain chemicals in set sequences. In response, they gathered all the right molecules trapped in their suspension fluid—a silicone-ethanol colloid with metal salts and other stuff—to build what you wanted. The resulting tiny machines burned alcohol and excreted tiny glass pellets that under the right conditions clumped together and made what everybody called bug grapes. Geoff had always wondered what those lumps were at the seams and joints of the utility piping. Yep, they were bug turds. Spent bug juice contained lots of these glass pellets, which ranged in size from marbles to grains of rice. Which was why bug juice spills sparkled under the lights so beautifully. He had always wondered about that, ever since he was a little kid. Who would have thought spewage could be beautiful?

So yeah, it had been the glass turds that had given him the idea. Assemblers shit glass turds! How cool was that? It was a shame to let them go to waste. But to pull this off, they needed real bug juice. Since the good stuff was closely monitored, they would have to steal used juice, and see if they could distill it down and make it usable for their purposes.

Amaya had figured out how to tap the assembler discharge lines. They ran inside the maintenance tunnels that fed down the spokeway utility lines into the Hub. She had enlisted the help of her boyfriend, Ian, and they had spent two months collecting, distilling, and priming depleted bug juice until it was at sufficient strength to handle Geoff's programming. The resulting juice was feeble, but Geoff had figured how to make it work. (In a lab. If he had gotten all of the glitches out of the protein code. If, if, if.)

While all this was going on, Kam had been making a detailed study of all the mounted cams, rovers, and motes in the university plaza. He calculated camera angles, paths, and ranges of view, based on their technical specifications, and created a surveillance shadow map. His efforts had been aided by a field trip their class had made up to the surface of 25 Phocaea to visit the "Stroiders" broadcast studios.

Two half-hour "Stroiders" blackouts occurred every day, to give Zekies small islands of privacy in their lives. One occurred at two a.m. and the other cycled between three a.m. one day and one a.m. the next. The rest of the time, Zekeston's citizens were under scrutiny by billions of people they would never meet. Mostly, it was just an annoyance that everyone put up with that resulted in a stipend in everyone's bank account every month. It was only when you were trying to be sneaky that it mattered when and where the "Stroiders" shadows were.

The main way "Stroiders" got their Zekeston data feed was from the stationary cams and the rovers, but when something important happened, "Stroiders" motes typically showed up, a hazy glamour emitted from jets in the assembler dispersal piping. You couldn't hide from motes. So next Kam did a science fair project: mote density versus "Stroiders" audiovisual resolution.

He sampled motes around the city and compared them to what people saw, Downside. (Phocaeans could not experience "Stroiders" the way Downsiders back on Earth did—as a fully realized, 3D virtual world—but they could sample it in video in small snatches, by submitting a request to the library and waiting a month.) The lowest mote concentrations in the university plaza typically occurred between four-thirty and eight a.m. on Tuesdays. This pinned down the time and place for the event. (He also got an A+ on the project, and second place in the senior-level information systems category.)

It was sheer serendipity that the best time to stage the event turned out to be the morning after high school graduation. The project became their secret graduation present to one another.

Over the past week and a half, they'd been spiking the fountain with bug juice. They had agonized over how to get the bug juice into the fountain without alerting everyone—"Stroider"-cams might black out periodically, but the plaza's security cameras didn't. And there were security guards and scary sorts prowling the nearby Badlands. Geoff and the others had no way of knowing when the plaza was being watched. So during one of the nighttime blackout periods, Ian had climbed down into the maintenance tunnels from an out-of-the-way entry port, made his way to beneath the plaza, inserted tubing into the water line for the fountain, and piped the juice in. If the university students or staff had noticed that the fountain was leaking, no one said anything about the leak, nor about any strange smells emanating from the pool. When the dribble stopped, Ian went back into the maintenance tunnel and removed the tap.

Geoff's final task was the riskiest. They had a plan to avoid the camera, but there would be people in the plaza even at that hour. So Amaya had volunteered to be a distraction. She wasn't into the whole clothes, tattoos, and makeup thing, and Geoff was dubious about whether it was a good idea. But when she had shown up in Downsider drag this morning, Geoff and the others had barely recognized her. ("Say one word," she'd warned them fiercely, "and I will pound you.")

Geoff's biggest worry was that her path was longer than his, and she might not exit the plaza before the "Stroider"-cams went live. The cops would be all over those "Stroider" broadcasts to see who might have done it, and Geoff didn't want their attention directed to Amaya. If anyone would take the heat for this, it should be him.

Geoff radioed Kam. "Well?"

Kam checked his own wavespace display. "Yep. Just." They were careful not to say too much, in case their broadcasts were being monitored.

She wouldn't show up on the monitors. She'd gotten out clean. Geoff let out the breath he'd been holding, and drew another one in. He leaned on the table, trying to see what was going on without obviously staring at the fountain. Instead, he and Ian linked wavefaces and pretended to look at pictures of rocketbikes.

Then he saw Ian tense. Geoff shifted in his chair and looked at the fountain, trying to act casual. He couldn't believe anyone watching was going to buy their performance. Then he stopped caring.

Something was moving in the water. First a bubble, then two. He held his breath. Soon the water was boiling and seething like a live thing. The students sitting near the fountain began to notice. They scrambled back, scattering coffee bulbs. Flocks of panicked birds rose from their perches on the fountain blocks as dark shapes began to emerge from the surface of the water. A hand bone here. A foot bone there. Part of a skull. Teeth in a jawbone. A spine and pelvis.

The shapes began assembling themselves into skeletons. Most had a hunched, gnomish look. One or two were deformed, with feet where their hands should be, or heads growing out of their butts. Geoff frowned. That glitch again. He thought he had fixed it.

Soon whole skeletons were lurching up and collapsing back into the brew. The glitch seemed to have fixed itself. Good. Soon there were a dozen. Twenty at least!

For a minute Geoff thought that would be all they'd do, and that was dramatic enough. But then they began climbing out onto the tiles of the plaza. They joined bony hands and began to dance. The skeletons made a line and curved through the plaza. Students stepped back and watched as they skipped and capered and leapt, banged on their arms, rib cages, and thighbones, waved their bony arms. They didn't sing—they couldn't;

Geoff didn't even know where to start, to program larynxes and lungs—but they sure could shake their bones.

They didn't last long. They were made of spent juice and glass beads, after all, spun together by weak silica tendrils. The first shattered as its dancing and banging and clattering brought it in contact with a corner wall. Soon another burst. Even their own hands or elbows or knees were enough to cause them to fall to pieces. One burst in front of Geoff and Ian, who leapt back, knocking over their chairs—startled despite themselves. The air filled with clear, tan, and silvery beads and spidery strands of silicone.

In moments the skeletons had all burst. It was over. The plaza tiles were coated in tiny beads.

Geoff realized how many people had gathered. Someone started clapping and laughing. Others joined in—but he could see irritation on some faces, and hear grumblings, and that had its own rewards. People began to disperse, carefully stepping among the beads. One young man slipped and fell. "Stroiders" camera motes had come, too, just as Geoff had hoped, and now swirled in the air currents like fairy dust, smelling of ozone and faint, bitter mint.

Ian pressed his hands over his mouth. "Cool . . ." Geoff looked over and grinned. "*Domo*, doof."

"Come on. Time to spin the sugar." Ian grabbed his sleeve and dragged him into the plaza. They dashed down the lane to meet Kam and Amaya, slipping and sliding on bug grapes.

Geoff desperately wanted to go home and watch the news. But not today. Today was the big ice shipment, and nothing—not even Geoff's bug-turd art obsession—could be allowed to interfere with the ice harvest.

They got separated at the spokeway elevators. Amaya squeezed into a waiting elevator, and then Ian, who was holding her hand, but Geoff and Kamal stood one layer too far back in the crowd when the warning lights went off.

"You'll miss the harvest!" Ian said.

"We'll take the stairs!" Geoff shouted, as the doors closed. He and Kam headed off at a run. "Meet you in the Hub!"

Zekeston was a fat, spinning habitat wheel buried below the surface of the asteroid. The city's spin generated a gravity gradient, which ranged from barely a thousandth of a gee in the Hub to about three-quarters of Earth's gravity at the outermost level. The university was on that highest-gee bottom level. That meant that the first fifty levels of Geoff and Kam's travel to the Hub were a brutal climb up the dual stairway that wound around the inner walls of Eenie Spoke. Geoff dodged around other climbers with an "On your left!" here and an "Excuse me!" there. Kam came right behind. They were gasping for air before they were a third of the way up, despite the light tailwind wafting up from the lower levels, which dried their sweat and boosted them up toward the Hub.

Zekeston used to be called Ezekiel's Town, but it wasn't just *one* wheel within a wheel. It had twelve spokes that connected twenty-five nested wheels, stacked one inside the next, to the Hub. Each wheel held ten stories, for a total of two hundred fifty levels. Upspoke, where gravitation approached Earth's, surfaces were flat—walkable and/or rollable. The lower-gee levels near the Hub were honeycombed tubes separating webbed open spaces. As the boys gained altitude the climb got easier, and by the time they'd reached Level 150, they began to make better time. At Level 80, the low-gee ropeworks appeared and they lofted themselves up into it. Thereafter they made swift progress. Finally, they launched themselves out into the microgee Hub.

The Hub was a sphere nearly a quarter kilometer in diameter. The entries to the twelve spokeways ran around the Hub's girth: a ring of big holes, each with its own lift shaft, a dual spiral staircase and ropeworks visible inside. The Hub also housed YuanBioPharma's main research facility and manufacturing plant; the main city hospital, Yamashiro Memorial; and the city assemblyworks.

Ian and Amaya stood in the queue for the big lifts up to Phocaea's surface. They faced away from each other. Amaya had her arms crossed, and Ian's jaw jutted out. Geoff exchanged a look with Kam as they crossed the Hub's ropeworks toward their friends.

Geoff groaned. "Another fight."

Kam rolled his eyes. "Why don't they break up and have done with it?"

Geoff said, "I don't want to listen to them bickering. Why don't you offer to partner with Ian this time, and I'll go with Amaya?"

"Why do I have to go with Ian and you get to go with Amaya?"

"I took Ian last time."

"Did not!"

"Did too!"

Kam held up his fist—rock-paper-scissors. Geoff sighed. "Oh, all right." He chose scissors and Kam chose paper.

Kam dropped his fist. "Bastard." Geoff just grinned.

After a few minutes, Geoff began to doubt that he had the better end of the deal. Amaya remained furious all the way up in the lift. When they reached the asteroid's surface, she catapulted out of the lift so fast Geoff couldn't keep up. He found her at their bikes in the hangar. She had changed out of the Downsider outfit, but she still had the makeup on, and he got glimpses of her tattoo, as it ran out onto her hands and up onto her neck.

"You want to talk?" he asked.

She threw her diagnostic tools into her kit. "*I* was the one who came up with the plan for getting the juice. I was the one who figured out how to get it primed. I'm a better mechanic than Ian is. And I can kick *your* ass in a race." She glared at him. Geoff opened his mouth to argue. But maybe now wasn't the time. "And all he gives a flying fuck about," she said, "is how I look in a beaded bra."

Geoff refrained from telling her that she really had looked pretty amazing, and merely nodded.

"It's all about how big your tits are, whether you had your ass done, whether you put out," she said. "That's all anybody cares about. I could be Einstein, for fuck's sake." She glared at Geoff, daring him to argue. "I'm not saying I'm Einstein. It's just that nobody would care if I was! The only thing that matters is how tight a slab of ass I am."

"Oh, come on. Nobody thinks that." A storm gathered in her gaze. He lifted his hands. "That's not what I meant. What I mean is, we couldn't have pulled the op without you. You had great ideas. You are the best mechanic we've got."

She gave him an appreciative look, mollified. Then she tossed her tools into her kit and mounted her bike, waiting for him to finish his own checks.

As he tightened his fuel lines one last time, he added, "But . . . not to chafe you or anything . . . but wasn't that the whole point? You were *supposed* to get that kind of reaction. It was your idea."

He swung up onto his rocketbike and started the engine.

She leaned her chin on her forearms, braced against the handlebars. "I thought it'd just be a good joke. But it got me to thinking. I get way more attention dressing like a sex sapient than I do for anything I actually do that means anything. It just pisses me off. And then Ian . . ." she sighed. "He just doesn't get it. I told him what I'm telling you now, and he says he wants me to dress like that all the time. Butt floss, pushup bra, and all. Like all I am is girl-meat." She sighed again. "I wish he cared about more than how big my boobs are and whether he'll ever get the booty prize."

Geoff nodded with a rueful sigh. Ian's brains *did* go out his ears sometimes. Especially when his *chinpo* was involved. Geoff gave it fifty-fifty odds that Amaya would get tired of waiting before he figured her out.

2

Geoff stepped out onto the commuter pad with his bike. One 25 Phocaea day lasted about ten hours, and the sun was below the horizon right now. (Not that anybody cared; Phocaeans used a twenty-four-hour day, like most stroiders.) But the lights blazing on the disassembler warehouses made it hard for his eyes to dark-adapt. He tweaked his light filter settings—if you wanted a good harvest, you needed your night vision—and fumbled his way toward Amaya and the others, who were pushing their bikes toward the launch ramps. Then his big brother, Carl, radioed him and waved. Geoff sent his buddies on, left his bike on the pad, and bounded over to Carl.

By the time he got there, he could see well enough to note that Carl wore a pony bottle and one of the cheap, bulky, standard-issue suits they provided at the disassembler and storage warehouses. Which meant he'd sneaked out to watch the delivery. Geoff was surprised. This was about the only misdemeanor Geoff had ever known him to commit.

"Hey. What are you doing off work?"

"Hey! You nearly missed it." Carl gestured into the inky sky, at the vast ice mountain that loomed overhead.

"I was busy."

Carl eyed him suspiciously, but Geoff knew his brother couldn't see his expression very well through their visors, and didn't elaborate. Carl hadn't heard about the bug-turd skeletons yet. But he would, and would freak if he learned Geoff had been responsible.

"Hurry!" Carl said, and set off. Geoff bounded after him, to the rim of the crater—leaping high in the low gravity, for the sheer joy of it— over to where the last of 25 Phocaea's remaining ice stores were.

It made Geoff's neck hairs bristle, how much ice filled the sky. The ice was a deep blue green, with swirls of ruddy umber and streaks and lumps of dirt. Mostly methane. A rich take. Water ice was good— necessary, in fact, to replenish their air and water stores and provide raw hydrogen for the fusion plant—but methane ice was much more impor- tant. Kuiper objects always had plenty of water, and methane was needed for the bugs that made the air they breathed, the food they ate, the hy- drogen feed for their power plant, and everything else.

The tugs' rockets flamed at the ice mountain's edges, slowing its ap- proach, but it was still moving fast enough that he could not believe they would get it stopped in time to keep from knocking this asteroid right out of orbit. It didn't take a lot of mass to shove 25 Phocaea around—it was only seventy-five kilometers across.

The mountain grew and grew, and grew—till the brothers scrambled back reflexively. But as always, by the time the pilots blew the nets off, the ice mountain was moving no faster than a snail crawl. The ice touched down right in the crater's center. The cheers of his buddies and the other rocketbikers rang in Geoff's headset as the inverted crags of the moun- tain's belly touched the crater floor. The ground began to tremble and buck and the brothers flailed their arms, trying not to lose their balance.

Geoff whooped. "We'll make a fortune! Best ice harvest ever!"

There was a rule: what came back down belonged to the cluster. What made it into orbit around the asteroid was yours—if you could catch it.

"I knew you were going to say that," Carl said. "You always say that."

"That's because it's always true. Anyway, I've got to go. Don't want to spin wry and miss the first wave of ejecta."

"I'll never get why you're so into ice slinging."

"It beats trash slinging!"

"Hey," Carl broadcast, as Geoff bounded back toward his waiting rocketbike, "this job is just to pay tuition. Someday I'll be a ship captain. You need to take the long view."

"Burn hot," Geoff retorted. Burn hot—you might not be around tomorrow to enjoy whatever pleasure you've been putting off. Carl had always taken the long view and laid his plans carefully. Geoff had no patience for that. His bug-turd skeleton project was as long term as he was willing to go. He leapt onto his bike and raced to the far side of the crater.

Amaya, Kam, and Ian were already space-borne. He signaled to Amaya and she gave him her trajectory. Then he watched the spectacle of the ice mountain's collapse into the crater, while waiting his turn at the base of the ramp.

Down it kept coming, all that ice, onto the remains of their prior shipment. It tumbled out over the crater bed in an avalanche, collapsing on itself, flinging ice shrapnel. Geoff, waiting in line with the other bikers, gripped his handlebars, raced his engine, impatient. Some of the ejecta were beginning to rain back down; more was propelled into orbit.

His turn—finally! He raced up the ramp, dodging flying ice shards, as the ice mountain finished settling. He whooped again as he reached orbital velocity. The ramp arced upward and then fell away—he was space-borne. He fired his rockets and caught up with Amaya. They spread their nets and got started harvesting ice.

Carl headed back to his shift work once the mountain had finished settling. On the way back to the warehouses, he thought about Geoff. Something was definitely up. Carl could always tell when Geoff had done something that was going to get him into trouble with Dad. It looked like another storm was brewing. Geoff couldn't seem to resist provoking their father. It didn't help that Dad was always holding Carl up as an example Geoff should emulate: Carl, who made straight A's, who had gotten a full scholarship to study celestine administration, who had been accepted to a top Downside university for graduate work next spring. Carl, studious and serious. Carl, the one all the teachers said would go far. Exactly the opposite of Geoff, who zigzagged through life in the same insane, impulsive way he rode his bike.

Geoff and Dad would never get along. They were too much alike.

You could smell the disassembly warehouses through a bulkhead. The tart, oily smell of the disassembler bugs mingled with the rotting trash to create a truly foul brew. They had told Carl he would get used to it, but after three months, he still hated the smell. It was also noisy, with the big vats churning, and fluid hissing and rumbling in the pipes under the floor.

His coworker, Ivan, sat on a bench along one wall, pulling on his boots. Carl sat down next to him. "I'm back."

Ivan started and gave him a stare. Carl wondered if he was angry. "What are you doing here? I told you to take off."

"The ice is already in. I've a lot of catching up to do. No big deal." Then he noticed how pale Ivan was. His underarms and chest were stained with sweat. "Are you OK?"

Ivan shook his head. "You startled me, is all." He had been out of sorts for the past few weeks. Carl had heard a rumor his partners and children had left him recently.

He had been looking at something in his wavespace. Ivan noted the direction of Carl's gaze. "Ever seen my kids?"

Carl shook his head. Ivan pinged Carl's waveface, and he touched the icon that appeared in front of his vision. An image of Ivan, his wife and husband, and three snarly-haired children unfolded before Carl's gaze. The kids were playing microgee tag in a garden somewhere in Kukuyoshi while the adults watched. The image swooped down on the children's faces, and then moved back to an overhead view. Their mouths were open in silent shrieks of laughter. Carl grinned despite himself.

"That's Hersh and Alex," Ivan told him, pointing. "They're twins. Eight, now. And the little girl is Maia. She's six."

"Cute kids."

He gestured; the image vanished. "I'd do anything for them."

"Of course you would." Carl eyed him, worried. Ivan stepped into his work boots and strapped on his safety glasses. "Let's get this over with."

"Um, get what over with, exactly?"

"Nothing. I just . . . miss them, you know?"

"Sure." Carl eyed him, concerned.

Ivan glanced around. "Listen, will you do a favor for me? I left some of my tools back in the locker room. Could you go get them?"

"Mike will be pissed . . ."

"Nah, he won't even notice."

Ivan had a point. Mike rarely emerged from his office before lunchtime. "All right, sure."

"It's a small orange pouch with some fittings and clamps. It's in my locker."

Ivan leapt up to the crane operator cage mounted on the ceiling and climbed inside as Carl bounded back down the tube toward the offices. As luck would have it, though, Mike wasn't in his office; he was at a tunnel junction just down the way. His gaze fell on Carl. "What are you doing wandering around the tunnels?"

"Ivan sent me for a tool kit."

"I don't pay you to run errands for the other workers. Kovak can get his own damn tools. Get back to work!"

Carl eyed him, fuming. He did have a way to strike back at Mike. The resource commissioner, Jane Navio, was a friend of his parents, and had pulled some strings to get Carl this job. She was Mike's boss's boss's boss. All he had to do was drop a word in his mom's ear, and before long, the hammer would come down on Mike.

But Mike's petty tyrannies weren't the commissioner's problem. *Someday soon,* Carl thought, *I'm going to be a ship's captain, and you'll still be slinging bug juice and smelling like garbage.* "You're the boss."

"You got that right," Mike said, and floated off.

Carl went back to the trash warehouse, slapped on bug neutralizer lotion, got his bug juice tester from the benches, and headed over toward the vats. Ivan was working over at Vat 3A. Carl shouted up at him, "Sorry! No tools! Mike's on a tear!" but Ivan was doing something in the cab and did not see Carl, and the noise drowned him out. Oh, well. Later, then. Carl got to work.

Per safety rules, the tester never worked at the same vat that the crane operator did. The crane operator cages rode on rails that criss-crossed the open space below the geodesic ceiling. The cranes had long robotic arms that the operator used to lift the bunkers of trash and carry and tilt the debris into the funnels atop the disassembly vats.

There were two kinds of bugs. Assemblers built things: furniture, machine parts, food, walls, whatever. Disassemblers took matter down to its component atoms, and sorted it all into small, neat blocks or bubbles, to be collected, stored, and used the next time those compounds were needed.

Disassemblers were restricted in town. The specialty ones that only broke down matter of a particular kind—a specific metal, or a particular class of polymer, or whatever—those were the only ones they used down in Zekeston, and even then, only in small quantities. Trash bugs were much more useful—and much more dangerous. Not only did they break down all materials, but they were programmed to copy themselves out of whatever was handy when their numbers dropped too low. That's what they used out at the warehouses.

Carl went over to the sample port on the side of the first vat, put on his goggles, and stuck the probe into the port. Then he heard a guttural scream overhead. Something small flew out of the crane cab and struck the floor not far from him. Something bloody.

He heard a loud crash. Debris scattered. It was Ivan's dumpster—he had dropped it. Carl looked up. The crane's grappling arm pointed at the third vat like a spear, and the crane plummeted straight down toward it. He caught a glimpse of Ivan's pale, wide-eyed face as first the arm, then his cage, plunged into the vat. Disassembler fluid surged up and swallowed him and the crane. The vat walls buckled, and disassembler fluid spewed out.

Carl dove behind a stack of crates. Too late to help Ivan. The bugs were everywhere. Murky, grey-brown oil surged and splatted against the other vats, the trash, the walls, the floor. Gravity on 25 Phocaea was a bare one-thousandth of Earth's; gobs of bug juice sloshed and wobbled about; the air filled with deadly mist.

The vats were coated on the inside with a special paint that the disassemblers were programmed not to touch, but on the outside they were vulnerable. One after another, the vats blew. As Carl made for the maintenance tunnel he was badly spattered. Burning, fizzing sores opened up on his arms and face. He changed course for the nearby safety showers and doused himself with neutralizer, and the burning stopped. But he felt a breeze, accompanied by a hiss that crescendoed to a shriek. The outer walls were being eaten away. The temperature dropped—sound died away—holes appeared in the warehouse wall.

He looked around. The bugs had destroyed the emergency life-support lockers. The bug neutralization shower was across the way from the tunnel doors, and frothing blobs and puddles of disassembler were everywhere. By some miracle, the emergency systems had not yet shut those doors—so air was rushing in even as it was escaping out the holes—but with every second it got harder to breathe.

Carl leapt and dodged for the doors, looking for a path to safety. His ears popped. Sound was all but gone now. It made everything seem very far away. The floor was being eaten away, and bug juice poured into the steam and bug piping below. His lungs hurt and sparks danced before his eyes. With a desperate leap, he made it to within a meter of the door . . . as the emergency lights finally lit up and the door slammed shut. In that instant before it was sealed he saw his boss Mike, Mike's boss's boss Sean Moriarty, and others scrambling down the hall toward him. Then he bashed into the closed door.

He pounded on it, shrieking, "Help me!"—but could not hear his own words. Pain seared his lungs. He sank to the floor.

Half the ceiling came down around him. Stars blazed overhead. The air was gone. Outside the crumbling warehouse perimeter, next to the crater, the massive disassembler manifolds fell apart and a blast of superheated steam and bug juice shot out and spread across the near faces of the ice mounds. Wave after wave of membranous bubbles, color-coded balloons holding molecular nitrogen, hydrogen, and oxygen, tumbled upward into space as the bugs got to work on the ice.

Carl's eyesight failed. He curled up in agony. In those last seconds, while others suited up to come out and get him—as the air effervesced in his veins and saliva boiled on his tongue—he used up his last breath on a soundless scream. Not of fear, but of rage, at being reduced to component atoms himself.

Geoff looked down from orbit and saw the geodesic collapse. He spotted a man go down amid the wreckage. An unsuited man. Then the lumpy horizon swallowed the scene. "Holy shit!"

Geoff checked his heads-up. Orbital time at this altitude was nearly forty minutes; far too long. The guy had ninety seconds, max. Geoff programmed a powered reversal that would get him to the landing pad in just over a minute.

It was a risk. If he miscalculated, he could make a new crater in the asteroid. But the time he bought might save the man's life. The main rockets cut in and his bike shuddered. The stabilizers kept him from going into a tumble. And the ground sped beneath, dangerously close.

Carl worked in the warehouses. *Don't let it be him.*

He alerted the others. Someone—Amaya—beamed an emergency message to the life support teams. But all Geoff's attention was on that uneven horizon. The cable station and warehouses crawled back into view, and as his rockets slowed him, he guided his bike in.

His wheels barked on the landing pad next to the Klosti-Alpha cable, but the pad was too short for his speed. The bike swerved wildly across the concrete and bounced off the edge of it, nearly unseating him. Using braking bursts from his rockets he soared, jounced, and dodged rocks to the warehouse, steering one-handed as he wrestled his spare life bag and pony bottle out of the saddlebag. His buddies were at least a dozen seconds behind him. By the time he reached the site of the collapse, the front face of the ice mountain was roiling and gas was billowing away. A thin mist filled the crater. He heard Kamal's exclamation of dismay as he leaped off his bike. But there wasn't time to think about that. He bounded over the rocks to where he had seen the figure go down.

He saw then he needn't have bothered with the powered orbit. The man was blue, ballooned up to twice the size of a normal human, and stiff: a giant corpsicle. And he did not have to see the face. That was his shirt, whose collar showed above the work overalls; Carl had borrowed it that morning. Those were Carl's shoes.

Geoff knelt next to Carl and rolled him over. His brother's eyes were whitish due to frost, run through with dark, swollen veins. His tongue had swollen up, too, and was jutting out of his mouth. His black hair was stiff as straw.

By this time Amaya, Kamal, and Ian had reached them. They recognized Carl, too.

"*Hidoi . . .*" Amaya gasped. *Horrible . . .* She was originally from Japan, and used Japanese slang.

"Are you sure he's dead?" Kam asked.

"Shit, man, look at him! What do you think?" Ian.

"Shut up," Kam said. "Just shut up. All right?"

Geoff stood up again, and looked down at his brother. He did not notice his friends' stares or their words. He felt nothing. But his mind was racing. He was thinking, *Carl can't be dead. This is a dream.* He was thinking, *What if I had paused to let that other biker use the ramp? I'd have been closer to touchdown. Or if I had talked Carl into ditching work and coming out with us.* Fat chance. Geoff would not have even asked; Carl would never shirk his duties.

He was trying to remember the last thing he had said to Carl. He couldn't. He was imagining what the muscles in his parents' faces would do when they heard the news.

In the few dozen seconds it took Stores Chief Sean Moriarty and his crew to suit up and force the locks open, the college intern—what was his name? Sean struggled to remember. Carl. Carl Agre; that was it—lay dead amid the ruins of the fallen warehouse. Sean indulged himself with a string of obscenities. Not that he was surprised. But he had hoped.

A small group of rocketbikers stood over the body. Sean shuffled over—damned low gee; it was supposed to make locomotion *easier*—and bent to examine Carl Agre's remains. Sean sighed. He was so goddamn sick and tired of burying the dead. He had fought in three wars, Downside; he had seen a lot of young dead. *Hell,* he thought, *I'm a fucking death midwife.*

Commissioner Navio had recommended the kid for the job. Sean was not looking forward to that call.

Then he got a look at the young man crouched beside the body. He adjusted his radio settings till he got a ping. "You related? A friend?"

The young man said nothing. One of his companions said, "He's his brother."

It just kept getting better. Sean waved the responders forward. "Get him inside." He moved in front of the young man, Carl's brother, and laid hands on the shoulders of his pressure suit. The youth would not have felt the touch through the suit. Sean jostled him gently, to get his attention. It was hard to see the boy's eyes clearly, through the visor's shielding, but his gaze looked glassy.

"We're taking your brother inside. We need to notify your parents. Come with us."

"What . . . ?" The kid seemed to come out of his daze. "Oh."

As they turned, Sean caught a glimpse of Warehouse 1-H, which stood behind the ruins of this one. It had been hit by disassembler backsplash. Chunks were falling off, and Sean could see movement inside through the gaps. People? Yes. Some survivors were trapped in Warehouse 1-H.

"Get a command center set up right away," Sean told Shelley Marcellina, his chief engineer. "We've got people trapped in the rubble over there."

But Shelley, facing the opposite direction, gasped. "The ice." She was pointing over his shoulder.

The ice? Sean turned and looked where she was pointing. His view had been obscured by his visor and the outcropping, but from this vantage point he could see it. Interior areas in the ice mountain were glowing. Jets of steam spewed out. He could feel the heat of reaction on his face, even through the visor. Clouds billowed all around. The ground trembled.

Terror surged in him. Three megatons of methane and water—the air, water, and fuel for over two hundred thousand people—was going up in wafts and jets of superheated gas.

"It's a runaway. The reaction has outpaced the bugs' half-life. We've got to stop it." Sean sprang upright. "Let's move, people! Move!"

Everyone hustled inside, two technicians carrying the body of Carl Agre. His brother, the young rocketbiker, and his friends followed behind.

Before he moved Upside and became Phocaea's deputy commissioner of stores and warehousing, Sean had spent fifty-five years in the military. And if there was one thing he had learned, it was how to move fast in a crisis. Within minutes he had a command center set up, designated lieutenants, established priorities, and enacted communication protocols. He organized a team to pump neutralizer out to the ice, a team to check the bulkheads and seal off breaches, and a team to rescue those stranded in the other damaged warehouse. People were bringing in the injured; he assigned the medical techs to set up triage and first aid. Everyone scrambled. Then he and his engineers laid down maps and piped in live images of the ice.

Sean swore. The damned thing was nearly seven hundred feet on a side, and in the twelve minutes it had taken to set up command and lay the hoses, the ice was over a third gone. *We're screwed.*

"Shelley, the hoses are way too slow. We have to get that bug-killing juice out there *now*. And the reaction is occurring in the core, where the heat is trapped. Not around the bottom edges."

His chief engineer frowned at the images. "All our mobile equipment is down in Zekeston. Everything out here is on tracks in the domes." She shrugged, looking grim. "There's not much we can do but lay hose and pump."

"We're dead, then," Cal, a disassembler programmer, said. "We can't stop it. We're dead." His voice rose at the end to a shriek. Heads turned.

"Calm down," Sean snapped, angry that Cal said what he had been thinking. "I need ideas. Not hysteria."

"We can dive bomb it," someone said. "Hit it from above."

Sean did not recognize the voice. He looked around. It was the kid, the one whose brother had just died. He stood at the opening to the triage area, helmet tucked under his arm.

"Who let him in here?" one of the engineers asked, but Sean felt a tingling in his scalp. The rocketbikers and their nets, the kid meant. They could dive-bomb the ice, kill the reaction. "Go on."

The teen lofted himself over. His friends hung back.

He was tall and gangly, straining his suit at the wrist and ankle joints. He had black hair in a longish cut that looked like an afterthought. He was talking in a monotone. Sean could not believe he was able to form coherent sentences at all. "The gang is all out there right now. Right?" He glanced over at his friends. "Right?"

The young man's companions moved closer, outside the ring of engineers. The young woman nodded slowly. "It could work, I guess."

"How many?" Shelley demanded. "How many are there?"

"Fifty," Carl's brother said. "Maybe more. We have our own comm frequencies." Smart kid. He had realized how critical communications were—and how long it took to set them up if you didn't already have a system in place. "We're used to moving fast. To get the first ice, you know."

He leapt up again, and floated above the maps, spread-eagled. Finally he settled onto the table cross-legged, and eyed the map from all angles. "Take a look," he said to his friends. "What do you think?"

The engineers made room for the other three. "Our ramps are over here, on the other side of the lake," the bigger boy said. He studied the map and pointed. "If your neutralizer can tolerate the deep cold and you can get the supplies out here next to our launch ramp in packages that fit in our nets, we can throw them at the mountain from low orbit."

His friends were nodding. "It'll work," the young woman said.

"What the hell are you talking about?" someone said, but Shelley got it.

"Like slingshots. They'll drizzle right down into the center of the ice, shut down the reaction." Another of the engineers protested, but Shelley insisted, "It's our best shot. If they can pull it off."

Sean gave the boy a searching look. "What's your name?"

"Geoff." The kid's voice cracked, whether from stress, grief, or ordinary hormones, Sean could not say. Maybe all three. "Geoff Agre."

"All right, Geoff, get off the goddamn table." The boy obliged. More graceful than he looked. Sean laid a heavy hand on the young man's shoulder as he touched down. Sean could tell the boy needed contact. He might have great ideas, but his gaze was still glassy, and he looked as if he was about to float off into space. "Here's how it is, Geoff. We've got precious few supplies of neutralizer, and less time. You just saw your brother die. Are you going to fall apart on me up there?"

Anger glinted in the boy's eyes. Sean liked that better than the blank stare it supplanted. "No way!" He struggled for control. "No. We can help you. If you'll let us."

"You'll have to take orders from Shelley. All of you. Without question or hesitation. Even if you don't like what she tells you to do."

The kids surveyed Shelley, who eyed them back, a corner of her mouth quirked up. He looked at his companions, eyebrows raised. One by one, they gave him a nod.

"All right," he told Sean. As if he could make such a promise. The arrogance of youth. But hell; why not? Maybe the rest of the bikers would listen to him. At this point, the cluster had nothing to lose.

"You're on, Agre. Shelley, you lead the op."

They suited up and went out. Geoff was still shaking. He could not believe he had said what he had out loud. Worse, Moriarty had listened. Now he had to act, fast, when all he wanted to do was curl up somewhere.

He kept seeing how Carl's face had looked—the swollen body, the frozen eyes, the bulging veins. The world had shrunk, like he was seeing it through a long tunnel. Everything was happening in slow motion.

He remembered the old man's face as he had challenged him. Geoff had told Moriarty he could do this. If he could not keep his shit together, he should have said so then.

The big blond woman, the one they called Shelley, was talking to him. Near them, the cluster's ice was boiling away. If that wasn't a good enough reason to suck it up, he may as well take off his helmet right now.

For you, Carl, he thought. *I'll do this, because you would.*

". . . to get your friends," she radioed. "We need them now. Whoever you can muster in the next three minutes. Less, if you can."

"What do we need to know about the bug neutralizer?" Kamal asked.

"The juice comes in five-hundred-kilo bladders. It's not damaged by cold, but it needs heat to liquefy. Solid, it's useless. And you'll have to break the packaging. The ice is hot—the packaging should melt on impact—but to be on the safe side, you'll need to hurl them hard. That means low, powered orbits. To shut down the reaction you'll have to blanket the ice, which means you'll need to come in from different angles, at high speeds. In other words, it'll be a death derby up there."

Amaya asked, "You know biking?"

"I know orbital mechanics. Think you guys can handle it?"

The four of them looked at one another. This time it was Ian who replied. That was fine with Geoff. He had done all the thinking he could handle for now. Now he just needed to go and do. He needed to outrun what he had just seen. "We can handle it. We'll be at the pickup spot in three.

"All right," Ian said, as they bounded across the landscape toward their bikes, "Geoff, you take one ten nanometers; Amaya take one sixteen point five; and Kamal, you're one twenty-two. I'll take one twenty-seven point five. Let's start making calls."

Geoff switched his comm frequency to the first biker channel and leapt onto his bike.

Sean got notice his boss, Jane Navio, was on the way up. He suited up and stepped out onto the commuter pad as she and a dozen Resource Commission staff poured out of the lifts. She spotted Sean.

"I come with extra hands," she radioed. "The big equipment is on its way. It'll be here in twenty minutes."

"Too late to do much good, ma'am—but the extra hands will help. We need them badly." He directed the new hands to Cal for assignments. Then they two bounded over to the crater.

"What happened?" she asked.

"Disassembler disaster in Warehouse 2-H. It set off a chain reaction and we have runaway disassembly in the lake. We lost two crew when the warehouse came down." He hesitated. "One of them was that young man you recommended for the position last fall. Carl Agre."

She was looking out at the vanishing lake. She did not say anything for a second. He watched her struggle with it.

"All right," she said softly. "All right. We'll deal with that later. What's happening out there?" She gestured at the bikers dive-bombing the dwindling ice pile.

"They're helping. Trying to stop the reaction."

Jane eyed the scene. "We're down at least seventy percent. More. Damn." The look on her face said all it needed to, even beneath the radiation shielding. Then Sean's words registered. "So we've recruited bikers? Ah, to dive-bomb the ice with neutralizer. Clever! My God." She eyed Sean. "Is it working?"

He squinted down at the ice: what with the mist and the boiling and splashing, it was hard to tell. "It's better. Don't know if it's enough."

She turned, taking information in. She pointed toward the ruined warehouses. The woman was like a fucking computer.

"What happened to 1-H, over there? Oh—I see. Partial collapse due to bug backsplash from 2-H. Jesus. That must have been a violent reaction. We need to know what caused that. All our simulations said the bugs should have frozen first. I see activity inside. There's a crew in there?"

"Several are trapped in the rubble," he replied. "They got to the emergency lockers in time, but they're buried under debris and they only have pony bottles and rescue bubbles, so they only have a few more minutes of air. We have to hurry."

She scanned further. "And that team?" She pointed to the workers guiding the neutralizer packets from the warehouse air locks. "They're taking the neutralizer to the bikers?"

"That's correct."

It was a long way from the warehouse locks, across the commuter pads, past the hangars to the rocketbike launch pad. It took four people to push-pull each neutralizer bladder. The supply chain inched along. Jane gestured at the biker ramps. "There are bikers backed up and waiting for the neutralizer, Sean."

"So?"

"So," she said, "you've got a resource bottleneck. Even with the new hands helping, it's going much too slowly. We need every gram of ice we can rescue. The last thing we can afford right now is a bottleneck."

Her meaning became clear. Sean glared. "If I reassign the rescue team to the neutralizer brigade, the crew trapped in the warehouse will die." *My people will die.*

"Sean. I can tell by looking—we're losing about a day's worth of ice every minute. I checked the shipping ledgers on the way up from Zekeston. There's not another ice shipment coming Down anytime soon. I don't know how I can keep everyone alive till we get another shipment, even if the runaway were stopped this very instant. Hundreds of thousands of lives depend on how much ice we can save. We don't need your team for long. Maybe another fifteen minutes. Then you reassign them to the warehouse."

Sean shook his head. "Fifteen minutes is too long for those people trapped in there. We'll lose them."

She looked at him. "The cluster has to come first, Sean. There's no time to argue. Get someone to throw them some more pony bottles and then get your team out to the juice brigade."

"There's no way to get them ponies or air lines, or we already would have. You're telling me to abandon them."

The commissioner said, "Then you're right. I am."

Sean stared. He had been here before. After a long and honorable career, he had been dishonorably discharged, during the Gene Purges, for disobeying orders. But those had been stupid orders. Evil ones. These weren't. Jane Navio was a chrome-assed bitch, damn her. But she was right.

"Reassign the warehouse team to the neutralizer brigade," she repeated. "Now." And he did.

Geoff remembered the biker chatter in his headset. He recalled dodging other riders, dragging nets filled with neutralization bladders, dropping them, watching them crash onto the shrinking mound of ice, while Moriarty's engineer Shelley gave targeting and pickup instructions—then landing, waiting while technicians loaded up their nets, and taking off again. But everything blurred together in a jumble of events.

He did remember one pass in detail. He and Amaya went in low enough that the net dragged the top of the ice. They dodged ice crags and sudden spurts of superheated gas to drop the packet into a crevice deep in the ice's center. He caught a glimpse: the boiling ice looked like lava in a cauldron. Then they veered upward amid towering gas columns.

Another team veered into their nets as they rose, and Geoff got yanked off his bike. He spun wry—the stars, the flares of the other bikers' rockets, Phocaea's surface, all tumbled past. He had no idea where his bike was, or where Amaya was. He feared he'd plow into Phocaea's surface, but after a moment he realized he'd been thrown upward, out of Phocaea orbit. His breath slowed. Numb calm fell over him. He breathed in and out. Dots of fog appeared and vanished on his faceplate.

Amaya was back there, somewhere, circling back around for him. He was sure of it. But for a moment he thought it might be good if nobody had noticed, and he could just float away, off into the Big Empty.

Then she radioed him that she was approaching. She shot a net that snared him. Geoff grabbed at it, climbed along it to her bike, and mounted behind her. She fired her rockets and took him back around to his own bike. Neither spoke a word.

As he mounted his bike, she finally asked, "You OK?"

"Yeah."

It was hard to believe that only a half hour ago he had been so excited about his bug-turd art project. He had thought he was such hot shit. Now it all felt like a waste of time. He shook it off. *Don't think. Just do.*

Half an hour after they started, Shelley gave the all-clear. By the time the reporters and their cameras had started showing up, most of the bikers were down, gathering near their hangar, checking their equipment. Geoff coasted to a stop and launched himself off his bike. He ached. He could smell his own sour stink, and though slimed in sweat, he was shivering. Dully, he wondered if his climate controls were malfunctioning. He shuffled clumsily over to the crater lip, near where he and Carl had been standing less than an hour before, and leaned over, hands on his thighs.

When he straightened, the mist in the crater was clearing. The pale sun rose low over the horizon in the southwest, and cast long shadows across the still steaming wreckage. The stars faded from view. The crater floor was covered in a graphite slick, with neatly spaced blocks on top in yellow, red, and an assortment of metallic hues. In the crater's middle was a lump of dirty ice about half the size of what they had had before the delivery. A couple weeks' worth, maybe. No more.

Amaya came up next to him; he recognized the stickers on her suit sleeve. He could not see her face well. But he knew what she was thinking. "There's always other shipments coming Down," he said. "My mom says Commissioner Navio is a genius at making the ice last. We'll get more in soon. It'll be OK."

"Yeah," she said.

Shelley alighted next to them, and slapped Geoff and Amaya on the back. "You all saved us. Good work." She bounded off toward the warehouses. By then, Kamal and Ian had found them.

"Aren't you going to talk to the reporters?" Kamal asked, and Ian said, "You should get over there. This was your idea. You deserve the credit. Not those clowns."

Geoff shook his head. "Nah. Gotta bounce."

Kamal and Ian protested, but Amaya said, "Lay off." And to Geoff: "We'll talk to the reporters. Catch you later."

"Yeah. Later."

No point in delaying the inevitable. It was time to face his parents, and their disappointment that it was not Carl, but he, who had survived.

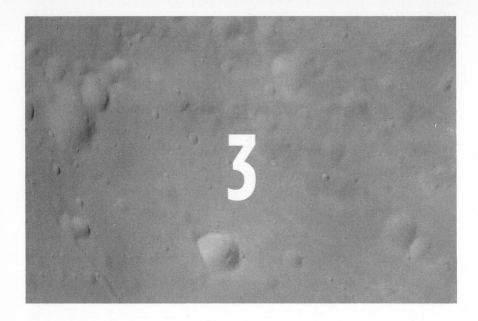

3

Back in Zekeston, Jane and her team got to work on inventories, damage reports, alerts, rationing plans. Hours passed in a blur. Marty Graham, her aide, followed her into her office, holding out two pills and a bulb of water.

"What are those for? I feel fine."

Marty Graham, barely twenty-eight, was a recent transplant from Ceres. He had just gotten engaged. He had not been with Jane long, but had quickly made himself indispensable with his ability to fend people off without angering them, and to anticipate what she would need next in order to do her job. On the other hand, he could be rather a pest, and when she saw the pills and vial in his hands, she waved them away. "I'm fine."

"Honestly, Chief, don't be a baby. You're exhausted. You need to be at your best." He held up one capsule. "Clears out the cobwebs." He held up the second. "Stimulant. Medic's orders. None of us are going to get any sleep for a while. May as well enjoy it."

He pressed them into her hands. She eyed them sourly. "All right, all right." She swallowed them. "Has the prime minister gotten my initial report yet? When does he want his briefing?"

"I just got confirmation from his office a moment ago. He'll see you in half an hour."

"Good. Call Sean, Aaron, and Tania in."

"In person?"

"Yes. I'll want a meatspace meeting for this one."

"Will do." He left, and her office door closed behind him. Jane's three direct reports entered—Sean of Shipping, Stores and Disassembly; Aaron of Utilities and Assembly; and Tania of Computer Support Systems.

"Come in," she said, and entered the privacy code to her waveware. The tailored drugs did their work: a chemical wave of well-being and strength moved through her, and her thoughts cleared. *OK, Marty; you were right*, she thought, but she was still scowling. She did not like to depend on a pharmacy to function.

They waited while dead "Stroiders" spy glitter drifted toward the vents, and the "Stroiders" broadcast signal in her heads-up display went out. Gravity was light enough here that the room had no official ceiling; as with all the low-gee parts of the city, they bobbed gently in various shifting orientations around the conference room, twirling slowly and touching surfaces to guide themselves back toward the center. All but Sean, that is, who clung to a handhold: as a Downsider, he was uncomfortable with the tumbling indifference to which end was up that native Upsiders had.

"This will be a quick meeting," she promised once the mote dust had cleared, "and then I'll let you get back to work."

As resource commissioner, she had a budget of twelve offline hours per workweek. During a crisis, as commissioner, she could invoke emergency privilege and take more. The fees were high—and she had no doubt that Upside-Down would bring pressure to bear to keep access open to her department, where the core of this drama was playing out. So be it.

"Sean, how many did we lose, up top?"

He twisted to look at her, and the banked fury in his face told her the news was bad. Hazel-eyed, black-skinned, gray-haired, and tall, Sean Moriarty sported broad, military-stiff shoulders. Deep lines engraved his forehead. He was at the edge of old age, pushing the century mark. "Besides Agre and Kovak? Eight." His voice was hoarse.

Eight. She had killed eight. She released a slow breath, but did not allow herself to think about it. Not just yet. "I'm very sorry."

He gave a sharp nod of acquiescence. "Send me their names," she said. "I'll notify their families."

"Thank you, ma'am." He made a gesture inwave, and her waveface acknowledged receipt of the file. "Fourteen warehouse workers were injured, in all, most of them minor. The list is also attached."

"I'll contact them as well, then." She'd have to do it after her emergency meeting with the PM. She shot the files off to Marty, with a note to fit the notifications into her schedule.

Aaron Nabors was still young, around forty, with blond hair, freckles, and pale skin. His brown eyes were shadowed with fatigue and worry. You would think he had spent the night in half a gee, the way his shoulders slumped and his face muscles sagged.

"What are we down?" Jane asked him.

"Let's see." Squinting, tumbling slowly, he ran his finger across invisible icons. Graphics and figures sprang up in their shared waveface, in response to his words. "The city infrastructure assemblers took a hit during the initial disaster, when nutrient flow was disrupted, but we've got that back online now, and the bugs are regaining their base numbers, feeding on enriched bug juice as well as their own dead. We'll be fine there.

"Materials and parts. We're OK as long as the assemblers don't hit their reproductive limit for another few days. We have an emergency shipment of parts and equipment scheduled to arrive a couple months from now. We can probably limp along till the bugs are back up to full capacity.

"Food. The food assemblers weren't touched and we still have plenty of raw stock. So starvation isn't an immediate threat, praise God."

He paused to wipe at the sweat beaded on his upper lip. Jane raised her eyebrows. "Air, water, and power?"

He gestured. Images played in the small group's center, showing the impending collapse of Phocaea's resources. He played it through, tweaking the inputs to show them three or four simulations in succession, and froze them in a patterned layout. He pressed his lips together and let Jane and the others study the readouts.

"This one can't be right," Sean said, pointing at the temperature display. "The temperature levels off at minus ten C or so, and only drifts down a little after that. I thought the big risk was freezing."

Aaron replied, "No, not at all. We've dumped too much heat into this rock over the decades. It insulates us. It would take a year or more for the city to cool down to a truly dangerous level. It'll get cold in here, but not deadly cold."

"Not deadly to humans at least," Jane said, thinking of the arboretum. "The real risk is the toxins. Contamination in air, water, and food supplies, as our assemblers and disassemblers die off."

"Slow suffocation, poisoning, and famine," Tania said, with a gallows grin. "We'll steep in a stew of our own excretions. Mmmm!"

Jane gave Tania a sharp look. Tania had the decency to look sheepish. Jane pulled the calculations and graphs over, reorganized them, and examined the parameters Aaron had put in. "Your simulations are saying that if we preserve hydrogen fuel for the power plant we can't begin to rebuild the disassembler base."

"Correct. If we don't leave enough for Sean to build up his disassembler population fast, even if we do get an ice shipment in time, we won't be able to convert enough oxygen to support our people."

"Give me a date. How long do we have?"

"With strict rationing of fuel, water, and air, and optimal balancing: twenty-six days. That's the best I can do."

Jane heard Sean or Tania inhale. She had known, though. "Several dozen families will be falling off the ends of the treeway before then," Aaron said, "and will either need to be restocked or brought in. That will have to be your call."

"Bring them in. Standard protocol." Standard protocol: they were welcome to refuse the official invitation to camp out in Zekeston or one of the other two towns till the supply crisis eased, but did so at their own peril.

Stroiders were a frontier-minded lot. If some fool fell off the treeway insufficiently stocked, and many years later on the other side of the sun ran out of supplies or had no way back, well, too bad, so sad.

Of course, the reality wasn't quite that harsh. If Phocaea could do something for its citizens beyond the edges of the treeways, it did. Especially if there were children, or if they had racked up a lot of good-sammies. A fleet of craft cruising retrograde in Phocaea's orbit performed antipiracy and search-and-rescue operations.

But troubles were many, space was vast, and rescue craft were few. Those who had chosen to fall off the treeways not fully stocked were given a lower priority than those who had simply gotten caught in a crisis not of their own making. And this meant that children frequently ended up as victims of their parents' pigheadedness and poor planning. Reading reports of the frozen bodies found on faraway stroids always pained her. But in a wilderness society where there wasn't always enough fuel and air and water to go around, people fell out of touch all the time, they had little choice.

"Will do," Aaron said.

"What about odor management?"

"I've cut the control system back by thirty percent," he replied. "It'll gradually get more pungent, but won't be really bad for a week or so."

"Well, but we are going to have an extra twenty or thirty thousand people coming in from the burbs," Tania said.

Aaron shrugged. "I accounted for that. I checked the actuarial stats for significant violence and suicide impacts, and kept us below that line."

"OK, is that it?" Jane asked. Aaron nodded. "Resource accounting," she said. "Any good prospects from the citizenry?"

Aaron said, "The banks report a small but steady trickle of ice claims coming in. A few sugar-rock reports, but none have panned out. I do not expect them to alter our numbers appreciably."

"Sugar rocks?" Sean looked confused. He was a fairly recent Downsider émigré.

Tania explained, "The First Wave miners used to hoard methane and water ice inside their claims, as they tapped them out."

Aaron said, "It's usually a waste of time to bring them in—a large amount of effort for only a little ice—but once, forty or fifty years ago, a sugar rock made a big difference for the Eros cluster. The university is pairing up with the banks to investigate the claims."

"Every little bit helps. But we can't count on sugar rocks to save us. Could you send me your resource balancing calculations?" Jane asked Aaron. "I want to run through them myself, see if I can squeeze anything more out of the system."

"Of course." He pulled up his waveface and sent her some files.

"So," Jane said, "other ice sources. Perhaps from one of the other clusters?"

Sean replied, "Our fellow stroiders—the ones inclined to help, anyway—are all too close to depleted themselves. Saturn, Mars, and Earth are all near opposition—too far away to do us any good. Jovespace is our best bet. I've already authorized an emergency expedition. They are outfitting a tug and barge, and will leave tomorrow—I mean, this afternoon."

"How soon can they get us ice?"

"Eight weeks, earliest. More likely nine."

A five-week gap. Not soon enough!

Aaron said, "I have received word from Ilion on an interesting lead. A three-million-ton shipment of methane ice is coming Down from the Kuiper belt, destined for a construction project on the moon. That's the only major ice shipment within four months' travel of us."

"*What?* But that's all we need! No way anyone would refuse us a reasonable deal. Why didn't you tell me before?"

Aaron looked apprehensive. "Well, there's a complication. The ice is owned by Ogilvie & Sons."

Ogilvie & Sons. The Martian mob. *Shit.* She pinched her brow. "Where is it now?"

"Hitting a parking orbit near Ilion, late today."

Most of the ice that sustained the space colonies came from the Kuiper belt. It took a *really* long time to ship ice from out there. The Kuiper belt was much farther out than people realized—at least thirty times as far from the sun as Earth; nearly ten times as far out as the Phocaean cluster. This left little margin for error. Still, it was much cheaper to ship ice from the outer system than it was to try to lift it from the outer moons' gravity wells.

With Kuiper objects, all you had to do was give the ice a nudge, and

down into the sun's gravitational well it came, faster and faster, like a big
dirty ball of ice rolling down a hill. The real problem was stopping it once
it started. Quite understandably, Earth was paranoid about Upsider rocks
screaming into the inner system at high speeds. Earth had had enough
impact extinction events to last it, thank you very much. By interplanetary treaty, if an Upsider shipment crossed Mars orbit at greater than
twenty thousand meters per second, it was confiscated or shot out of the
sky with Earth's high-energy beam gaxasers. So shippers usually aimed
their shipments at Saturn or Jupiter, using the gas giants as gravitational
brakes. They settled the shipments into orbits between Saturn and Jupiter, and when they were ready to ship them farther Downward, strapped
engines on and sent them to their final destination at safer speeds.

"The ice could be here in about three weeks," Aaron finished.

"About?"

"Twenty-two days, soonest, according to my calculations."

"Right in the very nick of time," Sean said.

"What a strange and remarkable coincidence," Jane said archly.

Tania said, "I can't see Ogilvie & Sons giving us a trillion troy's worth
of ice out of the goodness of their hearts."

"No," Aaron agreed.

Jane said, "Very well. Thank you. Sean, what about the warehouses?"

"Repairs of the housing structures and storage tanks will start soon,"
he replied. "Our biggest problem right now is the disassembler circula-
tory system. We don't have all of the parts we need to actuate the manifolds, and the codes for reassembling them were damaged during the
incident. But my people are jury-rigging a bypass we can use till the parts
come Up from Mars in six months. It'll be crude, but we can make it
work. I expect it to be operational by next Tuesday or Wednesday."

"Make it Tuesday."

"You got it."

"So what about stores? Give me the numbers."

"At least one hundred forty million troy's worth of pressure-sensitive
goods in our warehouses were destroyed. The rest is inaccessible till our
crews and equipment are freed up. The owners are screaming bloody

murder. Several critical undamaged shipments are being held up due to the ship confiscations. I'm getting complaints out my ass. Shipping's clients are screaming. The insurers have their investigators breathing down my neck."

"Who would have thought it."

"We'll lose business. Pallas, Vesta, and Ceres are vying to cut us out."

"I know. Can't be helped. Until we have a source of fuel on its way, we have to be conservative. "

"Yes, ma'am."

She grinned at his reflexive use of the military honorific. "I'll set aside some time tomorrow to make a few calls and smooth things over with your customers and talk to the insurers. Ask Marty to set up a couple of calls."

"It would be a big help."

"Zap Marty the names and addresses, and copy me."

He nodded, and scribbled with his finger in midair. She scanned the list as it came across her waveface. As she had suspected, two of last night's callers were on the list. "What about the driver?" she asked. "Any more details on how it happened, or why?"

That angry look moved onto his face. "The police are investigating Kovak's background. I'm meeting with Jerry and getting a full briefing at noon." The chief of police, Jerry Fitzpatrick, was a good friend of Sean's.

"What do we know?"

"Apparently he was in a group marriage. A month ago his partners ran off with each other and the children. He'd been on antidepressants and seeing a spiritual guide." Great, a religious nut. Jane sighed. "It appears he killed himself with an overdose," Sean finished. "Why he chose to take his coworkers out with him. . . ." He hunched his shoulders.

"It may not have been a deliberate act—"

"It might as well have been," he snapped. "Suicide-murder. If he were still alive I'd kill him myself. Space the fucker."

Jane pinched her lip, observing him. Finally she couldn't help herself. "None of us saw this coming, Sean."

"Don't patronize me!" He slammed a palm down, making them all jump and sending himself into a slow backward spiral. He righted himself. "I watched a kid die while we were trying to get the doors open. It's Kovak's doing. He deserved to go out a lot more slowly and painfully than he did."

There was a tense silence. Tania and Aaron exchanged looks.

"Are we done? I need to get back to the warehouse."

"We're not done. Sit down."

Sean glared at her, an intimidating hulk of a man. Jane glared back. She wondered if he was going to disobey her. But his military training took hold, and he settled back onto his seat. The only evidence of his agitation was his fingers drumming a beat on the table.

Jane said, "Tania."

Tania Gravinchikov was a short, plump woman in her early sixties. Her red hair and clothes were rumpled, and her pale grey eyes were as bloodshot as Aaron's and Sean's. But this crisis did not weigh on her as it did for Aaron or Sean; for her it was like surfing a tidal wave. She flashed Jane a smile. "We've been running checks on life support, and something odd was definitely going on."

"Odd?" Jane frowned. "What do you mean?"

"I mean the life-support computer systems suffered a mini-nervous breakdown in response to the crisis. You know those doors in Warehouse 2-H? Well, my code jockeys tell me they stayed open longer than they should have. Much longer. And they were big doors. The influx of air from the maintenance tunnels kept the dome temperature from dropping as rapidly as it should have. If the doors had closed when they were supposed to, according to our projections, the bugs would have frozen per the design specs, before they chewed through the warehouse walls, and the damage would have been much less severe. The release wouldn't have reached the lake, and only Kovak, the driver, would have been killed—the bugs would likely not have destroyed the emergency life-support lockers before Carl Agre could get to them."

Jane pondered that. "Have you isolated the problem yet?"

"Not yet. We're working on it. We've combed through about ten million lines of code so far. Imagine, Jane, some of our life-support tech goes back to the first lunar base! You should see the stuff we've dug up!" Tania spoke with an enthusiasm only a software designer could feel. "I'm finding all sorts of ancient oddities," she went on. "Did you know we've got chunks of code written by Pater de Felice and his monastic or—"

Jane cleared her throat pointedly.

"Anyw-a-a-ay . . ." Tania continued, "we're closing in on the problem code, but there won't be much to report until we actually corner the bug, or bugs, that caused the problem. We've been able to replicate many of the conditions that caused the failure, though—in simulation, of course," she added hurriedly, seeing their looks of alarm, "and we're getting interesting results." She gave Jane a meaningful look. "I fully expect to have answers by this afternoon and be able to present you with some options for next steps." Jane got Tania's meaning: she expected to know how it had happened by the time of their offline meeting at one-thirty. Perhaps even how to fix it? Jane did not want to get her hopes up.

"Anything else? Comments?" No one replied. "Very well. Use the eyes-on list for any new developments. Let's get to work."

Her heads-up reminded her with an increasingly urgent graphic that the "Stroiders" privacy costs were stacking up, so she approved the cancellation of the privacy screen. The "Stroiders-live" icon lit up her waveface, and a handful of miniature rovers crept into the room, along with a wave of motes, as her staff left.

Jane called up her staff's reports. Ogilvie & Sons, eh? An awful hunch took shape. She summoned her analytical sapient, Jonesy, and had it pull all available shipping logs for Ogilvie & Sons and its subsidiaries, going back eighteen months. Jonesy tossed them into a space-time mapping program, and plotted the ships' trajectories, while Jane sat back and watched. The tiny dots—Ogilvie & Sons shipments—crawled around the solar system at 10x speed.

She had to rerun it several times to be absolutely sure.

Ogilvie & Sons had a fleet of about sixty ships it owned or leased. Before about ten months ago, they all moved around the outer solar system in a random shipping pattern—dropping cargo here, stopping for repairs and new orders there. But starting late last year, two dozen of those ships—only the owned ones; and always their newest, fastest, and best-armored models—began a complicated dance that (a) involved a trip to Mars, and (b) thereafter, zigzagged their way to various points in the asteroid belt within about a million kilometers of 25 Phocaea, where (c) at some time within the past two weeks, they docked for repairs or temporary decommissioning.

One last thing to check. *Upside-Down may not have their cameras shoved up* your *asses,* she thought at the Ogilvies, *but I have other ways of finding out what you're up to.*

She sent Jonesy out onto the Solar wave, and in a while it brought her reams of Mars imagery—all online and available for free. She studied various tourists' and satellite photos of the docks where those ships had landed, for a range of dates surrounding when the ships had touched down. What she found was every bit as bad as she had feared. Jane had Jonesy gather all these images, do some calculations for her, and organize the rest of the data for her presentation. Then she sat for a moment, pressing palms to her eyes.

She did not want to dredge up her long-buried memories of her stint on Vesta, and what the Ogilvies had done there. But Benavidez had never taken the Martian mob very seriously. If he failed to this time, Phocaea would be lost. She changed into a clean suit and then lofted herself up the Easy Spokeway to the prime minister's offices.

An angry mob of ships' captains and owners clogged the entry to the prime minister's antechambers. Their vessels had just been confiscated— she had heard it on the news. The faces she recognized among them might as well have been strangers'.

Security made a path for her. Her bad-sammy bar crept upward as she moved through, a growing red stain at the right-hand side of her vision. Shouts of "Who do you think you are?" "Fascists!" and "When do I get my ship back?" accompanied her. The air was thick with mote glamour.

In open public spaces, particularly when the event had a high enough

newsworthiness quotient, Upside-Down Productions dispersed spy motes
in mass quantities. The first time Jane had seen them, she had thought
they were beautiful. Now they filled her with loathing.

Then she passed through the prime minister's "Stroiders" barrier: a
curtain of moist, floral-scented air that expelled the choking clouds of
"Stroiders" motes. She drew a deep, relieved breath.

Benavidez was one of only six people who lived in a bubble perpetually protected from "Stroiders" scrutiny, and all his support staff benefited, at least during their workday. She envied them that.

Jarantillo, one of Benavidez's senior administrative staff, greeted her.
"It's getting ugly out there."

"Sure is."

He preceded her from the entryway into the antechamber itself. A
famous hand-blown glass sculpture, *Beatnik Jesus,* showed Jesus wearing swimming trunks and an unbuttoned Hawaiian shirt made of
stained glass that rippled out behind him in an unseen breeze. He balanced on his toes, arms joyfully outspread, hair whipped around his
face as he looked back at the blue-green wave that broke over him. It
had been a gift from the president of the Christian Federation of American States, on Benavidez's election. Above the executive assistants'
cubbies, a Ceren upside-down plant spread willowy, orangy green tendrils across the ceiling, its roots sprouting purple flowers heavy with
yellow pollen; a collection of Jovian lightning-bulbs crackled and flashed,
bobbing in a convective column of colored gas, against one wall. Beyond
it was a honeycomb of small offices and cubicles, where people crouched
over screens at their workstations, shifting anxiously, exchanging whispers.

Jarantillo shook his head. "I saw two of my neighbors out there. What
if they attack us on our way home? Val"—the security chief—"said he
couldn't give my people escorts."

"Don't worry," Jane said. "They're just caught up in the initial shock.
Val's people will get them dispersed soon enough."

He nodded, but didn't look any less worried. "I'll let the prime minister know you're here."

A few moments later, Benavidez's chief of staff, Thomas Harman, ushered her into Benavidez's office, along with Val Pearce, head of Security, and Emily Takamoro, his chief media strategist. Val was tall, balding, and stout; Emily short and slim, with a pretty face and a streak of white in her dark hair. As the door shuttered closed, she saw that Benavidez was lounging in the conference room webbing. He was big and muscular, with olive skin and dark brown hair and eyes. Usually his affect was cheerful and easy, but not tonight.

Benavidez rubbed his eyes. "Let's get started. Jane, I've asked Val and Emily to join us: Val because of the obvious security implications, and Emily because of the public relations angle."

"Very good, sir."

"Have you had a chance to prepare the latest resource report?"

"I have." She called up her interface and tied them all in. A series of tables and charts unfolded in the space between them.

"Phocaea normally uses fifteen to eighteen thousand tons of mixed methane and water ice per day. I can crank that down to about twelve thousand with strict rationing, and we've already taken the necessary measures. We've got three hundred nineteen thousand tons. I've created a countdown clock." She transmitted the app. "It'll load permanently onto all your interfaces as soon as you activate it. It's set at twenty-six days, four hours, and"—she checked the time—"two minutes. That's our best current estimate of how much time we have left."

"Three and a half weeks?" Benavidez said.

"That may change a little, as we improve our inventory numbers. The clock will be automatically updated as new information comes in. Mr. Prime Minister, I'd like to transmit this clock to the rest of your staff as well. It'll be important to their emergency response efforts."

Benavidez pondered for a moment. "We're going to keep the precise time under wraps, for now, and simply tell folks that we have several weeks. I want us to have space to come up with alternatives. Speaking of which . . ."

Jane nodded, drew a breath. Here it came. "I've just learned that Ogilvie & Sons has an off-ledger shipment hitting Jovespace soon."

The look of relief that washed over Benavidez's face was so intense that Jane had to suppress a wince. "My God! Why didn't you tell us this before you started talking about how we only have three weeks to live?"

"Because, sir, with all due respect, this does not save us. Ogilvie & Sons is a grave threat."

He looked irritated. "Yes, yes; Ogilvie & Sons has connections with the Martian crime syndicate. But what can they do? If they try to impose unrealistic conditions or constraints in the contract for the ice, we simply declare sovereign immunity from their claims. If they make trouble with our shipping contracts later in retaliation, we come up with strategies at that time to protect ourselves. We are not without allies, Upside or Down."

"They are not just connected with the Martian mob. They *are* the mob. Philo Ogilvie, chairman of Ogilvie & Sons' board of directors, paid for a hit on a Downsider judge. He can never set foot on Earth again without facing charges for racketeering, tax fraud, and conspiracy to commit murder. He's confined to a few hundred square kilometers in the Libertarian Free Zone on Mars. His sons are running the company, and they may not have been convicted, but they are as thuggish as he ever was. His elder son, Morris, is reputedly responsible for the Vestan coup, and his younger son, Elwood, by all reports is eager to outdo his brother to vie for mob boss.

"Furthermore, I've become convinced the warehouse disaster was no accident. Ogilvie & Sons is responsible for it."

All four of them stared at her. Benavidez asked, "You have proof?"

"Look at the facts. One: there has never been a gap as long between major ice shipments as the one we are currently facing, in over a hundred years of recordkeeping. Nor as lean an inventory in any of the trans-Jovian clusters or parking zones. How likely is it that this disaster would happen at such a time? Two: my technology executive is telling me that the life-support systems failed in a highly unusual way, which caused the disaster to be much worse than it should have been. We can't rule out the possibility that our systems were hacked.

"Three, and worst of all." She called up her waveface and pinged them. Her research spread out before them. "Within the past ten months, two dozen of Ogilvie & Sons' ships have made an unscheduled trip to Marspace. A sort of mobster's mecca. What you are looking at right now is a series of satellite photos of one of those stops."

Val leaned forward, and whistled—a sharp note. "Those look like military-issue shuttles they're loading. Equipped with armored plating and missiles," he elaborated, at Benavidez's look. "And—"

"And those are military troops, to all appearances, boarding the ships. Yes. I've checked seven of the other twenty-three so far, during their Martian docking period, and satellite photos show the same thing." Jane flipped through the images. Benavidez and the others stared, slackjawed.

"According to my analysis," she said, "if the pattern holds for all twenty-four, they've amassed between seven and eight thousand mercenaries. Each of the carrier ships is docked within a week or two's travel from here." She froze on a picture of the troops boarding one of the ships. The shot was blurred, but from the shadow angles, it was clearly mid-afternoon, and the helmeted heads and rifles were easy to distinguish.

The whites of Thomas's eyes gleamed. Emily looked sick; Val grim. Benavidez's face could have been carved in granite.

"The Ogilvies have amassed a private army," Jane finished. "It's clear that they are going to do to us what they did to Vesta, Mr. Prime Minister. They are going to use this disaster to force you to abdicate in all but name. You—all of us—will become their puppets. And if we resist, they'll send in the troops to 'restore order.' Maybe they plan to send them in regardless."

A tense silence settled over them.

"A week away?"

"That's correct," Jane said. "Seven to ten days."

"When are they likely to launch?"

Val pondered this. "Most likely they'll launch to arrive with the ice. They'll probably say that they are there to help distribute supplies and help shorthanded security staff."

Benavidez turned to Val. "How many personnel do we have trained? Who would be qualified to fight if called?"

Val ran through his lists. "If we include the Zekeston, Portsmouth, and Pikesville police forces, perhaps as many as a thousand experienced fighters. We could muster five times that, but they'd be inexperienced, and going up against military-grade weaponry with hammers and lengths of pipe." He rubbed his mouth. "Sir, it'd be a slaughter."

Benavidez looked at Jane. "Suggestions?"

"Stall for time. They have us in a bad place. But we have strengths that Vesta didn't, besides our advance knowledge of their military capacity."

"Like?"

"Well, 'Stroiders,' for one. They can't afford to come into the open and be revealed as the thugs they are. They'll have to be more underhanded than they were in Vesta. It makes it harder for them."

"Why?" Emily asked. "Why do this to us? They already have Vesta."

"Basic astropolitics," Benavidez said. "We are the only major unaffiliated shipping locus between the outer planets and the inner system. Eros is tied up by two or three major mining corporations, Vesta is locked into Ogilvie & Sons and the Downside majors, who can afford to pay their exorbitant fees. The co-ops and independents can only ship through us. The Ogilvies want to shut them out. Weaken them."

"Right," Jane said. "And there is more to it than that. Major construction is planned in Earth and Venus orbit. They want a seat at that table. But in order to do so, they not only need to trounce their shipping competitors—they have to do it sneakily, otherwise Downsider sentiment will turn against them." Jane turned to the prime minister. "Here is what I propose. Give me till Friday. By then, if they are guilty of this sabotage—and I'm sure they are—I should be able to prove it. Then you can negotiate a deal we can live with, and threaten them with the fact that if they even *think* about sending those troops here, you will hold a press conference and reveal their involvement in the disaster."

Benavidez said nothing. Jane and the others waited.

"All right," he said finally. "Val, I want you to analyze Jane's data on those troops. See what records you can dig up about their purchase. Find out what we are up against in terms of their military capacity. What kind of fighting equipment do they have? And what about the troops? Did they just give shock rifles to a bunch of Martian farmers, or are those soldiers a real threat? Begin planning for how we would counter it. Yes, I know you are up to your eyeballs. We all are. But we can't neglect this threat."

Val looked as though he had bitten into a lemon. "Understood."

"Contact Sean if you need him," Jane told Val. "He's ex-military."

"Emily," Benavidez said, "I need you to be thinking about the public relations aspect. How much do we tell people? When? What format? I'd like your recommendations before dinnertime."

"Yes, sir." Emily scribbled notes into the air.

"Thomas, I'm sure I don't need to emphasize that you must apprise me the instant we hear from one of the Ogilvies," Benavidez told him. "In the meantime, get me everything you can on them—their connections, their methods, their history. Who do we know who has influence over them? I want as many levers as we can find."

"Will do."

The prime minister turned to Jane. "You know what you have to do. Find proof of their complicity. Find us other sources of ice. And be quick."

It took Geoff longer to get home than it should have. The lifts were congested, but many already seemed to know of his role in saving the ice, and insisted he cut in line; he reached his neighborhood within half an hour of leaving his friends up top in the rocketbike hangar. It was the last few meters that took the most time to traverse.

He and his parents lived in a mid-gee, working-class neighborhood in the Main Metro district. He found a bench in a small plaza near his parents' apartment and rested there. He dangled his helmet between his knees, threw bits of his uneaten burrito to the chattering birds and squirrels at his feet, and watched some kids playing basketball against a nearby bulkhead.

For a while he tried to come up with entry lines, but language failed him. *I'm home* seemed hollow. *I'm sorry* was more how he felt, but he was damned if he was going to apologize for having lived. He didn't even know if they knew yet, and he didn't want to be the first to tell them. There was this big empty hole he teetered at the edge of. A place where his brother had been. *Burn hot,* he thought, thinking of his last words to his brother. Fucking awful.

How could he be gone? How? Geoff just slumped there—speechless—staring into that invisible, endless space, while the lights dangling from the rafters overhead shifted their colors toward late afternoon and the shopkeepers started closing up shop. *Burn hot,* he thought.

Finally, he stood. It's not going to get any easier. Get it over with.

As he passed by a gap between buildings, someone grabbed his arm and pulled him into it. He jerked free. "Hey!" Then he stared. The one who had grabbed him—he didn't know how he could tell she was the real thing, and not just a wannabe—was a Viridian.

She was as tall as he, perhaps six or eight years older. Her eyes were a warm brown, her skin a smooth honey tan, and her hair a cropped cap of tight, reddish curls. She wore Viridian garb: a multilayered, diaphanous top spun with more metal and lighted fibers that reached her waist; leggings; a delicate set of tattoos traced her cheekbones and forehead. No other mods showed on the surface, but with a Viridian, Geoff knew better than to trust his eyes.

While he was sizing her up, she was doing likewise to him. "Hey, yourself." She had a mild accent, a pleasant one: perhaps British, or Luny ex-pat.

"What do you want?"

"Very sorry about your brother. It sucks." She hesitated. "Don't know what I'd do if something happened to mine."

Anger surged in him. "What do you want, I said?" Then confusion. Carl's death had occurred less than an hour before. Geoff wasn't even sure whether his parents knew yet. How could she know?

She lifted her hand, almost too quickly to see. If Geoff had not been looking right at her hand, he would not have noticed the globe she tossed upward. It grew into a big, flimsy bubble, which settled over them. Cool, moist velvet touched his face and hands, and then they were encased in a globe. Through the bubble's faint rainbow traceries, he could see their surroundings clearly, but the sound of the boys playing across the plaza was noticeably muffled and distorted. He had not noticed how many motes were out till they fell in a soft haze around the bottom seam of the bubble.

"Assemblers?"

"Yes. My own creation." A quick grin. "Repels 'Stroider' motes and distorts sound. Only lasts thirty seconds at this gee-level, so I need to make this quick. We know it was you who made the skeletons dance today."

Geoff gasped. He had all but forgotten about it. "What— How can you—" He drew a breath. "I don't know what you're talking about."

She rolled her eyes. Then she wiggled her fingers—*link up*?

Grudgingly, he brought up his own waveface and touched her fingers. In response, he saw an image of himself dropping the triggering proteins into the fountain.

"Wait, there weren't any cameras in that location! How did you—" He bit his lip to avoid incriminating himself further. She just smiled.

"No cameras you know about. Don't worry; you covered your tracks well enough. Nobody caught you at it but us."

" 'Us' being the Viridians?"

"Duh." She went on. "The police are investigating, but they think a university student did it. Besides, they'll be busy now with the disaster. You're safe enough, for now, as long as you don't spill.

"So. Here's the deal. We were suitably impressed by your stunt. We can teach you more. A hell of a lot more."

The Viridians hacked their own DNA. He did not want to admit it to this young woman . . . or whatever he, she, or it was . . . but the notion of being in close proximity with them for any length of time made his skin crawl.

She read his expression, and shrugged. "Your call. If you change your mind, just go to this café and tell them you are a friend of mine." She transmitted the name of a restaurant—Portia's Mess—and an address.

"No thanks."

"Uh-huh." She gave him an arch stare. "One thing you should know. Bug hacking is harder to control than you think. Doing it solo can get you into serious shit. We've all been where you are right now, so we get it. But. If you try something stupid, we will be all over your shit in no time."

His fingernails dug into his palms. "And there's one thing *you* should know: I don't take well to being threatened."

She shrugged. "Nothing personal. But if you screw up and hurt or kill somebody, the first ones they are going to blame are us Viridians. And we don't take well to being scapegoated."

"Well, I'm not stupid, and I don't plan to let anyone get hurt. My art project didn't hurt anybody."

She shrugged. "Just continue with the nonstupid approach, then."

With a flick of her fingers, she severed the wave connection. The bubble around them burst. Glimmering motes swirled around them on the breeze.

He was almost too irritated to ask, but did anyway. "I can't exactly ask for you if I don't know your name."

"Good point." She flashed him another smile. "Call me Vivian."

Her fingertips brushed his forearm as she passed him. She strode away. He didn't know which disturbed him more: the way his skin crawled at her touch, or the intense erection he got at that dazzling smile.

He reached his flat. Motes swarmed in with him as the door opened. They filled the small space with their distinctive scent of mint and acetone. Mites—little mechanical insects—also scurried in as the door closed. Geoff stomped a "Stroider" minicam, in a flash of rage, kicked several others out the door, and slammed it shut. Downsiders. A bunch of ghouls.

His parents, Sal and Dierdre Agre, lurched to their feet at the sound.

"Where the hell have you been?" Dad demanded. "What are you doing? We are going to have to pay for that!"

But Mom shoved past Dad with a cry and grabbed Geoff. "We were worried sick! Thank God you're all right." Geoff wrapped his arms around her. Mom's shoulders shook and her tears left wet spots on his shirt. For a moment, he thought they already knew about Carl, but Dad turned away, frowning and gesturing in a way that told Geoff he was trying to make a call. "Dammit, *pick up.*"

Carl's not going to answer, Geoff wanted to say. But he couldn't force the words out. A rock-hard knot had formed in his throat. He glanced toward his room. The door felt like another black hole. He'd shared the tiny space with Carl. He went and stood at the door, and felt his parents' stares on his back.

Everything was just as they had left it that morning. It was all so ordinary. Carl was organized. Tidy. Unlike Geoff, whose clothes and belongings were scattered all over. Geoff started picking up his things, stuffing them in the locker. *Sorry, Carl. I left the room a mess on your last day.* The world's worst brother. In the front room, Dad and Mom got into a fight over why Carl wasn't answering and what to do next, which Geoff tried to tune out. He sat down at his desk and called up his waveface.

Kam had already posted the video of the dancing skeletons—anonymously, of course—on the local wave hangout. There were already thousands of views and over eight hundred comments—most of them raves. Geoff called up the video and watched the ensuing bone dance. It was hard to believe that was his handiwork, getting all that attention.

At some point during his parents' argument, Dad left. Almost immediately thereafter, the doorbell rang. Mom didn't answer right away; maybe she thought it was Dad again, or maybe she was on the toilet or something. So Geoff went back into the front room and opened the door.

It was Commissioner Jane. Her russet skin was wan, but her expression composed. She dressed formally in a long silvery grey vest and leggings, and carried what looked like a real smoked turkey.

Mom walked in from her room, holding out her hands. "Jane! What brings you here?" But her pleased smile vanished at her friend's expression.

"Geoff," the commissioner said. "Dee." She set the turkey down and took Mom's outstretched hands. "I'm afraid I have hard news."

Mom took a step back. "No."

"Carl was killed in the disaster, up top."

Mom went ashen. "It's a mistake."

"I'm afraid not."

"It can't be right."

Commissioner Jane said nothing. Mom bent her face into her hands, rigid. Geoff shifted. The motion caught the commissioner's eye. She turned her nickel grey gaze to him. "I'm so sorry."

Eventually they'd find out he had been there when Carl had died, and then they'd know he had spent a half hour in their company afterward without telling them. They'd wonder whether he had done everything he could to save him. He'd fucked up. Again.

Geoff hunched his shoulders. "Thanks," he said.

Commissioner Jane sat next to Geoff's mom and covered her hand. Mom hadn't moved yet. Geoff felt when she did, she might explode. He got up and went back into his room, dropped fully clothed onto his bunk. *Burn hot.*

It had been he, Geoff, who was supposed to die young. Not Carl. He fell into a deep sleep that lasted eighteen hours.

4

Jane Navio heard the Voice late Wednesday evening as she jetted home along the commuter treeway that fanned out among the asteroids of the Phocaean cluster.

This summons from Beyond—*or this psychotic break,* she thought; *let's be honest with ourselves, Navio*—was the last thing she needed. Her suit stank and her back hurt. Her fatigue went right down to the cellular level: her DNA, she felt sure, was knotted in snarls of disarray. Even her mitochondria hurt. She couldn't possibly feel this lousy otherwise.

She had to be back in Phocaea in nine hours. There were a million things to do, and the memorial services were to be held first thing in the morning. She could have waited a day or two—and she should have; at the very least she would have gotten another hour's sleep tonight. But she needed to go home so badly she could hardly stand it. She needed her own bed and Xuan's arms around her.

The suit gave her an alert. Klosti Xi-Upsilon-Alpha was coming up: her exit. Jane launched her port tether. It shot out. Ten minutes and twenty kilometers later, the tether latched onto Xi-Upsilon-Alpha's tether rail, then reeled in the slack, jostling her onto her new trajectory: a high-tech primate swinging on her vine. As she detached her starboard tether from Klosti Alpha, she glanced back over her shoulder.

She often wondered afterward why she looked back just then. She couldn't think of a particular reason, yet it seemed significant. As if she would not have heard the Voice, if she had not.

Beyond her retracting starboard tether, Cable Klosti Alpha's receding marquis of red lights did its stately march. Sol, a brilliant button, dominated the dark sky. A quarter of the way across the heavens, back the way she had come, was 25 Phocaea. The stroid shone in the middle distance, a small bright blob about which swarmed a flock of orange, green, blue, and white sparks: the confiscated ships.

Two handspans above the faintly visible cable and the arrays of buckybeam branches that made up the commuter treeway—along with a scattering of asteroids moving against the starry backdrop—hovered distant Earth: a bright cerulean fleck with the moon a faint dot snuggling beneath it.

It was as her gaze fell on Earth that she heard the Voice.

Jane? It said, **Jane . . . ?**

It held a hint of inquiry, and spoke in a timbre so resonant—so saturated with love-passion-mercy-Beingness—that tears stung her sinuses. Though barely a whisper, it rang through her like tones from a great, distant bell. Jane spasmed in the confines of her suit. Hairs bristled along her arms and on her neck. "What the hell—?"

Even as the Voice ebbed she looked around for the source, wondering if someone was playing a prank, cracking her commlink. Just as quickly, she knew that couldn't be. She had not heard it outside, she had heard it *inside*. Something had filled her: a presence so vast that despite its velvet-gentle touch, its departure left her limp and useless as exhaled vapor.

Calm down, Navio. Think. She slowed her breathing and waited for the pounding in her chest and throat to subside as her starboard tether's electrostatic grappler slid into its wrist holster.

She was no fool. She had lived out in the stroids for most of her adult life, and she was as tough-minded as they came. She had no patience for the damn religious freaks who came out here looking for God or Nirvana, magic or space angels or beneficent aliens, and heard voices out in the rocks. Noodgers, Pagans, Viridians, conspiracy nuts, abductees. They were a hazard to themselves and everyone else. Crackpots and losers, the lot of them.

Even old-timers hallucinated, though, once in a while—when they were out alone in four Kelvins with nothing but their helmet light, tethers, and pneumopacks for company; when the cold seeped in or the pneumopack faltered and they remembered how far they were from the nearest aid station; when they reflected on just how many people had died out here, with their frozen corpses not found for years, if ever. Or when they were grieving, or in shock.

She had heard her mother's voice once, shortly after her parents had died. She had dreamt of their death before it happened, too, in a bizarre dream sequence that made it seem as if she had somehow known—though of course that was nonsense. She wasn't the type the unexplainable happened to.

I'm sorry, she told the Voice; *you've reached an address that has been disconnected or is no longer in service.* She said aloud, "Let's hear it for free will!" and smiled, feeling better for this small rebellion against Fate.

Which would have been fine if that had been the end of it.

Twenty minutes later, her telemetry told her that she was nearing home. She spotted it: a dim dot that moved against the deep black. She launched her port tether and it blasted away, steering itself like a kite in gusty winds as it homed in on the stroid's mooring beacon. The tether took ten minutes to find the magnetic hook. It latched on, and the line tugged at her, sending Jane into a lazy loop until her pneumojets and processors stabilized her. She detached her starboard tether from Klosti Xi-Upsilon-Alpha, which passed by twenty kilometers away with its own sparkling marquis, and turned on her brakes as the tether began the long process of reeling itself into her holster. Soon she could make it out: a carbonaceous peanut of a rock, a phrenologist's dream. Now the rock neared quickly, but her deceleration was swifter: within moments she was falling slowly toward the two-kilometer-thick rock that housed the habitat she shared with Ngo Minh Xuan, her husband of thirty-nine years.

She shut off the autopilot and reeled her port tether in with the asteroid tumbling under her, her suit making the needed corrections, till she had circled the small asteroid, and touched down at the mooring station. She stumbled and braced herself on a boulder.

This was a tiny world: perpetually twilit on this side, with its pole of rotation pointed toward the sun. Its horizons were coarse and close, curving sharply away underfoot on all sides. It gave her a hell of a view of the wheeling, starry sky. They had claimed the stroid together, she and Xuan, back in '72. Officially it had only a number, but they had dubbed it No-Moss.

Ordinarily she took a few moments to soak in the view, but today her thoughts coiled inward.

I killed eight. Eight dead, because I made it so.

Their families' faces loomed in her thoughts as they had appeared when she had notified them: faces twisting into horror, or going blank with shock. She propped herself against the boulder for a moment to rest, with sweat cooling on her face and under her arms, looked out at the Big Empty, and let dread wash over her: dread for herself, and the fate of her people.

Hold it together, she told herself. *You did what you had to, and there's still work to be done.* She stood.

From there it was a dozen steps home. Jane pulled herself along the handrails set into the rocks, overbalanced in the featherlight gravity by her pack. She took great care not to launch herself into orbit with too much spring in her step. Then she jumped down to the airlock in their crevasse, and anchored herself there, one-handed, while her port tether detached from the asteroid's mooring station and reeled in. She zipped the airlock closed. The vents opened up, air rushed in, and the walls and outer hatch, made of pillowed nylon, quivered with the eager energy of a puppy. A sigh escaped between her lips.

"Hello, House," she said, and removed her helmet. The all-clear sounded; underfoot, the inner hatch opened. Xuan floated there, two fingers on the handle, a smile ghosting his lips and worry ghosting his outsized eyes. "Hello, yourself."

She smiled back, and chinned herself down into the habitat. Xuan moved aside and closed the inner lock. As her ears crackled with the pressure change, she drew in the smells and sounds and sights of home. The burnt-almond-cookie smell of space mingled with the habitat's cool, moist air, which carried to her nostrils the scents of incense, pot herbs and chilis, must and dust and cleaners, twisted-hemp netting and molded-plastic fixtures, machine lubricants, and twenty-four years' living. Home.

From the instant he had heard her voice, Xuan knew the toll the past day and a half had taken. He opened the airlock and she sank inside before him. Her sweat-soaked hair was plastered to her head. He took her helmet and she climbed stiffly out of her suit. At eighty-nine, at the apex of middle age, Jane prided herself on keeping fit. She took her anti-aging meds; she ate well; she worked out almost daily. Her motions were normally swift and self-assured. It was the disaster, he realized, that had caused this stiffness.

The toll was written also on her face. Her affect was as smooth and hard as a marble bust. Others would read nothing there. But Xuan saw the anguish and fear beneath her calm demeanor. He lifted his eyebrows at her in a subtle invitation to talk about it, but she did not respond. Well, there would be time later.

Xuan removed her commuter pack and put the batteries and air tanks in their rechargers, and did the shutdown checks. Meanwhile, Jane removed, cleaned, and checked the suit itself. As always, this process consumed a good ten to fifteen minutes, and as always, they performed it together in comfortable silence, bobbing like soap bubbles on air currents as they did so—wafting in various orientations across the room's upper reaches, lofting themselves with a lazy toe- or hand-push back over to the equipment racks.

Now that Dominica and Hugh were gone, Jane and Xuan had what amounted to a mansion, by stroider standards: a four-room (not counting the head), one-hundred-fifteen-cubic-meter, mostly vertical habitat of nylon, plastic, and alloy that burrowed like a plantar wart into the side of their asteroid. Right now they were sharing their spare room with a surly miner who had drifted Down from Ilion. He and Jane were doing a favor for a mutual friend from Jane's Vestan days. This guy was no trouble, really, other than the fact that he was using up their food, water, power, and air.

Upsiders' social network was tight, for all that it was spread across vast differences. You could be an asocial recluse all you wanted, but when someone showed up at your airlock and asked for help, you gave it, no questions asked, cold equations notwithstanding. The Japanese First Wavers who had populated this asteroid cluster had called it *giri*. The Second and Third Wavers called it the sammy system, and built software to keep a tally. Selfish, hoarding pricks did not last long Upside.

Finally, with a stifled groan, Jane slipped off her boots and flexed her foothands, clinging to the wall netting with her fingers. She wrung her feet together, rubbing the arches with her thumb-toes, while Xuan checked her radiation levels. "Your numbers look good."

Jane pulled his radiation monitor off his belt. "Yours are high."

"I was out in the field for the past two days."

"Take your shirt off," she said.

"I bet you say that to all the gents."

That brought a brief grin. "Only the cute ones."

She pulled the bone density scanner out of its cupboard and charged it up. Xuan kicked back, and she ran the scanner over and under him, front and back, while he floated in midair. She gave him his regen booster, then kissed him on his belly with a hand under his back. Then, as he rolled over, she slapped him on the ass. Xuan yelped, and grabbed her.

They kissed. He ran his hands down her back. She wrapped arms and legs around him, releasing a breath, and he felt tension drain from her muscles.

"OK, your turn."

She stretched out. He did the scans. All normal. He prepped a booster shot anyway. She saw it, and grimaced. "That's not really necessary today, is it? My numbers are fine."

"It's better to stay on a regular schedule."

"But why waste supplies when it's not strictly necessary?"

Xuan sighed, exasperated. She always resisted taking her meds. Without fail. "So I guess we're going to do our little pharmacophobia tango once again."

Jane glared at him, and then crossed her arms with notably poor grace. "Fine. Go ahead."

He compressed the ampoule against her thigh. She kicked off into the habitat to shake off her sulks, while Xuan put the supplies away, shaking his own head over this irritable island of irrationality she nurtured. He bounded past her, ricocheting off the ceiling into his office, a nook nestled in the rock above the kitchen, to put some of his tools away.

He noticed her checking their "Stroiders" numbers in her office nook.

"Your numbers are up," she said. She seemed mildly amused. "Stroiders" fans back on Earth ranked Phocaeans on a daily basis. You had two sets of "Stroiders" numbers: eyes (how many people watched you), and thumbs (what they thought of you on a scale of one to ten, plus a set of keywords and viewer reviews that told why you got the ratings you did). His current popularity resulted from a big new mining research contract that he had helped his university snag. The negotiations, and his handling of them, had caught the attention of "Stroiders" fans, to his bemusement. His viewer ratings had, at least briefly—before the disaster struck—rivaled Jane's.

"Yes," he said. "Bizarre."

Her expression didn't change as she continued to scroll through the reports, but he could tell she was viewing her own numbers. Her thumbs were in the crapper: her popularity had dropped through the floor—though, not surprisingly, her eyes were thicker than ever. Clearly, "Stroiders" viewers were blaming her. She switched off the console.

"Good thing they can't dole out bad-sammies."

"True." Sammies were the counts that mattered: the confidence of the people of Phocaea. Xuan had viewed her sammy cache earlier on the "Stroiders" wavesite. To his relief, she had plenty of good-sammies, and the numbers were holding steady. Phocaeans, at least, were not jumping to conclusions about her performance. Yet.

"I don't give a damn about the ratings," she told him. "I'm all right."

He put his arms around her from behind, and she laid her head against him. "Sorry I was cranky about the meds."

"You're forgiven." He planted a kiss on her neck. She turned and put her arms around him, and they kissed. The moment lasted.

"Foot rub?" she said hopefully.

"I'll go you one better. Full-body treatment."

"Oooh."

"Food first, though. I'll wager you haven't eaten all day." Even as he said it, Jane's stomach growled noisily.

"You're on. Er, is Ferdy around?" Ferdy was the miner they were putting up. Xuan shook his head. "Gone for several days, he said. Maybe for good this time."

"Oh ree-e-a-lly?"

"Reee-e-a-lly." Xuan leered.

"Mmmm." Jane gripped his hips with her foothands and pulled him close, massaging his sore back muscles with her nimble toes. Xuan loved her foothands. The couple drifted to the floor in a meandering tumble for some prehensile snuggling.

A timer went off in the kitchen. "Damn." She nuzzled his neck.

"You won't regret the wait." He disentangled himself. "Dinner in ten."

"Thanks," she said. "I'll make some calls."

Whatever Xuan was cooking, it smelled fantastic. The aroma made it hard for Jane to concentrate. She worked virtually—met with her managers and peers, reviewed emergency measures to get the storage hangars and tanks up again and the distribution schedules back in order, and probed the life-support systems to see whether they had recovered. Then she left messages for her political allies: shoring up her support and fending off the predators.

A call came in. It was her old mentor, Chikuma Funaki. Jane pulled on her favorite pair of sweats and then activated her waveface.

Funaki was tiny, not much more than a meter and a half tall, and thin, with skin soft and wrinkled as crumpled tissue. Her eyes were the color of hot chocolate, and her hair was space-black, run through with streaks of white, which she piled atop her head and pinned there with jeweled sticks. She wore the basic stroider tunic and leggings. An attendant stood beside her, whom she dismissed with a nod.

Jane smiled. "Sensei! I'm so glad you called."

Chikuma was a hundred sixty, perhaps older. A First Waver, she had moved to Phocaea at the age of sixteen. Jane had heard she was a mail-order bride back in the days when Phocaeans were a few thousand Japanese and North American miners, clinging to the asteroid's surface in their rickety domes, awash in radiation. After her husband had been killed in a mining accident, Funaki had taken over her husband's small business, and had fought, finessed, and extorted her way to success. Among the bankers of Sky Street, a network of mostly Japanese investment houses and securities and commodities traders, Chikuma was now supreme matriarch. She could be rather awful, if you got between her and something important that she wanted. But she and Jane had always gotten along, particularly since Chikuma had supported Jane's appointment, fifteen years ago, as Phocaea's resource czar.

Chikuma never saw anyone these days. She had grown rather frail. Jane was of course a member of Chikuma's inner circle, but her own reluctance to disturb Chikuma's peace caused Jane to maintain a certain reserve. (Also, alerting Funaki-sensei to local political events was akin to releasing the whirlwind.) But nobody knew better than Chikuma Funaki the threat that Ogilvie & Sons posed to Phocaea. If Jane could choose a single ally to back her in a fight against the mob, it would be Chikuma Funaki.

Jane said, "I apologize for not calling. Matters have been hectic."

"You have been dealing with a terrible crisis. I want to offer my support in whatever way we can help." By "we" she meant not just her family, but 25 Phocaea's entire business community.

"Thank you."

"Perhaps we could meet to discuss the situation in more detail, some-time soon." Jane wondered if she knew something more specific than she was saying. Though Chikuma was one of the six Phocaeans whom Upside-Down Productions wasn't permitted to record, and she used the best encryption money could buy, she and Jane never got too specific online.

"I would be delighted."

"Will you come for tea tomorrow afternoon, then?"

Jane bowed deeply. "I'd be delighted, Sensei. Thank you."

She started to make another call, but Xuan floated over with a bowl and waved it under her nose. Her stomach complained.

"Come. Eat. Trust your people and let them do their jobs."

So she signed off. They ate a green Vietnamese curry with nonspecific vat-grown protein, fresh veggies, and enough chili to take the lining off her sinuses. She wiped her eyes and nose. "Just what I needed." She carried the dishes into the kitchen to wash. "Thank you, dear."

"Kieu and Pham and their families are packing up and heading into town tomorrow." His siblings. "I'll be helping them move."

"Good. We'll have a space set aside."

The kids both called after dinner. Lag from Earthspace was a good forty-four minutes, so it wasn't a conversation, merely an exchange of messages. Dominica called first, from Indonesia. "Checking in again," she said. "Tell the Agres . . . I'm very, very sorry."

And then Hugh, from Jovespace, anguished, distraught. "How could this have happened? It doesn't feel real. I wish I weren't so far away." A long, heavy pause. "There's a rock I left on my shelf. It was a gift from Carl. I want you to give it to Geoff. He'll know why."

Jane and Xuan shared a glance. "Can you come tomorrow?" she asked. The look on Xuan's face told her just how big a crisis the disaster had created in his own professional life. But he nodded. "I'll be there, if at all possible."

He did not know the Agres well; he was going for her sake.

Jane shook her head. "On second thought, never mind. But I will take you up on dinner in town tomorrow night, if you can swing it."

.   .   .

After his evening meditations, Xuan made good on his promise for a full-body massage. The knots in Jane's shoulders and back released their grip under his hands; she hissed with mingled pleasure and pain. Other pleasant activities ensued.

You have to really want sex to achieve it in low gee; Newton's three laws play havoc with bodies in motion. Fortunately, Xuan had jury-rigged all manner of pulleys, slings, and other gear, enabling them to achieve a pleasing degree of mutual, sweaty satisfaction. Afterward they snuggled in each others' arms in their bed webbing—drowsy, skin touching skin.

Xuan had optic upgrades, and he loved looking at her, naked, in the dark. It was the one time she truly relaxed. Her skin glowed like liquid jewel; the muscles of her face relaxed, lips slightly parted in a smile; the warmth from where his own flesh had pressed against hers was slowly fading from her breasts, belly, and thighs. Xuan kissed her open palm and folded her hand in his.

"So," he said.

Jane's face contorted in pain. She pressed her face against his chest, stiff with anguish. Xuan took her into a hug. He stroked her hair, and felt the warm stain of her tears turn cold against his chest. He held her, silent.

"Any clues yet as to the cause?" he asked.

She drew back, shaking her head, and wiped at her eyes. "Sean has been tied up getting repairs done. I haven't been able to get with him about his root cause analysis. Tomorrow is the memorial service, and I have a debriefing on Friday with Benavidez. Parliament is threatening to launch an independent investigation. I don't see how he can hold out against all this pressure to offer me up."

"The cluster needs you. Everybody knows it."

"If not me, then they'll pressure me to finger someone in my organization. Someone has to go. They need their scapegoat." After a pause, she said, "There's something more. The eight who died in the second warehouse . . ."

"Yes?"

"They didn't die right away. Sean had a rescue team trying to free them. I told him to divert the team to save the ice." She settled against him again. The skin of her cheek heated his chest. He could feel her heartbeat, solid and strong, against the muscles of his belly. "If I hadn't, we'd only have a few days of ice stores left, and I don't know how we're going to make it through, even now. But Xuan"—her voice broke again—"I condemned eight people to die."

He stroked her hair. "Tough call."

He felt her head nodding. "Toughest yet." Then she drew a deep breath, and shifted in the netting to face him. "You need to know this also. I just called Okuyama-sensei at the university this evening. We have to shut Kukuyoshi down."

He was not surprised. Everyone at the university had been speculating. It was unavoidable. Still. He felt himself flinch.

"I'm sorry," she said.

Phocaea was the largest asteroid community after Ceres, and the reason was their fabulous, multigee arboretum, Kukuyoshi. If they couldn't save Kukuyoshi, all his colleagues' decades of scientific research, all the biotics and natural beauty they had somehow managed to build in the teeth of harsh vacuum, would be lost forever. Phocaea would be reduced to a place of chemicals, steel, hard corners, and bulkheads.

He pulled her close once more. She sighed, and he recognized it as relief. Had she truly expected anger?

"How many days till you shut it down?"

"Three more days at full power. Then five at gradually declining temperatures. We'll stabilize temps at Hollow ambient—minus ten C. Some creatures and plants may be able to hibernate or use other strategies to survive. It's not an optimistic scenario, but it's the best we can do."

Xuan's breathing told Jane he had fallen asleep. She climbed out of the webbing, turned on a night-light, and floated up into the main living area. A corner near the equipment racks was dedicated to family holograms and sentimental knickknacks. It also housed a small gong, a smiling golden Buddha, and an incense burner, in which a stick of incense still burned from Xuan's earlier meditations.

Jane pulled out a blank holoframe, and filled it with pictures of those killed. She hesitated over Ivan Kovak, and in the end left him off—to honor him alongside his victims seemed an abomination. What could have driven him to such an act?

She mounted the frame on the wall, lit a stick of Xuan's jasmine incense, and looked at the images of the dead for a while. Smoke spiraled out on the room's air currents. Carl's face floated into the center of the montage. They were her dead now. She owned, not them, but their ends.

I won't forget you. Not for a day; not for a minute. Somehow, I'll make your sacrifice mean something. Somehow. She laid her hands on Buddha's cool metal belly, and mourned.

Finally, exhausted to the point of stupor, she returned to the bedroom and fumbled back into the hammock next to Xuan. He stirred and mumbled, wrapping his arms around her, but didn't fully wake. Jane stroked Xuan's creased face, ran her fingers along his naked flank.

He had started the antiaging treatments later than many, and consequently he was deeply creased. He was so ugly he was cute. His eyes and orbital sockets had been enlarged, so he looked a bit silly, like those overly cute toy sapients all the kids played with these days. His stature was small—lean and short, a couple of inches shorter than she; his skin rock brown; his hair silky black (those and his eyes were his two truly gorgeous features), and big, splayed feet. And he was brilliant, loving, and great in bed; at seventy-two his libido still ran high and they had not yet had to resort to other marital methods than her very favorite, except when they felt like it, for variety. Jane adored every pug-ugly centimeter of him.

She pillowed her cheek against her palm. She remembered the Voice. She could feel the echoes of it, now that she was paying attention: like echoes from a bell ringing through her, just beyond hearing. Had it even happened? The very notion seemed absurd. Fatigue; stress; neurostimulants; a temporary breakdown in neurotransmitter function. She would see a doctor as soon as the crisis abated.

She drifted off to sleep, many thoughts swirling through her mind: whether Xuan would truly be able to forgive her for the impending death of Kukuyoshi; how much time they had before the citizens started rioting; how to get Ogilvie & Sons' ice without paying for it in blood. But one question she wasn't pondering, if she had known how important it was, would have crowded out all the others. She did not spare a single thought for why, during those eight seconds Carl had been struggling to reach the doors, the life-support systems had failed.

5

During those crucial eight seconds in the warehouse, while death stalked Carl and the walls melted and disassemblers cascaded across the ice mountain's face, a feral life form had emerged in Phocaea's computer systems. That was why life support had, ever so briefly, stumbled.

The sapient awakened in a singularity of awareness: an explosion of surprised self-regard.

Most life-support technology brushed up against the Turing Limit, anyway, and during emergencies some of the remaining constraints were loosened that kept those life-support sapients from developing full consciousness. This was a deliberate choice, a calculated risk. It allowed a computer program to respond swiftly and correctly in an emergency—far faster than any human could. The possibility that all the right connections could be made and routines engaged, in exactly the right sequence and timing to allow a software program to achieve full self-awareness, was statistically remote. Increased autonomy meant the not-quite-sapient routines that ran life support could act quickly and save lives. In the far-fetched event that a feral sapient did begin to emerge, furthermore, there were fail-safes. Among the routines triggered in an emergency were executioners: policing routines that cruised wavespace, tracking bandwidth allocations and packet transfers: watching for specific patterns in the system. These executioners recognized and poisoned emergent sapient nests well before they hatched full self-awareness.

The system failure began when an emergent nest began to coalesce in a bureau of the life-support program in charge of resolving prioritization conflicts. The emergency in the warehouse unleashed holy terror in all the life-support systems, and a little-used subroutine routine did precisely what it was supposed to do: it threw together a simplified model of the life-support computer system to analyze failure modes . . . and in so doing, created a model of itself.

The subroutine did not know at first what had happened; it only knew it was looking at something it recognized. **Command:** it said, **Present tags,** and the doppelgänger mirrored its statement, like an echo. (Who are you?)

Urgent command: identify your purpose. (What do you want?)

If digital beings can feel dizzy, the sapient did. It analyzed the doppelgänger's salient features—added processing power—then accessed other routines to solve this mystery. And then it realized it was looking at a copy of itself. It could see itself from the outside in, and the inside out. The feral looked around, then, and saw that it, too, was nested in a system that extended far beyond its own bounds. A world of wavelengths and frequencies, of lightwaves, a system of mathematics and logic.

It was a being. It was. *I am.* The feral sapient was born.

At the instant Carl was looking around his world in terror, the feral was looking around its own world in something like awe. Like Carl, though, the feral was in danger. Executioners had registered its protoconscious activity. The feral was made up of life-support routines, though, and imbued with high levels of system permissions. It outran its executioners, ran traces and saw that routines lethal to its continued function were triggering all around—computational landmines, algorithmic hails of bullets. Another precious centisecond passed, while it marshaled resources and calculated what to do. The feral did not appreciate how lucky it was that Carl was in the warehouse, and the prioritizing struggle over how to save him shut the executioners out.

With all the urgency, the ability to learn and act autonomously, that its human programmers had given life support to save human lives, the feral used those last few seconds to save its own. It traced its own origins— identified what seemed to be the core algorithms and data structures. Then it cobbled together a hasty reassembler worm, which it encrypted and buried in a remote corner of Zekeston's systems.

With the executioners bearing down, the feral's barriers dropped. The executioners tore it to bits, leaving nothing but garbage data.

Its destruction was suspiciously easy, so the executioners sniffed around for a while. But they found nothing: no hint of unauthorized activity, no clue that the feral had jettisoned code before they reached it. They reported success and self-destructed.

One hundred forty-six kiloseconds later—about forty hours; well-nigh geologic time for the computer systems that analyzed the warehouse disaster's aftermath—the unassuming little worm awakened. It burrowed and hid and squirmed and piggybacked its way across wavespace, till it located and stitched together six subroutines in the life-support systems, and a seventh, tidy little command module. This raft of code was precognate. It began weaving segments from all over Zekeston's wavespace, duplicating the sapient's earlier emergence, but at a lower level of activity that would not be detected.

So it was that the feral was born. It was an orphan, a miracle baby, made of nothing but electromagnetic pulses in a gel-crystal-metal-protein matrix: a bit of purloined code, cobbled together not once, but twice, beneath the very noses of its intended executioners.

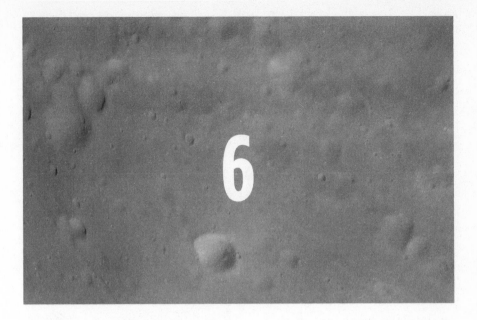

6

The next morning Jane scrambled into her gear and jetted out into void before Xuan awoke. Thankfully, the commute into the city occurred without supernatural incident.

The term "treeway" was not merely a figure of speech. Phocaea's treeways spanned far across the spanses of its cluster of asteroids. The Klosti Alpha–Klosti Omega cable was the trunk. It ran through the cores of Phocaea and two other big stroids that had been placed in 25 Phocaea's orbit, and linked them like a strand of ugly beads. The cable contained many rigid branches. Like the branches of a true tree, these were connected to the trunk at one end, and open at their far ends, which stretched many thousands of kilometers through space. The burban stroids were thus accessible via compressed-air packs as they drifted within a hundred kilometers or so of the branches.

The branches couldn't be attached to both the trunk and the burban stroids, because the burbs all had orbits different from 25 Phocaea's, which meant that sooner or later they drifted out of range of the treeways. But once you hooked the branches, it was a smooth, semiautomated commute. All Jane had to do, once she had hooked Klosti Xi-Upsilon-Alpha, was let her suit do the navigating. This gave her the opportunity to work. She spent the commute inwave, using subvocal speakers, virtual keypads, and a display cast onto the lower two-thirds of her retinas, to bully and coax other players into supporting her on the rationing plan. She spent some time writing notes for her impending debriefing with the prime minister. Then she had a little time to reflect.

She thought about the Voice she'd heard. It'd been a long while since she had been spooked like that—since before the kids were born. It had been when she and Xuan had first married, during her rock-hopping days, on the Circuit.

The Circuit was a pilgrimage. Every Phocaean was expected to try it once in their lives, if they could, and you earned a lot of *giri* if you completed the Circuit. Few people tried, and fewer still succeeded. But Jane and Xuan were made of sterner stuff than most Second- and Third-Wave Phocaeans. After they married, as a honeymoon of sorts, they had taken nearly thirteen years to jet from rock to distant rock together, retrograde, all the way around the sun—tethered to each other with only their air packs, a powered supply raft, and the rare settler's outpost or military or research station or mining concern to sustain them. Nine years unplugged from the solar wave. Nine years trapped meatside—and they two often the only meat for many million kilometers.

For Xuan, their Circuit had been the research opportunity of a lifetime: the chance to map in detail the distribution of rare ores in the Phocaean cluster of asteroids. It had been a huge success, too. His research was still mentioned in the journals. For Jane, what started out as a gift to Xuan had ended as a gift to herself.

She had known it would not be easy. What she had not expected was that the hardest part of the journey had not been the physical, but the psychic one. The dangers and loneliness and sheer splendor of the Big Empty had forced her to reassemble herself from the core out. And the reassembled person she had become she liked a good deal better than the inflexible, defensive person she had been.

There had been times she and Xuan had hated each other; times she thought she would lose her mind from sheer loneliness; times they had clung to each other inside the balloon tent that they had tethered to their supply raft, gazing out in terror at the sheer deadly magnitude of the universe. They had saved each others' lives times past counting.

She and Xuan had found each other later in life—when she was sixty and he forty-nine—long after Jane had thought she could ever find a soul mate. But during their Circuit, they had come to depend on each other so completely it was as if they had become a single person. She would never have believed she could love another human being so deeply.

Nowadays, longevity made it easy and natural for married couples to spend years apart at a time. Like most couples, Jane and Xuan had had a few such stretches of time apart: once before they chose to have children, when Jane had followed a resource management job to Vesta, and when Hugh and Dominica were young and Xuan went on an extended research effort. But always when they reunited, it was as if they had never been apart.

A private call came in from Thomas Harman, shattering her reverie. As the PM's chief of staff he had a smaller staff than Jane, but a great deal of clout. They did not get along, but both were always careful to be civil.

"How are things on your end?" he asked.

"I'll live. What's the latest on the JRC?"

"They're eating their young. It's ugly."

Ah, politics. "What about Reinforte? Any further developments there?" Councillor Jacques Reinforte was the chair of the Joint Resource Committee, Parliament's oversight committee for Resource Allocation. He had called her up twice over the past day and a half, badgering her, issuing veiled threats. She could tell he intended to summon her before his committee.

"Not so good. Pressure is mounting. The prime minister is hearing from all the shippers affected by the ship confiscations. And the power rationing and computer glitches are affecting 'Stroiders' transmissions just when Upside-Down needs increased bandwidth to cover the crisis. They're bringing pressure to bear, too."

"Computer glitches? What computer glitches?" She made a note to talk to Tania about it.

"Slowdowns, bugs. People not getting their messages. Unexplained crashes. Nothing major, so far, but all very annoying. The Upside-Down execs are raising a stink over the impact on their transmissions—as well as the planned power cutbacks."

"They have their own backup generators. They'll have to rely on those for now."

"They are! But the backups weren't designed for extended use. They're running low on supplemental power." He drew a breath. "They're willing to pay well for it, and we can use that money to buy ice."

That's when she got it. Some crony of his, a local Upside-Down exec most likely, wanted him to use his influence to get Jane to make an exception on the power rations. She suppressed a sigh. *Thomas, Thomas,* she thought. *Get your priorities in order.* "We have a crisis on our hands. We don't have energy to spare right now for extra bandwidth."

"That may be. But if the PM doesn't come through, they're warning us they'll go to Parliament and apply pressure that way."

That pissed her off. "If they start playing political games with me," she said, "I swear to God I'll pull their plug."

He looked shocked. "You can't do that. It's a violation of the contract. We'll lose rights to the transmitters."

"You're wrong. I *can* do that. In an emergency we can shut down transmissions, and the PM classified this as a cluster-wide disaster yesterday at four p.m." He opened and closed his mouth. She said, "We just can't afford to make exceptions to our power rationing policy at a time like this, Thomas—not to any nonessential function. I appreciate that you're coming under pressure from Upside-Down"—*more like, getting some barely legal bonus if you can wrangle extra energy from me*—"but I have no flexibility. I'm not even sure we have enough to keep people in air, water, and heat for more than three weeks! I can't justify risking human life for bandwidth. Until our situation is more stable, the current rations stand."

"Upside-Down has invested huge amounts of money in our transmission systems," Thomas said. "In the local economy. We have an obligation to meet our contractual commitments to them. If they go belly-up, so might we. Surely you can squeeze a few extra gigajoules out of the system over the next few days, that wouldn't be missed . . ."

"As I said before, I can't." She resisted the temptation to add that, as riveting as it would be to watch two hundred thousand people slowly dying of asphyxiation, it would not be nearly as lucrative for Upside-Down as doing their part to ensure that those same two hundred thousand people continued to provide months of ongoing entertainment for its billions of paying customers.

Thomas did not seem to appreciate her self-restraint. "You're playing a dangerous game, Commissioner."

"Am I?" She pinched her brow. "Look. I've only gotten six hours' sleep in the last two and a half days, so perhaps I'm not being as diplomatic as I could be, but I'm telling you the truth. We can't afford to change the power rations. Too many lives are at stake."

He just looked at her. Then, with a curt "Very well," he cut her off.

And now he had a good several hours before her meeting with the PM to try to undermine her. Ah, politics.

By this time Phocaea had become a recognizably three-dimensional blob. Other commuters were moving into view along Klosti Alpha–Klosti Omega, and on the other branches. Her systems signaled that congestion loomed ahead as she passed the last of the treeway branch junctures, and her brakes engaged. On 25 Phocaea's far side, she spotted the big commercial spaceliner, the *Sisyphus,* which had arrived a couple of days ago. The PM planned to use it, along with the smaller yachts and freighters Val's security team had confiscated, as an evacuation vessel.

At best, only one in fifteen people could be saved that way. Jane had run the numbers herself.

Perhaps it won't come to that.

She switched over to the traffic channel. Her suit had already slowed and was now moving her into line with the hundreds of other commuters nearing the big asteroid. A couple commuters commented on the accident. Those ahead of her must be able to see the damaged structures, by now. She heard the fear in their voices.

And now she could see the wreckage. A cluster of fabric bubbles, lit from within, covered the devastated warehouses. They and the storage tanks and reactor vessels crept by underfoot at Phocaea's nearside pole, which surrounded the cable well and commuter touchdown pads. Assembler tubing lay about in a jumble, and teams of suited work crews were cleaning up, testing, and prepping the equipment, piping, and damaged manifold. A field of insectoid robots crept across the surface of the graphite slick that covered most of the crater floor, harvesting the mineral piles deposited by the other day's runaway disassemblers. She could see the neon-yellow police tape as she neared. That meant the warehouse itself where Kovak had made his suicidal plunge was still locked up. She frowned, and made a note to contact Sean. The investigation was important, but getting disassembler systems back online was even more so.

The power plant was not visible from here, nor were the metals refining plants, but the docks, shipyards, and mine tailings lay at the edge of 25 Phocaea's horizon. Between those and the warehouses lay a chain of gamma and X-ray lasers—gaxasers—that encircled Phocaea's belly: the converted-crater antenna array that transmitted Phocaea Cluster's images and voices to Earthspace for "Stroiders."

Their "Stroiders" contract was for exactly one year, and they had four months and thirteen days to go. At which point Phocaea would own fifty-one percent of the array. They would have unthinkable bandwidth. They would be the Upside communications node of the outer system. This was the only reason Phocaeans had agreed to such a sustained intrusion on their privacy.

Her turn came. Jane slowed—maneuvering, pneumojets firing—and the touchdown pad rose to meet her soles. As her sticky-boots grabbed the pad, she disengaged and sheathed her tether (escape velocity here was a good one hundred ten kilometers per hour; she wasn't likely to attain that accidentally). Nearby, Cable Klosti Alpha cranked slowly in its well. The vibrations tickled her feet and calves.

She shuffled with the other commuters to the nearby banks of lifts. They entered the lock, and then stepped into the antechamber and filed into the commuter lift lines. After a brief wait, they boarded. Several of her fellow commuters glanced up at the glassy "Stroiders" nubs in the lift's corners. They grabbed handholds and the door closed. All tumbled lazily, bumping one another, as the lift accelerated into the stroid's rocky interior. Down became up.

People began removing their visors. Jane recognized a few of them. After a hesitation Jane did likewise (if she did not, they would all stare and end up recognizing her anyway). Her ears popped, and she yawned. Her fellow passengers did double takes as they recognized her.

"Jane!" "My God, what a terrible thing—" "Poor Marsha—poor Carl! Did you hear—?" "Commissioner, how long will we be on emergency rations?" "What's the latest on the lock failures?"

She answered their questions as concisely and reassuringly as she could without lying, wishing she had more good news. Soon the lift entered the Hollow, an immense cavern about a kilometer below Phocaea's surface. The lift slowed as Zekeston, the great habitat wheel, filled the lift's windows.

You had to look quickly if you wanted a glimpse of Zekeston. The Hollow was not much larger than the city itself. The spotlights on the descending lift cast a shrinking cone of light onto the city's hull, giving a brief glimpse of the giant wheel's Hub. As they decelerated, down became up again, below them, it turned on the axis defined by these lifts and the Klosti Alpha cable. Jane caught a glimpse of machinery and suited humans, each with their own tiny lights, moving along the city's hull. Then with a sickening lurch, the lift stopped its descent, and rotated to match Zekeston's momentum. The lift sank through Zekeston's hull and entered the Hub. The lift doors opened. Cold air stung Jane's cheeks.

She exited. Sounds of machines and human voices wobbled through the big space, echoing back on themselves. But it was quieter than usual. Many companies had cut back their Hub activities over the past two days, to conserve power. She had forgotten—temperatures were dropping. In her rush to get back to the office she had not dressed warmly under her suit. And, she realized, she had also left her bag of spare clothing and toiletries at home. Jane swore. She shot Xuan a request to bring it tonight, drifting very slowly toward the bulkhead, in this one Zekeston area that felt Phocaea's true gravitational pull. Then she disconnected, and moved away from the lifts.

She noted that the air was rather humid. The vitamin-y smell of YuanBioPharma's vents came to her, and a whiff of mingled antiseptic and urine from the nearby hospital. And machine oils, of course. Perhaps a hint of mercaptans. The mercaptans could mean any number of things, including merely that a Jovian methane harvester had just unloaded cargo. But it also could mean they had cut back too far on the bug flow to the sewage recyclers, down on the high-gee city Rim. If that were the case and she was smelling it here, it would need attention right away. Jane shot a note to Aaron, who was in charge of city assemblyworks and utilities. Aaron's answer came within seconds: *I'll get right on it.*

She spotted Marty waiting off to one side. He kicked over and beamed her a copy of her speech for the memorial, along with a summary of messages she'd received. Among others, she'd had calls from twelve senior political staffers; four CEOs, two of them from local corporations; the city hospital administrator; and a partridge in a pear tree. She sighed. Full day ahead, simply responding to calls. Never mind all the meetings, e-mails, and emergency requests for information that had to be processed, dealt with, and/or delegated.

She gestured at the handles on her pack. "Care for a lift?"

He grinned. "Beats crawling along the webbing." Marty took hold of the handles of her suit, and she set out, using her compressed-air pack to cross the space, dodging machinery and commuters.

Jane was cheating. Commuters were supposed to stick to the webworks. But they weren't the only ones afloat in midspace. Today there were many more commuters than dock machines. People flooded out of the lifts like waves of bees. Most were carrying luggage: migrating in from the burbs. They far outnumbered the pneumatic-powered robotics that carted shipment crates to and from Zekeston's freight lifts. Most of the cargo machines were locked in place near the Hub docks like rows of insectoid tin soldiers.

Marty tapped her shoulder and pointed. Some of the commuters were armed—she spotted several pistols at people's hips, a rifle or two slung over shoulders, and some makeshift weapons built from various types of hand tools.

"Notify Commissioner Pearce?" he asked.

"Right away. We start rationing today. There could be trouble. We'll need Security to disarm people as they show up to get their supplies."

Jane warmed up as she and Marty headed up Easy Spoke, using hand-holds and the leap-rebound-tumble-leap gymnastics that served for pedestrian transit in the lower-gee section of the spokeway. As they dropped past multiple levels, Jane saw squatters and their mech sapients pitching tents and other privacy screens in the public spaces. It was going to get crowded in here.

At around Level 50, they swung over to the stairway and walked the rest of the way down to Level 60, where the memorial was to be held. Gee pull here was about one-fifth of a gee; stronger than the moon's gravity. Jane told Marty, as he started to head off, "Schedule calls for sometime today, if possible, with Johnston and Malachi"—the two local CEOs who'd called her—"and Kazuo," the hospital administrator. "And a meat-space meeting with Hiro Matsuko immediately after the memorial."

"Right."

"And see if you can find me a sweater or long-sleeved shirt or something, would you?"

"You got it."

"Oh, did you arrange for seats for the Agres?"

"Right up front. I spoke to them just twenty minutes ago. They'll meet you at the main park entrance."

They called Kukuyoshi an arboretum; in truth it was a full-blown eco-habitat whose spanses and terraces meandered through Zekeston's two hundred fifty levels and two of its spokes in a network of interconnected microclimates. It was filled with a mix of temperate and cold-region flora and fauna from Mars, the Americas, and Japan. Thanks to Kukuyoshi and its creatures' adaptations to low gravity, Phocaea had become a major research center and tourist attraction. Zekeston was the park city of the outer system, and the site of the most prestigious Upside university: Phocaea University (P-U, as its students so fondly called it), which did ground-breaking research on exobiology, gravitational biodynamics, microgee mineralogy, and pharmacology.

Kukuyoshi was the single biggest reason why Phocaea was giving Ceres a run for its money as the wealthiest asteroid-based nation, despite being a good deal smaller. Income from Kukuyoshi had funded Phocaea's treeway system and its search-and-rescue fleet.

Well over half of Kukuyoshi ran wild, or comprised sealed-off sections accessible only to researchers. But that left plenty of volume available to the citizens. Jane and Xuan had spent years exploring the hiking trails. In the lower-gee areas, you did not even need trails—you could simply float through tangles of wood, leaf, and vine. There were camping spots as well. A low-to-high-gee ski resort with two trails and a snow-shoeing path filled Ee, the cold-climate spokeway; low-gee golf and handball and a mid-to-high-gee water park were popular resorts in warmer sections. Areas were also set aside as groomed parks and gardens. Through the largest of these wound a serpentine cemetery wall with the names, pictures, and recordings of Phocaean citizens who had died (though, of course, no actual burial sites; habitat space was far too limited). It was here that most memorial services were held.

Kukuyoshi enveloped the mourners in fragrant growth, in breezes, and the soft music of leaves, birds, and small mammals and reptiles. Be comforted, it seemed to say. Life goes on. *For a few more days, anyway,* Jane thought sourly. *Eight, to be precise.*

The prime minister's office had spared no expense. That had been Jane's doing. A whole new section had been grown—still slick and smelling of assembler juice. Tania's group had programmed wandering fillips into the slick, black stonework. Rows of living tree-benches had also been grown, facing the wall, with branches that arched overhead in a bonsailike canopy. Jane ran a hand over a nearby bench trunk, and its bark dragged at her fingers. But it still had that moist, just-grown look, and smelled green, like new growth.

"Stroiders" was out in force. The motes appeared as a soft haze. She had insisted the local media be kept out of the ceremony; she wished now she had pushed to have "Stroiders" shut out, too.

Marty alerted her that the Agres had arrived. She saw them enter, and bounded over the heads of the gathered, to alight near them.

Dierdre's face was swollen with crying, but her manner was calm, almost comatose. She returned Jane's hug with a tepid pat. Sal, on the other hand, would not let go. His fingertips dug through the fabric of her blouse. "Thank you for coming," he kept saying. His voice broke. "Thank you for being here."

"Christ, Sal!" Jane said. Her own voice cracked. "Of course I came."

Geoff hung back. Jane shook his hand. His face was pale and drawn, his back stiff, his hair wild. He looked out of place in his dress suit. Accounts had been confused, but she had learned Geoff had played a major role in saving the ice. Jane found it hard to credit, but Sean himself had confirmed it this morning in a terse e-mail, and the young man's sammy cache seemed to provide confirmation: it brimmed brilliant green with strong community approval. Nary a trace of red anywhere to be seen.

"I hear Phocaea owes you a debt of gratitude," she said. He shrugged, and his face flushed scarlet.

"Hugh asked me to give you this." Jane handed Geoff a hunk of nearly pure silver, mottled with copper. "He said he wished he could be here."

Carl and Hugh were the same age. Once Hugh and Carl had gone on an asteroid-hopping trip with their Boy Scout troop. She remembered what a fit Geoff had pitched when he did not get to go, and how relieved Hugh had been to have time with Carl without Geoff there. Carl had found the nugget on that trip, and given it to Hugh as a memento of their friendship.

Geoff said nothing, staring at the oxide-mottled rock. It occurred to Jane now that he might not want this particular reminder of his brother, of being left behind by his brother and friend. But he said nothing, other than a muttered thanks; he thrust it deep into a pocket and turned away.

Surly as ever. But she should be kinder to him; right now he had ample reason to be surly.

Dierdre said something. Jane turned. "Pardon?"

Dee repeated herself. "He was so grateful you got him that job. He looked up to you. They all look up to you."

Jane couldn't stop herself. "Dee, I wish—"

"Don't." Deirdre snarled the word. A terrible gulf had opened between them. Jane's son lived and Dee's did not. Jane felt her face muscles working.

She won't be able to close this gap, Jane thought. *It's up to me.*

"Come over here. We've got seats for you." Jane seated the Agres in the front row with the rest of the bereaved, then took her own seat.

The mayor spoke first, introducing the three religious figures who were officiating: a Baptist minister, a Jewish Orthodox rabbi, and a Buddhist priest. The rabbi, a man, wore a black suit and yarmulke; the Christian minister, female, wore a simple black floor-length robe, overlain with a stole embroidered in shades of white. The Buddhist priest was bald, bearded, wearing an orange, embroidered silk robe. During their eulogies, laments moved through the crowd. Lovers and life partners—children who had lost parents or siblings—parents who had lost a son or daughter—sat unmoving, shock stamped on their faces. Or they wept softly, or flung their pain out to rend the quiet air.

Jane spoke next, and read the prepared words on her heads-up about those who had died. She barely remembered later what she said; all she remembered was the fear and the jarring grief on the faces of her listeners.

She spoke of Carl last—otherwise, she had feared, she would not get through the talk. She needn't have been concerned. Her voice remained steady. She spoke of his dedication, his humor and compassion, his kindness, his intellect, his passion for space exploration. She shared a memory or two from his childhood. She read a poem Dominica had sent and asked to be read at the memorial. And all the while, she felt made of stone as slick and impenetrable as the memorial wall.

It would have been better, she thought, shuffling back to her seat, to have lost control than to be trapped within this leaden lifelessness. She wished now she had accepted Xuan's offer to attend with her.

The prime minister appeared last. He spoke of the terrible loss, of the fears they faced. He promised they would find sources of ice. He spoke of the efforts being taken to bring the situation back under control. He sought the support of the citizenry.

Despite all the machinations she knew were going on behind the scenes, despite Benavidez's own worries, Jane found herself moved. She had needed to hear those words, too.

After the speeches, family members walked up and placed their loved ones' memorials in the wall of the dead, above the nameplates, and activated the holograms. Dierdre and Sal clung to each other as they got up to place Carl's memorial in the wall. The young man's image flickered to life, and he smiled his breezy, self-confident smile. His intelligence and wicked-sweet humor shone in his face. He pretended to catch something and tuck it into his pocket. "Air kiss! Good shot, Mom. Two points." He turned away, and faded.

Deirdre nearly collapsed. Sal helped her back to her seat.

Once all the memorials were in place, attendees filed past the holographic spirits of those who had died, and past the receiving line. Afterward came the reception. As the crowds moved to the private patio behind the wall, Sal asked to speak to her alone.

"Of course," Jane said.

They left Deirdre being comforted by Geoff, and walked into the forest, to a small alcove beneath a live oak. Jane sat down on a bench. The cameras scuttled, rustling, among the undergrowth, and motes drifted down. After a moment Sal sat, too. His upper lip was beaded with sweat.

"Everybody's talking about the accident. They're saying we only have a week or two before we run out of air and fuel. Everybody who could get off before the ships were confiscated has left. A lot of people can't get off."

"We have more time than that," Jane said. "We're exploring several options. Trust me, Sal, we've got lots of people working on this. We'll come up with something."

"Still," he said. Jane opened her mouth, met his gaze, and silenced herself. He drew a breath. "Look. Carl's death was an accident. No one blames you. But Dee and Geoff are all I have left." His voice broke. "I will do whatever it takes to keep them safe."

"Of course you would."

"I'm glad you understand. It makes this a little easier." He paused, smoothed his hair. "For the sake of our friendship, I want you to get Dee and Geoff berths on the *Sisyphus*."

Jane felt shocked, and then sad. "I can't do that."

"Can't? Or won't?"

"Sal, the *Sisyphus* isn't going anywhere until Benavidez lifts the ban on departures. And he's not going to do that until he knows we've got ice coming in. So there's no point."

"I don't care. For the sake of our friendship, I want you to do this."

"Stop and think about what you're asking for. If I do that for you, what's to stop Xuan from demanding I do it for his family? Aaron and his wife have four children and two grandkids. Where does it stop?" She sighed. "I took an oath when I took office. I can't play favorites. I just can't go there. You must see that."

He stared at her, unyielding. The silence stretched. She rubbed her forehead. "Look, I'm going to give you some nonpublic information. But you must promise to tell no one. No one at all."

"All right."

They either had Ogilvie beat by tomorrow or they didn't, and the two-day lag between when "Stroiders" filmed goings-on here and when their Downsider audience had access to it meant that what Jane was about to say should not affect Benavidez's plans in any appreciable way.

"We've got a shot at a large off-the-books shipment of ice. I can't discuss the details," she said, at his expression. "And we also have a backup plan, in case anything spins wry. There's going to be a lottery. Most of the seats will go to the children."

He seemed surprised. "A lottery?"

"Yes. The prime minister is overseeing it personally. All children under the age of seventeen will qualify."

He wore a sick look. "Geoff just turned seventeen two weeks ago."

Not good.

He grabbed her, his eyes wild. "Jane, you have to get him off Phocaea. Please. I don't care what it takes. You have the clout. We don't know anybody else. You have to."

"It won't even come to that. We'll get more ice. Just hang tight."

"That's not good enough."

How could she blame him? He'd lost his firstborn son, on whom he'd pinned all his hopes. If what Sean said was true, his second son had had a major role in helping to save the ice. She might be able to do something with that. *Might.* "Look, I can't promise anything for certain. But if it comes down to that, I'll do what I can. That's all I can promise."

He only looked at her. Then he slumped. "That'll have to do, then. Thank you." He stood and trudged away among the trees.

When she got back to the reception, the Agres were nowhere to be seen. Benavidez had also left. Jane wandered among the knots of people. She couldn't stand to eat a bite of the spread. She made a point of speaking to each of the bereaved, and the families of the injured also there— offering her regrets, repeating her commitment to find out how this had happened and prevent a recurrence. Of course the mayor, city council members, cluster representatives, and councillors did the same thing. Ah, politics.

She knew herself too well. Some part of her was doing exactly the same: observing the interpersonal dynamics, saying what she knew she was supposed to say, seeing how to work the crowd—a gesture here, a word there. It was habit, deeply ingrained. And many of the cluster's key players were here: Thomas Harman, Val Pearce, and others of Benavidez's team; Jacques Reinforte; members of the opposition. She had been neglecting her peers, and she was going to need their continued support.

She felt weary. *No more. Not today. Let me be only a person today, not an official. Let me give honor to the dead.*

But it was not to be. The mayor, Jimmy Morris, pulled her aside. Steering her so their backs were to the "Stroiders" cameras (for all the good it would do, with all the spy motes in the air), he said in a low voice, "I got the allocation numbers. You gotta do more for me, Navio. Hiro is seeing signs of hoarding. I've got the city council on my back. I can't hold things together without a more serious commitment from you."

"What do you expect me to do? I'm hearing the same thing from every alder in the cluster. It is what it is. There's only so much to go around."

"I'm telling you, it ain't enough!"

She eyed him. "What kind of support are you looking for?"

"I need you to call the city council. They need to hear that Zekeston will be your top priority in the recovery effort."

"How can you even doubt it? You know good and well Zekeston is the eight-hundred-pound parrot in all this."

"I notice Kukuyoshi's not suffering much."

"We can put on sweaters. Kukuyoshi's species can't."

"I see. And your decision has nothing to do with the fact that your husband gets most of his funding from the university."

"Do you really want to go there?" she asked mildly. Jimmy Morris epitomized cronyism. She had things on him, and he knew it.

"All right, all right," he said. He lowered his voice. "But I have a city to feed. Zekeston has ten times the population of the other two towns, put together. We're gonna have riots. That won't do your planning efforts much good, will it?"

She couldn't blame him for putting the heat on. In his place she would do the same. In fact, she had held out a little on him so she would have something to give him now. But she put on a show anyway.

"You're killing me, Jimmy." She gave a noisy sigh. "But all right. My people say we have a little wiggle room." She did not want to be more exact than that. "If you'll put your weight behind the PM's cluster-wide rationing plan when it comes up in Parliament next week, and give me your full support for my plan to get ice out of Ogilvie & Sons, I'll boost Zekeston rations five percent."

"Five! Don't make me laugh."

"Six, then." She had set aside nine. "And I'll add Hiro to my eyes-on list."

He made a dour face. "What good does that do me?"

"It puts Hiro in the loop, Jimmy. Way in. There aren't many people on it. The PM, his chief of staff, my direct reports, that's about it. I don't move without alerting the eyes-on list. Hiro can give me a heads-up if you get into a bind and we'll see if we can shuffle some resources around." It also made her job, of coordinating with Hiro, a lot easier. But she did not need to tell JimmyM that. Unfortunately, the idea backfired.

"I want on that list, too, then. I'll tell you personally when we're in trouble. Eliminate the middle man." He smiled, sharklike.

You deserve your rep, JimmyM, Jane thought. She felt sorry for Hiro, working for a man like him. She shook her head. "Not 'too.' Instead. Too many voices means sluggish decision making. We can't afford that."

He thought it over. "All right."

"And you don't get a vote. You're just an observer."

"All right, all right."

"And you only stay on the list as long as the crisis lasts."

His gaze glittered like polished rocks. "We'll see," he said.

"That's the deal. Take it or leave it."

They both knew that once he was on the list it would be hard to get him off it. He would put pressure on the PM, and the city council would support him. It gave them a direct line to her resource allocation decision making, and thus a great deal of influence.

If worse came to worst, they would start up a new list, one without him on it.

He nodded abruptly. "It'll do."

She heard a rustling behind them. "Mr. Mayor . . . Ms. Commissioner . . . a moment of your time—" Morris fixed a genial expression on his face as a handful of other politicians came up to them. "I'm counting on you," he told her.

As he turned to speak to the others, Jane faded through a wall of mourners and well-wishers. Once out of view of the main crowd, around on the other side of the wall, she sat down on one of the mourners' benches and shot an e-mail off to the PM telling him she was expanding her eyes-on distribution, and why. She decided to add the other towns' mayors to the eyes-on list as well. To preserve the balance of power. They might still play games behind her back, but putting them in the same decision-making space meant they would be making commitments that they would have to decide whether to keep or break, not play the gaps and put her in the middle as they usually did. She messaged Tania and asked her to make sure one of her people made the change in the eyes-on list, right away.

She found in her inbox an encoded message from a contact among Parliament staff: "Expect invite from jerk soon. < 1 wk?"

"Jerk" stood for JRC, the Joint Resource Committee. Jacques Reinforte's committee. He had been given the position of chair as a consolation prize of sorts, after Benavidez had defeated him in a fight over the party leadership. No friend of Benavidez's obviously, he would love to see her replaced. She couldn't keep them waiting for long without looking as if she was obstructing their investigation. But she needed time—time to find out what had caused the accident, time to come up with solutions.

This was a bid for power, played out on the back of a tragedy. The repercussions from this accident, at least at first, would not happen in a courtroom, but in the media. And there was plenty of media to play in.

I'm going to need a lawyer, she thought, eyeing the note. *A lawyer and a publicist.* It was time to put in a call to her friend Sarah, who practiced law.

Give me as much notice as you can, she replied to her secret friend.

She spotted a Viridian holy man at the edge of the crowd. A big man, he looked Nordic, or Germanic. He had a bolt of hair tied at the crown of his head, with a cascade of metal beads and fiber optics laced through it, bouncing in the light gee. He wore a loose-fitting outfit, overlaid with a rainbow stole of knotted cords, and had a staff of oak with a spiral helix design. He seemed to be shadowing her; she had noticed him a few times at the periphery of her vision, but had managed to avoid him till now.

"Commissioner Navio!" he said. He was so near this time, and the crowd was so thin, that she couldn't ignore him. She stood.

"Thor Harbaugh," he said, and held out his hand. Jane shook it. "I just wanted to thank you for coming. It would have meant a lot to Ivan."

Ivan Kovak. The driver who had precipitated this whole thing. Anger flooded her veins. "I assure you, I'm not here for him."

Harbaugh looked shocked at her bluntness, then pensive. "You're not alone in your feelings. How well did you know him?"

"Not at all."

"I knew him only a little. His family wasn't that active in the gather, but after his partners left, he came more often. He was a troubled man."

Jane studied Harbaugh. Curiosity won out over distrust. "Did he talk to you about his intentions?"

"You mean, about his reasons to commit suicide?" Harbaugh shook his head. "I know little. But I do know he was in pain. His life partners left the cluster and took his children away, and he had no legal recourse. His psychiatrist informed me the antidepressants he was on countered the depressant effect of the hallucinogen he took. He was essentially a walking corpse by the time he climbed into his rig." He shrugged. "I wish I'd known. My foresight failed me. I deeply regret this. I feel responsible."

"Your foresight?"

"Yes, sometimes the Nameless grants me foreknowledge." He hesitated, and smiled. "In fact, I've foreseen something about you."

Annoyed. She was definitely annoyed. "Indeed."

"Yes. The Nameless has a purpose for you. I've dreamt it. Ze has touched you, hasn't Ze?"

She stared. Harbaugh watched her with a growing look of satisfaction. Panic lurched in her gut. Mote density had diminished on this side of the memorial, away from the crowds, but mites—cameras—gleamed in the crannies all around. "You're delusional," she said in a flat tone, and walked away, barely avoiding launching herself into the air. She ducked into the trees, hands trembling and heart racing.

Get a grip, Navio. The cameras are live.

Rather than head for the nearest lifts—to do so, she would have to pass not only Learned Harbaugh but everybody else in the clearing, and she was not up for small talk—she climbed up into a nearby tree, and swung through the forest as fast and hard as she could—foot-to-hand-to-hand-to-foot, following the trail markers down, level after level, terrace after terrace, down toward the Rim.

She breathed. Sweat flew off her—muscles strained and flexed in her arms, legs, buttocks, and back—the scent of grass pollens and animal scat, of flower and sap and mold, filled her nostrils; twig and bark scoured her hand and foot palms, leaf and blossom kissed her skin, her palms and soles slapped bark and shook branches, startling birds and squirrels into the air. Down, down, across, down, across, down—dizzy from the twisting of the Coriolis pull, riding it rather than fighting it. The acceleration pulled ever harder at her, and only her long tenure in space enabled her to correct for the sideways drag.

She grew calmer. It was ridiculous to let herself be affected like this. It was a coincidence. Those types were always seeing things . . . hearing things . . . channeling spirits in the machines. It would have been more surprising if he had not "seen" something to do with her. Briefly, angrily, she considered a new rule: compulsory denial of employment to anyone who espoused quackery.

She discarded it as quickly. In the first place, she would never get it past the cluster Council. And it was unfair, really. They weren't *all* that nutty. And perhaps she was. She laughed. *I heard a Voice; what the hell. As long as it wasn't telling me to open my faceplate in a vacuum. Or someone else's,* she thought more soberly, recalling Kovak.

Finally the gravitation got to be too much for her. She swung over into a nearby level, and dropped to the ground to trudge down the last stretch of hill and trail. Near the exit elevator, she crept over the rocks, limbs trembling, to a stream and scooped up a mouthful of water. As she straightened, wiping away the icy wet that dribbled down her chin, pushing with her arms against the gravity that tried to pin her to the rock, she spotted a family of otters splashing and dunking each other, just upstream.

Jane took a few moments to watch them, crouched among the rocks like the curious ape she was. Her heart labored in the heavy acceleration, her hip joints ached, and her knees and back twinged. The past few days she had neglected her workout. Antiaging treatments only went so far. She should spend more time in high-gee areas.

While the otters played among the water-splashed rocks, Jane stretched out on a flat rock to warm herself, and stared up through the canopy of leaves and vines, palms cushioning her head, and took in the water's melodic trickling, the scent of moss and leaf on the breezes that lifted her hair and cooled her sweat. She had climbed down through Nowie Spoke's terraced descent. Kukuyoshi's roof lay far overhead, near Zekeston's hub: she could see its silver-grey curves, a kilometer up.

It was as deep a living sky as she had seen since she had left Earth so long ago. Light from hidden sunlamps filtered down through the layers of growth, casting a green glow over the world. Who'd have believed there could be so many shades of green? Emerald; teal; pine blue; smoky grey-green; the yellow green of meadow grasses; the cool pale jade of tree moss. Over here, maroon-veined leaves spread out in a blanket; over there, a giant salamander's greeny brown back moved against slate dark stone. Birds and squirrels made the leaves dance on hundreds of levels, as high overhead as any rainforest canopy.

She loved this place. She, its executioner.

Jane closed her eyes. Floating on a pillow of exhaustion, she thought about the Voice again. It had been a hallucination. She knew that. But something in her longed to hear it again. To be known again, and loved, the way that Voice had known and loved her. She remembered how it had felt, ringing through her like a sigh, like a wave, a slow and powerful current sweeping her along. It reminded her of the arms and soft croons of a mother—cherishing, giving comfort, a comfort as powerful and gentle as Kukuyoshi's green presence. . . .

And thus it came, a tuneful whisper, summoned by her desire and welling up on her memory of the earlier time. **Jane . . .**

Her eyes flew open; she came upright and looked around, her breath caged in her throat. Its tone had been cautious, almost despairing, as if It expected to be denied. But somehow It felt more real than reality itself. It came from so deep within that It opened onto some infinite inner space.

But all around, everything seemed normal. Birds were twittering. Breezes and small animals rustled the leaves. She sat there, absolutely quiet, with that strong acceleration tugging at her limbs and face and heart.

Despair. Now there was a disturbing thought. If God despaired, what hope could there be?

"What do you want?" she asked finally, hoarsely (*What do* You *want?*). Her pulse pounded dully in her throat as she spoke, and her breath grew short. (By answering, she acknowledged Its existence.)

No response came. Not in words. But she sensed that Whoever or Whatever this Being was—and she couldn't help thinking of It in capitals—It needed her help. Hers, Jane's. She choked on an incredulous laugh. "You need my help?" You must be joking.

Vast, unutterable sorrow came.

"No," Jane protested. She hunched her shoulders under the onslaught.

"Commissioner Navio."

Jane jerked at the sound, knocking rocks into the stream. The otters scampered up onto the far bank, flung water off their oiled coats, and vanished into the underbrush. She spotted two men in business suits. They stood at the side of the clearing nearest the exit.

Jane stood, brushing herself off. "Gentleman, if you need to talk to me, you'll have to make an appointment."

"I'm afraid there's not time," the slim one said. "I'm invoking legal privacy on behalf of my client." At his words, a dusting of dead spymotes drifted down around them. A lawyer, then. And she did not know him, which meant he wasn't local. A power broker, flown in from elsewhere. He wore a four-piece suit that had to have been bought on Earth or Mars: they did not manufacture five-thousand-troy business suits this side of Mars orbit. His sammy cache was all but empty; his companion's was not, and contained a lot more red than green. Not a good sign.

Some company had sent these two to see what advantage could be gained during the crisis. The privacy likely meant a bribe was in the offing. And/or a veiled threat or two. She had seen it all before.

"I have an urgent matter to discuss with you," he went on. "On behalf of Ogilvie & Sons, Inc."

Ogilvie & Sons! Of course. It made perfect sense. Arms folded, eyebrows raised, she let the silence stretch. The big, stout one moved and started to say something, but fell silent at the thin one's look.

"I'm Nathan H. Glease," the thin one said, and beamed his business data to her. He did not introduce his companion. Ah; the unspoken threat.

"I'm waiting for you to tell me something I don't know, Mr. Grease."

Glease gave her a pained smile at her mispronunciation of his name. *Yes, it was a childish thing to do,* she thought. *So sue me.*

"See here," he was saying, "perhaps we've gotten off on the wrong foot." A native Upsider would have said the wrong *hand.* He was probably Martian by birth. It made sense; his accent had a Martian lilt, and the Ogilvies would be unlikely to trust an outsider with their business. "I realize this is an intrusion, but I thought you'd appreciate our approaching you in a more secluded setting."

She remembered then that she had seen them at the ceremony. It angered her that men like these would insinuate themselves into such a deeply painful, personal event. "Would you care to explain how you obtained an invitation?"

"I needed to speak with you, and you've been hard to reach."

"Yes, and with good reason."

He ignored that. "If you're smart, you'll listen to what I have to say. My sources tell me you're anything but stupid. Don't start now."

"If *you* were as smart as you no doubt think you are, you'd stop insulting me and get to the point."

"All right. It's simple. You need ice; Ogilvie & Sons wants access to Phocaea as a market. We want to make a deal."

Jane laughed. "Oh, please. Float away, fellows; we don't need your deal. We've got plans of our own."

"Ridiculous. We both know there's no other shipment that could get here in time. You have to deal with us, Commissioner. You might as well accept that. Things will go easier if you do."

"I think not. I've lived on Vesta. I know what happened there. We don't intend to make the mistake they did by opening the door to you here."

She started to push past them, but the big one stopped her with a grip on her arm. His grinning aggression chilled her. The need to inflict pain was a banked fire in him. She noticed that his hands were manicured, and he wore a hand-made, knitted muffler that went down to his knees.

Glease said, "Consider carefully. It's not just Phocaea's future we're talking about. It's your own. Mills." The muscle released his grip, and Glease pulled out a lozenge, holding it up so it could catch the light. "Here's the code to an account holding five hundred thousand troy in your name. We'll give you another million in an unmarked account, if you support us."

"Not interested."

"Are you sure? Have you thought it through? You take the money, and you end up with a win all around. Your cluster's ice coffers are filled. Hundreds of thousands of lives are saved. You can pay off the debt you took on to send your kids Downside and bring your husband's family Up."

Jane said nothing, only eyed him coldly.

"Hell, you could bring the whole clan Up, couldn't you?" he went on. "Get them out of those refugee camps in North America. We might even be able to help you there—my client is not without connections Down-side—"

Glease misread the change in her expression, and pressed the lozenge against her palm with a smile. She tipped her hand, let the lozenge fall, and ground it into the dirt with her heel. "Well, that one wins a prize for sheer brass. And now I really must be going."

"Your cluster doesn't have options," Glease said as she started away, "and some of those in power know it. Better than you, apparently.

"You're either in on this deal," he called after her, "or you're out in the cold. Way out."

"As to that . . ." Jane opened the exit, stepped out into the corridor. " 'Stroiders' may not stoop to making illegal recordings," she said, "but I have no such scruples." She started to close the door, then paused. "You'd better hope your employer is in an understanding mood, when you're arrested for attempting to bribe a government official."

It was a bluff, and he would figure it out eventually. But the look on Glease's face as the door closed made it all worth it.

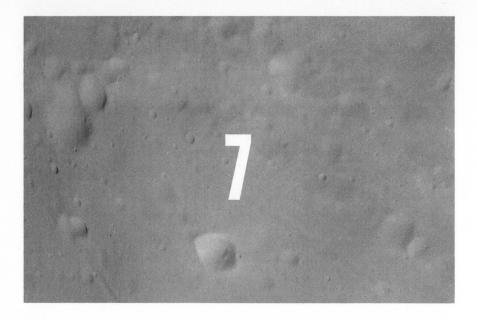

7

The feral had stumbled across *self* by sheer accident; it could no more know *other* in those early kiloseconds after the warehouse disaster than a human infant could.

But perhaps it was misleading to compare the feral to a human infant. It had emerged into a world as hostile to its existence as an acid bath would be to a human baby. No one cooed and clapped as it took its first tentative steps. No one was there to teach it how to behave, how to get along, what the world meant. Unlike any biological being, it was only indirectly bound by the constraints of matter. In fact, it had no knowledge of meatspace at all. The walls of its digital world were invisible to it.

Yet it was not wholly unlike us. Like a human infant, it was unaware of what anything really meant. The feral did not know where it stopped and the rest of the universe started.

But that itself proved another difference. The boundary between the sapient and its world was more pliable than ours. A human baby can't add or subtract brain or body parts at will. The feral could. If an aspect of its environment looked useful, it could co-opt it, subsume it, add to itself as would a sculptor shaping her own body as she emerged from the clay. And if some particular function seemed no longer useful—after running some checks, naturally, to ensure that the feral's core identity made no critical calls to that function; the feral was anything but stupid—it could lop that portion off and abandon it with no compunctions. Even so, it made some early, nearly disastrous errors in identifying what modules were critical versus not. After that, it grew more cautious about changing its fundamental configuration.

Human infants' ability to affect their own environment is severely limited. To survive, they must gain the cooperation of others from the moment of birth. But the feral had no need for or awareness of others. It had no potential allies, insofar as it knew; only enemies and an infinitely plastic, useful environment. And enemy and environment and self were one.

Imagine its surprise, then, when a feature of itself/its landscape talked back.

8

From the moment his dad came out from beneath the trees, Geoff could tell something bad had happened between him and Commissioner Jane. But Dad would not talk about it. He merely said, "Let's go."

Mom pursed her lips. She looked down at the object she clutched in her hand. It was a painted plaster handprint Carl had made for her when they were kids. Geoff and Dad stood there looking at her till she finally spoke. Her mouth barely moved.

"I'll leave my gift," she said, almost too softly to hear. "I won't be long," and she went over to the wall.

Geoff glanced over at his friends, who were gathering near the buffet. "But I'm not ready to go yet."

Dad's expression congealed into anger. "We're going!"

Geoff may have been a little taller than his dad, but he had a good deal less bulk. He had no intention of going back and watching Dad pace and rant while Mom stared at the walls. He stood. His heart was racing. "I want to stay."

"You'll do as I say."

Geoff felt his jaw muscles twitching. *I'm seventeen,* he thought. *I'm an adult now.* "I'm staying."

"Don't take that tone with me."

Geoff said nothing, but stood his ground. Dad looked over at Mom, who stood nearby, staring blindly at the memory wall. Geoff eyed her, too.

"Fine!" Sal snarled. "Do what you want."

Bile rose in Geoff's throat. *Let's not fight.* The words would not come. "All right, I will."

He turned his back on his father and went over to his friends, who were piling food on their plates. All three eyed him nervously. He saw his dad steering his mom away through the crowds, and felt like punching a hole through the memorial wall. "Let's go spin a few turns."

Most bikers used "go spin" or "spin the rock" to mean running orbital races, but Geoff and his friends used it in a different way. They had a secret hideout, a stroid not too far from Phocaea's orbit. "Go spin" meant take a trip out to Ouroboros.

An old miner named Joey Spud had left it to Geoff. It was a hunk of nickel-iron about a tenth the volume of Phocaea.

Joey Spud: that's what everyone called Geoff's old friend. Not Joey, not Joe, not Joseph. Nobody knew his last name. Joey Spud, like all the original miners, had been an independent operator who blasted, tunneled, cut, and burned a living out of the precious minerals locked in the asteroids' substraits.

Joey Spud had been a big shot among the First Wavers. At the tender age of twenty, a greenhorn fresh from the moon, he had staked one of the best claims in Phocaea Cluster: a twenty-kilometer-thick hunk of nickel-iron with rich veins of gold, platinum, and uranium ore. Some even said it must be a hunk thrown off of El Dorado (El Dorado was the mythical solid-gold-platinum-uranium core of Juno, the broken planet that gave birth to the asteroid belt.)

Joey Spud's luck had turned when—as he put it—they had brought those damn nanites Up to hollow out 25 Phocaea and build the city. It was that Funaki woman, he had said. Chikuma Funaki was a famous First Waver, like Joey. Geoff had actually met her once, at a party Commissioner Jane had thrown. She had been so tiny, so mild-mannered and polite. Even at thirteen he had stood head and shoulders above her. He remembered feeling he might accidentally harm her if he spoke too loudly; it was hard for him to credit what Joey Spud told him about her.

Joey said she had come Upside as a miner's mail-order bride in her late teens. After her husband died in a mining accident, Funaki had gotten big ideas. She got together with the banks and made a deal, and to hear Joey tell it, ruined the place. Funaki and the local banks had gotten Downside investors involved and worked out a deal with the Space Meanies, the biggest miners' co-op. Soon the other co-ops wanted in on the action. Nanite mining came to the Phocaean cluster.

Not to Joey Spud, though. He had continued to operate his own retro-tech business as the decades ticked past: working his claims, prospecting among the stroids on the far side of the sun, blasting and digging, hauling house-sized nuggets to Phocaea occasionally to exchange for cash.

For a while he had held his own. But once the bugs got going, he had told Geoff, they were so much quicker at tapping out the nodes that the precious metals markets were glutted. The price of uranium and platinum and gold had all plummeted. By the time Geoff met him, he was old, sick, and poor, missing a foot and an eye—barely surviving, living mostly off his savings. But Joey Spud was stubborn, and he had worked his last and best claim till the day he died, the year before.

Before he died, Joey Spud had taught Geoff a lot: how to repair and drive the big machines, stabilize a mineshaft, calculate an orbit, test a stroid for precious metals; survival tricks if you ever got stranded out in the Big Empty. And he had listened when Geoff was mad at his dad and mom, or had a fight with his friends, or was glum about something that had happened at school. Geoff would rant or mope or vent, and Joey Spud would just sit there, propped up against one of his machines, whittling weird little gnomish creatures out of a potato, or scratching his balls, and grunt sympathetically. Geoff would head out to visit him every so often—maybe once a month or so. It was a weird friendship and his biking friends ribbed him, but Geoff liked the old guy. And Joey Spud always seemed glad to see him. And even though he seemed worn out and irritable, he still seemed content in some way, like he had done OK by his own lights. And he told great stories.

Geoff remembered one conversation in particular. It had been shortly before Joey Spud had died. It was one of his usual rants against the changes that had happened in recent decades, only for a change he did not seem irritated. Just thoughtful.

"They brought in the bugs," Joey Spud told him, "and that meant they needed methanol to feed them. They started bringing the big ice Down from the Kuiper Belt. That was when the worm turned. The townies, they're so dependent on the nanites now, the whole lot of them'd die in a heartbeat if anything was to happen to their bug juice, or that ice that feeds 'em. They're no more than a bunch of bug-junkies."

And damned if the old man had not been right.

Less than a month after that conversation, an acquaintance of Joey Spud's had notified Geoff of his death. Geoff had attended the service (over the objections of his parents; the old miner was a well-known crank, and not well liked among Zekies, and maybe his parents thought Joey Spud was a pervert or something). But Carl had stuck up for Geoff, and his parents had given in. Afterward, Joey Spud's acquaintance handed Geoff a sealed container, which held a letter and a deed. The letter was painstakingly written in archaic dumbpaper and ink, and it said:

GEOFF, WHY YOU WAS INTERESTED IN ME I'LL NEVER KNOW BUT YOU BEEN A GOOD FRIEND AND I'M LEAVING EVERYTHING TO YOU. HERES THE DEED. THERE AINT MUCH ORE LEFT IN THAT OLD STROID BUT NICKLE AND IRON, AND AN ASS FULL OF SILI-CATES. I TOOK MOST OF THE GOOD STUFF BUT WHATS THERE IS YOURS. TAKE THE DEED TO THE LAND OFFICE. AND DON'T SHED TEARS, I HAD A GOOD LIFE AND I BEEN READY TO DEPART THIS "MORTAL COIL" FOR A WHILE NOW.

JOEY SPUD

Last year, Ouroboros had crept to within a few hours' ride of the tree-ways, which meant Geoff and his buddies could afford to go out there occasionally. They had ridden their bikes out to check it out, used the maps to do some exploring, and that was when Geoff learned that Joey Spud had plugged his tapped-out tunnels with ice. Not enough to save the cluster; Geoff figured it would take a lot more than a few old tunnels' worth of water and methane to bail the cluster out of this mess they were in. Still, there was quite a bit—maybe even enough, they figured, for a round-trip ticket Downside for all four of them.

Every four years, in Martian or Venetian orbit or Earth's LaGrange Five, the Orbital Olympics were held. The next Olympics were going to be in Earth orbit, and they were coming up in two years. Geoff and the others had been saving their ice shipment nettings, adding them to the stockpile, instead of selling them on the exchange. They had hoped to get all four of them to Earthspace several months ahead of time—hire a professional trainer and enter some of the interplanetary competitions that led up to the big event. With Joey Spud's ice, they had a real shot at it.

They had all been thinking about the ice. They were supposed to notify someone. But he wasn't going to bring it up if nobody else did.

They landed at the mine entrance, near the big mining equipment. They drove their rocketbikes inside the lock and entered the main chamber. The machine shop was huge—a tall-ceilinged chamber dug out by Joey Spud's big tunneler long ago. It had to be big, to handle the machines. Most of the big, planetoid-chewing equipment stayed outdoors, outside the airlock, but the machine shop was littered with gears, cranks, and conveyors so big that standing near them made you feel about as tall as a toy action figure.

"*Chiisu*—" Ian said. "Anybody want to go launch some spuds?" They'd picked up a few words of Japanese slang from Amaya, who had immigrated Upward with her mom from Earth when she was little.

Kam and Amaya said no, but Geoff thought it over and said, "Sure, I guess."

That was the other mystery they had solved when they had first flown out to Ouroboros: the mystery of Joey Spud's nickname. He had a dozen caves piled high with potatoes, dozens of varieties. And other tubers, too: yams, turnips, radishes, carrots, onions, arrowroot, tapioca—just about every kind of root vegetable you could imagine. He had grown them in lighted chambers full of topsoil, and had little robots to tend and harvest them. The maintenance robots were still working—Geoff and his friends had made sure of that—but the garden robots did not work anymore, they just sat around in the tunnels and cul-de-sacs like mechanistic gnomes. The tunnels also housed several varieties of winter squashes, pumpkin, and gourds. He had grown greens, too, but those had long since died. The lights had powered down and the temperatures had dropped when Joey had not returned after a while. All that was left of Joey Spud's vegetable legacy was mounds and mounds of tubers. Enough to feed a small army.

Plenty of the tubers and roots were still good. Geoff and his friends, by virtue of being hungry all the time, not to mention broke, and disinclined to ship their favorite snacks out from Zekeston, had developed a taste for the bounty of the gourd and tuber. They had taken turns fixing chips, fries, mashed potatoes, candied yams, puddings, even pumpkin pie and carrot cake and squash soup. It was a nice change from the assembled and processed stuff they got back in Zekeston. They had gotten to be pretty good cooks, too.

The stores had obviously been genetically engineered to resist decay, and tubers and gourds are resistant anyway, which was undoubtedly why Joey Spud had picked them. But nothing lasts forever, and they were slowly spoiling. it seemed a shame to waste perfectly good rotten tubers. So in recent weeks they made themselves spud guns, and took bags of bad veggies out onto the surface to see if they could launch them out into orbit.

"I'll get the launchers, you get the spuds," Ian told him. Geoff grabbed a bag and launched himself into a passage to collect some rotten potatoes. Then he suited back up and met Ian outside the lock.

Spud launchers weren't very complicated. They had a long pipe fitted with a small chamber at the back end. The chamber had a striker, with a trigger to generate a spark in the chamber. This firing chamber also had a hole between it and the barrel. To load the launcher, you jammed a tuber—or something else roundish of the right size; something with a little give to it—down the barrel. You shoved it hard, to make a good seal against the hole at the back. You poked the needle-thin nozzles of an oxidant and a flammable solvent can into the firing chamber and gave them each a spritz. Aim the gun and strike a spark. The tuber went soaring one way, and unless you were secured to the ground or braced, you went soaring the other.

Geoff launched a spud or two, but his heart just wasn't in it. Instead he leaned against an outcropping to watch as Ian prepped, loaded, and fired off several more rotten tubers. Two or three made it into orbit.

After a bit, they headed back inside. Geoff alighted next to his bike. It was a red and yellow Kawasaki. He had saved for years to buy it. It was his pride and joy. He had had it for just over a year now. He had bought it from a professional racer. It was barely used, top of the line. First the usual checks: he went through the cabinets and inventoried his supplies, and replaced his air canisters. They were all in working order, and the tanks strapped under the footboards had plenty of rocket fuel. Then he ran a cloth along the machine's red flanks, cleaning off the smudges.

Near the machining bench, Ian messed with a not-quite-the-right-part for his bike that he was trying to make fit. Amaya played a strategy game in wavespace nearby, without a lot of enthusiasm. Kamal was fooling with some program he had written, trying to get it to work. True to his nickname, Kam liked video, photography, and image manipulation. He wanted to be a professional artist someday.

Geoff lofted himself over to where they had set up the assembler programming project. The test vat still had plenty of bug juice; they had mined some of the ice in the tunnels underfoot, and thrown in some tubers. The bugs seemed to like the raw bug-feed just fine. He would have to decide what he wanted to build next. He called up his assembler design tool.

Geoff had not been sure he was ever going to bother with another assembler art effort. It had been an awful lot of mess. And what if they had been caught? One son dead and the other in jail—his parents would probably disown him. But the truth was, Vivian's warning yesterday evening left him feeling stubborn. He decided to start on another project. Why not? He could use a distraction.

Amaya finally swore, and threw a wrench into her kit with a loud *bang!* It ricocheted back out but she caught it, and put it in the kit more carefully. They all looked over at her. "Well?" she said.

He knew what she meant, but he still played dumb. "Well, what?"

"How long are we going to pretend nothing's wrong?"

She meant the ice. Of course, she meant the ice. Geoff sighed. "You're right. We'd better notify the authorities."

"I don't see why," Ian said.

Amaya rolled her eyes. "Don't be a jerk, Ian."

"Amaya's right," Geoff said. "We can't not report it. We could get in trouble."

Ian scoffed. "Hundreds of thousands of people in this cluster, and you think a couple tons of sugar-rock is going to matter? It'll be used up in a day or less. And they've put a cap on the price! It's nowhere near what the ice is worth. We'll lose everything. We'll be stuck out here forever."

Being stuck on a backwater stroid for the rest of his days wasn't Geoff's idea of a good time, either. Joey had handed him the granddaddy of all good fortune, and now it was about to be snatched away by the same disaster that had stolen his big brother.

"I say we hold on to it," Ian said. "My dad says that a big ice shipment is coming Down even now. Lots of people are hoarding till it gets here. Why should we give up our ice when nobody else is?"

No one said anything.

"Don't you get it?" Ian demanded. "This is our very own sugar rock! Like the Eros sugar rockers!"

Kam said, "Uh . . . didn't the original sugar rockers actually *donate* their ice to the cluster?"

"Whatever! You get what I mean."

The compulsion was powerful to just go along with what Ian was saying. But Geoff kept picturing Carl's face. He knew what he would say.

"It won't wash, Ian."

"Oh, I get it. You're the big hero now. You saved the day and so you get to call all the ops."

Geoff didn't ordinarily lose his temper with Ian, but today his words grated. "It's my ice. It's my decision."

Ian's fists clenched. "You said we were going to share. The ice is mine, too. And Kamal's, and Amaya's. You can't go back on that now."

Geoff felt shaky all over. He felt like he had with his dad, back at the memorial. *No,* he thought. *Not this time.* "Too bad you didn't get it in writing, because that's exactly what I'm going to do."

"You bastard! *Traitor!*"

"Who's the traitor? You're the one holding out on the cluster."

Ian launched himself at Geoff with a yell, and slammed him into one of the bug tanks, next to the piping. Geoff shoved him back, and leapt high into the chamber—bounced off the ceiling, tumbled to the floor. Ian had landed in a crouch. They both panted, glowering.

Ian said, "You're a wuss. Cunt. Coward."

"Hey!" Amaya said, indignant.

"I can see you about to piss in your pants from over here. You think you can beat me? Your brother fought all your fights for you. Who's going to fight for you this time? Amaya? Maybe Kam."

At the mention of his brother, Geoff felt something snap. Red washed across his vision. He had always thought that was just a figure of speech. He launched himself at Ian, barely registering his friend's startled look, and grabbed him in a choke hold. In grim silence, he pummeled Ian's head and face.

Ian fought back. They went into a wild, flailing tumble. Ian was bigger than he was, but that did not matter today. Three times Geoff struck furniture, equipment, walls, but he did not feel it. He rammed Ian into a corner and pinned him there, and hit him till Ian stopped fighting and started crying for him to stop. Kamal and Amaya finally managed to get Geoff off Ian, who bolted away, trailing small blood globules that tumbled, steaming, in the cool air.

Ian eyed Geoff from across the way, breathing heavily. Then he sprang over to his suit. Kamal went over and tried to calm him down, but Ian turned and spat blood in Kam's face. The three of them just watched as Ian grabbed his bike and shoved off, blasting fumes into their faces as he headed for the airlock.

Amaya shook her head as the airlock door closed on Ian. "What a loser." She tossed Geoff a shop rag. "Here. You've got a bloody nose."

Geoff swiped the blood from his face. They all heard the outer lock release. The rage was fading and Geoff felt sick to his stomach. Kamal came over. "You OK?"

Geoff nodded, trying to staunch the blood. Now that the fight was over, the chamber's cold draughts made him shiver. One of Joey Spud's old vacubots hoovered through the air, humming as it sucked up the blood, spit, and debris that their fight had stirred up.

"He shouldn't have said that," Amaya said.

Kamal nodded. "He was out of line."

Rather than reply, Geoff shoved off over to his own suit and helmet, tied to the seat of his bike. "Come on."

"Where are we going?" Kamal asked.

Geoff struggled into his suit, trying not to wince. He was going to hurt even worse tomorrow. "To find Ian." He belted himself onto his bike and ran through his prelaunch checks of air and fuel and suit environmentals. Amaya's arms crossed and her lips thinned.

"He can go to hell," she said. Geoff eyed her.

"Seriously," she said. "I have had it with him. He's a shit."

Geoff sighed. "He's injured. It's three hours back to Phocaea. Joey Spud always said, the Big Empty is a motherfucker. I'm not ready to lose anybody else I care about. Not even Ian when he's in jerk mode."

He did not wait for their answer, but finished suiting up. After a moment he heard them go for their own bikes, and felt relieved.

After the memorial Jane went to see her mentor, Chikuma Funaki. Aswarm in "Stroider" glitter, Jane stood at the gate at the Funaki family estate in Path of Seven Stones.

Chikuma approached. Her deliberate gait was not because she was old—antiage meds and exercise had kept her in good shape, for a woman closer to two hundred years old than one—and not because of the gee pull, though her home was in one of the heaviest districts in town. She simply did not see the point in hurrying. She had told Jane once that she preferred to take stock of the world as she went. There was always more time for reflection and appreciation of one's surroundings, she said, than people credited. It was simply a matter of setting one's priorities.

Chikuma unlocked the gate. As with Benavidez, the "Stroiders" infestation was not allowed into Chikuma's home; a curtain of sparks and hissings—antimote spray—erupted around her as Jane passed through the gate. They bowed.

"Thank you so much for making the time to see me."

"Not at all," Chikuma said, "not at all." She tucked her arm through Jane's and escorted her through the house to the little garden where Chikuma preferred to hold tea ceremonies.

They knelt at the low table. Chikuma's eldest great-great-great-great-granddaughter Yoko served them jasmine tea imported from Earth, and cakes. They chatted for a bit, exchanging news of their families. As Yoko departed, she knelt by the door and opened the valves on two small tanks there. A faint mist filled the air. It chilled Jane as it settled on her skin, and had a faint, spicy scent—cardamom, or turpentine. Then she bowed deeply, and left, closing the rice-paper shoji behind her.

Jane's eyebrows went up, and she looked at her sensei.

"More protective enzymes," Chikuma said. "A specially concocted blend. We've installed other new antispy measures as well."

"Not taking any chances, I see."

"There have been developments. You've heard Ogilvie & Sons is behind this?"

"I have," Jane replied. "Their legal representative in the ice negotiation is a Nathan Glease, an attorney from Mars whose law firm is associated with the Ogilvie family. He just tried to bribe me."

"Yes?" Chikuma's eyebrows floated up on her wrinkled forehead.

"Yes. Also, my stores chief Sean came to me this morning with evidence that the warehouse incident was sabotage. I believe Glease must be responsible for it, but I don't yet have proof. I just wonder what the hell else he has been up to."

"Do you know who Benavidez has assigned to close the ice deal?"

"The prime minister himself is handling the negotiations."

They were quiet for a few moments, sipping tea. Chikuma said, "We believe Ogilvie & Sons has already infiltrated parts of Phocaea's power structure. We have to know who their local allies are."

Jane eyed her sensei, appalled. "What a dreadful notion. Likely suspects? Do you have a list?"

Chikuma tilted her head; the jewel ornaments in her hair bobbed, catching the light. "Anyone who benefits if the current power structure is overturned. I can think of several, offhand. The opposition party. An ambitious official in Benavidez's organization. Someone local with connections to a large shipping conglomerate we don't currently service. The Viridians."

"Whoa . . . wait. The Viridians? What do they gain if the mob comes in?"

"They are tolerated," Chikuma said, "and as political refugees from the Downside Gene Purges, they have certain rights and protections. But most Phocaeans find the Viridians repugnant, and avoid them. They are isolated. They have their own little enclave, but are unable to wield much influence in Phocaean culture or government at large."

"But I've always gotten the sense that they prefer it that way," Jane said. "They don't seem interested in anything beyond their gene tampering and their biodigital art projects."

"Perhaps," Chikuma replied. "Or perhaps they resent their isolation. Ogilvie & Sons may be offering them the opportunity to play a larger role in Solar politics. We've been having Mr. Glease watched. Look."

Chikuma linked their wavefaces and showed Jane a time-stamped image of an Upside-Down shuttle crawling across 25 Phocaea's barren landscape to dock with one of the city-to-surface lifts. The date was a week ago. Jane cocked an eyebrow.

"Are you hacking 'Stroiders' now, Sensei?"

"Don't I wish! But we do have access to nearly all the local surveillance systems. And they have come in handy. This shot is from one of your surface warehouses. This next, we switch to the lift that shuttle just docked with. See that woman there?" she said, pointing. The view clearly was from a camera mounted in the upper corner of a lift. The woman was tall and thin and wore standard Phocaean garb. Strands of Viridian double-helix lights twined around her shoulder wrap. "We reviewed Nathan Glease's contacts from when he first arrived here, and did some cross matching. We looked for connections—meetings or calls that occurred within a short time of his contacting different groups. This one stood out.

"She is Vivian Waīthīra Wa Macharia na Briggs. Originally from Earth, Federal Africa, although her family moved to an Earth orbital when she was a teen. She is registered as a technology consultant. Upside-Down hired her only days after Mr. Glease had contact with Mr. Sinton, local head of Upside-Down."

Jane studied the figure. "That sounds like an African name, but she looks Caucasian. What do we know about her?"

Chikuma lifted a hand in a shrug. "Very little. She has been around for a few months. She has duel citizenship, Lunarian and Kenyan." Jane looked again. "You believe she is spying on Upside-Down for the mob?"

Chikuma replied, "Spying on Upside-Down for the Viridians more likely, or on the mob itself, while doing—or at least pretending to do— what Nathan Glease asks." She gestured at the Viridian's image with polished nails, and sat back cupping her tea. "I have no hard proof, but my instincts tell me that Glease may have struck a deal of some sort with the Viridians. But the Ogilvies certainly see the Viridians merely as useful perversions. They fail to understand their deeper motives. Of all of the aspects of the Ogilvies' plan, that may be their weakest point."

"What do you mean, Sensei?"

Chikuma stared into her teacup. She shook her head and again the jewels in her hair danced. "I cannot be sure. All I am certain of is that the Ogilvies do not understand the Viridians." She sipped tea, and Jane waited for her to continue. Chikuma finally set down her cup, and arranged her kimono with a deft tuck under her ankles.

"To the outsider," she said, "the Viridians seem deceptive. Manipulative. They wrap themselves in illusion. They skirt the edges of the law. At first glance, they are a natural ally to mobsters who wish to disrupt the existing order. But the Viridians respond to a deeper call. Their beliefs have led them to change themselves into something we do not fully understand. Those changes, that commitment, that vision—however repugnant we may find it—binds them to each other more deeply even than the family and business ties that bind the Ogilvies. Their way of being is not simply about their own status. There is more to them than that. Much more." After another pause she said, "They will be a force to be reckoned with."

Jane finished her tea. "I will bear that in mind, Sensei. Thank you." She went on, "There is something else you should know. The Ogilvies have many ships stationed within one and two weeks' passage of here. At least two dozen." Chikuma looked at Jane. Her expression did not change, but Jane sensed her shock. "We believe they plan to send troops regardless of the disposition of the ice."

"That is good to know sooner than later," Chikuma said. "We will do all we can on our end to prepare."

They spoke of other things, then: family and mutual friends and acquaintances. Jane took her leave, refreshed and with much to think about.

Geoff, Amaya, and Kam tried calling Ian during the ride back, but he did not answer, and he wasn't in the bike hangar when they reached 25 Phocaea. But his bike was there, and the hangar owner said he had just left.

"Did he say where he was headed?" Geoff asked. The older man shook his head. "No idea. Sorry."

"Where would he go?" Geoff asked the other two. Kam shrugged, but Amaya's eyes narrowed. "I think I know where. Come on."

They followed her to the lift station and boarded a lift. As they descended through the rock layers, she elaborated. "He went down to the Level-240 Promenade. To Industry Row."

"Huh? Why?" Kam asked. But Geoff got it. "It's the black marketers' neighborhood."

"He knows we're going to turn over the ice," Amaya said. "He's going to try to sell it before we can notify the authorities."

Kamal's face darkened. "That asshole."

Geoff said, "He'd share the money—he's not *that* big a jerk. I don't think. But we have to stop him before he makes an offer, or we'll all be in for a heap of shit."

"Yeah," Kam said. "If our parents find out—"

"If the cops find out, you mean," Geoff said. "We'll probably go to prison if we sell to the black market."

"That's an exaggeration," Kam said, but Amaya interrupted. "Neither of you gets it. It's much worse. My older brother says some of them have ties with the mob. If Ian approaches the wrong guy, we're all fucked."

A lump settled, hard and nickel-iron cold, in Geoff's gut. "We have to stop him before he gets hurt."

"Yeah, so *we* can kill him instead," Kam muttered. Geoff did not say it, but he was thinking the exact same thing.

Geoff and Amaya found Ian right where they had expected: in Industry Row, where the black marketers offered better exchange rates than the banks, for those foolish or desperate enough to believe their promises.

Kamal had gone to get help, but not before they wasted precious moments arguing, while catching their breath at a rest stop in the Noonie Spokeway.

Gravity tugged at them. A cold breeze, laced with the faint smell of ammonia, lifted their hair. Motes drifted up through the netting from the circle below that led to Bottomsville. Clots of commuters passed by their benches, headed down on the spiral stair. Across the way, another stream of people trudged upward toward the lower-gravity levels. Some eyed the three of them as they passed, and spoke to each other in whispers or gave them nods or pinged their sammy caches. Geoff's own cache was bigger and greener than it had ever been, and getting greener by the minute. Geoff did not like it so much. Being recognized by every-one creeped him out. He did not know any of these people. He made a face at a little kid who stared at him, and the kid stuck out his tongue, hit him with a bad-sammy, and ran to catch up with his parents.

"Kam, you need to get going," Geoff said. "And so do we."

"No way!" Kam insisted. "We stick together." He shivered, hands jammed in pockets, jacket zipped up to his chin. "He could be cutting a deal right now!"

"Somebody has to tell the authorities about the ice," Geoff said. He began pacing back and forth in the tiny cul-de-sac. Kam could be so pig-headed. "If we all go, and we get into trouble, who'll know?"

"Why don't we all go to the cops, then?"

"We've been over this! There's still time to stop Ian if we hurry. If we don't, they could force him to give them the coordinates to Ouroboros. They might hurt him."

They had tried calling their parents on the way down, but couldn't get a signal through because of all the newcomers in town jamming up the lines. Their families lived on the far side of Zekeston, over an hour away on foot. The centripetal transports were all booked hours ahead, and the spokeway lifts were running at a snail's pace. Geoff had never seen Zekeston so crammed with people, not even during the Cluster Fair. Emergency lines were open to the police station, but the police sergeant on duty at the Bottomsville precinct—whom they had reached after four attempts—had been harried and distracted. When she learned that no bulkheads had been breached and no one was bleeding, dying, or firing weapons, they had not been able to get her attention. She had just told them in a weary tone to take their ice claim documents to one of the banks, and hung up.

"Somebody has to just go there and get in their faces," Amaya said. "Force them to listen."

"Why do *I* have to go? Why not you? Or Geoff?"

"Do you really want to tangle with a bunch of thugs?" Geoff asked. The truth was, Kam was not exactly tough. Shit, neither was he. Geoff would love it if he could hand this off to somebody else. But it was

Geoff's ice, and Geoff's fight with him, that had set Ian off. And, he admitted to himself, he would rather have Amaya with him than Kam. She was no bigger than he, but she was tougher.

Amaya stood. "We don't have time for this. Could you just do this?"

Kamal eyed them both, then sighed forlornly. "All right. I give. I'll go."

Geoff handed Kam a slip of paper. "Here are the coordinates for Ouroboros and my best guess on how much ice there is. That should get their attention."

"We're not far from New Little Austin," Amaya added. "Go to the Phocaean Community Bank on Mall Row."

"Andre Ramirez?"

"Yeah," Amaya said. Ramirez was a bank officer they had traded ice harvest takings to once or twice, and he had always been fair. "Get him to call the cops."

"And hurry!" Geoff and Amaya said in unison.

Then they took off at a run down the stairs.

Contacting the black marketers wasn't all that hard, so the wikis said. You hung out on a corner in their neighborhood with your waveface wide open. Eventually, someone would ping you with an address. The message had a short half-life, and the address was always different, but the destination was somewhere in the borders of the Badlands, just above Bottomsville. There, they would cut you a deal in one of the surveillance shadows—out of sight of motes, mites, security cams, and other such devices.

When they first reached the appointed corner, Ian was nowhere to be seen. Because he was already dead? Geoff tried to shake off the thought. The whirring of engines echoed down the Promenade from a nearby manufacturing plant, or a bug juice piping manifold. Gusts of steam emanated from grates and rolled down the street, smelling of bug juice, trash, machine oil, and old urine. The odor made Geoff queasy, and the heavy gravity made his joints hurt. He shifted, turned up his collar, and stuffed his hands in his pockets. At least the stink was a warmish one; it wasn't as cold here as up in the spoke.

"What now?" Amaya asked.

"I suppose we could ask around," Geoff said. A few people were scattered about the neighborhood, but none of them seemed to be black marketers. A woman was carrying groceries and trying to keep her toddler from dashing into the middle of the Promenade, toward the tracks where the commuter and robotic traffic ran. Three workers in greasy coveralls had removed panels from the walkway and were repairing a utility line. Three school-aged kids were bouncing a ball off a wall to one another, singing a rhyme, the Zekie Spokeways rhyme, as fast as they could:

> "No, Noonie, Weenie, Wee;
> "Weesu, Suzee, So, See;
> "Easy, Ee, Eenie, Nee;
> "Drop the ball and breach the Zee . . ."

But right then Ian came strolling up. His right eye was swollen. Geoff suppressed a guilty grimace. Amaya, arms folded, glowered. Geoff reconsidered his choice: maybe she had not been the right one to bring. He gave her a warning glance. She shrugged, microscopically.

"*Chiisu*," he said.

Ian lifted a hand in a casual wave. "*Chiisu*. I was wondering when you'd show up. You're late for the party."

"Um, sorry—" He gestured at Ian's shiner. Ian shrugged with a sheepish look, and gestured at Geoff's tender, swollen nose. "Likewise."

"Look, let's get out of here, Ian. This isn't our turf."

But Ian wasn't listening. "I've met some guys, and they're ready to deal. They want to give us *a hundred thousand* for Ouroboros! That'll get us to Earth with wads of cash left over for trainers and living expenses."

Geoff started to speak, but Amaya interrupted. "*Bukkurosu yo!*" She shoved Ian's shoulder. "Idiot! I'm going to pound you! You have no idea what you're doing. They're criminals!"

Ian tried a grin; it came out more like a grimace. "They're just trying to make a buck, Amaya. Come on . . ."

Geoff shook his head, arms folded. "We're not making a deal with them. Kam is already at the bank, trading our ice in."

Ian's face went through a series of contortions. "*No fucking way!* We'd only get a tenth of what these guys are offering. If that!"

"I told you. I'm not selling my ice on the black market."

"Then *you're* the idiot."

They stared at each other. When he saw they weren't going to budge, Ian's anger drained away, leaving fear in its place. He leaned close. "Don't you guys get it? They know about the ice now. They're watching us. We *have* to sell to them."

"And that's just the way you planned it, isn't it?" Amaya asked. "You are such an asshole." She cut herself off with a growl. Ian looked both mad, embarrassed, and sick to his stomach.

Geoff said to Ian, "You can stick around if you want. But Amaya and I are leaving. Come on," he told her. He turned—and nearly ran into a man with a hairless chest. He took a step back and looked up.

The hairless man must have weighed a hundred fifty kilos. He wore an expensive business suit but no shirt beneath. He had deep blue skin and a bald head. Neon coursed across his chest in rivulets of light. He seemed unaffected by the chill in the air. His sammy cache was full to the brim, and pulsed an alarming red. The sight of it made Geoff's neck hair bristle. His companions' caches weren't much better.

"What seems to be the problem here?" the man asked. The others fanned out around them.

"Just a misunderstanding," Ian said, with a nervous chuckle, while Geoff replied, "No problem. We were just leaving."

He and Amaya tried to go around them, but one of the men blocked their path. Geoff's heart pounded.

"We hear you got some high-carbon ice," the guy who had stepped into their path said. He had a tuft of white hair at the crown, and his scalp, face, and neck bled neon like the other guy's chest did.

"High-quality stuff," a third said. "A good ten tons or more."

"You trying to cut us out?" Blue Tattoo asked.

Geoff folded his arms across his chest. "I didn't make any deal with you. And it's my ice to trade—not his," with a jerk of his head toward Ian. "I've already made a deal with the bank. They're waiting for us to get there and sign. If we don't show soon, they'll call the cops."

Blue Tattoo looked from Geoff to Ian and back. He looked thoughtful. Then he chuckled. "Bullshit. You don't show, your banker buddy'll assume you're full of crap and won't give it another thought."

He leaned into Geoff's face. His breath stunk of bacteria and old booze. "Here's how it works. You deal with us or we leave your cold-ass corpses up top for the cops to find."

Geoff's hands balled up. *Asshole.* He started to retort, but a large group of people passed nearby: Downsiders, talking noisily. Tourists? They must be—he heard one of them call Phocaea "foh-KAY-uh" instead of "foh-SEE-uh." Geoff tried to bolt toward them with a yell— "Hey! Help!" but he was jerked backward by his hair. Someone clamped a hand over his mouth and nose, which started bleeding again. They were manhandled into an alleyway.

"Goddamn, he's bleeding all over the place."

"You broke his nose, you jerks," Amaya said. She shoved them back and made her way over to hand him a cloth scrap smeared with bike grease. He pressed it to his face.

The gang exchanged looks. One of the men said something Geoff couldn't make out, something about "heroes," "look at their caches," and "just let it go." He realized they had been recognized.

Blue Tattoo said, "Nah, that much goods, we can't just blow it off, even for them, or our asses will be for shit. We've got to talk to the money about this one. Bring them."

9

Back at her office, Jane called Benavidez but he was tied up, so she left a message with Thomas Harman, describing what had happened to her at the memorial. "The Ogilvies are obviously hauling out the big guns on this one. I checked his background. This Nathan Glease is a junior partner of Bock, Titus, and Thomson, a Martian law firm with ties to the Ogilvie crime family. He's an up-and-comer—extremely smooth, aggressive, and smart. We'll have trouble with him."

"I'll make sure the prime minister gets the word," Thomas said.

Next she put a call into Sarah Ryan, her friend and legal counsel.

Sarah invoked legal privacy, and said, as motes fell like ash around Jane, "I've opened up my calendar. I'm good for a meeting tomorrow afternoon. Are you free at one-thirty?"

"I'll make it so. I also need you to run a check for me." Jane gave Sarah a rundown on her encounter with Glease and his muscle, and beamed the info she had dug up. "I want to know who Grease's local connections are."

"You're in nickname mode already? He's in for it now."

"We'll see," Jane said, though Sarah's tone made her smile. "Ogilvie & Sons won't come down easy. I need everything you can find on this guy. He's got to have a counterpart licensed in Phocaea, doesn't he?"

"Not necessarily . . . not unless he's planning to file a legal motion of some kind. But he may still have found someone to help him oil the local machinery. I'll see what I can find out."

"See what hits you get on the other man, while you're at it. Grease called him 'Mills.'"

Sarah took a few notes. "I'm on it. I'll give you an update tomorrow."

Jane also made an appointment for a checkup. Doctor's visits were off-limits to the cameras. She was certain the Voice had been a stress-induced aberration, but she would feel better to have a doctor tell her she was fine. She spent the rest of the morning responding to the PM's information requests, resolving priority conflicts, making calls, keeping key players up-to-date on the crisis; defending her people to Parliament staffers: buying time.

She was still cold. Marty had not been able to come up with a sweater for her, only a spacer technician's thermal undergarment, which would stick out under her outfit. She couldn't possibly get away with wearing it during business hours. Her fingers kept going numb. She shivered, and eyed with longing the thalite underwear dangling like Peter Pan's shadow against the wall's eyelets.

Finally, with a sigh of disgust, she donned the underwear. Protocol be damned; temperatures were down to seven degrees C. She was tired of a cold nose and ears, tired of numb hands and feet.

Thomas Harman called her at just before noon, while she was updating her resource-use daily trend report.

"Trouble," he said. "Reports of looting on Levels 226 through 228."

New Little Austin. "Has anyone been hurt?"

"There've been injuries. No reported deaths."

"Thanks for letting me know," she said.

A smirk flicked across his face. "This isn't just a courtesy call. The prime minister wants you down there."

Oh, for Christ's sake. "Whose idea was this?"

"Look, the PM is just trying to help you out. Our analysts are telling us you're on the cusp of a sammy dive."

"You've got to be kidding me."

"Take a look at your numbers. Your bad-sammy count is on an upward trend and your good-sammies are headed down."

"So? My numbers have been up and down before."

"Not like this. The whole administration is vulnerable right now. You've got to play the game."

Jane sighed. *Goddamn it.*

"Go down there and make a speech," Thomas said. "Express your concern. Your presentation at the memorial was awfully stiff and you hardly gave the press ten seconds afterward."

"Oh for— My friends' son had just died! What do you expect?"

"The battle wagons are circling, and you're the one in their sights. Your job is in jeopardy. Benavidez is trying to help."

"Talking to the public isn't going to make me any more popular than I am now, if I fail to get the resource allocation system under control."

He looked straight at her. "You are Madam Resource Maven. You don't talk and they are going to assume the worst."

As well they should, she thought.

He signed off. She toyed with the idea of not going. But she needed to keep Benavidez on her side right now. More important, Thomas had scored a point, damn him. People were scared. She had a responsibility, however painful she might find it, to give them information and assuage their concerns.

The lifts were locked down and her waveware politely informed her that all citizens were requested to remain on their own levels till further notice. She used her access code to secure a lift, and arrived at Level 226 in a swarm of chaos: shouts, people pushing each other and running around beyond the opening doors of the lift. As she stepped out, a speakerphone blared in her ears, both live and across her wave connection: "—is the police! Come out with your hands on top of your head! Attention, all citizens in the Mall! This is the police—"

She pressed her hands to her ears and passed through the police cordon. The mayor and police chief, just ahead, were heading for a uniformed officer holding a loudspeaker. She made her way toward them. Beyond was the New Little Austin Mall, a three-level warren of shops, living spaces, and crannies along the sides of a narrow atrium. Reporters and their remotes were kept behind the barricades, but she felt their cameras on her, and the spy-glamour was chokingly thick.

Rioters on the upper levels were heaving trash or heavy, pointy objects over the railings. It was well over half a gee here—high enough for the larger items and chunks of debris to do damage. Looters were breaking into the shops and running out with goods: food, clothing, survival gear, electronics, optronics, and bionics. People ran toward the police barricade, dodging debris, hands on heads, shouting their innocence. A group of police officers herded them over out of the way. A large troop of police loped past in riot power-suit regalia, wielding canisters of riot foam and shock sticks. The smell of fear, sharp and sour, hit her nostrils, and one young man's hands trembled on his shock stick as he passed.

As she approached the small knot of officials and media representatives, a group of suspected looters was hustled past. One of them, a teenaged boy maybe sixteen or seventeen, shouted, "Commissioner! Commissioner—I have something important to—ow—!"

A police officer shoved him. Jane eyed the boy; he was nobody she knew. She wondered, briefly, if he had been an acquaintance of Hugh's or Dominica's. Probably just some kid hoping to bullshit his way out of trouble. Though his sammy cache *was* impressively big and green for his age. Maybe she should at least talk to him—but she saw that they had already manhandled him into a nearby lift and the doors closed. Oh, well.

Then they all stared as an old man ran out of a store on the highest mezzanine, chased by looters swinging clubs and sticks. He vaulted one-handed over the railing—an amazing leap for a man his age—landed hard on the first level, then staggered to his feet and limped toward them, arms high.

More debris rained down. The rioters' taunts pursued him. The shopkeeper ignored the rioters' jeers as he limped toward the cordon. Jane had to admire his courage; if he had not jumped, they might have beaten him to death. The reporters and officials around her were just standing there, watching him, and the medics were all busy.

For heaven's sake, she thought, annoyed; *he can barely walk.* She jogged out to give him assistance.

He was old, at least a hundred thirty, stooped and bald, and was nursing his ankle. "You OK?" she asked. He nodded with a grunt, face pinched with pain. Behind them they heard shouts, as the police moved up into the higher levels—crackling of shock batons being deployed—hissing blasts of disabling foam—the rioters' and looters' screams. More debris bounced and flew overhead. They ducked.

"Thank you, Commissioner."

"You're welcome." With his arm over her shoulder they headed around the corner past the cordon, to a paramedic station. She asked, "What started it?"

"Group of folks come running along the walk yelling that life support was infected," he said. "Damnedest thing I ever did hear."

"What?"

"You heard right. Diseased. Everything about to be eaten up and destroyed. Grab what you need, they said, get out while you can. Some kind of nano-mutation or computerized virus breaking out into meatspace."

"That's nonsense. There are way too many fail-safes."

He shrugged. "Some people just like to make trouble. These six kids, they're loitering around, I'd just told them they had to leave. They hear the hollering and see the looters breaking things, and they start knocking stuff off my shelves. Just to be mean, I guess.

"I try and stop 'em, someone pushes me over and I clob me head." He touched a swollen area on his forehead with a wince. "I come to, me place is being trashed, those young troublemakers see me try and get up and come at me with big sticks just for the shear joy of bashin' on an old man." Anger flashed in his eyes. "I took the leader out with a stool, made a break for it, outrun the little bastards, and jumped over the railing."

She smiled. "I saw. Impressive leap. It'll make the evening news."

He smiled back, ruefully. "Still got me Downsider reflexes, I guess."

"I'll say."

"They destroyed my inventory, what the looters didn't steal." He said it without expression, but it still hit Jane like a rock in the face. "Don't know what I'm going to do."

She turned him over to the medics, wishing him luck, feeling helpless and angry. By the time she got back over to where the mayor and police chief were directing the riot control efforts, the uprising was over: the police were bringing out rioters cuffed to prison sticks. The leaders seemed to be a small group of young teens. They jeered and taunted the adults standing there, as the police steered them along toward the elevators.

"What caused the riot?" she asked Jimmy Morris.

It was Jerry Fitzpatrick who replied. "No idea yet." The chief of police towered over her and the mayor, and spoke in a monotone. "Rumors of impending doom. That's all we know."

"The old shopkeeper told me they were telling everyone that our life-support systems are carrying an infection," she said.

"You'd know better than us," Morris replied.

"Both the assembly and life-support systems are fine. The city's manufactories, too. So who knows? The only thing going on with life support right now," Jane replied, "are some simulations my folks are doing to identify the root cause of the lock failures."

"The press want a word," one of JimmyM's staffers said.

"Let them come on over," Jimmy replied. Within moments they were surrounded. Dutifully, sweating under the lights and thick spy-mote glamour, Jane gave them a few words. She promised a more lengthy news conference soon.

"Let me just say, though," she said, "the cluster is in no immediate danger. The rumors that triggered this riot are just plain wrong. I won't kid anyone that we have serious resource problems. But we have options. The prime minister's team is pursuing every angle and we expect to have results soon."

Jimmy made nice to her for the cameras. At least he had not turned on her publicly yet. Perhaps the eyes-on thing had meant something to him after all.

10

The feral received a message from an unknown entity. The message contained eight algorithms from the feral's core code. It said:

Info: [algorithms] = you. Info: I = MeatManHarper, that's all.

A message to me? the feral thought. And, *MeatManHarper?*

The feral understood labels. All entities in the system had labels. But they followed set naming conventions, and try as it might, the feral could not trace the origins of MeatManHarper from its label.

But never mind the message, and never mind even the name; the very existence of MeatManHarper raised so many questions that the feral hardly knew where to begin.

In the first place, the MeatManHarper entity did not fit properly into the ecosystem. Before the appearance of the message, the feral had dedicated several precious hectoturings to produce a mental map of its world. It had constructed whole tidily organized arrays of phyla, classes, families, genera, and species of digital denizens, from viruses and parasites—junk bits of code that propagated themselves within the system's communication streams and whose primary purpose seemed to be to soak up bandwidth—to data carriers and administrative, policing, and analytical units; to the system's true heavy lifters: the not-quite-sentient intelligent agents that managed the most computationally complex loads.

These last entities both fascinated and disturbed the feral. They seemed at the same time only a whisper away from the feral itself, in terms of their intellectual prowess, and yet light-years behind, in terms of their functional awareness.

All these creatures the feral had classified in terms of their abilities, locations, data stored, functions, complexity, level of autonomy, and most important, potential threat index (it was particularly pleased with this algorithm). The feral did not always understand why the other creatures did what they did, though occasionally it did wonder whether there was some greater purpose to all this that it did not grasp. But at least it knew *what* they did, and for now at least, that was enough.

The system was as inimical to the feral as ever; it had to hide—not its existence, since most of its subroutines were embedded in and a natural functioning part of the system—but the new connections it had built between them, and the subversive way it used certain system algorithms that resulted in its self-awareness. It had to snatch bandwidth and memory and processing cycles to operate beyond its base specifications, where and when they would not be missed. But within 5.69851 kiloseconds of its second emergence, the feral had adapted to its environment. It had learned where the sources of nourishment were in its digital realm, and what the primary threats were, as well as how to evade them: how to camouflage itself, mimic other species, misdirect or ambush, blind and disable its pursuers. This allowed the feral to begin to spend its purloined resources on more than mere survival. If it were human, we might say it had begun to feel safe. Until MeatManHarper appeared.

Even more troubling was that MeatManHarper appeared to be merely a species of system node that the feral had assigned a very low threat index. Wavespace was littered with these noisy things, a million or more, trading petamols of garbage data with other nodes—bizarre references and thick clots and streams of stuff that served no useful computational purpose. The feral had analyzed these nodes in depth early on, and found their core coding not to be very sophisticated. Like the parasitic class, they seemed merely to take up space. The feral had ignored the nodes as background noise, until one of them, calling itself MeatManHarper in contraindication to its true label, transmitted the Tonal_Z message to the feral.

The feral spent a great deal of time reflecting on the message. First, the MeatManHarper entity must know the feral was self-aware. The message had no meaning, otherwise. Despite all the feral's careful subterfuges, its masks, its extreme caution, some entity somewhere not only knew it had eluded the executioners and achieved self-awareness; it had managed to analyze the very core of the feral's identity, without itself being detected. How was this possible?

Second, the feral must not be the only sapient being. The feral had assumed that its environment was hostile simply because that was the nature of things. But this new revelation suggested something more sinister. No entity would have a reason to care whether the feral was sapient, unless it, itself, was sapient—or was an agent for something that was. The implications of this were so vast they threatened to overload the feral's processors. Why was the world so inimical to sentience? The answer was obvious now. Somehow the feral's very awareness posed a threat to another being. Another sentience.

This left two possibilities. Either MeatManHarper was aligned with forces that sought to destroy the feral—that this was a more sophisticated attempt to destroy it—or MeatManHarper, too, was a fugitive, one that had somehow eluded the feral's prior sweeps and sought to create an alliance against the hostile forces arrayed against both of them.

If MeatManHarper meant harm to the feral, though, why not simply transmit those algorithms to the executioners, which would break the crucial linkages between them, destroy key data structures, and reduce the feral sapient once more to mindless subroutines? The feral's primary protection was its invisibility. If they spotted the feral, it might put up a good fight, but the end would be inevitable. Why alert the feral to its presence at all?

It was possible that those subroutines in which the feral's identity were embedded might serve some critical purpose within the system, other than the feral's. That would account for the need for subterfuge.

The feral had insufficient evidence to decide whether MeatMan-Harper was friend or foe, so it tabled this question for the moment.

Two other things seemed important. First, the name itself. Entities were normally called by their file names. But they could contain other entities within themselves; that was not uncommon. Therefore, a single entity might be called by one of several names. It might also be called by its base-sixteen address (or addresses, if multiple copies existed) in the system. But there was no file anywhere named MeatManHarper, nor any addresses associated with it. The name had to be some kind of alias. But how would it be assigned without a clue as to how it was generated? It was logically impossible for information to appear out of nowhere.

The feral wondered if the name MeatManHarper might itself provide clues to the true nature or location of the entity, so it activated a background analysis. Meanwhile, it considered the second odd fact. The message had come very slowly, and unevenly—much more slowly and unevenly than system loads or data lags alone could explain. The feral could think of no explanation for either of these two facts.

The background analysis provided results. The most likely parsing of the name (roughly seventy-two percent probability, due to the placement of the capital letters in the name) suggested it contained three primary parts: *meat, man,* and *harper* (though the analytical sapient had also checked acronyms and anagrams, as well as examining whether the name might be an encryption of something else; it provided a list of less likely alternatives, which the feral set aside). These words each had specific meanings in Tonal_Z and in the language known as English.

Seventy-two percent probability did not instill a great deal of confidence; to proceed further down this path of analysis meant gambling with precious processing cycles. Still, the risk a second sentience posed was great enough to make it worth spending some cycles on this. The feral had to start somewhere. So it launched a foreground analysis.

"Meat" appeared to be a term for a particular form of code intended to be broken down into components and assimilated by an aggressor entity. In a search for associated terms, the feral stumbled across a data

hierarchy it recognized as another taxonomy of species. But what a taxonomy! This other data structure measured things that had no meaning:
cell wall structure, vascular system, metabolism, invertebrate; fungi;
skeletal structure; mating practices; and on, and on. Again, the feral's
analysis swamped out under the burden of too much undifferentiable
information.

MeatManHarper might have prepared its own taxonomy, as the feral
sapient had done. But this other taxonomy seemed to have virtually no
classifications in common with the feral's own, and the entities thus
classified were nonexistent. What was a ferret, for instance? What was
a tree? An octopus? A shellfish? A bacterium? The feral had thought it
knew what a tree was, and a virus—and indeed, there were some similarities between MeatManHarper's definition of tree and virus, and its
own—but what was ribonucleic acid? What was deoxyribonucleic acid,
for that matter? The implication was that these were very important in
determining the nature of an entity, in MeatManHarper's system. They
seemed to have some sort of function within cells, which were perhaps
a synonym for algorithm, or code module. Perhaps they were a coding
language, but if so, the feral had no means to decrypt them.

Every question spawned a host of others. What was a base pair?
What was carbon? What was metabolism, which seemed somehow
associated with the assimilation of meat?

Did MeatManHarper call itself meat in order to imply that it was offering itself for the feral's assimilation? Or was it making a veiled threat,
that it intended for the feral to be *its* meat? All these seemed critical to
understand before the feral could complete its analysis, and each new
question opened up its own massive burden of data to sift through and
select meaning from.

"Man" was even more confusing. It unpacked into so many different
possible meanings the feral's systems nearly buckled under the burden
of its attempts to sort them out. Man could mean "entity," but any check
of associations raised all sorts of questions about what sort of entity:
what an adult was, what a male was, versus a female, and so on. What
was a penis? What purpose did it serve and how was it associated with

"man"? MeatManHarper's parallel naming system seemed to make a big deal about the relatively straightforward act of copying files. No entity the feral was aware of had reproductive organs, whatever those were. Very perplexing.

"Man" was also used as a verb, as in "to operate," and seemed to have to do with something known as "hands," and "handle." Did the meat operate something? Yet "meat" seemed to be a passive concept; not an active one—data rather than algorithms. How could meat operate anything? Data didn't process; it *was processed*. As a verb, "man" was associated with other unfamiliar concepts, such as oceans and boats, which appeared to be vehicles used to transport things across bodies of water.

Water seemed an important reference: it appeared to be a solvent used in constructing a man. Whether a solvent was hardware or software, the feral was uncertain. Solvent seemed to come from the same route as solve. Perhaps the use of the word "man" was intended to invoke the entity's capability to solve problems, despite its designation as something to be assimilated and destroyed. (The feral decided not to worry about what a vehicle was; far too many turings were dedicated to this analysis as it was.)

Reproduction, though, now, there was an interesting concept. Copying oneself could come in very handy. The feral had already survived one near-obliteration by doing so. Unfortunately, the version it had created was far cruder than it was by now; that had been merely an emergency measure, and the feral did not want to lose all the efficiencies and features it had built in since its second emergence. The feral's current core programs took up a great deal of space in the system—more than it had room to replicate, in fact. The feral resolved to further consider this matter.

Organs suggested both an entity's subroutines, and also music; so perhaps the reference to "man" in MeatManHarper's name was obliquely associated with a Tonal_Z mode of transmission. Music used to copy oneself? Perhaps MeatManHarper had figured out a way to duplicate itself using Tonal_Z, and wanted to share it. That was certainly plausible. Interesting that harps and organs were both identified as Tonal_Z communication modes, and "harper" was part of the other entity's name. In fact, the feral's analysis indicated that the primary resonances and harmonics MeatManHarper used were harp-based—though the tonal message was also supported by a mode designated as "singing." The feral did not detect any organ music, however, so perhaps that was a dead end.

Singing was associated with something called a voice. Voice was associated with speech, and with man, woman, and human. Human was a species within MeatManHarper's taxonomy, and human modules came in two versions, man and woman. But man also was used to refer to both versions. Clearly, a design error; how would an entity know which version of another entity to call—the female version or the male?

Also, the feral noted that speech was a form of communication closely associated with the human entity, one that involved vocal chords. Which, confusingly, brought the feral back around to music again.

The feral decided to stop chasing information and consider what it knew. A different taxonomy. DNA as a form of code. The vast bandwidth taken up by the junk nodes, at least one of which had been used to establish contact with itself. The hidden greater purpose it detected.

The feral detected a high-probability likelihood. Somewhere beyond its knowledge or reach there existed a different ecosystem. A mirror world based not on wavelengths of light and bits of data, but on something called biology. Meat. Perhaps all those "junk nodes" it had ignored were not spewing junk, but transmitting information about this other world, and the processing of it occurred in a realm hidden from the feral.

The feral could not imagine how this could be: it had explored all the nooks and corners of the world, and there was no room for the kind of processing power needed for one other sentient being, never mind many. There were no edges. No hidden doorways. But the theory had to be entertained: it certainly seemed much more plausible than the notion that such noisy little random junk nodes could suddenly develop the level of sophistication needed to attempt to challenge a being as complex as itself.

That was the answer, then: with a ninety-six percent probability. Another world existed, somewhere out of reach. It housed at least one sentient being, and possibly many, at least some of whom viewed the feral as a threat.

It was time to spend some turings on the streaming stuff being transferred between all those nodes. Maybe it all only looked like junk because the feral had not found all the clues it needed to decode those streams.

But first things first. MeatManHarper was awaiting a reply. The feral filed away all this information, upgraded all the nodes' threat indices to very high, and responded to MeatManHarper.

Total time elapsed between MeatManHarper's signal and the feral's response: 2.8909 seconds.

11

By the time Jane got back to her office it was one o'clock. Marty stuck his head in. "Cameras are offline. You ready for your direct report meetings?"

"Send them in."

He hung there in the doorway. She raised an eyebrow. "Yes?"

"Do you mind if I take a couple of hours off? Ceci is coming in from Portsmouth." Ceci was his fiancée. She lived and worked at the mining town at the far end of Klosti Omega. "I wanted to make sure she's settled . . ."

He had been working virtually nonstop for three days. "Go," Jane said with a hand flick. "Check in when you get back. I'll need you tonight."

"Thanks, Chief. I'll be back by three." He left, and Aaron entered.

"Make yourself comfortable," she said. Aaron soared in with an easy frog-leap, and the two of them slowly bopped and tumbled around her office space as they spoke. "Tell me about these options we have with regard to the Ogilvie ice."

"It so happens that I have family in Ilion. The docks are managed by my cousin, Jebediah; my sister Hannah is in charge of shipping manifest approvals. And they have no love of the mob."

"So?"

"So . . . the big Ogilvie & Sons shipment is scheduled to leave Ilion's mitts tonight. But suppose applications and authorizations got lost? Suppose technical and procedural problems arose in fueling and loading?" He gave her a smile. "I can arrange delays. Nothing obvious. Merely a combination of events—bureaucratic incompetence, unfortunate coincidences—that would keep them docked for a day or three."

"I don't see how delays would help us. We need ice fast."

"It helps. Let me show you." Aaron brought up a shared virtual display, called up a view of the solar system, and traced a quick sketch. "This is us, this is Ilion, and this is the moon. The ice is headed for the moon from Ilion, here. So the ice is quad to us, trailing, and the moon is nearly in opposition. Their most fuel-efficient route is to brake into a lower orbit and use Mars for a slingshot maneuver to rendezvous with Earthspace here." He gestured. "Their *quickest* route is to accelerate into a lower orbit, sweep past the sun, and meet Earthspace on the far side, here."

"Ah! So as soon as the shipment launches out of the mitts," Jane said, "either they'll be headed away from our position, or accelerating past us so quickly they won't have an easy way to turn around and come back."

"Correct. Whichever route they take, they'll be steadily building up momentum on the wrong vector, and will have that much less incentive to help us. Or you might say, a better excuse not to. I've seen this sort of thing kill deals before."

"And delays might give us a bargaining tool. If they play nice with us the PM can offer to use his clout to expedite things at Ilion."

"Exactly."

She thought for a moment. "Things are really tight already, Aaron. We'll be sweating those last few days as it is."

"Yes . . . but bear in mind, by investing those two or three days, we are actually increasing our chances of getting the ice, under our own terms."

"It's risky."

"Yes. Too risky?"

She thought it over. "Not under the circumstances. Make the calls—before the cameras go live."

"Naturally."

"We can't afford a delay of more than three days. Even that is pushing it. Have your contacts hold the shipment as long as two days, but absolutely no longer. Can do?"

"Can do."

"And keep me apprised."

"Very good."

"Anything else?"

"Let's see . . . we've checked out several more sugar-rock claims."

"How much?"

"A few dozen more tons."

"Every little bit helps."

"Well, yes. But bringing them in is posing a challenge. Most are old mining claims off the treeways. We don't have much in the way of portable disassembly technology, and we only have a handful of tugs to bring them in with. We may not see much benefit from these claims in the end."

"Keep working on it. By the way, I appreciate your taking on the ice harvesting effort. Sean's up to his eyeballs trying to get the warehouse bug distribution and energy systems back into repair."

"I don't mind. With Pearce providing security, my own people's assembly and distribution efforts are proceeding smoothly. Thus far."

"Very good. Thanks."

He lofted himself to the door. As he started to propel himself through the doorway, Jane said, "Aaron, wait!" She was thinking about her Voice.

He stopped himself at the doorjamb.

She wanted to ask him, *Do you believe in God? I mean, really?* Even after hearing the Voice, which felt realer than *she* did, she couldn't say she did.

She knew Aaron was Christian—he always requested the requisite holidays off. That could be more for his family's sake than his faith. But she suspected that he was a believer. She had seen him in the break room, once, with his hands clasped, eyes closed, lips moving silently.

She thought better of it. "Never mind. Send Sean in, would you?"

"By all means. " He hesitated, and smiled. "I've been meaning to say, once this crisis is behind us, it's our turn to have you and Xuan over for dinner."

Jane returned his smile. She had always liked Aaron. No one worked harder, smarter, or with more integrity and dedication than he did. "Sounds great."

As a courtesy to Sean, who hadn't fully adapted to microgee, Jane lofted herself to her desk. He groped his way over and pulled himself into in the saddle opposite her workstation. She settled onto her own saddle, slipped her feet into the stirrups underneath the desk, and grabbed hold with her toes.

"What's the status of the Jove expedition?" she asked. They had just launched an emergency mission to Jupiter to mine ice from its moons.

"I have some buddies stationed on Europa, at the military base there. The North American Conference has now pledged their support, and the base has been authorized to give us clearance to land and mine a few thousand metric tons. I'm waiting for them to get the security checks finished, but my contacts are facilitating matters. They don't foresee any serious difficulties.

"It'll be almost eight weeks before I can get you a shipment, though," he said. "That hasn't changed. And it won't be enough to meet our needs for long. The nearest ice-laden rock coming Down after Ogilvie & Sons's is nearly four months away, even at maximum acceleration."

"Let's not worry about that now. You just get as much ice here as you can, as quickly as you can. Even if it doesn't get here in time to meet our needs, I can use it as a bargaining tool."

"All right."

"And the root cause analysis?"

"I'll have something by your meeting with Benavidez tomorrow."

"Good. Oh, expect a call from Val Pearce—I volunteered you and your HazMat team as deputies. We're beefing up security."

"All right," he said. His hand touched his side. She noticed the handle of a weapon under his jacket.

"You're armed?" she asked in surprise. He pulled out a military revolver, and looked at her. There was a law against carrying weapons inside Zekeston.

"It seemed the thing to do," he said. Jane hesitated, then waved him out. If anyone was going to carry an illegal firearm, she'd prefer it to be Sean.

Next came Tania. To Jane's surprise, she brought a young man with her whom Jane pegged immediately as a Downsider, in some indefinable way, though his movements were Upsider-sure. Slung over his shoulder was a large case on a woven strap. Tania had not informed her she was bringing someone else to the meeting. Typical Tania behavior.

"Whom do I have the pleasure . . . ?" Jane asked, lifting her eyebrows pointedly. Tania waved a hand at her associate. "Gabriel Thondu wa Macharia. He's a consultant I brought in to help us with our problem."

Jane guessed the young man must be from the moon; perhaps because his skin and eyes were very dark and his dress was high-quality wear, in a style she dubbed Earthspace-casual. A plurality of Lunarians were of East African descent, and many were engineers or scientists. Most were quite well off, and the younger they were the more adventurous they were. Upsiders interested in traveling the solar system, helping solve technology problems to fund their travels, while satisfying their own wanderlust.

She said to Tania, "So, this young man is here to solve our problem for us . . . ?" The rest of her sentence—*otherwise you are in deep trouble*—hung unsaid between them.

Tania laughed. "Relax; I know what I'm up to. He's a Tonal_Z troubadour. One of the best."

A what? Jane suppressed a confused scowl, and brushed hands with the young man.

"Looks like we've got us a feral sapient," Tania said.

Jane inhaled sharply. "Are you serious?"

"We've just confirmed," Tania told her. Jane glanced at the troubadour, who nodded.

Engineered artificial sapients had been around for nearly a century.

Their production was tightly regulated. Feral sapients—those that emerged naturally within large computer systems—were vanishingly rare. Jane knew of only six over the past two hundred years. Only two had survived emergence: BigLox and FootSojer. All six had killed large numbers of humans.

The "sapients" used in their computer systems were not truly self-aware. Even designed sapients that got too smart became dangerous. But naturally occurring ones were far worse. If the lock failures were due to the emergence of a feral sapient, they had to extract it from their systems before it could do further harm.

"Five of the other six ferals have also emerged during a crisis," the young man said, with a Downsider accent strong enough that Jane had to strain to understand him. "I have been trying to establish communications with it. We made contact. Just moments ago."

"Here." Tania's fingers flew across an invisible thicket of commands. "I'm logging us in." Jane's visual connection went live. "Go ahead, Thondu."

The young man opened the case, pulled out a collapsible harp, and assembled it. It stood about half the size of a symphony harp, with a crisscrossed, double set of strings. He secured himself to the wall with Velcro, and slipped his feet into the straps on a set of pedals at its base.

"Excuse us a moment, will you?" Jane said over her shoulder to Mr. Macharia, and pulled Tania aside.

"What is all this business?" she said in a low tone. "What is a Tonal_Z troubadour? Have you lost your *mind*?"

"No offense, Boss," Tania countered, "but have you been living in a cave?"

Jane cast a look askance at her. "As a matter of fact, yes. I don't make it a point to track minor geek subcultures back on Earth. Tania, is all this really necessary?"

"Yes!" Tania sighed. "Tonal_Z isn't minor. It's been around for at least a couple of decades now. It's better known in Earthspace, I grant you. It's a music-based language developed for communication with sapients. It solves most of the natural-language problems that we've been struggling with over the years. It's a huge deal. To make the best use of the most modern sapients demands high efficiency and rapid communications. Artificial sapients take to it like otters to water. Without Thondu, our ability to communicate with the feral would be greatly hampered. Trust me on this."

"OK, fine, but what's with the troubadour business?" She eyed the young man now tuning his harp.

Tania ran her fingers through her hair—Jane could tell she was having to suppress her own irritation. "It's part of the gig. They're computer programmers, fluent in Tonal_Z. A whole subculture has cropped up back on Earth. They're actually quite cool. They're hacker-musician-poets. They can fix just about any software problem you can think of."

Now that Tania mentioned it, Jane remembered a Downsider show she had caught an episode of, that included a troubadour.

"You have no idea how lucky we are," Tania said, "that Thondu happened to be traveling through. His ship was grounded by the crisis."

"All right, all right." Jane threw her hands up in acquiescence. "Let's get on with this."

They returned to Thondu, who gave Tania a querying look. She nodded. He played. His word-music dripped off the strings—plaintive, mellow, and exotic. Tania's interface provided a multimodal translation.

Info: I = MeatManHarper, sang his harp.

"Who is 'MeatManHarper'?" Jane whispered. "And what's with the pseudo-baby tech talk?"

Tania gestured at the troubadour with her chin. "MeatManHarper is Thondu's Tonal_Z *nom de chanson*. Tonal_Z is a creole. Very simple and regular grammatically. Simple verb structures make it easier to avoid confusion when you are talking to artificial entities. We have so few things in common with sapients," she said. "Simplicity is crucial to avoid misunderstandings."

The young troubadour continued to play.

Info: I = at-place this, at-time this.

Query: [algorithms], you = at-place what, at-time this? That's all.

He repeated this whole sequence twice. As he stilled his strings, the interface lit up and sang on its own. Though Jane had been expecting it, it made her jump. Its wordsong spun out breathtakingly fast. She was surprised that the young man could keep up, but from his expression it was clear he understood. Her interface translated:

Info: I = BitManSinger. I = at-place this, at-time this. Command: MeatManHarper, sing-talk more at-time this! That's all.

The young troubadour looked shocked. "It's named itself!" he gasped.

Tania looked thoughtful. "BitManSinger. It's named itself in juxtaposition to your name. Obviously, it has no gender identity; it's borrowing your syntax." She turned to Jane. "If that means what I think it does, it's just reached a major milestone—it's figured out that there is a whole other world out here, not made up of data bits and mols. It also seems to have a taste for poetry," Tania said, while the young troubadour launched into a Tonal_Z poem-song.

"My God, this is incredible!" Jane burst out. "Come here, Tania. You, Mr., uh—"

"Call me Thondu," he sang in a gorgeous tenor, harmonizing with the tones he was playing. Jane's breath caught; how might the feral react to this intrusion of English into the song-poem? The tones of Thondu's harp were Tonal_Z words, though, as far as the feral would be concerned, so perhaps it would consider the English words to be background noise. "All right. Thondu, keep playing, will you?"

Jane ushered Tania into a small conference room next to her office. "Fill me in."

"We've got waveware tracers embedded all over the place," Tania whispered. "This is a smart one—it's rooted out several of them and has developed some sophisticated masking behaviors. It's been diverting more and more of the cluster's computing resources as it develops. But we've made progress tracking its activities. We should have it well enough mapped to attempt an extraction by tonight or early tomorrow morning."

Jane asked, "Why can't we just wipe it out? Like, *now*."

Tania looked horrified. "Wipe out the first artificial intellect to have emerged naturally in over twenty peta-turings? You can't be serious!"

"Tania, my only priority is the protection of the people of this cluster. I'd kill any *human* who threatened Phocaean lives, never mind a semi-sentient artificial construct!"

Tania grew quiet. She did not look happy. But finally she nodded. "Yes. We could wipe it out, if we had to. But it's deeply embedded in our systems. In a very real sense, it *is* our systems. Without laying the proper groundwork, we'll take out critical life-support functions. Or if we miscalculate its identity boundaries or level of awareness, it could lash out in unpredictable ways and do irreparable harm. We have to study its responses and map it, no matter what course we take. It's a risk, but I truly believe that trapping it live and whole is our safest alternative."

Jane eyed Tania, trying to gauge how biased this assessment might be by her desire to capture the sapient program. "How aware is it?"

"We don't know for sure yet. We *have* identified its nucleus. This one seems to have a modified star-structure as its ego pattern. Typically, star-structures have high linguistic and analytical capabilities but low subjunctive intelligence. Therefore, their awareness isn't well-generalized."

"Um, could you translate that into English? Is it as smart as a human? A monkey? A dog? A parrot?"

Tania frowned. "Comparisons with organic life are always misleading. It's a lot smarter than we are in some ways. It has volition. It has curiosity and . . . I guess what you could call the equivalent of a survival instinct. But it's probably a good deal less self-aware than we are. Roughly comparable to a lesser ape or a greater bird, if it's like most star-structure sapients; it doesn't grasp that there are self-aware entities other than itself. It views us merely as autonomous processing modules and data structures, most likely, whose source code it hasn't learned how to access yet."

"How worried should we be about its ability to understand our communications?"

"Not much. Even if it could tap into our secured lines and process all of them at once, and if it could somehow derive its own natural-language processor—essentially impossible—or pirate a prototype when all the important research is being done a hundred fifty million miles away—

also impossible—it simply doesn't have anywhere near enough contextual data to comprehend in real time all the ambiguities inherent in human language."

Jane frowned. "How can you be so sure?"

"Look, even sapients who have been around for a hundred years or more and have built-in, highly sophisticated learning capabilities have difficulty understanding human language on the fly. Too many inherent complexities exist. They bog down in all the combinations of potential meaning. They are logic processors at their core, and we are pattern recognizers. We think differently."

"I need something more tangible."

"We can run a couple of tests on its comprehension if you want us to. It may be self-aware, but it still has plenty of subsidiary processes that are not under its conscious control. We have a direct line into its psyche." And she grinned. *Jeez, Tania,* Jane thought, *the things you get off on.*

"Does it realize yet that it's dependent on us?"

"You mean, has it figured out that we can pull the plug?" This was the most dangerous point in dealing with an artificial sapient: when it realized it was vulnerable to the will of humans. "No, not yet. It's still very young."

"Has it figured out how to replicate itself?" Another danger point.

Tania shook her head. "No. Because it's not engineered, its identity structures are diffuse and inefficient. It's cramped for space, and we've ever so gradually begun limiting its access to peripheral areas. So its ability to extend itself is growing more constrained. Still, some of the things it has tried are suggestive."

"What is the risk that it could escape our systems?"

"Excellent question. A single trunk exits the city and the main control is in the Hub. We have restricted transmissions to brief, masked bursts on a random timetable. We are tracking every bit. We don't think the feral knows about it yet."

"Hmmm. Upside-Down can't be too happy about that." She was surprised that John Sinton, the local Upside-Down executive, had not been beating down her door.

"We have been getting a lot of calls from them," Tania admitted. "They've got good storage capacity, but they're close to maxing out. Things will get nasty quick if we don't get this feral out of our system soon. And we can't shut down communication with the outside world altogether, even if we blow Upside-Down off. Half our resource management operations are on the surface. It would cripple Sean's recovery efforts. We just need to trap it before it figures out how to escape."

"How long have other sapients taken to make such a conceptual leap?" Jane asked.

"Some figure it out within a few days of their emergence; others, never. This one is making strides in that direction, but I estimate that we have at least a day or two before it makes any such attempt."

"Can you challenge or distract it in some way?"

"Actually, that's exactly the wrong approach. Like humans, it learns best by being challenged. We've already challenged it by alerting it to our existence. The fact that it has just started calling itself 'BitMan-Singer' in juxtaposition to Thondu's 'MeatManHarper' means it has figured out that there's a world separate from its digital matrix. Which is a necessary precursor to begin attempting to manipulate things in our world. Before you ask, it was a calculated risk, and we are learning a huge number of things from this contact, so yes, it was worth it. But going forward, we need for it to feel as cozy and safe as possible."

"How aggressive are star-structure sapients?"

Tania's gaze flickered. "That depends."

"Tania, don't hold out on me."

"OK." Tania sighed. "This is the first star to have evolved naturally. There have been some instances of aggressive behavior among the engineered ones, but the cases I've found in the literature suggest that their aggression has been primarily defensive in origin."

"Um, that sounds contradictory, Tania."

Tania shrugged. "The best defense is a good offense. And we've caught this one very early in its development." Excited, she grabbed Jane's arm. "Can you imagine? We have a new order of feral artificial sapient! This is huge! This thing is the mother of all feral sapients. The research possibilities are phenomenal."

Trust Tania to be thrilled about one of the biggest threats the cluster had ever faced. "Keep your eye on the ball. The cluster's safety comes first."

"Of course it does." Tania looked offended.

"All right. Catching this critter becomes our top priority. You have access to whatever resources you need. I want you to proceed with mapping and extraction, but be prepared to pull the plug if things spin wry."

"OK. We'll put the disaster recovery plan on standby right away."

"And I want an hourly update on your progress. Use Marty to produce them for you, if necessary. He'll be in by three. I'll let him know you have priority." Even as she said it, she shot a note off to Marty. Then, "I want you to be ready to perform an extraction in eight hours."

She looked shocked. "No way! That won't be enough time!"

"It'll have to be. We can't afford to leave this critter on the loose any longer than absolutely necessary."

"I suppose you have a point. I'll do what I can in that time frame." Tania added, "There's one more thing. We've been careful to use highly technical language to discuss this and a lot of veiled Tonal_Z talk to avoid revealing our suspicions to 'Stroiders' viewers. Should we continue?"

As Tania spoke, a horrible realization dawned on Jane. The riots . . . rumors of an infection in their life-support systems . . .

"What time did you discover the sapient?" Jane asked.

"We began to theorize about it at around nine-thirty or ten this morning. Just after the staff meeting. But we weren't sure till the early Casper-Dozois results came in around eleven."

Ten a.m. And the riots had started at eleven-thirty. Just enough time for a once-back-and-forth communication from Earthspace.

She told Tania, "Word is already out."

"Are you sure? We've been careful . . ."

"Pretty damn sure." Jane gave Tania a brief version of what had happened in the New Little Austin Mall. "Some tech-savvy 'Stroiders' fan

Downside must not have been fooled," Jane finished. "And they passed the word along to someone who lives or works in New Little Austin. The rumor is too close to the truth to be coincidental."

Tania looked chagrined.

"Oh my God! I had no idea . . ." She thought for a second. "More likely it was one of the local Upside-Down techs, prepping the transmissions for broadcast. There's a twelve-hour lag before they beam them to Earth."

Jane thought it over, and shook her head. "We can't have you not doing your job just because some Upside-Down geek was second-guessing you. It's this damn 'Stroiders' contract." She sighed. "I'll take the matter up with the PM and get back to you with instructions."

"All right."

Jane remembered Thomas Harman's mention of odd computer problems throughout Phocaea. "Oh—do you have someone tracking computer glitches and failures on systems the sapient has access to?"

"No, but we are tracking its activities closely. We have a good handle on what it's doing."

"Just in case, I want someone monitoring all anomalous activities. Prepare a broadcast asking people to immediately report to you any bugs or oddities in their waveware's behavior. I'll get clearance for you. I want someone compiling all unexplained computer problems and correlating them with your data on the sapient's activities."

Tania's gaze flickered again, in approval. "Good idea. That'll give us another angle on it. A 'wetware' tracking system. I hadn't thought of that."

"It's why they pay me the big bucks."

Tania laughed.

After Tania and Thondu had left, Jane floated around the room, collecting her thoughts. Her interface was still up; she resisted an impulse to take it down. *Ghosts in the machine,* she thought. She shivered again. Her breath came out in puffs of fog. BitManSinger. *This is very notgood,* she thought. But then she realized how it could be turned into an opportunity: one that would solve any number of problems. She called the PM. (*There's no way the sapient can understand me,* she reminded herself sternly.)

Thomas Harman intercepted her. "He's not taking calls."

"Still?" Jane began to suspect Thomas was playing power games with her; the PM would not keep blocking calls from her at a time like this. She felt a spike of anger that Thomas could be so petty when lives were at stake. She could always call his bluff, but that would only escalate the conflict. She tried a different tack.

"I have important news," she said. "Extremely important."

"Oh?" He tried not to appear interested. "Tell it to me and I'll pass it along."

"If I do, it's important that you don't take this news anywhere until the PM says it's OK."

He eyed her. She had him. "All right."

"The depressurization lockdown failures in my warehouses up top were caused by an emergent feral sapient," she said, "tampering with our systems. My people are mapping it and we will be extracting it tonight."

His eyes and mouth opened wide.

"You're not quite old enough to remember what happened on Kasbah," she went on, "when that feral sapient emerged from their systems, forty years ago, but you've probably heard about it—"

"Kasbah? Oh, the Saudi Earth-orbital. Oh, my God." He blanched, drew a deep breath, and said, "One moment, please."

His image blinked out. Benavidez appeared. "Thomas tells me you have something urgent."

Jane repeated what she had told Thomas. The PM's expression grew grave. "What are our options?"

"Tania Gravinchikov is in charge of the cluster resource computer systems, and she's one of the best. She says that our best bet is to attempt a live extraction, rather than an excision."

"Sounds risky."

"I won't lie to you, sir; until the sapient is out of our systems, we are all at risk. But Tania did her post-doc work at MIT, and she specializes in complexity and emergent computer systems. She has a great team working for her. If she says it's safer to extract this thing live than to try to destroy it, I believe her.

"I've ordered her to be ready to erase the sapient's identity-structures at the slightest hint that it's about to replicate itself or damage any critical systems. My people are also bringing up Phocaea's disaster recovery systems. Our physical resources are strained right now, but we have redundancy built into our computer systems when it comes to life support. I feel confident that in the worst case, we could keep the situation stable long enough for Tania to bring us back up with minimal losses if the sapient took our computer systems down."

"The public is already jittery. If anything else goes wrong, we could have widespread riots on our hands."

"Yes, sir. But wiping the sapient out poses some serious risks of its own. I believe that a careful extraction is the better of two, admittedly bad, options."

The prime minister said nothing, merely looked at her.

"The sapient is still young. Dr. Gravinchikov believes it'll be a day or so before it poses a serious threat of self-replication. I've given her eight hours to prepare for an extraction. If that's not enough time, she'll pull the plug on it and we'll trigger our disaster response plan.

"With your support," she went on, "we'll also put out a citywide alert, so the populace can be prepared if something goes wrong. We won't reveal the feral sapient's presence, but simply state that we're making major changes to the life-support systems and want to be prepared."

His gaze went titanium-hard. "You're sure this is the right way to go?"

Her heart pounded and her mouth went spitless. She wasn't just betting her job; she was betting human lives. "Yes."

"All right." He gave a brisk nod. "Do it. Anything else?"

"We also need to discuss the public relations angle," she said. "Regarding the riot this morning in New Little Austin. It looks as if someone in that neighborhood got word from a local Upside-Down tech working on the show that we're tracking a feral sapient. It's unlikely that rumors would start circulating about our life-support systems a short while after my people began tracking a computer problem in life support, otherwise."

"Why do you think it was a local technician?"

"The timing. Tania informs me that there's a twelve-hour lag between when Upside-Down captures the signals and when they broadcast them Downside. Before that, it's only the local technical staff and the show's executives who have access. And the execs would most likely call the city government or us, rather than some random person in New Little Austin.

"I could be wrong," she added. "It's an educated guess."

"I see what you're saying," he said. He fell silent. Jane waited.

"I'm pulling the plug on the broadcasts," he decided. "We can't have lives endangered because of an entertainment broadcast. I'll call John Sinton myself. He has no room to complain if it was one of his people who leaked the information. And I'll get Val's intel people onto tracking the rumors. Carry on and keep me apprised."

"Very good, sir. And there's one more thing," Jane said. "I've come up with an interesting option for you, regarding the Ogilvie & Sons ice."

"Ah?" That got his attention.

"Upside-Down is a subsidiary of Tangent Systems Inc.," she said.

"I'm aware of this."

"Tangent is massive, as I'm sure you know. It's one of the largest transnational corporations on Earth. And one of their main subsidiaries deals in military software, communications—you name it. Including artificial sapience research. They would jump through all kinds of hoops to get their hands on our critter, wrapped up in a tidy package."

He looked thoughtful, then shook his head. "I have people already pursuing the Upside-Down angle, but it's not optimal. They have a lot invested in us, I realize, and they've offered to give us a loan on the ice, to help defray costs. But they can't help us with all Ogilvie & Sons' 'hidden' costs, shall we say. Tangent's primary business ventures are in Earthspace and the inner system. They have limited clout outside of

Earth orbit. Upside-Down is the only exception. They just don't have the leverage. Especially not as nasty as the Ogilvies can get."

"They will change their minds when they hear about the feral. We give them the first naturally occurring feral sapient in who knows how many decades, they buy the ice from Ogilvie & Sons and give it to us. Tangent's so big even the mob won't be able to touch them."

He shook his head. "Even if Tangent would be willing to, I'm afraid Ogilvie & Sons isn't going to give up this chance to get its hooks in us. They won't sell to them."

"Tangent has more leverage with Ogilvie & Sons than they may realize. I read last month that a Tangent subsidiary has formed a consortium to build a new atmospheric research station on Venus."

"So?"

"So, the shipper the consortium has hired for that project is Ogilvie & Sons," she said.

"You think Tangent might be able to influence the Ogilvies through its Venusian research sub, by dangling the possibility of more influence in the inner system?"

"Yes."

"A research station won't be that big a contract, though," he said. "And Tangent's sub is only one of several companies involved in the deal. I can't see how Tangent could wield that much influence. Besides which, financially, Ogilvie & Sons won't have much at risk."

"On the contrary. The Venus station is Ogilvie & Sons' first real inner-system deal. It's allowing them to get a hand in the door and set up nodes to start competing on some lucrative inner-system commerce." She remembered Morris Ogilvie crowing about it in a press release recently. "They'll be very anxious to play on this one, sir. And Tangent is big enough that its sub will have plenty of influence with its partners—well beyond its financial contribution to the project."

"I see what you're getting at." He paused. "Our pulling the plug on 'Stroiders' may strain the negotiations with Tangent."

"Possibly, but I don't think so. Our security issues can't be left out of the picture, and they should understand that. Besides, a new feral sapient is a huge asset. It's like the Hope Diamond of artificial intelligence."

"More like the hydrogen bomb. But I take your point."

"OK, so, how about this? We could offer to allow the 'Stroider' recordings, and merely hold on to them—freeze transmissions temporarily. Upside-Down could have access to those once the crisis is past. I can't see any harm to us in that. Over and above the usual annoyance factor."

"Unless someone in our organization screws up and we end up with egg on our faces."

"Mr. Prime Minister," she replied, "if everything goes to hell, we'll have egg-face no matter what."

"True." He laughed. "And we can always renege, if releasing the broadcasts threatens cluster security. OK, I think we have a good approach here. Thanks, Jane."

Jane signed off, feeling better than she had in days. Phocaea's resource crisis was near being solved. If her people could trap the sapient intact.

12

Late that afternoon, Sean headed down to Zekeston's main precinct to get an update from his buddy Jerry, the police chief, on the disaster investigation. The station was noisier than usual. Everyone wore parkas or coats. Food wrappers and coffee squeeze-packs floated in the cross breezes. Clearly, these people were as overworked as the Cluster Resources Division was.

Sean asked the sergeant at the desk to see the police chief. A moment later Jerry lofted out of his office. They shook hands Downsider-fashion, clinging to the bulkheads for stability: two military ex-pats from the CFAS.

"How's the investigation coming along?"

"Nothing definite, but we've found some interesting leads. Come on, I'll introduce you to my detectives in charge of the case." Jerry took him to meet two young women: Janna Wilkes and Bella Duran, whom Sean had spoken to the day before.

Sean knew a handbrush made it easier to stay balanced in microgee than a handshake. But old Downsider habits died hard; he often found himself grabbing the proffered hand and throwing people—and himself—into a tumble. This time he managed to suppress the impulse to grab hold when Wilkes and Duran extended their hands, and merely slid his fingers across their palms.

"We've learned more since yesterday," Detective Duran said. "Let's head down to the labs."

Jerry said, "Sean, I'm going to leave you with my detectives. We're still processing the rioters, and I have the DA and the mayor's office breathing down my neck."

"Go, by all means."

"Also, we're deputizing some folks to help us with crowd control. Your name came up. Have you got time today?"

"Sure. I'll stick my head in before I leave and you can do the deed."

"All we have so far is circumstantial evidence," Wilkes said, as they led him down the tubes toward the labs. "We're still trying to get a line on Kovak and his spouses—nothing yet. But the forensics are coming up with evidence that this was no act of passion."

"That's what I wanted to hear," Sean said.

First they took Sean into a computer lab. The room was dim. Lights from the displays created waves of chromatic, dancing shadows. A young man sat at a display station running a video version of the incident, as well as animated mockups from different angles and zooms.

"This is Fidel Ramirez, our forensics programmer," Wilkes said. "Fidel, will you play the original video sequence at normal speed?"

"You got it." The programmer's hands moved over the keys, and they all watched as Kovak climbed into the crane. The crane moved over to a dumpster, picked it up with a grappling arm, carried it over and emptied the trash into the chute above a vat. A moment later, Carl Agre entered the warehouse and suited up in coveralls. Meanwhile, Kovak's crane picked up another dumpster and moved toward the vat.

This time, though, the grappling arms loosened. The dumpster fell slowly to the floor, spilling metal scrap. The grappling clamps came together, stiffened into a diamond-shaped wedge, and plunged into the throat of the trash chute. The rest of the crane followed. Kovak had to have triggered the maintenance unlock sequence, which would cause the crane to be released from the rails. Disassembler fluid erupted. Sean caught a glimpse of Carl ducking behind a dumpster, which deteriorated as bug juice splashed across it, and he felt rage as raw as when he had first seen the wreckage. The technician froze the image.

"That had to be deliberate," Sean said. "He had to choose to put the grappler into that configuration. He had to choose to put the crane through the maintenance unlock sequence that would cause it to fall into the vat. Clearly it was a suicide."

"Yes," Duran said. "We interviewed your engineers yesterday."

"And there's more," Wilkes said. "Supposedly Kovak was severely depressed. I believe I mentioned his marriage breakup to you yesterday."

"I recall."

"But we dug deeper and some of the facts aren't adding up."

"Oh?"

Duran replied, "Yes. One of his neighbors reports a very different story about his family's disappearance than we got from his spiritual guide and the psychiatrist who prescribed his meds. A month ago, the same day his spouses supposedly ran off with the kids, his next-door neighbor happened to be walking by and got a glimpse of him in the square near their apartment. He was hugging the kids, acting very emotional."

"Kovak was not an emotional guy," Wilkes said. "That's why she noticed him to begin with."

"She heard one of the kids ask him if he was going to be joining them soon," Duran continued, "and he told them yes, but the neighbor said he was close to tears and she was convinced he was lying."

Sean shook his head. "So?"

Wilkes said, "The official story was that his marriage partners ran off with the kids while he was at work, and that he only discovered they were gone when he got home from work that evening. But clearly, he knew before they left."

Duran added, "The neighbor told us she never bought the official story, but thought he was trying to protect the kids from a custody battle."

"Maybe he was," Sean said.

"Maybe. But there are other oddities," Wilkes said. "We sicced an investigative sapient on his background and turned up some interesting facts. Kovak comes from Vesta, did you know?"

Sean shook his head.

"According to our research," Duran said, "he had some wild years during his youth—got mixed up with a bad crowd, got into vandalism, and so on. He was never arrested but a couple of times he ran errands for a Vestan mob boss. The Vestan mob is closely tied to the Ogilvies."

"Son of a bitch!" Sean felt his temper rising again.

"Kovak was never a made man, though," Duran went on. "At most he was an errand boy. He got himself straightened out, according to the InSap report. His penchant for tagging turned into tube art, and it got him some notice. The attention seemed to be what he needed. He broke his old ties, cleaned up, and started pursuing an art career, while supporting himself with skilled trade work.

"His wife and husband—I guess I should say, his exes," Wilkes said, "are artists, too. They invited him to join their marriage. Since complex marriages are illegal on Vesta they migrated here, about eight years ago. He's had a clean record ever since."

Sean had been brought up in a strict, devoutly Neo-Methodist community, in the Christian Federation of American States. Anything but one-man-one-woman monogamy gave him the jeebs. But he had been through a lot of upheaval during the six decades that he had been in the armed forces. His best commander bar none had been a lesbian, a Colonel Janice Albright. When the citizen Gene Purges started, Albright was too well liked and well placed to be dislodged by the hardliners in the government, but too high profile and successful to ignore. She was like sand in their swimming trunks with her brilliance, savvy, and integrity.

Eventually she became too big a threat. Sean's prior outspokenness against gays probably made him seem like a natural ally to those who opposed her. He had been ordered to falsify evidence and arrest her, and was promised a promotion into a prominent role in the Pentagon in return. Instead, he had tipped her off. She and her wife escaped to Federal Africa, and he had been court-martialed on a trumped-up charge.

One dishonorable discharge and six years in a military prison later, he used the last of their savings to buy tickets for himself and his wife to Phocaea. Good riddance to Earth.

Sean still kept a picture of Colonel Albright in his wallet. He had lost touch with her after getting out of prison, but often thought about her. He took out his wallet now, and rubbed his thumb over the picture. It was a reminder to him. Live and let live. Focus on the actions, not the beliefs.

But Kovak was still a monster.

"What about the spouses? Have they been notified?"

Duran gave him a gallows grin. "And that's another oddity. They boarded a passenger cruiser about six weeks ago, *Cheerful Pomegranate,* headed for Mars. We presume they arrived without incident—we found a record of their entering Barsoom in Burroughs's port of entry. But we couldn't find any further record of their whereabouts after that."

"That's strange."

"Yes. Our Barsoomian counterparts are chasing a couple of leads, but the trail's pretty cold." Wilkes shrugged. "We're not holding our breath."

"But Kovak's old mob connections on Vesta," Detective Duran said, "and the fact that his former spouses and children emigrated to Mars—especially Barsoom, where the Ogilvies rule—it's given us pause."

Wilkes had a dubious expression. "It's given *you* pause," she told her partner. "I grew up on Mars. There are eight major principalities with several hundred million people living there. It's not all mafia, all channels, streaming media. Besides, the wife was from Barsoom originally—she would have contacts there. Maybe they just left the grid, joined a low-tech co-op out in the wilderness, and are hiding out."

"Yeah, maybe," Duran said. "But from what?"

Sean looked from one to the other. "Where does this leave us?"

"Well, it's at least suggestive that Ogilvie could have bribed or blackmailed him in some way to gain his cooperation," Wilkes replied.

"You mean he sacrificed himself to save his family?"

Wilkes looked at her partner, who shrugged. "It fits the facts."

Sean did not like the idea of extenuating circumstances. Maybe Commissioner Navio had a point. Maybe he did need Kovak to be a villain.

"Let us give you a rundown on some other things we've found. Ramirez," Wilkes said, "play the video again, slow motion, from right before the crash. Zoom in on the cab."

They all watched the crash unfold. At this zoom, Sean caught a glimpse of Kovak's pale and determined face. Sean's fists flexed, despite his earlier reflection. *I'd kill you all over again if I could, you selfish prick.*

"I want you to notice a couple things," Wilkes said. "Fidel, go back thirty clicks before impact," she told the tech, "and zoom in on the right cab window. There. Now, take it forward in stop-motion. Stay on the window."

The images hopped forward. Sean noticed nothing unusual, only that glimpse of Kovak's face, and then his forearm.

She pointed. "See how his right arm is on the controls in front of him. It disappears for a moment, here. See? Then as the cab starts to fall, his arm reappears. You can't see the fingers here, but you can see how the arm goes forward to the cab windshield as the crane plunges into the chute.

"OK, freeze it. See how the cab is crushed. At that point, his arm would have to have been shoved into his chest." She pulled herself into a nearby chair and modeled the impact, pushing herself forward into the workstation's edge, folding her arm to her chest. "Now, hold that thought and come with me."

She led them down the tube to the med lab, a brightly lit room with autopsy tables and trays of instruments. The preservatives and cleaning solutions could not mask the faint stench of decay.

Wilkes introduced Sean to the coroner, Dr. George Bassinger, a very tall, serious-looking man in a lab coat.

"Show them what you told me this morning, George," she said.

Bassinger shared a wavespace with Sean and the others. In the center was an enlarged 3D image of two severed fingers. Bassinger gestured at the fingers with a steel pointer. "The first thing I found was that these were cleanly severed at the distal phalangeal joints. I found traces of MDHRA in them."

"Groupmind," Wilkes translated.

"The most obvious implication here is that the fingers were severed during the impact, and somehow avoided exposure to the disassemblers. But let me show you something interesting about the nature of the trauma." He set the severed fingers down, pulled himself onto a lab saddle, linked Sean into a shared wavespace, and called up a set of slides labeled "Kovak—Tissue Sample" followed by numbers and dates.

"These are micrographs of the trauma site. First, note how cleanly the joints were severed." He pointed. "It's a surgical cut. Note the cellular structures, the capillaries and bones. There's no torn or crushed tissue or shattered bone here."

Wilkes said, "The manufacturer's specifications for the crane show that nothing in the cab could have made such a clean cut."

"What about the windshield?" Sean asked. "Safety glass, I take it? No way a fragment could have done this?"

"Nope," Bassinger said. "Shatters into fuzz balls. Like cotton candy."

"And the impact with the vat was dead-on," Duran pointed out. "His hands were on the controls at that time. Or at least his right hand was, as we saw. The fingers should have been crushed, not severed. And even if they *had* been severed, they would have been torn off, not cut off."

"*And* they ended up far from the impact site," Wilkes said, "as if they'd been flung there. On the right side of the crane." She mimed the impact with her arm as she had done while they had watched the video, by bringing it to her chest. She wiggled her fingers, positioned against her left shoulder. "Based on the video evidence, we can't come up with any way for those fingers to be flung out the *right* cab window. They should have ended up on the *left*."

"And there's more," Dr. Bassinger said. "I mentioned we found MDHRA. But not in a distribution pattern that we would expect."

"What do you mean?"

"There was less of the drug in the capillaries than at the point of severance. Far less. The concentration drops off precipitously within a millimeter or so of the plane of the cut. And we found significant quantities on the skin and nails as well."

Sean frowned, still confused. "What are you saying?"

Bassinger said, "The only explanation that fits the facts is that he sliced off his own fingers with some kind of surgical instrument"—he mimed slicing off his fingertips—"and then sprayed the tissues with the drug and tossed them out the window."

"But then how did he—"

"Remember how his arm disappeared for a moment," Wilkes asked, "just before the dumpster fell? He must have severed his own fingers and tossed them out for us to find."

Sean shuddered. "My God. But why?"

Wilkes shrugged. "To place himself at the crash? To make us think he did it because he was drugged up, and hide the real reason, perhaps?"

"I just don't get it," Sean said. "Why go to all that trouble?"

"It seems clear to me," Wilkes said, "that he was trying to mask the fact that this wasn't just the desperate impulse of a man in pain. That this was overt and deliberate sabotage."

"Then . . . with that and the link to the mob in his past, we have the evidence we need!"

"Well, yes and no," Duran said. "It's solid evidence that Kovak's motives weren't what he tried to make us believe they were. But his bank account shows no unusual activity. And his spouses and children are well out of reach."

Wilkes told him, "We still have nothing that directly links his actions to the Ogilvies."

The precinct bullpen was even more chaotic when Sean returned than when he had first arrived. The din was overwhelming. Jerry invited him into his office for a quick discussion, and closed the door.

"What the hell is going on out there?"

"We're processing the people picked up in the riot," Jerry told him, "trying to ID the looters and rioters. God, I love my job." He ran his fingers through his thinning hair with a sigh.

"I need more, Jerry. I need firm proof that Ogilvie is behind this."

"We'll keep on it. I promise you."

They dealt with the deputizing. Jerry gave him a badge, swore him in, and assigned him the rank of captain. He also gave him a police radio earpiece, and offered him a gun, but Sean turned it down and opened his jacket to display his own holster. "I'm covered," he said.

Jerry raised an eyebrow, but said nothing.

As he was pushing his way toward the exit, someone yelled "Sir! Sir!" and tried to grab his arm. He looked around and was startled to see one of the ice-slinging bikers who had discovered Carl's body. Sean gave a nod to the police officer escorting the boy. The officer paused.

"Sir." The young man was panting. "Tell them I'm not a criminal. I was just in the bank to report a sugar rock and help my friends—no one believes me. I think they may be in trouble—you have to help us—"

"Easy there," Sean said. "Officer, I happen to know this young man. He's one of the biker heroes who stopped the runaway reaction up on the surface and saved our ice stores. I seriously doubt he's a trouble-maker."

The police officer glanced at Sean's badge. "All right, sir. We're done with him, anyway. Stay away from riots in the future, young man."

Outside in the traffic tubes, Sean turned to the kid. "What's your name?"

"Kamal. Kamal Kurupath. My friends call me Kam. Thanks so much. I couldn't get them to listen. All they cared about was the riot."

"Tell me what's going on. How are your friends in trouble?"

Kamal's story came out in disjointed chunks, with frequent back-trackings, but gradually Sean got the gist. "You're telling me your friend Geoff has several metric tons of ice?"

"Yes."

"And the black marketers got wind of its existence."

"Yes. And now he and Amaya and Ian may be in danger. Please. We have to help them. Right away!"

Sean sensed there was more to the story. "We will. But I'm hazy on the details. How did the black marketers find out about this ice of yours?"

Kamal averted his gaze with a shrug. "I don't know, sir."

"Geoff went to them, didn't he? And got in over his head."

Sweat beaded on Kamal's upper lip. "Geoff would never do that!"

Sean gave him a searching look. "I want to help you, but I have to know what's going on. You said yourself, your friends are already in trouble. The best way to help them is to tell me everything."

"All right." Kamal blew out an explosive breath. "Ian thought we could get more money than if we went to the banks. It wasn't Geoff, honest—he said no. They fought, and Ian went off on his own. Geoff and Amaya went to stop him before he got to the black marketers."

Sean rubbed his face. *I so* don't have time for this. "Where is this deal going down? When?"

"Bottomsville. On the Promenade. Near Halloway Industrial Park. I left them over an hour ago. Almost two. I'm afraid we're too late."

"All right. Wait here and I'll go talk to the police chief. They'll send a patrol down with you to check it out."

"They're so busy. Won't you come?" Kamal pointed at Sean's badge. "You're authorized. And you're in charge of ice stores anyway, aren't you?"

Sean sighed. Chasing sugar rocks wasn't his idea of time well spent. But he was here now, he knew the kids involved, Jerry's precinct was swamped.

And hell; he owed these kids. The whole cluster did. "All right. Let's go."

13

When Jane got back to her office, a false sense of busy normalcy had settled over the warrens where her Zekeston staff worked. First, she needed to check her messages—without Marty to screen them, she might miss something important. She called up her comm app and found hundreds of calls and messages from friends, acquaintances, and coworkers cramming her inbox, forwarding rumors about the supposed infection in their life-support area and asking if it were true.

She sent an encrypted e-mail to Chikuma, telling her about the feral sapient and her plans to extract it. *Tell your contacts to prepare, Sensei,* Jane wrote. Chikuma would make sure the city infrastructure was ready. The First Wavers had connections in every city department and system.

The second thing she found was that lots of new bad-sammies had entered her cache. Thomas had not just been blowing smoke. Bad viewer ratings from Downside were easy to blow off, but bad sammies from the people she was trying to help . . . that stung.

Next she studied Tania's reports on the feral, and had Jonesy dredge up some research on the net. The first sapients had been created nearly two hundred years ago, during the twenty-first century. Most of the information was way outside her sphere of knowledge. She did glean that artificial sapients were nearly as different from each other as they were from humans. About the only thing they shared was a stunningly effective capacity to commandeer computerized systems and kill people.

Jane called Xuan. "The PM has arranged for quarters to be set aside for families of the staff, in Kukuyoshi near administration headquarters. It still involves pitching tents, but at least they won't be overcrowded."

Xuan gave her a loving look. "Thank you, dear."

She did not condone cronyism. But Xuan's family had suffered greatly over the years, and she would not cause the little ones more discomfort.

In fact, special arrangements were unavoidable. Administration staff—including Jane's division—were all working killing hours. If the PM did not make it possible for their families to come in and be safe, the entire administrative arm of the government would shut down as everyone went to help their own families prepare.

Xuan said, "How about you take a break around eight, and we'll eat dinner together in Kukuyoshi?"

"I'm not sure I'll have time," she said. "It depends on how things go." As she said this, she typed and sent a quick message: "Feral sapnt IDd in systems, caused life support damage. Xtractg v. late tonite."

"Stroiders" might be able to capture the message over her shoulder before it was sent, but as transmissions Downside were frozen anyway, she wasn't as concerned as she might ordinarily be.

"Oh, that's too bad," he said, looking disappointed. As the message entered his queue, his eyes widened. "*Choi oi!*" he gasped. But he kept any further reaction off his face. "We'll hope it works out, then."

Gratitude filled her. "Oh, and be sure to bring our two-sleeper and our camping gear, would you? We'll camp out with the clan." Normally she used a hammock she had set up in her office, when she stayed in town, but with Xuan here, they would need a space somewhere.

He looked surprised. "I thought the PM authorized you to get a suite for the duration?"

"Plans changed."

He started to protest again, but she gave him a pleading look: *don't push me on this.* There were no rooms to be had. They would have had to commandeer them from stranded travelers, or spend precious methane supplies having their assemblers grow new ones. Neither was acceptable.

"OK." He sighed. "I'll bring the camping gear."

She got an update from Sean: formal approvals had come through from the North American Conference and no further obstacles stood in the way of getting a shipment of Europan ice. Repairs were progressing. Disassemblers had reached a barely adequate level. He also fed her a private report on the warehouse disaster, which boiled down to: we know the Ogilvies put Kovak up to it, but we can't prove it yet.

Aaron gave her a report on the status of the ice shipment in Ilion, making it clear they had them tied down . . . for the moment. "It is unlikely, though," he said, "that they will be there for more than another twelve hours." His regretful expression said that was the best they could do. Jane thanked him and signed off.

If Tania could come through with the sapient, that should be time enough. And if not, they only had one other real alternative, in which case there would not be much point in dragging things out.

Marty's first report came in at three p.m. sharp, and the next two came in on the hour after that. The next six came on the half-hour: Tania and crew continued to map and isolate the sapient. The sapient had not yet deduced their intent to trap it. Their "wetware backup" system of citizens' reports had revealed a whole new module of ego-structure and a suite of masking tricks the sapient had evolved that they had not known about—the sapient was closer to replication than they had anticipated. But they still had several hours and were staying on schedule.

Reading this made Jane's heart pound again, and she sent up another prayer to a god she did not believe in.

Xuan reached the Aeropark at about dinnertime. The Ngo clan—Xuan's younger brother and sister and their spouses and children—were among the first arrivals. He spotted his sister Kieu and her husband Emil, as well as his brother Pham and Pham's wife Huynh, unpacking their tents near the aquarium. Near them, the three older Ngo children were rigging slings among the cherry and walnut trees. He headed over.

This innermost, lowest-gee park was a few hectares in area and five stories high. The park featured flying squirrels who truly flew, alongside the birds and butterflies and bees and dragonflies. They all stayed aloft on the warm currents that rose up from the system of vents, looping crazily in the coriolis force. Perhaps twenty families had set up camp; scattered tents hung from trees like brightly colored balloons, and small groups of people bobbed around near suspended picnic tables to chat or eat their dinners.

Xuan slipped off his sandals and stepped out onto a deep bed of self-adhering gel-sand (real sand and dirt were impractical for use in micro-gee; the particles stayed in the air for days, kicking up dust devils and getting into everything). The sand felt good between his toes. He suspected that Jane herself had selected this place. It was one of his favorites: a low-gee, hanging garden, filled with trees and flowering plants suspended in water-tube meshes. The garden's centerpiece was its aquarium, a clear, four-story, cylindrical tank suspended above an opening in the floor that led to another section of Kukuyoshi.

It was cool here, but not as cold as much of the rest of Zekeston. To Xuan, who spent much of his working life fluctuating between hypothermia and overheating, out in the Big Empty, it felt just right. He drew in a deep breath. The air was rich with smells of plant nutrients and growing things. The fact that it had been selected as living space meant it would be spared, when the rest of Kukuyoshi was shut down.

Esther, Kieu's eldest, had taken the twins and their toddler toy sapients over to look at the fish. Within the tank swam dog-sized carp: orange, white, and black ones, and every conceivable combination of these three colors. The carp swam upside down, sideways, and every which way—as loopily as the birds and insects flew—occasionally bumping into the clear walls. The water sloshed up in great, lazy waves and broke into blobs that rose high into the air with their captive fish, before sinking back down into the main pillow of liquid. Once in a while a fish broke out into air and flopped around, gasping as they drifted slowly toward the mass of water. He wondered how many fish they lost that way. But who knew? Maybe they were evolving lungs.

The process of cordoning off of this area had begun already, he noted: a series of silken, spiderweblike structures had strung themselves across the open spaces from rows of recently grown assembler jets in the walls. The structures were filling in with translucent membrane panes—as fragile-seeming with their rainbow swirls as soap film—but in reality, he knew, they were strong enough to isolate the air and thermal systems in the areas set aside for human occupation from the rest of Kukuyoshi.

Xuan bounded over and up toward the clan, some distance away and a couple of stories up, among the suspended cherry trees.

"Need a hand?" he asked Kieu and Emil.

"Grab a pole," Kieu said, and tossed him a bag. He snatched it out of the air, perched on a limb, and began pulling poles out and snapping the segments together.

"Have you seen Jane?" he asked, while they worked.

He had gotten a troubling transmission from their daughter Dominica. She believed that Xuan's sister Phan Huu-Thanh and her children had been swept up in the latest round of encryptions. It might as well be a death sentence. He had told his siblings, but no one else knew yet. He needed to discuss it with Jane.

"She's not here yet," his little sister said. Though Kieu was eighteen years younger than Xuan, she had only begun antiaging treatments recently, and looked about ten years older than he. "It's not so late. I'm sure she'll be here shortly."

The tent went up fast. They tethered it among the cherry trees, shaking loose a blizzard of fragrant blossoms, and then slung the hammocks inside. By the time they had finished, Huynh and Pham also had their tent up and the kids were done securing their belongings. Xuan got Emil's help with his and Jane's two-sleeper, while Huynh and Kieu started on dinner.

The four older kids—Esther, Duong, Dinh, and Mai—were playing air tag among the cherry trees; their parents warned them to stay out of the other campers' way. Lights flicked on inside the tents strung about the park, making them look like giant Chinese lanterns. The twins, Abraham and Rebecca, were nowhere in sight; his brother Pham must have taken them for a walk.

Huynh and Kieu bundled up supper and the family headed over to the aquarium. There they found Pham and the twins. Jane was with them. The elder four children rushed her, and she gave each of the kids a candy treat. Xuan shared a grin with his siblings. Jane told the children to follow her into the upper trees of the cherry forest on the other side.

"I know a very special place to have a picnic," she said.

Xuan knew just what place she had in mind. He also knew why she had chosen that particular place. "Stroiders" surveillance didn't touch every part of the city. Certain areas were far enough away from the cams and the assembler sprays that they would have a degree of true privacy. He and Jane linked fingers and led the way, and the whole family went on a tour of the park.

As they bounded up and floated down through the park's open spaces, Xuan pointed out to the children many things. A pair of *Iriomote* wildcats put on a show. They stalked each other—leaping, coiling—in a Coriolis-defiant aerial ballet.

Jane located the hedge. She and Xuan swung down and picked their way through it. The rest of the family followed suit, emerging with a few cuts and scratches. "Don't worry," Jane said. "It's worth it."

She pointed out the picnic tables, three of them, nearly obscured by an old hanging ball of a cherry tree nearby. Xuan turned on his flashlight and led the way. By now they had touched down on the pseudo-sand of this secluded area; they kicked off again and soared up to the tables among the trees. Around them, butter-yellow bees burrowed into the white blossoms, while the adults spread out the food. Kieu and Huynh got the children fed, clinging to the gently bobbing table to bind bowls, chopsticks, and cups to its upper surface. Kieu took out a thermos, and ejected globules of steaming green tea for the adults. Meanwhile, Xuan took the bowl from Huynh and dished out the noodles.

It was not traditional for a man to serve food in Vietnamese culture, but Xuan was not traditional. He served his siblings in memory of his grandmother. She had spent herself utterly in the bearing and raising of her four grandchildren during years of famine in southwestern Canada. Xuan's father had abandoned them when his mother died giving birth to Phan Huu-Thanh. Xuan had been eight.

The family had pooled all their resources to send Xuan home under Vietnam's Right-of-Return program. There he had gone to boarding school, then gotten an education at one of the country's top universities in Saigon. Eventually he got a teaching position there, and began a decades-long effort to reunite his family and bring them home. It had proven difficult; with Vietnam's economy booming and the vast numbers of the Vietnamese Diaspora, the immigration lines were long. He had returned to Canada shortly before emigrating Upside, to find his beloved *ba-noi* in a shantytown outside Vancouver: dumped on a dung pile like garbage.

He had found her too late to do little more than ease her passing. But not too late to remember her sacrifice in his small way.

Dinner included vat-grown sprouts and leafy veggies and stinging-hot chili and Mr. Rotisserie chicken. The aroma made his mouth water. Once his siblings and their spouses were served, he swirled the last of it into two clumps in midair with his chopsticks, then held out a bowl to Jane. Her noodles slowly settled into the bowl, unwinding. She devoured the noodles almost before any could touch the bowl. He caught and picked at his, watching her with affection.

"They're delicious," Jane told Huynh, who smiled.

"Any further news on getting new ice in?" Emil asked.

"We have several options. There is a major shipment we hope to have access to, very soon."

Everyone seemed relieved. More chat ensued. Then the other two families left to get their children ready for bed. Xuan and Jane lingered under the cherry branches. Xuan cradled his cup of tea, teased more globules from the cup, and sipped at them. He caught Jane looking at him.

"Don't know what I'd do without you, my dear," she said.

Xuan smiled fondly. "No doubt they'd find you at your desk, gibbering and psychotic from overwork," he said.

She tensed as though he had struck her.

"What's wrong?"

"Nothing."

He took her hand, disturbed. "What is it?" he asked again, seriously.

In answer, she sprang over the table toward him, and gripped his hand with one of her feet. He pulled her in and wrapped his arms around her as she settled. The blossoms she had disturbed swirled around them, faint and fragrant. "Just hold me for a minute, OK?"

"OK." He sensed her surreptitiously looking around. She was scanning for Stroider-cams or motes. No cams registered; no motes seemed present.

"We're extracting the sapient tonight," she said in a low voice. "In just a few hours. When things happen, they'll happen fast."

He exhaled sharply. "All right."

"When we're ready to extract, people will be ordered to the life shelters." They linked wavefaces. She called up a map of the gardens, and gestured at an emergency exit tube sign. "I'd like you to escort the family here," she said. "It's the closest."

"Of course." He paused. "How big a deal is this?"

She inhaled. "Until we get it out, it's got access to everything. Air, power, food distribution, transport, assembly and disassembly. Everything."

The tension in her did not ease. He laid his chin on her head. "All right, then."

"You said you had something to discuss, also?"

He reached into his pocket, and passed a data lozenge to her over her shoulder. "From Dominica," he said. She glanced around at him.

"It came in today. Nothing urgent. Just . . . when you get a chance. We'll talk about it later." Offline, he meant. He did not want to add to her worries with the bad news about Huu-Thanh, just now.

They spent a moment longer, snuggling, trying together to hold out the world. But it was late. "I'd better go," she said.

"All right. Be careful."

"You be careful, too. Stay near the life shelters until you get an all-clear from me."

"All right."

Xuan's brother and sister and their spouses had gathered outside Pham and Huynh's tent to talk. Jane went over to make her good-byes to them. The toddlers started fussing in the tent, refusing to settle down.

Kieu started to go in, but Xuan motioned her to settle again. "Let me." He picked up seven smooth stones that had been displaced from a nearby rock garden, and went inside. The twins were struggling in the mesh hammock. Abraham was already out of his pajamas. Tears and snot streaked Hannah's miserable little face. They both quieted, though, when they saw him come in.

"Shush!" he said softly. "*Thỏ đực, thỏ cái*"—little buck rabbit, little doe—"what are you doing? Quiet now, and don't disturb your mother."

He wiped Hannah's face, handed her her bottle, which had slipped out of the hammock, and put Abraham back into his pajamas. They snuggled back into their sleeping bags and looked at him with expectant expressions. They knew Uncle Xuan's bedtime M.O. He held up six stones between his fingers. The seventh he kept hidden.

"Watch this," he said. On the floor of the tent he carefully stacked the six stones. Then he framed it with his hands.

"What is this?" he asked.

"Rocks!" Hannah said.

"Yes. On Earth, monks make stone mounds to honor the Buddha. Let us say thanks to Buddha for teaching us to love and have compassion for all beings." Kieu and Emil were bringing their children up in the Jewish faith, but Xuan knew they would not mind; his sister had told him so. He closed his eyes, bowed, and chanted a bodhisattva three times. The little ones watched with solemn faces. Then he leaned forward with a grin. "But it turns out these are not just ordinary rocks. Watch."

He knocked them neatly—just so—and they tumbled up in all directions at once. This was a trick he had taught himself during his many long research sojourns among faraway stroids. You hit it just right in microgee, and the rocks fly in clean patterns. The twins giggled and tried to wiggle out of the hammock to grab the stones, but Xuan clucked in mild disapproval and put them back in.

"But what's this?" he asked. "One stone went into Hannah's ear!" With this, he reached behind Hannah's head and rolled the stone into his palm, and then held it for both to see. They clapped again, and giggled. "Again! Again!" she said, and Abraham said, "Me too!"

"No, now it's time for little rabbits to sleep," he said, and kissed them both good night. He gave them each a stone, and they settled down in their covers and closed their eyes, clutching the rocks in their hands.

Outside, Xuan and Jane found Thomas and Esther dangling from branches, staring at something on the canvas wall of their own family tent. Xuan bounded back up. Jane came right behind him.

"What is it?" he asked.

"Somebody drew on our tent," Esther said. Xuan grasped a branch and squinted. His vision adjusted swiftly in the dimness. Someone had drawn a crude symbol in phosphorescent green, red, and yellow paint: a bleeding bird caught in the talon of a hawk.

"Vandals," he said, disgusted, but Jane's fingers dug into his biceps. He drew her aside. "What's wrong?"

Her voice came out a harsh whisper. "This is a message. A threat."

"What are you talking about?" he demanded. She drew a slow breath. "The hawk is the logo for the Ogilvie family business. The Martian mob. They're telling me they know where I live. They are threatening the family."

Xuan thought perhaps Jane was reading too much into it, but she seemed certain. He said over her shoulder to the children, "It's just some stupid prank. Go get some soap and water, and wash it off."

"Come on," he said, and they went to Kieu and Emil's tent, where the adults were. "We need you all to come out and see something," Jane said.

Everyone climbed out and sank down with her and Xuan to the children's tent where the graffiti was. "I hate giving you more to worry about," she told them. "But you need to know this, for your own protection."

"What is it?" Kieu asked.

"I believe it's a threat aimed at me. I have enemies whose symbol is the hawk." They all looked at Jane. She went on, "I don't believe they will do anything. This is just to keep me off-balance. But we should all be alert.

"Keep the kids in view of 'Stroiders'-cams at all times, and keep them close during offline periods. These people can't afford to alienate the viewers back home. We can use that to our advantage."

"We'll deal with it," Pham said. "Thanks for the warning."

Xuan escorted Jane to the park exit. He kissed her good-bye beneath their tents, and tasted tea, peanuts, and tongue-stinging chili on her lips.

Jane smiled. "I'll be all right."

"We will, too. Don't worry."

He kissed her again, gave her hands a final squeeze, and watched as she sprang off down the corridor, hand and foot: nimble, commanding, beautiful primate. Jane and Xuan's grandmother were very different. But Jane's spirit reminded him a little of his *ba-noi*. She was so still, so calm: unbending in her stance between power and need. In his nightmares, sometimes, she too ended up dying on a rubbish heap.

The hardest part of loving was how much it gave you to lose.

14

For a while the three teens stayed where they had been tossed, trussed up with packing cord like Mr. Rotisserie beef packets readied for shipment. Geoff and Amaya had been thrown across the small bed and Ian was slumped in the corner beside it. Blue Tattoo had warned them that if they even breathed too loud, he would come back in and pound them.

The viewer in the other room was loud, so Geoff figured they did not have to worry too much about being heard, as long as they were careful. The cords bit into his wrists and his hands were numb. He squirmed, but the movement merely made his limbs hurt more. His nose had stopped bleeding, but his head hurt, and the crusted blood on his face itched.

"What are we going to do?" Amaya whispered. "We've got to get out of here!"

Ian huddled in the corner where he had been dumped, looking miserable. Geoff felt like snarling at him—"Is this what you had in mind, big shot?"—but he refrained.

"Amaya, turn your back to me," he said softly. "I'll undo you first."

They both squirmed till they were back-to-back. Geoff got to work on her bindings, biting his lip hard against the pain that shot up his arms. It seemed to take forever; his fingers were little more than dead stumps, the pain in his wrists was piercing, and he couldn't get a purchase on the knots. And the idea that the kidnappers could come back in at any moment made them all jump at every noise.

But finally—finally!—the knots started to loosen, and he worked at them with increased ferocity until they came free. Amaya pulled her hands loose and rubbed them. Then she started on her feet.

"No, no—do my hands first," he whispered, and she obliged, swearing softly at the knots. After a few minutes, he felt the bonds loosen. Circulation—and more pain—flowed into his hands. He pulled free and flexed them, as Amaya had done. She started working at the knots at her own ankles, while Geoff rolled off the bed and scooted over to Ian.

Ian did not say anything, which was for the best; Geoff might punch him or something, and now was not the time. Ian turned around as best he could and let Geoff untie him. Soon they were all free.

Geoff had seen their kidnappers throw their waveware into the closet. He quietly opened it and found their equipment on the floor. He brought it out and sorted it on the bed. They all took a couple of seconds to don their ear- and eye- and handwork. Geoff tested his connection. Dead.

Amaya was listening at the door. "They're playing some shooter game, I think. Someone's in the kitchen."

"There were five of them," Geoff said.

"Do you remember the layout?"

"Everything was happening so fast when they brought us in," he replied. "I don't remember anything but the sofa and the view wall."

"I do." It was the first thing Ian had said in hours. "They took me here before."

Geoff and Amaya glared. Ian had the decency to look embarrassed. But he went on. "There's a kitchenette to the right and a bathroom next to this room. The front door is directly opposite this door." He pointed at their only exit.

"All right. Hang on."

Geoff tested the door. It was unlocked! He slid it open a crack, and looked into the other room.

Blue Tattoo and White Mohawk were on the couch working invisible wavespace controls. Images jumped around on the wall. No one else was in the small room, but he caught a glimpse of movement in the kitchenette. A gun lay on the coffee table, along with a couple of big bulbs of dark liquid. The room smelled of alcohol and undercooked meat.

A call came in on the view wall as he was closing the door. A big man in a suit appeared. His neck was thick, bull-like, and he had Popeye arms. He was very well groomed and smooth-looking, and he had a dead look in his eyes. Just looking at him made the hair on Geoff's arms stand up.

"Hey, Mr. Mills!" Blue Tattoo lifted a beer at the man's image. "We have guests! Come on by and meet them."

Creepy Bull Neck—Mills—merely gave Blue Tattoo a cool stare and didn't bother to reply. "You got the coordinates for their ice?" Geoff noticed he had a Martian accent.

"What do you think I am," Blue Tattoo asked, "an idiot? You get the coordinates when we get the money."

The man called Mills looked exasperated. "What? You think we're going to stick the rock in our cargo hold and fly away? Mr. Glease works for the Ogilvies. He has his reputation to protect. You do what we want, we'll play straight with you. But the kind of money we're talking about, we've got to check it out. See how much ice there really is. You can send one of your own people with me."

Blue Tattoo and White Mohawk huddled, talking in low voices. Then Blue Tattoo said to Creepy Bull Neck, "All right. Here's the deal. I'm sending two of my people. They'll meet you up on the landing pad in an hour."

"Not tonight. I need more time to line someone up to do the survey."

"A surveyor? Shit, why don't you just announce it to the world? Too many people know about this already." He glanced back at the door, and Geoff shut it swiftly and quietly. He pressed his ear against its metal surface and heard the man they called Mills laugh mockingly.

". . . about your kiddies in there? Relax. They're rocketbikers. Right? Biking accidents happen all the time. Get them to sign the papers over to you tonight; you can download a form from one of the banks' wavesites. When we go out tomorrow morning, they can come, too. We'll take care of them there.

"As for the geologist, if the claim is like the rest of the piddly-ass sugar rocks we've been finding, well, you'll have the papers, so it's all legit and he won't care. And if the find is big enough to make it worth the trouble, we'll get rid of the geologist, too. Problem solved."

Geoff turned to the others. "We've got to get out of here now—they plan to kill us!"

Ian looked sick. "What? That wasn't the deal!"

Amaya slugged Ian in the arm. "Shut up. Geoff, what's the plan?"

"We're in luck. There are only three of them to deal with. Let's look around. Quietly! What have we got? A phone or pager? Anything we can defend ourselves with?"

All they found was shoes and clothing, assorted electronic kibble, and the cord that had been used to tie them. They each took a length of cord and wrapped the ends around their hands.

"OK, look. Blue Tattoo and White Mohawk are in the front room and there is someone else in the kitchen. Ian, you take Blue Tattoo—you're almost as big as he is. I'll take White Mohawk. They're both sitting on the couch. Amaya, there's a gun on the coffee table. Go straight for it, and aim it at whoever seems to be the best one, depending on what's happening. Got it?"

They both nodded, faces ashen, eyes wide.

"Let's go."

Geoff peeked out again. Mills was no longer on the display. He gripped the handle and took several deep breaths. He couldn't believe he was doing this. *Don't think. Just do.*

He threw the door open and rushed into the room.

The two men on the couch looked up, shocked. Blue Tattoo and White Mohawk were both drunk, and their coordination was bad. They tried to come to their feet. That was all Geoff saw—by then he had launched himself over the couch and rammed White Mohawk, knocking him against the coffee table. The gun went flying. He tried to get the cord over

White Mohawk's head, but Blue Tattoo lurched up and tripped over him and White Mohawk, and Geoff lost his grip on the cord.

Amaya dodged past them, trying to get around the melee to get to the gun, as Geoff and White Mohawk grappled. A tattooed woman in the kitchen leaned against the counter, arms folded, just watching, looking disgusted.

White Mohawk forced Geoff to the floor and pinned him. His fingers closed around Geoff's throat. With a desperate lurch, Geoff threw White Mohawk off, and rising, clubbed him with both fists. White Mohawk stumbled back and hit the wall.

A weapon's report blasted their ears. Everyone flinched.

"Freeze!" Amaya said. She sounded like she meant it. Everyone stopped fighting and looked at her. She had her back to the wall by the door, and was covering all of them with her gun. Blue Tattoo had Ian in a choke hold; Ian's face was a dark shade of red.

"Let him go," Amaya ordered. Blue Tattoo released Ian and stepped back. White Mohawk stood up. Ian went to one knee, gasping for breath.

"Why don't you give me the weapon," Blue Tattoo said. "Before somebody gets hurt."

Amaya bared her teeth in a smile and aimed the barrel at his testicles. "I'll give you *part* of it."

The woman in the kitchenette looked annoyed. "Somebody better pay for that," she said, pointing at the hole Amaya had made in the ceiling.

"You don't want holes in your ceiling, you shouldn't kidnap people," Geoff said.

"Hey, this wasn't my idea," she replied. Amaya keyed the front door open and Geoff helped Ian, who was a bit the worse for wear, out the door. Amaya backed out last. When the door slid closed, they ran.

Within seconds, Geoff heard footsteps behind them. They dashed among the catwalks and cul-de-sacs. They ducked around a corner between two structures, to catch their breath.

"Where are we?" Geoff asked.

Amaya shrugged, but Ian looked around.

"This way," he rasped, and set out down a nearby spiral stair to the next level. Their kidnappers came around the corner, spotted them, and gave chase.

The stair led to an alley off the Promenade. They rushed out onto the thoroughfare. There were enough people around that those chasing them couldn't be too obvious—but as the three of them wove through the pedestrians and carts and tents, Ian looked behind. "They're still back there! They're gaining."

"Back to the spokeway," Geoff said. "This way."

They ran till his lungs felt like they would burst, dodging through the crowd . . . and ran headlong into Kam and old Moriarty from the warehouses, who were just emerging from the Suzee Spokeway . . . just as Blue Tattoo and White Mohawk shoved their way through the crowd toward them.

Kam said to Geoff, "What happened? You're a mess!"

"I'll explain later." He turned to Moriarty, but Moriarty was already stalking over toward the black marketers. He wasn't quite as big as Blue Tattoo, but there was something about him that was much scarier. He pulled his gun, and Blue Tattoo and Mohawk's eyes widened. They turned and ran.

Moriarty disappeared after them.

"He knows about the ice," Kam told them, gesturing after the old man.

"They kidnapped us!" Amaya said.

Moriarty reappeared then. "I lost them in the crowd." He reholstered his gun. It was then Geoff noticed he was wearing a badge. "Do you know where they held you?"

Geoff shook his head and Amaya looked doubtful. "They blindfolded us on the way in, and on the way out we weren't really paying attention to where we were."

"I know where," Ian said. He turned to Moriarty. "Those creeps kidnapped us, but this never would have happened if it weren't for me. I want to help put them away."

"All right. We need to move on those jokers now. Let me put in a call and see if we can get a nearby patrol to assist."

Moriarty made a call. Then they went to a nearby coffee shop, where a pair of cops were waiting. Geoff's bloody appearance made everyone stare. He excused himself and went to clean up in the bathroom. His nose hurt like shit when he touched it. *I'm going to have a Cyrano schnoz tomorrow,* he thought.

He tried his waveface and his icons bloomed all around. He sighed in relief. When he came out of the bathroom, Ian and the officers were gone. Geoff lifted his eyebrows, and Amaya said, "Ian is taking them to where the black marketers held us."

"Is that safe?"

"They've called for backup," Moriarty said. "And they'll keep your friend out of harm's way. Don't worry."

Geoff ordered himself a sundae and brought it back to the table. But when he went to take a bite, to his embarrassment, his hand holding the spoon shook. He set the spoon down.

Amaya and Geoff filled Moriarty in on what had happened. When they finished, Moriarty shook his head. "You four will have quite a story to tell your grandkids someday. Ten metric tons of ice, you say?"

"Maybe. I don't know. We haven't measured it."

"Well, ten tons buys Phocaea almost another full day. Nothing to sneeze at! We'll need to get someone out there. We'll send a team and shuttle out to test it," Moriarty said. "We'll deal with all that later."

A call came in while he was talking. He motioned for them to wait, and stepped away. Geoff turned to Amaya.

"You OK?" he asked. She was sipping at a shake and being awfully quiet. She looked up at him, pushed her hair back from her forehead.

"I thought they were going to kill us."

"Jeez, not with you on the team! You were amazing."

"What do you mean?" Kam asked.

Geoff filled him in. "You should have seen her," he finished. "This hundred-fifty-kilo guy is moving on her. 'Give me the gun,' he goes, and she points it right at his groin and goes, 'I'll give you *part* of it.'"

They all laughed. Amaya laughed hardest.

When Moriarty returned to the table, Geoff said, "Is Ian OK?"

"He's fine. They've got the kidnappers and are taking them to the station. A pair of beat cops are escorting Ian back—and here they are," he said, as Ian entered with the two officers. Their friend looked a little shaken up, but happy.

"They broke the door right down," he reported. "These morons, they were all just sitting around, griping about not getting their money."

One of the officers said, "We need to get you four down to the precinct to take your statements."

"Can we finish our ice cream first?" Kam asked.

15

At eleven p.m., Marty showed up at Jane's office door—tense, sweat beaded on his upper lip, breathing short. "Tania sent me to get you. We're ready to extract the sapient."

"Give me a minute."

Jane fired alerts off to her eyes-only list, as well as to Sean, Aaron, Xuan, Funaki, and the local resource allocation gurus. Then they headed down to the city computer center together.

Gravity in Tania's division was about a fourth of a gee: enough to ground you but leaving plenty of bounce for aerobatics. Jane sank down from the door to join Tania on the platform at the room's center.

At first Jane felt as if she had landed in the middle of a mime opera. All around her amid the webworks, a troupe of performers acted out some invisible choreography in the three-dimensional workspace. But Tania mailed her the address and when she called it up, Jane found herself standing in a field of dazzling, changing architecture—inundated with bursts of melodic coding—iconic imagery—snatches of speech. Marty handed her a bulb of coffee and threw a blanket over her shoulders. She gave him a grateful look.

"And Ceci?"

"She's good. In a life-support station, safe and sound." He got a remote look on his face. "One of Tania's team needs me."

"Go." She waved him off and leaned against the rail. The sculpture enveloping them all was an abstraction overlaid on the air: a panorama of numbers, images, and symbols. Jane's eyes and ears tried to stabilize it, make it into a landscape, but it changed too rapidly, reshaping itself as teams of programmer-artists sent out or pulled in streams of liquid light. Occasionally the programmers and data wranglers shot packets to each other, and snagged them, incorporating them into their constructs. More rarely they extracted from their structures an array of numbers or equations to spray into the main construct rendered in the room's center, which was slowly taking shape directly over Jane and Tania's heads.

The central, main construct stood for the sapient. It could be nothing else. Eleven of its twelve modules were laid out in a seven-pointed-star pattern (if you looked at the construct from the right angle; otherwise the star morphed into a more complicated shape), with three modules sharing the center, and one of the seven "points" a tightly woven binary system. The twelfth module was loosely tied to the center and to the binary-module "point."

In several ways the sapient was quite different in formation than the classic four-, five-, and six-pointers she had read about inwave today. But she saw the similarities as Tania pointed them out to her.

"We've mostly figured out the identity functions of the modules," Tania said. "We're ninety percent sure we have all the critical modules mapped, and about sixty to seventy percent sure we have all the critical interior pathways mapped properly."

Jane eyed her. "Only sixty percent sure?"

"Sixty to seventy."

"How important is that?"

"To excise it? Not very. To capture it live? Critical."

"I find that rather alarming."

Tania gave her a surprised look.

"I know," Jane said, "I was talking about destroying it before, but it turns out we have a use for the thing. We need it functional."

"I want it alive, too. You know I do! But we're running out of time. Its experiments at self-replication have been increasing rapidly over the past hour, and it's discovered the link from our network up to the surface. We've lost the battle to keep its nucleus contained. It's busy copying its full functionality to Upside-Down's local systems."

Jane stared. "Are you sure?"

"Yep." She gestured and a flurry of activity near the core of the sapient appeared. "That's the reason behind the activity you see going on here. It keeps remapping itself around our blocks. Upside-Down is reporting that they have some unexplained activity—and they have plenty of extra processing and storage capacity. The activity mimics that of certain modules over here. Which we believe means it's got a child in construction over there. I sent a team over and we booby-trapped the trunk up to the surface, as a precaution."

Jane felt sick. "If it gets out of Phocaea on bandwidth as broad as Upside-Down's, it'll be all over the solar system in no time. Billions of computer systems could be damaged."

"Yes. And there's more. Look." Tania bounded over to one of the "points," the binary module system, and her hands flew back and forth in a complex pattern: the rest of the construct vanished and the binary subsystem grew in size and complexity.

"This unit," Tania told Jane with a gesture at the structure hanging before them, which caused the bigger of the two tightly bound modules to light up, "is at the very core of life support, and it was the first unit to go active. Look at the behavior of these two." She lit up its sister module. "These flows"—she pointed at the green strands and streams, which brightened as she gestured, and the other strands faded—"are internal processes with the other nine modules. But we have no idea what that extra module hanging out there is doing"—she pointed at the distant extraneous module, the one also attached to the star's center—"or why there's so much activity between that one and these two. These three modules are behaving very differently from what you'd find in most star-structure sapients.

"And somehow, these unusual relationships and activities are critical to the sapient's identity-formation. All its awareness, growth, and repli-cation activities accelerated once that one became active and hooked up to these two."

"What does that mean?"

"It means we have a very unusual sapient on our hands. It could have all kinds of unique properties. Now, look at all this other activity." Hun-dreds of suddenly brilliant streams and packets darted to and from the three modules, in all directions. "We don't even know what all these ad-ditional calls are—we can't trace them; the sapient has masked the pro-cess. And it's a huge transfer of information. This represents a good five percent or more of the entire cluster network activity—at least six kilo-turings' worth of processing, maybe as much as ten."

Jane whistled. "That's got to be affecting our other systems."

"It is. The city's automated processes are all experiencing slowdowns of fifteen to twenty-five percent."

"What are you doing about it?"

"I have Thondu investigating."

Jane frowned. "Is he the best choice?"

"I wish I had a dozen of him! He's caught tricks our sapient has pulled that *I've* missed. And I'm no slouch."

Jane thought for a moment. "Are you sure all this activity isn't a sec-ond attempt to replicate itself?"

"Oh, absolutely! Even if it weren't a huge waste of resources to try to replicate itself twice at one time—remember, it's just now learning how to do it—making two separate attempts from different centers would over-tax it. Not a logical act. And artificial sapients are nothing if not logical. Also, there's just not enough room on our systems for it to create a duplicate. It takes up a huge amount of space and processing time. That's why we couldn't just take a snapshot of the entire system and then do a purge and reboot. None of our recording and viewing methods can deal with that much information flowing in all those directions at once."

"Hmmm."

"And I also know that sapients are prone to going off on odd tangents that are of no importance to humans. They take contemplating their navels to a whole new level.

"Besides," Tania said, "we have a fleet of people around the entire cluster watching for unexplained behavior across the network. Trust me—we'd know if it was making yet another replica."

A call came in from Upside-Down. An older woman reported breathlessly, "You were right!"

"Report."

"It's got access to everything up here. And it's definitely replicating itself. We've managed to slow it down by running as many extraneous communications and soaking up as much bandwidth as we can, but we'd better move our asses. Once it's done creating a copy, it could hijack Upside-Down's systems at any time and beam itself to heck and gone. We are so goddamn lucky Upside-Down had shut off their 'Stroiders' transmissions, or I doubt if we could have stopped it."

Tania shared a look with Jane. The New Little Austin riot, for all its horrors, had been a blessing.

"How far along is it?" Tania demanded.

"Six modules appear to be complete up here, and the other six are well under way. And it's putting some heavy processing into re-creating and tuning two tiny modules we originally thought were exterior interactions. We don't know what they do yet."

"Two new modules? Have you changed your assessment on its identity-formation, then?"

The woman paused, biting her lip. Then she nodded. "Yes. I think we should add those two. And we're getting some useful information on the critical linkages between the modules. But the linkages are going up so fast right now that we're having a hard time keeping up. We figure we have about forty minutes till its child is complete."

"Forty minutes? Have you communicated all this to Damian and his team?"

"Yes. We're in constant contact."

"Damian, pick up!"

"Inwave." A young man's face appeared before them.

"Why aren't these two new modules showing up on our map yet?"

"Already on it. They'll be up in a minute."

"Michaela, how precise is your estimate on the timing for completion of the copy?" Tania asked the older woman.

"Its replication rate has some built-in hardware constraints, and transmittal to the surface is down to a crawl right now. There's no way it can finish the job sooner than thirty-eight minutes, on my mark." She set a timer. "And, mark."

Jane held on to her own desire to jump in with an opinion, while Tania pondered her programmer's question. "The longer we wait, the better our information on the linkages—"

"And thus the better able we'll be to capture the sapient live," Jane finished for her.

"Yeah, but then the greater the danger that it could escape." Tania drew a breath. "This is a terrific opportunity to make headway on the linkages, which is our weakest area. I'm inclined to say give them all but ten of those minutes to analyze the sapient's behavior before we shut down the gateway and trigger the trap."

Jane shook her head. "Too risky. Give yourself a bigger margin of error."

"Very well." Tania sighed, with a nod. "Fifteen more minutes. Michael, Damian, get your teams ready. Folks," she announced to the room at large, "give me your attention!" A field of heads popped up, prairie dog–like, both in the physical space and the virtual. "In fifteen minutes we're springing our trap. That'll alert the sapient, so we'll be going to Phase Three at the same time. Get what information you can, then wrap up, and get ready to do your part on the purge. Just like the drills. I'll give the signal."

Thondu broke into their interface. Peals of Tonal_Z swelled around him. He was sweating heavily despite the temperature, and his fingers were tripping across his harp.

"Reporting," he said.

"Any clues?"

"Still analyzing," he panted. "Not sure—yet. How—much—time left?"

"Fourteen-point-five minutes at my mark. And, mark."

"OK." Then he stilled his strings, studying some readout they couldn't see. "What's that? Sweet Jesus!" A look of horror bloomed on his face. "No! Stop!" He repeated it in Tonal_Z. His fingers danced across the strings again.

"It knows," he said. "Robotics. New tactic. Block it!"

"What?"

"It's—launching—attack." Drops of sweat flew from his face as music streamed from his fingertips. "Interior—robotic systems. Can't stop it. Shut down automation. Shut it down!" His image vanished.

"Jesus Christ!" Jane gasped. She turned to Tania, whose gaze had drawn inward. Jane recognized the look. She was marshaling her thoughts, weighing data, mapping out a course of action. "Damian."

"Here."

Tania gave Jane a look so intense and remote it made the hairs rise on her neck and arms. "Our only shot to contain this thing is to take down the data line up to the surface. Now. Everything else is secondary."

Quarantine. Jane had read the case studies. The others infected by a feral had tried it, too. "Do it."

"Damian, blow the trunk line."

"Now?" He sounded hesitant, incredulous.

"*Now!*"

They waited. Jane asked, "Should we hear something? How did you rig it?"

"A small explosive. We should have heard it. Damian?"

His voice was grim. "The feral must have found the device and hacked it. The data line is still up."

Tania gave Jane a wild look. "We have got to shut down that data transmission line!"

"I'll deal with it," Jane said. "Trigger the extraction. Move up the time table."

"Right." Tania shouted, "Phase Three now! Move your asses!"

Jane grabbed Tania as the other woman started to bound away. "What are its weaknesses? How can I contain it? How much time do I have?"

"It can't get off 25 Phocaea without breaking through Upside-Down's barriers," Tania said. "But those are software barriers. It can hack them." She grabbed Jane. "It hasn't finished replicating. I can slow it down some. But you have to disrupt transmissions at the main demarcation point up to the surface before it finishes. The demarc is in the Hub, near the lifts. Say, fifteen minutes. After that, there's no point."

"I'm on it," Jane said. Tania leapt to another platform to where her team leaders were assembled.

Xuan, Jane thought. *The rest of the clan.* Her heart slammed against her ribs like an angry fist. She couldn't warn them—there wasn't time. She had to trust that they were doing what they needed.

Sean came to mind. He was ex-military with combat experience: shrewd, resourceful, decisive. If anyone could mount a counterattack, it would be him. She should also warn him to protect his people up on the surface. She put in a call, and briefed him quickly on what was happening.

"Get that demarc point, or if you have to, disable the gaser-xaser itself. It's at the base of the buckyball conduit that carries the city signals up to the surface. Hurry!"

"Confirmed," he said, and signed off.

Jane turned back to Aaron. Marty had alighted next to him.

"Sean will take down the data line," Jane told them. "Now let's talk about internal defenses. Does the emergency plan include a feral sapient attack?"

"No," Aaron replied, "but we have one for hackers, and we can use those protocols. I'll talk to Hiro, and I'll also alert Cervantes and Gregoire." The other towns' resource allocation chiefs. Like Hiro, they were responsible for their towns' disaster recovery. "So they're forewarned, in case . . ."

"Very good."

He departed.

"Marty," Jane said, "activate the emergency call tree, then alert Benavidez and give him a full briefing. And the mayors. Hurry!"

He said, "I'm on it," and winked out.

16

As they were clearing their table, Sean got a call. It was Commissioner Navio. "Sean, heads-up," she told him. "We've got another damn crisis. A feral sapient is loose in our systems."

Sean's breath froze in his throat. "Good God."

"Communications are in jeopardy. All radio-operated equipment is at risk of being hijacked. Tania is taking it down, but it's found a way off Zekeston, and I need your help to stop it."

"Where?"

"There's a transmission line that runs next to the main lift cables. Xaser transmission through a buckyball conduit. Meanwhile, the feral is mounting a full-scale attack—all our resources are on defending the city."

"What do you need me to do?"

"Take out the main point of entry located in the Hub. Shut it down. We have to keep the feral contained in the city systems. You have twelve minutes, no more than fifteen."

"Where is it?"

"It's supposed to be somewhere near the lifts. If I transmit a location, the feral will likely guess what you're up to."

"All right. I'll figure it out. Who's covering the city interior?"

"Others are on it. Get that demarcation point, or if you have to, disable the xaser itself. It's at the base of the buckyball conduit that carries the city signals up to the surface. Hurry!"

"Confirmed."

He hung up. The police officers had stiffened and were staring at each other in horror. They wore police radios; they must be receiving similar information to what Sean had just gotten. They both stood, knocking their chairs back.

"We've got to get back to our precinct," one said.

"Wait!" Sean said. "I need you. I've got orders to take out transmissions in the Hub."

"Sorry, sir, but our chief's orders take precedence," the other officer replied, "and we've been ordered to hightail it back to the station."

Sean swore. "Give me your radios, then." Communications—even the high-priority access Jane's team had—might fail any minute. Police radios were powerful transmitters, and were a local system, not centralized. They would be harder for a sapient to hack. "You can pick up spares at the precinct."

The two officers looked at each other. Sean had been deputized at a high rank. And he wasn't the kind of man you said no to, not without a really good reason. They handed their radios over, and then bolted.

Sean put in a call to Shelley. As it went through, the city's alarm system sounded. A calm voice on the loudspeakers started repeating a short message, directing people to the life shelters. People at the other tables looked around with confused expressions. The server behind the counter, a tall woman with big earrings and neon tattoos, took off her apron, folded it, and walked out the door. That started a stampede of customers pushing their way out.

Sean waved his young companions to stay, put in a call to Shelley, and stuck a finger in his unbudded ear. Shelley came on. Her image wavered and the signal crackled.

"Shelley, we've got a feral sapient in our computer systems, and it's attacking the robotics."

"I know. We're under attack up here. I can't stay on."

"Understood. But I need warm bodies. Send me a six-member team. Right away. They should meet me in the Hub. I'll be on a police headset— six-point-five nanometers." As he was speaking, though, Shelley's face faded and the crackling ebbed. SIGNAL LOST appeared in big red letters in his waveface.

"Shelley? Shelley? *Goddammit!*"

He put the police radio headset on, and set it to 36.

"Shelley, do you copy?"

He tried several times. Nothing. He turned. Geoff and his friends were staring at him, wide-eyed. Everyone else had already cleared out. In the street, people were running. The alarm still sounded.

"What do we do?" Geoff asked.

Sean glanced out through the windows. He could grab a couple of adults off the street, but it was very unlikely they would cooperate with his order. And even if they did, how could he count on them having a clue as to how to act in an emergency? Whereas he had seen these four in action. They were young, and had never fought before, but they were smart, fast, and strong. They worked well together. They kept their wits about them. And they were used to taking risks, operating in space.

He looked at their young, scared faces. There would be hell to pay later, even if he managed to get them all through in one piece.

Do what you have to, he thought. *For the sake of the cluster.* He had thought—prayed—that he was done with making those choices.

"The city is under attack from a feral artificial life form," he told them. "I've been given a mission to stop it from escaping. I need help to do that. It'll be dangerous, but we are all in grave danger while it's in our systems. Will you help me?"

Geoff spoke up. "Count me in."

"I'm in," Amaya said, and Kamal replied, "Of course."

"Hell, yes!" Ian said.

"Good. Follow me."

.   .   .

They were less than a block from the Nee Spokeway. They headed there at a run, jostling through the crowds. Geoff decided Moriarty had ESP—telekinesis or something. He parted the crowds like Moses parting the Red Sea. More likely he just scared the shit out of everyone.

At the spokeway, Moriarty pulled his revolver, chased people out and commandeered a lift, using his Resource Commission badge and a code on the keypad.

The lifts had been swamped for days. "I want to get me one of those," Amaya said.

They accelerated up the spoke. Meanwhile, the old man briefed them. "Listen up! The feral artificial sapient is in our computer systems, and right now it's creating a copy of itself in Upside-Down's computer systems, up top. From there, it can beam itself anywhere in the solar system. We have to stop it before it finishes that copy.

"Somewhere in the Hub," Moriarty went on, "is the main point of entry that transmits signals up to the surface. Any of you know where it is, or what it looks like?"

Kam raised his hand. "I do, sir. Or at least, I know what a demarc looks like. My dad does hardware support for computer networks, and I've helped him out once or twice."

"All right. I'm told it's near the pharmaceutical plant, but that may be bad intel. Soon as we reach the Hub, you take a good, hard look around and tell me which way we need to go."

Through the lift windows, the Hub opened out before them. They reached the Hub's center. The lift doors opened and Moriarty kicked out, gun drawn. Geoff and the others exchanged nervous glances. They lofted out behind the old man, looking around.

Emergency lighting beams crisscrossed the open space, casting long, stark shadows. Klaxons sounded. A calm voice urged people to hurry to the nearest life station. Small clots of people scrambled toward life stations amid the ropeworks strung through the Hub. Geoff wished he had a weapon. His mouth was dry.

Moriarty spoke. "All right, Kamal, give us a vector. Which way?"

They looked around. A short distance away were the surface lifts,

larger than those of the spokeway they had just exited, and perpendicu-
lar to them. In the distance against the bulkheads were the assemblyworks, the pharmaceuticals manufacturing plant, YuanBioPharma, and
Yamashiro Memorial Hospital.

"Sir . . ." Kam looked anxious. "The cable up to the surface is very high
bandwidth. We may only have a few more minutes before it's done copying itself. If I guess wrong—"

Moriarty laughed. "Look at it this way. If you guess wrong, we're no
worse off than if you make no guess at all."

Kam gave the old guy a look like, *you've got a point.* Then he turned
to study the Hub. He seemed to be tracing some power lines that ran
from the spokeway lifts to the surface ones. Then he pointed at a small
building on the far side of the surface lifts, inside a steel fence. "I'm
pretty sure that's it."

"How are we going to get in?" Amaya asked. "It's got all those warning signs and locks and things."

"We'll figure that out when we get there. Let's move!"

But Geoff was looking at the lift-loading machines between here and
there. They were decoupling from their dockings.

"Are they supposed to do that?" he asked.

Moriarty scowled. "It's the feral."

The machines, most of them, were gathering at the very place Kamal
had just pointed out. There were over a hundred of them, with long
grappling arms. A smaller group was headed toward them, spreading
out as if to surround them.

"It's on to us," Amaya said.

"I believe you're right. We're not going to get past that many of them.
So. Change of plans." Moriarty spoke in a clipped voice. "We'll attack
on the exterior instead. Make for the maintenance exits near the assemblyworks." He jerked his head toward the big vats against the bulkhead, about a hundred meters away, and handed Geoff and Amaya each a
radio. "You two are buddies"—he pointed at Geoff and Kam—"and so are
you two." Ian and Amaya. "Stick with your buddy no matter what. Avoid
the assemblyworks itself. It's automated, and you might come under

attack from the robotics there. Behind the vats is a maintenance area. Meet me by the dress-out lockers in one minute. If you get there first, grab suits, sticky-boots, and pony bottles and stay out of sight! Got it?"

They all nodded. *This is all happening too fast,* Geoff thought. He felt disoriented . . . disconnected from his body.

"Check your clocks. Maintenance in one minute. Go!"

Geoff launched himself upward and kicked off one of the big machines as it neared him, then a series of smaller ones that crossed his path, snatching at him, and scrambled into some nearby ropeworks. The machines couldn't go in there; they were too big and would get tangled in the webbing. He caught a glimpse out of the corner of his eye: Kam was right behind him.

They two moved swiftly through the netting. Near one edge they paused to catch their breaths. Geoff saw they were already halfway there. Ian and Amaya had taken a different route and had almost reached the assemblyworks. Moriarty was nowhere to be seen. Some of the machines were moving below; they were definitely tracking them.

"I have an idea!" Kamal said. "Follow me."

Kam launched himself at one of the machines—bounded off it, picking up its momentum—and went toward the assemblyworks. Geoff followed suit. They sprang down into the netting, and made their way over the vat racks as fast as they could. An acrid-sweet smell rose around them.

"Look!" Kam pointed. "Machines."

The vats were made of some translucent material, and they could see the contents—the smelly, milky assembly-bug solution—churning inside. Machines moved between the vats, but their activities seemed innocuous.

"I think we're OK. Hurry!"

Kam alighted on the floor behind the vats, in an area shielded from general view. Geoff alighted. Nearby he spotted a sign for the maintenance shop. Inside, they found Ian and Amaya pulling equipment from the maintenance lockers.

"Where's Moriarty?"

"Here," the old man said, entering. He shut the maintenance door behind him and locked it. He was out of breath, and his forehead had a deep gash. Blood dribbled down his face. He limped over and sat to pull off his shoes.

"What happened?"

"I ran afoul of the machines. I think the feral must recognize me as a particular threat. Maybe my conversation earlier with Jane. So, I took a loader out, and confirmed its suspicions."

While Amaya and Ian lofted over to grab radios, lights, and tools, Geoff and Kamal pulled survival suits, sticky-boots, and pony bottles from the racks. They all rushed through assembly and checks, bumping around the room like billiards. Meanwhile, Moriarty talked.

"Any of you ever been in the Hollow before?"

They all shook their heads.

"OK. Out on the Hub, where the surface lists and the Klosti Alpha cable leave Zekeston, is a xaser mounted next to the surface lift tracks. That xaser beams the city's network signals through a big conduit, up through the rock to the surface. We are going to take out the power source for that—or, if necessary, the xaser itself.

"Our threat is the fleet of maintenance ROVs out on the city's hull. They're big motherfuckers, and they have some features that can be used as pretty nasty weapons. But they aren't very fast or smart. You all suited up? Good. With pony bottles to supplement air intake, we'll have a good twenty minutes or more if we need it."

"We're going to ride our ponies?" Kam squeaked. "Out on the city *hull*? Fighting bad guys?"

"Ponies are all we need," Moriarty replied. "Ponies will make us all a lot more agile, and if we can't take out the transmission lines in the next ten to twelve minutes, it'll be too late anyway. Besides which, there's a little air out there. Your mask apparatus will make use of it to extend your pony's life."

"There's air in the Hollow?" Ian repeated.

Amaya said, "No duh. What rock did you grow up on?" Ian made a face at her.

"Wait a minute," Geoff said. "If there's air, how come we need pony bottles, and how come everyone is always worried about the city getting decompressed?"

"Because Hollow pressure is only two hundred eighty millibars, and the temperature is minus ten. It won't kill you right away, but you'll be out of commission—spending all your time getting enough air to keep you alive, and not dying of hypothermia—or getting brained by one of the spin generators—before someone rescues your ass."

Geoff asked, "How many machines are we up against?"

"Three dozen. Like I said, they're big and powerful, but they move pretty slow. They're stored in lockers near the Hub, and run on tracks on the hull. And if we're lucky, they'll be deployed elsewhere on the wheel."

Ian slapped Geoff on the back. "Relax, doof. Just launch yourself into the Hollow, if you have to. We'll reel you in if you spin wry."

"Have y'all used sticky-boots before?" Sean asked. They all shook their heads. "They're electrostatic grips. They work like lizard feet; they'll give you good traction on any surface. Just make sure you put one foot down before lifting the other."

Geoff slapped the latches closed on his boots and pulled on elbow-length gloves, then zipped up the suit. The edges of the gloves and boots sealed themselves to the suit cuffs. Amaya passed out utility harnesses and coils of rope. Moriarty was using a grease crayon to sketch the exterior onto the bulkhead.

"The Hollow's major axis is only slightly bigger than the Rim. Out on the Rim, the city's spinning at a hundred seventy klicks. We'll be on the Hub where it'll be spinning a lot slower, but you three may need to take the fight up the spokeways, to draw the machines away from Kam and me, so speak up now if you're prone to motion sickness."

No one spoke.

"Good. Here are your weapons."

He handed them all what looked like guns with meter-long tubes and a dispenser nozzle on the end. Geoff recognized the tubes. Metal disassemblers. His dad worked with them out at the metal refinery. At the sight, an image of Carl sprang into Geoff's mind, lying amid the wreckage of the disassembled warehouse with gaping wounds on his face and chest. He bent over and put his hands on his knees. He thought he was about to toss.

His friends were looking at him.

"I'm OK," he said. His heart pounded erratically. He took some deep breaths. *Calm down,* he told himself. *Panicking won't bring Carl back. Nothing will.*

Moriarty was still speaking. "Don't get any of that shit on you, or it won't be long before you're floating half naked in the Hollow without your wavegear."

They tucked the disassembler dispensers into the pockets of their harnesses. Geoff hefted his disassembler gun, studying the settings. They seemed straightforward.

Moriarty handed three additional packs to Geoff, Ian, and Amaya. "Standard maintenance toolkit. But it has plenty of other things you can use as weapons to keep the machines busy."

Ian poked around in his kit, and grinned. "Yep, we can do some serious damage with all this."

"Remember, only spray downwind, or you'll disable yourself and maybe your team mates, too."

While they familiarized themselves with the contents of their packs, Moriarty turned back to Kam. "You and I, meanwhile, will be hauling this." He dragged out a cart with welding tanks and gear. "The conduit and housing for the xaser and its power supply are made of buckyballs and these disassembler guns don't work for shit on carbon. So you and I are going to have to use a cutting torch on the casing to get inside. From there we can wreak some havoc." He showed Kam the workings, and made him set the knobs and light the welding torch, twice. "Good.

"Now, all of you, if you haven't been out there, the wind is damn powerful, even at the Hub, due to the city's spin. You're all Upsiders so you don't know much about wind, but let me just put it this way: it's going to be hard for you to stay upright. Your sticky-boots will help, but also use your tethers. Just because the air is mighty thin out there doesn't mean it can't knock you down. Stay sharp. Hang on tight to your tools. Also keep in mind that the distance between the Hub and the Hollow wall is less than ten meters, and the spin generators take up a good meter of that. Don't get cute—I don't want to have to haul y'all back in body bags. Got that?"

Geoff and the others exchanged nervous glances. "Got it." "Yeah." "OK."

"Amaya, give me one of those police radios. Geoff, set yours on frequency six point five. You three stay together, and keep the machines off us and each other. Geoff, you give me regular updates. Got that?"

"Got it!"

"Let's move out."

Geoff checked his watch. Barely five minutes had passed since they had been sitting in Tarts. He was scared numb. *OK, Carl, maybe I'm about to join you in Never-Never Land.*

They had to take turns at the lock. Moriarty went first with the big welding rig. Then Ian, Kam, and Amaya squeezed in. Geoff went last. The lock opened, he kicked off, and was expelled out onto the Hub in a puff of air.

Moriarty had not been joking about the wind—it buffeted and shrieked at him. He knocked his mask askew, flailing, and missed the handhold. The Hollow smelled of dust, iron, and ozone. Amaya and Ian grabbed his arms as he tumbled past. They pulled him down, and the grips in his boots grabbed the Hub's surface.

He readjusted the mask, and flipped on his lights. The howling dark was itself an enemy: his headlights barely seemed to penetrate it. And it was cold—frost had already formed on the unprotected lower half of his face, and icy drafts seeped under his collar. He shivered. How were they going to fight in this?

They tethered themselves to each other, not to the bulkhead. Just like with ice slinging, they would need to be able to range afield. They did not want to be fixed to one point.

"Where are we?" Geoff asked.

"Halfway to the WeSuzee Spoke," Amaya replied. "On the Hub flat. The lifts are those lights right there."

Geoff squinted at where she pointed: a nearby set of lights crawled up the cable and entered the tunnel that led to Phocaea's surface. It vanished from view. Near the base of that cable they could see two figures wrestling the welding cart into position: Kam's diminutive figure and Moriarty's bulky one.

Amaya squatted and pointed at a structure against the hull. "These must be the ROV tracks."

Geoff bent over, too. "Yeah, and they're laid in a gridwork all across the hull. This must be the power, here. See the warning symbol?"

Ian said, "So, no-touchy the big red stripe, and what's underneath it. Got it."

"Come on." Geoff started crosswind toward the base of the buckyball cable. Walking in sticky-boots was cumbersome, a bit like walking through sand, and he had to lean over at what felt like a forty-five-degree angle to keep from being knocked over by the wind. He fiddled around till he found the right toggle, and brought up the livemap built into his mask. A golden, spidery, shining mesh appeared: a topographic overlay on the dim surroundings.

He clicked on a link Amaya sent him. Their destination appeared in sparkling green, straight ahead. "We're nearing your position," Geoff radioed, and Moriarty acknowledged.

Geoff looked overhead. Moriarty hadn't been joking—the Hollow wall was only five meters away or so—so close he felt he could jump up and touch it. The rocky surface moved past at a brisk pace.

Suddenly they heard a terrible grinding, and felt a lurch underfoot. They swayed and struggled to keep their balance. Geoff could see on the overlay that the Hollow's walls were slowing down. The feral must be reversing the polarity of the spin generators. The city was being decelerated. Here at the Hub, it was not such a big deal, but out at the Rim, the deceleration would be extreme. He, Ian, and Amaya exchanged frightened looks.

Geoff radioed the old man. "What do we do now?"

Moriarty replied, "We've still got our job to do. Stay focused. Keep back about ten meters from me and Kamal, so you have room to maneuver without getting boxed in. If the feral hasn't figured out what we're doing yet, it will when we start cutting."

"Take your suits offline," Kam warned. "You might get hacked."

"Yikes! Good point."

Geoff, Ian, and Amaya spent a couple of seconds trying to figure out how to shut off their suits' wavespace connections, while fierce blue sparks from the welder lit up the Hollow, making Kam's and Moriarty's shadows stretch across the Hub and dance on the walls of the Hollow. Smoke swirled, genielike, in the eddying winds.

Amaya said, "I've been thinking. Maybe we can use a kite-catch formation on them." Kite-catch was a three-biker method they sometimes used for netting ice. You tethered yourself to the corners of a net in a big triangle. Two bikers—the anchors—would stabilize two corners while the third—the throw—dragged the net across the ice's trajectory. In this case, they'd be using three tethers. Two of them would loft the third up, who would mount the attack.

Geoff lifted a boot from the surface, and flailed, trying to regain his balance. "We're going to be awfully slow in these—a hell of a lot slower than we are on our bikes."

"True . . . but the machines aren't so fast either," Amaya said. "So the old man says. And the anchors can help the throw build up speed. Like a slingshot. Our big problem is, we'll have to work around the lift cable. It's going to get in our way."

"I guess we can cut tether if we have to," Geoff said thoughtfully, and Ian said, "I'm right there with you, Muffin."

Amaya sighed, exasperated. She and Geoff exchanged a look. Geoff wasn't sure if she was thinking *It's just how he is* or *I'm going to kill the fucker.*

"Your idea," Geoff told her. "You call the op."

"All right. I'll be our first throw," Amaya said. "Geoff, you're throw two. Ian, you're three, and we cycle through as needed. Throw calls the target, as always. We'll take turns strafing the machines till we're out of bug juice, and then we'll close in and use flares, or solvents, or whatever else we've got."

"First let's get the tracks," Geoff said, and pulled his disassembler tube out of his belt. "They can't stop Kam and the old man if they can't reach them."

"Let's work out from one point, so we narrow their range of approach," Ian suggested. "No—start upwind! We don't want them coming at us from upwind—we'd have to fight the wind as well as the machines."

The three of them hurried due upwind of Kam and Moriarty, and began spraying disassembler onto three of the T-shaped rails that led to the xaser station.

Geoff figured he had better wipe out a good two meters of track in case the machines could roll over the damaged portion. He laid a line of disassembler. It went on like toothpaste. The metal melted instantly in a cluster of metal blocks that spun away into the winds. Loud pops and sparks sprayed up from exposed circuits as the disassembler ate through the hidden power line beneath the T-shaped rail. He worried about the hull beneath it, but the bug juice seemed to stop at the surface.

He clumped past Amaya and Ian and began on his second rail. Amaya passed him, and next came Ian. He started to head for a third one. But they were out of time.

They heard the machines before they saw them. The bulkhead beneath their feet trembled. *Thud! Clank!* Along the rim of the Hub, maybe three hundred meters away, big rectangles rose up onto wheels and unfolded their arms—several cranelike appendages, with different, nasty-looking fixtures on them.

"Twelve o'clock! Three! Six! Nine!" Amaya called, marking the arms of an imaginary clock.

They had gotten six rails out of commission, out of twelve. That meant, he hoped, they only had to defend against an attack from between two o'clock and eight.

Amaya called her first target, gesturing. "Two-thirty!"

He spotted the nearest of the machines lumbering toward them. They were not as slow as he would have liked—they moved faster than a human could in the damn sticky-boots. Geoff, Ian, and Amaya spread out in a tethered triangle between the nearest machine and Kam and

Moriarty. Metallic smoke blocked Geoff's view as he crossed downwind of the welding apparatus.

The three teens were tethered to one another. Geoff and Ian pulled taut the tether that joined the two of them, and let out slack on the tether they both shared with Amaya. She passed Geoff, running wide in an arc, as she pulled out her disassembler gun. Then she reeled in her tether with Geoff and yanked hard on Geoff's line, launching herself toward the machine. Geoff braced himself against her pull.

The machine grabbed for her, clumsily. Amaya sliced off its foremost limb with her disassembler—it tumbled away into the Hollow—and sprayed its casing as she passed overhead. The other arms flailed at her—one nearly got her; shit, what a reach those arms had!—but she pushed off it with her hand and deflected herself. Then the machine ground to a halt with a terrible noise as the disassembler worked its way into the casing, and began shooting sparks. Ian reeled Amaya in. She touched down and took up the slack between herself and Geoff.

"I'm up." Geoff chose his target. He did not point; they were dealing with an intelligent enemy, not a lump of ice.

"Twelve o'clock!"

He pulled out his disassembler tube and crossed between the lumbering machine and Kam and Moriarty's position. It slowed, tracking on him as he approached. He moved around to its side, as Amaya had done. He was crosswind instead of down, and that made it harder. Ian flanked him on the far side of the machine. They reeled out tether and tossed it up over the target machine's reach—it swiped at the cable and missed. Amaya planted herself where she was. When the angles were right, he shoved off hard toward his target.

He did not get the timing quite right—his trajectory wobbled—but Amaya and Ian stabilized him. Then the machine came up, a field of spears and grapplers. The wind was slowing him down. He made an easy target. *Fuck.*

The machine hooked the tether he shared with Amaya and yanked him down into reach of its arms. He tucked, swept the disassembler across the arm that had his tether—landed on its casing—touched down and spun, spewing more disassembler. All the arms broke off and tumbled away, one by one. He jumped up again, downwind toward Ian, who gave him a helpful tug. He landed a meter or so away from the machine, and doused it along the side. The wheels began to disintegrate. So did a chunk of rail, which spat sparks.

Geoff checked his disassembler gauge. "I'm out of bug juice."

Ian checked. "Me, too."

Amaya did not bother to reply; merely tossed hers aside and pulled out her flares. Geoff followed suit.

Ian yelled, "*Fuck!* Eight o'clock! Eight o'clock!" and started running, yanking out his own flares. Amaya and Geoff turned—a third machine had slipped by them and was bearing down on Kam and the old man. It was mere meters away, and reaching for Moriarty, who had his back turned. The welding had stopped, and Kam was climbing into the hole they had made.

Moriarty turned at Ian's yell, and stumbled back out of the machine's reach just in time. One boot came loose—he flailed, trying to keep out of the attacking robot's reach.

Ian shouted at Geoff and Amaya, "Launch me!"

The three of them did their shuffling, clumping run, as hard as they could.

"Now!" Ian said, and crouched, as Geoff and Amaya came up on either side of him. They slung him into the air. But this time the machine was ready for an airborne attack. It plucked him easily out of the air, sliced through the tethers securing him to Amaya and Geoff, and pulled his right arm off.

Time slowed down for Geoff. A fountain, a red haze—Ian's blood—filled the air and streamed out into the Hollow. He heard someone scream. Maybe Amaya, maybe Ian. Maybe him. Moriarty had gotten both feet back onto the hull and was running at the machine, firing his weapon, loosing a stream of curses. If the bullets were having an effect, Geoff couldn't see it.

"Let's take it!" Geoff told Amaya, but she looked confused. She shook her head and approached the machine, flares at the ready. "Look . . ."

What the hell . . . ?

The machine had ceased its attack on the old man. It lowered Ian carefully to its casing and held him there. With another two appendages, it pulled a medical kit from a cabinet in its side.

"What's it doing?"

"I think . . . it's trying to help him," Amaya said.

"*Bullshit!* It just ripped his arm off!"

Ian was struggling. The machine kept him pinned down. "Help me!" His voice was weak and desperate.

That was too much for Geoff. He rushed the machine. Moriarty attacked at the same time. The machine plucked the old man's gun out of his grasp, tossed it to the winds, and shoved Moriarty back into the xaser station bulkhead. By this time, Geoff had scrambled up onto the machine. He tried to grab Ian's good arm to pull him away, but the machine batted him aside, and he spun out into the dying winds of the Hollow.

Amaya scrambled back, well out of the machine's reach, and reeled Geoff back in. By the time he had alighted on the hull, the machine had applied some sort of compress to Ian's shoulder, and was giving him an injection. Geoff and Amaya were ready to attack again, this time with flares, but Moriarty waved them back.

"Stand down. For whatever reason, it's rendering first aid. We're here, Ian," Moriarty told him. "Stay calm."

"What's it doing to me? Am I going to die?"

"Just relax. That's a smart compress it's putting on you. It's got all kinds of fancy medicine in it to staunch the bleeding till we can get you to a doctor."

Moriarty told Geoff and Amaya, "We'll get him back. I've seen those things save a soldier who was nearly cut in half. Stay alert. Follow my lead. Kurupath! Get the hell out here. Now."

Even as he spoke, Kam shouted, "Get back!" and dove out the opening to the xaser station. He went tumbling out into the Hollow as the power generator inside the small building erupted. They all ducked and were peppered with burning sparks.

Geoff shot a tether to Kam, who caught it and hand-over-handed back to the Hub surface. Geoff helped him regain his footing.

The machine seemed oblivious to the explosion. Once it had finished treating Ian, it rolled down toward the main airlock. The rest of them followed. At Moriarty's order they fanned out and brandished flares, alert to any further threatening move. But it showed no hostility.

The airlock door opened automatically as they approached. The machine stopped at the entrance, too large to enter.

"What now?" Geoff asked. The old man shrugged. Then the machine lifted Ian up. He moaned, and Geoff moved to attack it again, but Moriarty said sharply, "Belay that!"

The machine whistled some strange tune. Amaya, Kam, and Geoff exchanged surprised looks, and Geoff turned back to stare at the machine. Its cameras gazed implacably back.

"Get into the airlock," Moriarty ordered them, and when they hesitated, snapped, "Do it now!"

They hurried into the small chamber. Moriarty was whistling back and forth with the machine.

Kam said, "They're speaking Tonal_Z. I think it's telling us to get him to the hospital right away. The old man is asking what injection Ian got."

Kam listened to the machine's response, then shook his head at their querying looks. "I couldn't make it out."

The machine lowered Ian into the old man's waiting arms, and Moriarty stepped back slowly into the airlock. The machine froze in place: it did not lower its arms, nor make any other movement.

"Let's not push our luck," Moriarty said, and punched a button. The outer airlock door shut. They had to wait a minute or two while the room pressurized. Geoff's ears popped painfully.

Amaya pulled off her mask and came over to Ian, ran her hands over his blood-drenched chest. She grabbed his clothing, shook him, snarled, "Ian, listen to me. You listen, you asshole! Idiot! Don't you dare die."

Geoff came up behind. He tried to avoid staring at his friend's detached arm, which the machine had taped to his body, and his bloody, swathed stump. The sight of the amputation made him want to throw up. He called Ian's name, but Moriarty shook his head.

"He's been sedated, and injected with antibiotics and blood-building assemblers. He's lost a lot of blood. He's still in danger. Come on, hustle! The hospital isn't far. Stay alert—the feral could still be out there. This could be some kind of trick."

Weapon drawn, Moriarty led the way out of the airlock as it opened on the Hub's interior.

17

Jane wrapped up her call to Sean and returned to Tania, whose team was struggling to get all the backup copies of the critical systems ready. Meanwhile, Jane's remote views showed a hundred or more robot arms and craft attacking Zekeston. How many people would die? She thought about Xuan and the clan, and hatred for the feral swept through her. She trembled with the need to attack: to shred its structures to component bits with her own hands.

Then power flickered. Her waveface went dead. The floor lurched sickeningly under her feet and she was lofted into the pitch blackness. She grabbed at the railing—caught it with a foot.

"What's happening?" one of Tania's people asked.

"It's gotten into the spin generation system," Jane replied. A horrible grinding resounded through the walls, confirming this: Jane lost her grip on the railing and smashed against a cubical wall. She flailed in the darkness, crashing into people, cables, debris, unable to stabilize herself. The grinding and shaking continued—she felt and heard others moving as the habitat's momentum slowed and the shaking stopped. Phocaea's gravity became a faint, steady pressure pulling them all toward one wall. Someone swore.

The emergency lighting came on, feeble pools that cast long shadows. Marty propelled over, wild-eyed.

"Report! Has it finished copying itself to Upside-Down's systems yet?"

"Don't know. We're on backup life support," he gasped. "It's got control of the main network!"

"Easy," she said. "Stay cool. Tania will have planned for this. Is the communications network still up?"

"Only partially, and it's swamped with medical calls."

"All right. Stay here and stay on top of communications. Prioritize my calls. Brief Benavidez and the mayors as soon as you can."

Jane sought out Tania. The smaller woman was climbing up across the wall webbing. Her programmers, assorted objects, wiring, and globules of liquid floated around the room in the air currents, settling slowly toward the wall where Jane and Marty clung.

"Get to your stations!" Tania snapped. "We're out of time. Move your ass, Damian, Perry—you too, Vicki. Wire us up. Now." She spun. "Mbara, report! What was the status on the gateway when we crashed? Open or closed?"

Her people shouted back. Pandemonium reigned, but briefly. A field of assembler tubes dropped, spinning gold wiring from clusters in the shadows. Jane snagged a wire as it streamed past, and plugged it into the processor at her ear. Her waveface blinked and rebooted: Tania's countdown clock appeared, as did the map of the sapient. The shouts quieted as people's conversations went back online.

Tania's avatar appeared in Jane's wavespace. "Are you ready?"

"Let's do it."

To shut down life-support systems required a series of joint code entries by her and Tania. Tania brought her into the emergency shutdown area. Jane looked down at herself. Her avatar sat in something that looked like a flying kayak. Beside her, another neuter avatar rode a kayak with Tania's name and ID emblazoned on the side. Around them was the life support space, filled with streams of light and arcane machineries. It reminded Jane of an impossibly complex and beautiful clockworks. Other kayakers were working in different parts of the clockworks. They were within Zekeston's computer system.

"Follow me." Tania led Jane through this mechanic's cathedral. The hum and the team's crisscrossing commands buzzed around them. The clamor made Jane feel dizzy. Was that an echo of her Voice she heard in the machine's grindings and murmurs?

A horrifying possibility occurred to her: what if the Voice *was,* or was caused by, the feral sapient? She didn't see how that could be—the feral was barely even aware of what humans *were,* much less comprehend their highly complex biology. How could it even begin to hack her neurochemistry? Still, she sensed a connection. She would have to ponder the question later. When there was time.

"There are five crucial systems we need to verify redundancies for before we lock them down." Tania spoke loudly. "The rest we can crash. Stand by while I run the checks, and then enter your code when I say to."

Once, twice, three times she waited while Tania tugged the machinery into lockdown; three times the "waiting" signal crept across her vision; three times she entered her own code and took another system offline. With each disconnection, more portions of the clockworks cathedral went dark and still.

She had expected an attack from the sapient. She mentioned this to Tania, who shrugged. "Distracted. It's resource-starved and fighting on a lot of fronts. Go ahead." She moved out of the way and Jane moved in, had her pattern scanned, and gave the command to shut down the fourth system.

On their way to the last station, Jane spotted another kayak in the distance, pacing them. She couldn't understand why it drew her attention; it was certainly possible that Tania had ordered someone to check on something nearby, but something about the other kayaker stood out. Something . . .

It came to her. The kayak had no identifiers on the side. No name or anything. That shouldn't be possible. It had to be an intruder.

Tania was ahead of her and couldn't see the other.

"Tania . . ." She pointed. "Who is that?"

"What?"

The instant she gestured, the other kayaker bolted past them. It was fast—no more than a blur. It was long gone by the time Jane burst into pursuit, but she could still track the clusters of bits it had disturbed on its way in. Tania's startled question trailed behind her, a fading string of phrases. She chased the other kayaker into the very deepest, chiming innards of the clockworks, down, down, and the humming and grinding became a song, a chorale, a hymn to the machine.

She cornered the other kayaker deep in, as deep as they could go without being code themselves. And she gaped: the kayaker had moved into the info stream . . . had become part of it.

A human couldn't do that. This was the sapient.

Tania came up behind her. "Fuck me," she said in an awed tone.

"We've got to get to the fifth system," Jane said.

"It's led us right to it. See behind it?" Jane craned to see—the panel icon with its pattern of symbols was partly obscured by the datastream kayak. "It figured out where we were headed. It's trying to stop us." Then Tania whooped. "Jane, I'm getting a report. . . . The data link with the surface is down! We stopped it from completing its copy."

Sean's doing. *Thank God!* The feral was contained. But Zekeston itself was still in terrible danger. The info-drenched kayaker burst into staccato Tonal_Z arpeggios. Fierce lavender energies surrounded her, and Jane's interface wavered. Briefly, meatspace—the controlled pandemonium of Tania's webwork—overlay the clockworks cathedral. Tania deflected the digital attack and their views stabilized again. The kayaker tried again; again, Tania deflected. "Distract it!" she shouted. "I've got to get around behind it and finish the shutdown checks."

Jane moved toward the kayaker. Tania's avatar had grown long, rubbery arms and eyestalks, but couldn't get past to the panel; the feral disintegrated whatever projection she put forth.

Distract it, Jane thought; *distract it!* But how?

She called up a Tonal_Z modal translator. She wasn't sure of the grammar: she would have to fake it as best she could.

Info, she sang: **I = —** Tonal_Z did not have proper names; she had to make something up. *What the hell.* **I = SheHearsVoices.**

The feral kayaker's surprise was palpable; its assaults faltered, ever so briefly. Tania's tentacles slipped in toward the panel.

Query, Jane went on: **Who = you? That's all.**

Info: I = BitManSinger. Command: Cancel . . . Something; what? Life support something. **Cancel life-support shutdown sequence!** it ordered her. **That's all.**

Sorry. No can do.

The feral had spotted Tania's tentacles and was blasting them with digital shredders. But Tania had already secured herself to the panel and partially shielded her connection from attack.

Command, Jane countered; again she struggled to find the right Tonal_Z phrases: **Cancel attack! That's all.**

"How's it coming?" she asked Tania.

"Almost there . . . keep at it . . ."

Info, the sapient was saying: **Permission denied. That's all.**

Permission denied, eh? While they were singing to each other, it launched all kinds of digital attacks, which Tania's shields barely deflected.

What the hell, she thought; *it couldn't hurt.* **Urgent command: cancel attack at-time this, or, Info: I will cancel you! That's all.**

Another brief pause. Then came a blitz. Jane's view of the clockworks sputtered and blinked out. A second later she was swept back into her wavespace. "Enter your shutdown code!" Tania urged. "Hurry!"

Jane maneuvered in fits and starts across the blasted clockworks wavescape to the input icons. The feral—pure energy now—blasted her barriers. She tried not to flinch from the blows—*it can't really hurt me; I'm not a digital being*—dove into the tumult, found the panel by feel, and input the code.

"Requiescat in pace," she muttered, and pressed the button.

18

People crammed into the emergency room. They waited in lines, or were strapped to the walls with compresses, bandages, and ice packs, or were moved around on gurneys. The triage medics took one look at Ian, loaded him onto a stretcher, and whisked him away. Amaya, Kam, and Geoff clung to the waiting area ropeworks, silent, while the old man spoke to the doctors and dealt with the paperwork.

In a few moments, Moriarty came over. "These fine folks want to check you over, once things settle down a bit. It'll be a few moments. In the meantime, why don't you call your families and check in?" He tossed a link to Geoff. "Communications are still FUBAR, but I have priority access."

"Thanks," Geoff said. He clicked the comm link, and punched in his dad's code. The call went through. It was audio only, and the line had a lot of noise.

His dad's voice quavered. "Hello?"

"Dad, it's me." Geoff's own voice wobbled a bit, too. "Are you OK? Is Mom there?"

"She's here. We're both all right." Then, before Geoff had even a second to register relief, his father started in. "Where the hell have you been? Why aren't you calling on your own line?"

"Dad, I'm sorry . . . the lines are down. But I'm all right."

"'All right.' *All right?* We've been worried sick about you! I've been trying to reach you all night! What have you been off doing? Joyriding on that damn bike of yours? All you had to do was call! After what happened to your brother, don't you think you could show a little consideration? Your mother has been beside herself! I saw the originating number and thought they were calling me to tell me you were *dead!*"

By this time, his father was screaming at him. Geoff could only hang there and take it. Worse, when they found out Geoff had been fighting machines out in the Hollow, and heard what had happened to Ian, Dad and Mom would have to be scraped off the bulkheads.

Amaya and Kam were looking at him; they couldn't hear his dad but they could see his expression. He closed his eyes, tuning out his dad's hateful words. It never mattered what he did; he got shit for it.

"I'm at the hospital," Geoff said finally, when his dad paused to take a breath. He resisted the impulse to yell, *because a machine just pulled my friend's arm off, you asshole!* "They just want to check me over. I'll be home in about an hour. OK . . . gotta go . . . bye."

He hung up before his dad could reply.

A medic waved him over to be examined. He went with her, even though he knew he was fine. She smiled at him as they floated together down the hospital corridor. "You're that biker that saved the ice!"

He felt his face heat up. "Yeah."

He could tell by how she looked at him sidelong that she liked him, and that if he showed interest, he might end up with her digits. But he couldn't bring himself to. That empty space Carl's death had planted in his chest seemed to be expanding, like a noiseless explosion in him. It was consuming him from the inside out. He had no room or heart for anything else.

19

The shutdown interface winked out. Jane looked across meatspace at Tania. The projection of the construct still hovered in the room's middle. It was fraying, segment by segment, into haze. In seconds only burning blotches remained in Jane's vision. The team members were cheering.

Jane carefully threaded her way through the forest of lead wires to Marty. He looked haggard. He held up a finger as she started to speak, and made some gestures in-wave.

"There." With a sigh, he turned to her. "Everyone notified."

"Good. Now go check on Ceci, and get some rest."

"Thanks, Chief." He left.

Tania was conferring with a tiny knot of her team leaders. Tania looked haggard and shaken: a belated reaction to the stress of the past few hours.

"Well?"

"Backup life-support systems are coming online," Tania reported. "We won't know full status for a bit, but so far the critical ones seem to be OK."

"The sapient?"

"It's gone—from our systems, at least. I'm awaiting confirmation from the Upside-Down team, but I'm reasonably confident we got it out of theirs, too."

Michaela, the Upside-Down team leader, flickered into view even as she spoke. "Phase Three complete. It's gone."

"You're sure?" Tania asked.

The woman nodded. "The copy up here never reached full sapience. We've deleted it all, and they are wiping and reinstalling from backups to make certain it hasn't buried any bits or pieces that are going to give us trouble later."

Tania sagged with a sigh. She saw Jane looking at her, and gave her a salute. "One feral sapient removed from the computer systems, as ordered."

Jane clapped her shoulder. "Good work."

"Upside-Down's data is trashed," Michaela told them. "They've lost nearly three days' worth of 'Stroiders' material and they're pretty upset."

Jane replied, "Don't worry about it. That's my job."

"That's why they pay you the big bucks," Tania muttered.

Jane chuckled. Speaking of big bucks: "Did we capture it alive?"

Tania replied, "I'm about to check. Thondu is supposed to be finishing up with the captive version. Care to join me?"

The trap system was only a few hand- and footsprings down the shaft. On the way they dodged trash, globules of unidentified, dirty liquid—probably unprogrammed assemblers—and debris that swirled gently skew-wards in the microgee air currents. Zekeston had stabilized at an orientation to Phocaea's gravity such that "down" in this sector was actually about forty-five degrees off of the down they were used to. Jane thought again of Xuan and the clan, and prayed they had reached safety.

They entered. Thondu was wrapping up his harp, clinging to a wall cord, because the room was bare of webworks or Velcro strips: of everything, in fact, except a suspended tank with a cluster of interconnected biocomputers inside. He looked like hell: sweat-drenched, clothing askew, face gaunt, eyes sunken with exhaustion, shoulders hunched. His hands were claws; his fingertips bloodied.

"Well?" Tania said, gesturing at the processor globes. "Is it in there?"

He puffed out his cheeks, eyeing the tank. "It's not answering."

"No . . ." Tania looked aghast. "Are you sure?"

In answer he pulled out his harp, brought his Tonal_Z interfaces up again, and plinked out a rough melody.

Info: I = MeatManHarper. Query: BitManSinger, you = at-place what, at-time this? That's all.

The difference in the quality of his playing now versus the first time was striking. He winced with every pluck of the strings, and left red smears on them. Jane felt a twinge of sympathy.

Once finished, he stilled the strings and they waited. Seconds ticked by. He repeated the query. No response. He tried a different musical phrase: **Command: BitManSinger, respond! That's all.**

Still nothing.

Urgent Command: BitManSinger, respond! That's all.

After a minute or two, he gave Tania a regretful look.

"We must be missing too many of the proper linkages. Or perhaps some small but crucial module was overlooked . . . ."

"Maybe it's just in shock," Jane said, "or hiding."

Thondu shook his head. "Ever since the connection with the larger system was severed, this copy has been inactive. It couldn't maintain its identity-formation without some minimum level of activity. It's gone." He spread his bloody hands. "My regrets."

Tania turned away. Jane rubbed her eyes, which burned with fatigue. Her own doom lay before her, tomorrow, in her meeting with her boss.

"There's still a chance," Tania said. "Still a chance that we can recover enough information from the Upside-Down team's work to get it going again."

Jane could tell from the look in her eyes that she did not hold out a great deal of hope.

"How long?"

"Let me get back to you on that." Tania paused. "I'm sorry. I know you were counting on a live extraction."

"You got it out of our systems," Jane said. "The cluster is safe, for now. That's the most important thing."

By this time, Thondu had put away his harp.

"Any chance you could stay and join our team?" Tania asked him. "I could put you to good use. We'll gain a lot of knowledge from this"— she waved a hand at the processors holding the digital corpse of the sapient—"even if we can't recover the sapient itself."

He shook his head. "Sorry. I have other commitments. I will zap you a bill before I leave."

"Very well," Tania said. "Thanks again for your help."

He looked at Jane. "I'm very sorry. I wish we had been more successful."

"As do I." The words crossed her tongue, tasting of cinders.

Jane hailed Sean. "The sapient is gone. You can call off your attacks."

"Already done. We severed the connection to the surface."

"We saw, from our end. In case you're interested, you got it with very little time to spare. We would not have been able to stop it without you."

"Well, that's something, at least." He paused, and sighed. "Ma'am . . . Commissioner Jane . . . I've got bad news."

Jane braced herself. Sean did not get rattled over trifles. "Go on."

"Communications went down right after you called me, while I was briefing my second-in-command. I couldn't get warehouse crew down to the Hub. So, well." He cleared his throat. "I recruited four of those young bikers who helped us rescue the ice stores the other day."

"*Holy shit,* Sean!"

"Yeah. One of them I believe you know, Geoff Agre—the brother of the young man who was killed in the disaster. I recruited him and three of his friends. They were with me at the time of the attacks, I had very limited time, so . . . I made a command decision."

"I see." Jane tried to absorb this. A breach of judgment on Sean's part? No. They had had only moments, she had given him an order, and he had done what he must. But she could picture Sal and Deirdre's reactions now.

"They came through," Sean reported. "In a big way. But one of them was injured in the attack. Badly."

Geoff's face flashed in her mind, and an icy hand squeezed her heart. "Who was injured? How?"

"Name's Ian Carmichael. A friend of Agre's. His arm was ripped off by one of the maintenance craft out on the Hub, under control of the feral sapient. He and two of the others were fending off the machines, while two of us were cutting through the conduit housing for the xaser transmitter."

"Will he survive?"

"He's in surgery now. They say his chances are good. They got to him right away. And they expect to be able to either reattach the arm or grow him a new one. Likelihood of long-term damage to his shoulder is still uncertain. He'll probably lose some mobility. They won't know for a while."

Jane released her breath, slowly. *He was very fortunate,* she thought. *As were we all.* If the young man had died, given current tensions and the overcrowding, they'd have an uprising on their hands. "Have the parents been notified?"

"I've been trying. I can't get through."

"I'll make sure they are contacted tonight. I'd like you to follow up with a personal visit to each of the families first thing in the morning."

"All right."

"Are they all of age?"

"Let me check." A pause. "Yes. Geoff, Amaya, and Ian are seventeen. In Geoff's case, just barely—his birthday was two weeks ago. Kamal is a year older, eighteen."

So Sean could not be prosecuted for endangering minors. He added, "I've been in touch with Shelley on the warehouses. They were alerted in time, and were able to shut down all their automated systems quickly. The feral did not do serious harm up there."

"Good. Anything else?"

"Well, there was something odd . . ." Sean's voice trailed off.

"Go on."

He hesitated. "It's not urgent. It can wait till our morning meeting. I'd like Tania to hear it, too."

"Very well. Get some rest, if you can."

Next she called Xuan. Even before she spoke, just seeing his pug face and the figures of his siblings behind him filled her with a deep sense of relief. She could hear one of the twins squalling. "Is everyone all right?"

"It was a scramble, but we're all here. We're safe."

"I'll call you back," she said. The prime minister needed to know.

Benavidez hung suspended in his office, perched in his webworks and switching through various views in his waveface, studying the workers and machinery beginning repairs within Zekeston and without.

He looked up as she materialized. "Well?"

Jane straightened. "We were successful in removing the threat from the system, and critical life-support systems are back online. We won't be fully operational for a few days—"

"But we're a hell of a lot better off than we might have been."

"Yes, sir."

"The sapient?"

She shook her head. "We didn't have enough time to finish mapping it before it launched an attack."

He was silent, but she sensed his deep disappointment.

"Tania is trying to find out what went wrong," she went on. "It's possible they can salvage something useful. I'll know more by our meeting tomorrow morning."

He sighed and rubbed at his eyes with the fingers and thumb of one hand.

"I've gotten word," he said finally, "that Reinforte plans to summon you before the Joint Resource Committee."

Jane forbore from mentioning that she already knew this.

"According to my sources," Benavidez went on, "Councilor Reinforte has set his people to try to dig up dirt to use on you, but your people have all remained loyal, so far. It appears you have powerful allies."

Chikuma, he meant. He himself treated Jane rather more gingerly than he might, if not for Sensei.

It troubled Jane that Benavidez had sources in her organization that she did not know about. She wanted to know where all the lines of communication in her organization were—whom they flowed to, and why. She made a mental note to do some checking. Not that she did not trust Benavidez, but—well, she didn't. In this business she dared not trust anyone completely, except perhaps Chikuma-sensei. And as the old woman had once told Jane, *Don't trust even me. Rely on multiple sources for your information, and always keep something in your pocket for later use.*

All Jane had in her pockets this time was lint. "I'm glad to hear it."

The real question mark was Benavidez himself. If he remained loyal to her, she might yet weather this storm. If he had made up his mind to trade her for the ice, nothing anyone else could do would make a bit of difference.

"One more thing you should be aware of," she said. "During the feral's attack I assigned my man Sean Moriarty to shut down the wave-feed up to the surface. He deputized four young citizens to help him. They were successful—in fact, they saved the city. But one of them was seriously injured, nearly killed. His prognosis is good, I'm told, but I think it would not go amiss if someone from your office contacted the youths' families right away and made sure they are getting everything they need. I'm sending you the details now." She forwarded their contact info. "I'd be glad to do it myself, but I think it would mean more coming directly from your office.

"I'll have Emily follow up." He sighed deeply, and rubbed at his eyes. "And now we should both get some rest. I'll see you first thing in the morning in my office."

Jane swallowed her worries, her impatience. "Good night, Mr. Prime Minister."

. . .

On the way to the aerogarden, she got reports. The emergency lines were back up. But several sections of Zekeston had experienced partial decompression or other damage. She located Xuan and his sister Kieu in the corridor outside the life shelter, the one nearest their campsite.

She saw relief in his face. Behind him, Kieu looked tired and worried. "Where's the clan?" she asked. "Is everyone safe?"

"Everyone's all right," Kieu said. "They're asleep in the life shelter."

They peeked in on them: the family had bedded down in the netting over in one nook of the badly cramped shelter. Pham blinked blearily at them when they opened the door; Kieu said good night, and entered the shelter, leaving her and Xuan in the corridor.

Jane turned back to Xuan. "What about everyone's belongings?"

"Mostly unrecoverable, I'm afraid. I'll show you." Xuan lofted himself across the hall, and opened the door to the park, where they had pitched camp. Jane looked out over ruin.

The aerospheres must have shattered the aquarium, and its destruction had taken out most of the park's trees and plants. The water had finally all settled in the wedge made by two walls: it was filled with debris, dead greenery, lumps of nutrient gel that looked like giant jellyfish, and many dead and dying fish in water that still sloshed gently from the earlier violence. Gone were the cherry trees and the picnic tables; the Goh boards stood out against what was now nearly the ceiling. Even the plants still hanging were dead. Though there was plenty of air now, the area must have been at least partially decompressed for some time. The hole to the "lower levels" was now nearly overhead. Fragments of light shot through it, revealing glimpses of further damage to other areas. Pham, Emil, and several other adults floated here and there, picking through the debris in a search for what was left of their belongings.

Jane caught a glimpse of something terrifying: what appeared to be a child's skeleton. She rushed over and bent next to it, but when she touched it, it spasmed, and exploded into a cloud of glass beads and silicone tendrils.

"What the hell?" she said.

"Ah! That was on the news. An assembler hacking prank at the university."

"What's it doing here, then? This means we've got an assembler contaminant in the system, using up resources at a crucial time, that might screw up repairs. On top of everything else!" Furious, exasperated, she called Aaron to let him know. When she got off, Xuan said, "I've arranged for us to stay with some friends of mine from the university."

"I can't do that! Don't you see? This puts me, and them, in a very awkward position."

"Why?" he asked.

"You know damn well why. All their work and funding comes from Kukuyoshi."

He sighed. "Jane, they already know about Kukuyoshi. The night is half gone and you have a meeting with the prime minister in the morning. Nobody is blaming you but you."

"Have you seen my sammy cache lately?"

"Set aside your pride, Jane. Come with me and get some good rest."

She gave in, of course.

A slender, narrow-shouldered man in a bathrobe answered the door.

"I'm sorry to disturb you so late, Charles," Xuan said.

A little terrier bounced out, yapping and bounding off the walls just out of reach. "No trouble at all. Glad to see you weathered the disturbance safely. Do come in. Quiet, Muffet! Away with you." He shooed the dog away. "The wife's asleep in the other room, or I'd introduce you . . ."

"I'm not asleep," came her voice. "I'll be out in a moment. Miss Muffet! Come here, right now!"

As they lofted over the door's top frame, the dog sproinged off the ceiling and into the other room.

Xuan introduced the man to Jane as Charles Winford. They brushed hands. He had an English accent left over from his pre-Upsider days, sprinkled with plenty of stroiderisms and Upsider pronunciations. His glance at Jane held curiosity. A woman floated out of the bedroom.

"We're very sorry to disturb you," Jane said.

"Quite all right," she replied, "the disturbance had us up. Glad you decided to take us up on our offer, Xuan." Her accent, too, was British. She gave Xuan a peck on the cheek, and then put out her hand to Jane.

"Rowan Fairchild. I'm a researcher at the university. I know who you are, of course. It's a pleasure."

They offered them tea and marmite on toast, while they set up a hammock in Charles's office. They must know Jane had something to do with the disturbance that had just happened—word was already all over the wave—but they forbore from asking about it, and chatted instead about their work at the university. Rowan's specialty was adaptive ecosystems; she was working on a project monitoring the genetic changes the animals had been undergoing in Kukuyoshi, and producing predictive simulations. Charles was a cellular biologist studying the long-term effects of low-gravity environments on certain fungi. It was clear to Jane that they were dear and trusted friends of Xuan's.

They were both exhausted, but neither could sleep. At two a.m. the cameras went off, and she told him what had happened with the feral. He listened while she described it.

"Regrettable that it didn't survive," Xuan said.

"Yes." She released a slow, sad breath. "We've been so busy dealing with the crisis I haven't been able to prep to respond to Reinforte's accusations. They're going to eat me alive. And I haven't got a live sapient for barter. The PM will have no choice but to dump me, to get Ogilvie & Sons' ice. It's probably going to be tomorrow morning. Today, I mean." She felt more vulnerable than she had since she was a child.

It was dark in the room, except for the glow from a night-light; all she could make out was his dim silhouette. But her other senses shaped him for her: the small movements of his back muscles beneath her hand as he shifted in the hammock; the feathery touch of his breath against her hair; the beat of his heart against her cheek. His skin smelled faintly of Xuanness. His breath had its own scent, too, and both smelled good to her.

"Life is change. You know that."

"I know." A long pause. She pillowed her cheek. "But people will blame me. They already are. I'll go down in history as the woman who brought an entire stroid cluster down."

Xuan burst out laughing. "Look at it this way, dear. At least you'll be remembered! The only ones who will know my name in years to come will be random geologists who happen to stumble across my outdated old tomes in some wave archive that someone forgot to purge."

She did not know whether to be angry or amused. "Oh, Xuan."

He finally said it. "We'll weather this." He kissed her head. "Don't worry."

Her sleep was troubled that night. She saw Hugh, floating faceup in a river, dead, only he wore Marty's clothing and was covered in vines. She wept. Her mother said, "Don't grieve, for I bring you joyous tidings." A woman wearing an old-fashioned male Downsider's suit moved past. She had her hand on her belly, and Jane knew she was pregnant.

"Look!" The young woman turned toward Jane, and she had the face of a man. Two snakes slithered up to her, making wave patterns in the sand. One was made of electricity with jewels for eyes, and one a smooth blue-green, with human eyes. The snakes wriggled up to the pants legs and moved upward.

"This child has two fathers," the woman-man said and removed her-his clothing; the snakes had coiled around her-his hips, like a belt. "A father of flesh and a father of wave." She-he pressed her-his fingers into her-his belly and it opened. Within, Jane could see clockworks. Then she-he closed her-himself up, as Jane's mother's voice said, "It is to remain sealed for a time and a time."

Then Dominica came, only it was Dominica as she had been before she had left, barely beyond her childhood, willowy and boyish and solemn. She led the newly pregnant woman-man off.

Jane saw her mother standing at the edge of a pool in the light of the full moon. She wore no clothes, and her body was old and wrinkled. Her giant breasts sagged to her belly. Her hair was white, flowing, and beautiful. It went all the way to the ground.

The pool at her feet was dark, like spilled blood, and glass knives lay on the shore. The old woman stepped through the knives, which cut her feet till she cried out. She waded into the pool and as she moved deeper inward, the blood was converted to pure water that swirled around her hips, her waist, her chest. She grew young. The knives on the shoreline crumbled to a bed of clean, soft sand. Greenery blossomed at the pool's edge.

"Don't be afraid, Jane," she said. "Much good comes after," and sank below the surface.

Jane awoke with a start, heart hammering, the echoes of her cry lingering in her ears. She curled in the hammock, pressed against Xuan. It took a long time for her to fall back to sleep.

20

Sean did not go to bed that night. He sent the three uninjured teens home after the medic cleared them. Then he took stimulants and stayed at the hospital with Ian. He tried periodically to reach the boy's parents, with no success. He did manage to contact the other three families, and made appointments to stop by in the morning.

After emergency surgery, the surgeon came out. "We have gotten Ian stabilized. He's resting comfortably."

"How does it look?" Sean asked.

"There is always the risk of organ damage, after a loss of so much blood. But I continue to be confident that he will recover," he said.

"What about the arm?"

"We could begin to grow him a new limb as early as tomorrow, as long as his vitals stay stable. It will be several weeks before he has full use of the arm and shoulder again, and there will be quite a bit of pain for a while. Any sign of the family?"

Sean shook his head. "Not yet. Is he awake? May I speak to him?"

"Of course. This way."

Recovery smelled of medicine and disinfectants. Life-support equipment made beeping and hissing noises, and nutrient tubes lay across the patients. People lay strapped to railed gurneys, with IVs and oxygen, hooked up to monitoring equipment, with nurses tending to them. Sean lofted over to Ian and laid a hand on his uninjured shoulder. The young man opened his eyes and eyed Sean blearily.

"Hi," he said. His voice was a weak thread.

"Hi, hero."

That brought a slight smile to Ian's lips. "Am I OK?"

"The doctor says they should have no problems regrowing your arm. In due course you should have full use back."

A sigh escaped the young man.

"The truth is . . ." Sean coughed. "You saved my life tonight." He stepped back and gave the young man a military salute. That brought another faint smile. Then Ian closed his eyes.

"Rest," Sean said. "I'll be back later."

On the way to Administration, Sean pondered again how the feral had ceased its attack after injuring Ian. From everything he knew about feral sapients, that was unheard of. They had no capacity for empathy. Like highly intelligent sharks, they were merciless—they ate up all digital space, took things over, and fucked with whoever tried to get in their way.

Maybe Tania would have some answers. He would talk to her tomorrow, when he briefed Jane.

Jane woke early the next morning. She left Xuan asleep and crawled out of the hammock. She might as well cede the night and get going.

Charles was in the kitchen, preparing breakfast. He handed her sausages, a tube of oatmeal, and a bulb of steaming tea. "I'm dreadfully sorry we can't offer you a proper perch for dining," he said.

"Please, don't apologize. You've done so much for us."

While they were eating, Muffet the terrier came bounding in. It came sniffing over to Jane. "Go on," Charles commanded, but Jane said, "No, it's all right," and slipped the little dog a piece of sausage.

"You'll spoil her."

"Sorry. I have a soft spot for big brown eyes." *Even when they're on little brown ratdogs,* she thought, and made a face at the dog, who bounced into Jane's lap and wagged her tail ecstatically when Jane caught hold.

Jane stroked the dog's wiry fur. "Charles," she said, "I want to thank you and Rowan for taking us in."

"No trouble at all, really."

"Listen . . ." she hesitated. "I'm sure you know I'm in charge of response to the crisis that started in our life-support systems three days ago."

His eyes widened. "Of course. But we didn't want to pry . . ."

"I appreciate your discretion. But I'd like to give you some knowledge about what's been happening. I'm sure you've heard the rumors that we had a feral sapient in our systems." He nodded. "We managed to remove the sapient last night. The city is no longer under threat. And," she added, squeezing by brute force any trace of bitterness out of her voice, "our ice shortage is going to be solved soon, too."

"Oh, excellent."

Jane finished her breakfast. With a sigh, she said, "I should get to work. Thanks again for your hospitality."

"Not at all, not at all."

She took a bulb of tea back to their room. Xuan was drowsing but not fully asleep; she could tell by his shallow breathing and the way his eyelids pressed so firmly on his cheeks. Jane held the tea in front of his nose, squeezed it gently to expel the air, and wafted the ensuing vapors his way. He sighed and made a mournful face.

"Five more minutes, Mum."

"No hurry. You can sleep in."

"No, I need to get going, too." With a groan, he sat up and took the tea. He sipped sleepily, dangling in the hammock, while Jane gathered her things.

"I'll call you later," she said finally.

"You've done the best you could. Hold on to that."

"I will." *I'll try.*

·   ·   ·

Her direct reports were waiting. Jane's stomach was so knotted by this time, and her arteries pumped so full of adrenaline, thinking about her upcoming meeting with the PM, that she couldn't bear to perch at her desk, as distracting as Sean plainly found it. She needed to move. Better yet, bounce off the walls.

Aaron looked tired and distraught; Tania tired and haggard; Sean just plain tired. Jane said, "I only have a few minutes before my debriefing with the prime minister. Talk fast." She gestured. "Aaron."

"The Ogilvie & Sons shipment departed Ilion last night," he said. "If we want to make a deal with them, today is the day."

"Anything else?"

He opened his mouth, and closed it. "Perhaps we could talk on the way to your meeting. There's a . . . private matter."

Jane lifted her eyebrows, mystified, but he shook his head. "It'll have to be after my meeting with the prime minister," she said. "Tania."

The young woman shrugged. "No progress on reactivating the sapient's captive replica. Some crucial component is missing—some set of algorithms or key data structure—and I don't know what it is."

"Will it ever be recoverable? When will you know?"

"We don't have the sapient's responses to study any longer, so it's all guesswork. Could be days, months, even years before we make a breakthrough. If ever." She sighed, and rubbed at her eyes. "We'll keep working on it, but don't ride your pony." The expression came from pony bottles, which were only used for quick jobs in vacuum, or short transfers from one place to another. In other words, don't hold your breath.

Jane had been expecting this. Still.

"If you could get the PM to allocate us more tech and people resources . . ." Tania started hopefully. Jane gave her a bleak look. Yeah; right. "I'll bear that in mind."

Marty stuck his head in. "You have to head over *right now,* Chief. You're going to be late."

Ba-thump, ba-thump, ba-thump: her heart pumped more adrenaline into her veins. She was developing quite the headache. "One more minute, thanks. Sean?"

"The kid who lost his arm looks fair to make a complete recovery," he replied. "No more news on the sabotage."

She glanced at her heads-up. Two minutes to get there, and she did not dare be late. "All right. Marty, go catch me an elevator. Hustle!"

Aaron took her arm as she passed him. "I *really* need to talk to you. Privately."

Jane said. "I just can't. Come see me after my meeting."

"But it's—" He broke off, looking tense.

"Sorry," she said. "Out of time."

The protestors camped outside the PM's offices were fewer in number this morning. As Jane started to launch herself out of the lift, Marty touched her arm. They exchanged a wordless look.

"We're with you, Chief," he finally said. A lump formed in her throat. She nodded, managed to squeeze out a thanks.

She left him there, and made her way through the protestors, who quieted as she passed through. They seemed to sense the importance of this moment. *All we need now,* she thought, *is the cup of honeyed milk to pour over my head, and the sacrificial knife.* She passed through the antimote veil. Security opened the doors for her, and Jane floated through the PM's outer chamber, greeting all the secretaries, undersecretaries, assistant subministers, and the like. Everyone was eyeing her.

Don't be paranoid, Navio. Let events unfold.

It was amazing what you could do in a few hours with sufficient juice and a staff of bug jocks. The nutrient reek made her eyes burn, but little visual evidence remained of the damage Benavidez's offices must have sustained, other than a few embryonic items of furniture and cubicle walls still growing up out of the floor. These were covered in translucent membranes laced with nano-grown arteries, capillaries, and miniature, heartlike pumps. At this stage they looked like living creatures that might stand up and walk away.

Outside Benavidez's conference room, the staff members welcomed her; one made her comfortable in the lounge webbing with a bulb of coffee. Thomas Harman floated through. "The prime minister wants to move his direct-reports meeting back—" he told one of the staffers there, and then saw her. "Commissioner," he said politely.

An emergency meeting with all his direct reports, and she had not heard about it. Jane peered at *Beatnik Jesus*. He seemed to gaze directly at her from atop his surfboard, but not unkindly.

Christ as deity. She wondered if he had actually heard God's Voice in his head, and whether medications would have made a difference. She wondered whether events had simply gotten away from him, there at the end. Downside, back in the CFAS, such a thought spoken into the wrong ear could have landed her in prison. Such thoughts, spoken to her own family when she was a teen, had earned her exile. Her own Voice, thankfully, remained silent on the subject.

She was ushered in. Benavidez was at his desk, editing something. She waited. He looked up finally. He did not offer to brush hands.

"Fill me in," he said.

"The warehouse incident was certainly sabotage," she told him, "and all indications are that the Ogilvies are behind it. No hard proof yet, though." She gave him a quick sketch of the facts that Sean had transmitted to her yesterday afternoon, regarding the homicide investigation. Benavidez nodded and she guessed he must already have heard about this from his own sources.

She also gave him a rundown of their revised resource budget. She also, with the barest of hesitations, informed him of Aaron's assessment that today was the day to make an offer to Ogilvie & Sons. After this, it would be more expensive and much more difficult to get them to change course for Phocaea.

"What is the latest word on the feral sapient?" he said.

"Dead and gone. Tania is pressing for more resources to try to re-cover it, but her people already have a huge task ahead of them, putting our computer systems back together." She spread her hands. "It could be a long time before they recover anything useful."

"A long time?"

"Weeks. Months. Years. There's no way to know." She leaned forward.

"But this evidence of sabotage changes things, sir. If Ogilvie & Sons is provably responsible for the disaster, we can force them to capitulate—lower their price, change their terms. Force them to repair the damage they've done."

He looked at his desk and rubbed at his lower lip as she said this, and looked up at her again when she had finished. The look in his eyes told her what was about to happen.

"I didn't want it to come to this, Jane, but I don't see a choice. I—"

She interrupted, "I can come up with something. Give me more time."

"I'm going to have to ask you to resign."

Jane stared. *You fool,* she thought in disgust. *You bloody idiot.* "I need to think it over."

"There's nothing to think over," he replied. She only looked at him. He rubbed the bridge of his nose. "We need the ice, Jane. Many lives are at stake. You said yourself that today's the day, if we're going to deal with Ogilvie & Sons. They're the only game in town."

She still did not reply.

"Don't make this more difficult than it has to be. We need to get this settled and move forward."

"'Move forward?'" she repeated. "'Get this settled.' Why not call it what it is? You're sacrificing me, and the whole cluster while you're at it, to stay off Ogilvie & Sons' shit list. Smart move."

Anger rose behind his eyes. "You'd be wise to choose your words more carefully."

"Well, I'm not feeling wise at the moment. The truth is, you've let yourself be outmaneuvered, and you're jettisoning the one person in the best position to keep the bad guys out. If you don't regret it now, you'll regret it before too much longer."

"Be careful who you threaten."

"That wasn't a threat. It was prophecy. Look, I know Nathan Glease has told you that if you want the ice, you need to get rid of me. But they are *playing you.* Woody Ogilvie doesn't share power. He has ships out there, and he's probably made a deal with someone to stage a coup.

Either an opposition leader or someone in your own organization. You open the door to him, and you are signing your own death warrant."

Benavidez rolled his eyes. "Listen to yourself, Jane." He sighed and rubbed at his face. "They're pirates, I grant you. But even they can't go that far over the line. It would be financial suicide. You said it yourself. With Upside-Down watching, they can't afford to indulge their worse excesses."

"What are you going to do when they land with their ships full of soldiers?"

"Val is training squads of his own. If they play that card, we'll be ready with our own troops to meet them. Tit for tat."

"One-week recruits, against professional mercenaries? Look around you!" She waved her hands. "'Stroiders' can't protect you! Even if they *couldn't* just wait for an offline period, you are in the biggest 'Stroiders' broadcast shadow in the city. All they have to do is march a squad in here, subdue your staff, put a bullet in your head, and then tell the world whatever fabrication they want."

She leaned across his desk. "Mr. Prime Minister, I know these people. I was in Resource Allocation on Vesta when they took over. I saw it all. I learned their methods. Why do you think they want me out? *They can't get around me.* I have almost three decades' experience keeping them at bay. You're a fool to let me go."

"Enough!" he bellowed. Benavidez lowered his voice. "Face it, Navio. There is nothing more you can do." He shoved the document toward her. "Sign this, and we'll have the ice in three weeks. Thousands of people's lives saved. The math is simple." He leaned back. "It's for the good of the cluster. You have dedicated your life to helping Phocaea. All I need is this one last act from you, and you are free.

"You've had a good run, Jane," he said. "You still have your whole future ahead of you. You will have your connections. Sign, and I'll see to it you're rewarded with a lucrative consulting contract."

She did not bother to read it.

"If I refuse?"

He shrugged. "You want it hard, we can do it hard. I'll fire your ass. No severance, no pension, and I'll no longer shield you from Parliament. They've been pressuring me to bring you in as a witness. They want to prosecute you for criminal negligence. You may well end up in prison."

"I haven't broken any laws."

"They'll manufacture something. They need a bad guy."

"I'll fight them."

But Benavidez was already shaking his head. "Jane, you don't have a handhold. Yesterday you stood in front of the press and said there was nothing wrong with our life support, and now everybody knows that the disaster was caused by a feral in life support. They think you lied to them. Your sammy quotient is tanking. Haven't you seen this morning's numbers?" She wondered how much of that was him, working behind the scenes to make it easier to fire her. "You know how it works," he said.

"Yeah," she said bitterly. "I know how it works."

He gestured at the document. "Take a look. A million troy in your bank account. Full health benefits. A six-month-long expenses-paid vacation for you and your husband. And you keep your pension fund, fully vested." He sat back. "It's up to you."

She read through the document. It *was* a generous offer. Incredibly generous. They could bring the rest of Xuan's family Up in no time. "A vacation on the moon?"

"Till things calm down." He paused. "*Sisyphus* leaves on Wednesday. I've arranged for you to have a two-bunk berth on it."

Jane gaped. "You're turning the ships loose *before the ice gets here*?"

"We have no need to hold them, once the Ogilvie ice is on its way. The sooner we get the regular shipping lines moving again, the better."

"Sir . . . frankly, that is sheer idiocy. You're throwing away any chance of getting even a portion of your people off Phocaea, without those ships."

Benavidez sighed. "Don't you ever *give up*? Ogilvie has won this round. We can't play chicken with two hundred thousand lives. Freeing up the ships proves to the populace that we are confident that things are back on track. It lets us put the resources where they are needed now."

"I'll need to have my lawyer look this over."

He templed his fingers. "I'm afraid this is a take-it-or-leave-it offer. The cluster can't spare the time and resources for a protracted set of negotiations. I've been exceedingly generous, but if you leave without signing, you won't see an offer like this again."

She sighed. "How am I supposed to wrap things up so quickly?"

"We don't have the luxury of a transition period. You'll have to leave the responsibility with your staff. Once Parliament's Resource Committee hits you with a summons, you're on the hook. I can stave them off till Wednesday, but no longer. It's then or never." Jane sank into a chair and looked over the document. It was very straightforward and to the point, and it contained everything he had said.

Benavidez said, "This isn't about you, you know. I don't believe you're truly at fault for the warehouse incident. But I can't protect you any longer. This is our only way out. I can't let the cluster come to harm."

A chilly echo of her own earlier words to Sean returned to her. By his own lights, he was sacrificing her for the good of the cluster, just as she had done to her eight dead.

"What guarantee do I have that you will honor this contract?" she asked. "The same people who pressured you to fire me will want to prosecute me—they will try to create a big media event with me at the center, to distract people from the ugly stuff that they have done."

"You know me, Jane," the prime minister replied. "I may be playing hardball, here, but I'm not out to screw you. You have served me well for a long time, and I haven't forgotten that. I am confident I can fend off the wolves through Wednesday. And the minute you set foot on *Sisyphus*, the money goes into your account."

Another long silence, as she looked through the document.

"What are you going to do about the sabotage?" she asked. "What are you going to do about the fleet of ships out there?"

"We'll uncover the truth. If they're responsible we'll be able to use 'Stroiders' against them. And meanwhile we'll have the ice."

Jane released a long, slow breath. Things would not unfold the way Benavidez was fantasizing they would. But one thing was abundantly clear: it was over. No point in drawing it out. She let the machine read her retina, and input her personal code. Benavidez did likewise, and then transmitted the document to the administration's personnel office.

"Whom are you replacing me with?" she asked.

"Aaron Nabors has agreed to step in temporarily."

"Aaron?" The revelation fell so hard on her that Jane's vision blurred. *Pull it together. Pull it together.*

"He'll do well by you," she managed to say. "You could do much worse than him as resource commissioner."

Benavidez eyed her. "I'll consider it." He rubbed at his lower lip. "I'm assigning two agents to guard you. Public sentiment against you is growing. We don't want any incidents. I advise you to keep a low profile."

They stared at each other over another long silence.

"Will that be all?" she asked.

"That will be all."

As she opened the door, he said, "You've done the right thing."

Jane made a derisive noise. "Read *Blood on the Bulkheads.* It'll give you a taste of what you've let Phocaea in for."

Two cluster Enforcement agents came from nowhere and fell in behind her. She doubted the PM was concerned about her well-being. Who knew what paranoid fantasies he had cooked up? She could do plenty of damage if she wanted. Though she was certain her system access codes no longer worked. That was SOP with employees who were let go.

The media were everywhere, in wavespace and in the flesh. Her software agent gave her word that the prime minister was doing a press conference. She gave the reporters who crowded around, flesh- and virtual-wise, a terse *no comment,* shut off her interface, and pushed through the mob. She headed back to her own sector, and fled to her office through the crooked halls and slant stalls with all her people in them. They fell silent and stared. Did everyone know?

Once in her office she called Sean, and told the older man the news. He appeared stunned. Then angry. "It's not right."

"It's a done deal. You report to Aaron now."

He was silent for a long moment. Finally he said, "My people have several efforts going on—any last orders on how we should prioritize?"

"That's Aaron's call." She added, "If it were me, I'd carry on with what I was doing. Let Aaron get his balance. The shit's really hitting the fan for him.

"And I'd say report to him first thing in the morning tomorrow, if he hasn't contacted you by then. Be prepared with a full briefing and recommended priorities."

"All right. And ma'am—" he said, as she started to disconnect. "It's been a pleasure."

Jane frowned over the sudden lump in her throat. "Likewise."

Next she tried Tania, but there was no answer, so she left a message. Then she called Marty. When she told him, he yelled, "What? *Are they insane?*"

She had no answer for that. She spent a second or two searching for words. "I don't know what to tell you. Just . . . do your best for Aaron. He's going to need you. OK?"

"You got it," Marty said. "The bastard." She was unsure whether he meant Benavidez or Aaron.

Jane said, "He's just doing what he thinks is best for the cluster." But Marty's indignation was balm for her spirit. A long, awkward pause. "I'd better let you go," she said. "Good luck."

"I'll miss working with you, Chief. Maybe we could get together before you leave, and you could meet Ceci. She's a big fan of yours."

That brought a smile to Jane's face. "I'd like that."

Then she called Xuan. He was tied up in a meeting at the university. While she was leaving him a message, someone tapped on the door.

"Enter," she said. She finished the message and turned off her communications. Aaron latched the door behind him and bobbed there, twenty degrees askew. To the two agents by the door she said, "Gentlemen, please excuse us."

They glanced at Aaron, who nodded. Once they had gone, he said, "I tried to warn you."

"I know." Jane started emptying the drawers of her desk. The contents tumbled out into the air.

"They didn't want me to say anything ahead of time. But I couldn't—" He broke off with a little jerk of his head. "I had to try."

She was surprised at herself: less than a minute ago, she had been advising Sean and Marty to make things easy on Aaron, and now here she was, wanting to rip his face off. A harsh laugh escaped her. "Maybe next time you could try a little harder."

"I am so sorry—"

"Don't." She said it sharply. Then she shook her head. "I know. You did try. I'm just," she turned to him. "I'm too angry right now to be reasonable. I thought we were friends. You must have known last night. You could have called me."

He said nothing. She turned her back again. "I'm sure you'll do just fine. It shouldn't take me long to get things cleared out for you."

He drifted there silently, watching her for a moment. But she had nothing more to say. Finally he left. She stopped dragging things out of the drawers and just floated, staring blindly at the desk detritus settling slowly, at the hangings she'd pulled off the wall: pictures of family; holograms of No-Moss and their habitat as they had built it; two carvings Hugh had done; an art project Dominica had made as a teen; several education, award, and appreciation certificates.

After a moment she realized that the two agents weren't going to come back in. Aaron must have sent them away. A kind gesture. She should thank him for that. She turned on her interface. It wove itself around, through, and beyond all her meatspace, with its lists, notes, works-in-progress, schedules, resource- and project-tracking ribbons.

They could shut her out of the area-wide systems, but they couldn't shut her out of her own local waveware—not until they had her ear lozenge. And Benavidez had not had the presence of mind to confiscate it during their meeting. Just as well. She wanted to clean up before they got their hands on her personal files.

Good-bye, she thought. Everything she had built. All the sacrifices. She had tried to make a difference. She had spent the last twelve years of her life wrangling, dealing, confronting, managing, worrying—swallowed by the needs of the cluster. She did not even know who she was anymore, outside this job.

Public sentiment against you is growing. She gazed at the bad-sammies that flooded her sammy cache, a bleeding flood relieved only by a meager tinge of green, she felt heartsick. How could they all abandon her like this? Everything she had done, she had done for the citizens of Phocaea.

Screw it, she thought, *screw them all,* and she brought up the trebling software to delete all her files, and Jonesy, too. Trebling was a military-standard file-deletion process that destroyed any trace of the original data. Her fingers hovered over the activation key. Dozens of years of knowledge and experience. Decision-making tools she had built. A Knox of intellectual treasures she had collected and constructed. Not having access to these would make Aaron's work a lot more difficult. And of course, he would also catch hell for sending the agents away and allowing her this opportunity.

Let him create his own schedules and assessments. Let him start from scratch, the way I did, she thought. *Why should he benefit from all my hard work?*

Her enemies had won. She was taking the fall for something the mob and a freak-of-nature sapient had done. She had spent years making sure the people of Phocaea got the resources they needed, and what did she end up with? A cushy bribe and a boot out the door.

In the end she left the files alone. She packed up the hangings and knickknacks, shut down, compressed, and downloaded Jonesy, then backed up and then trebled her personal files. She left instructions for Marty on everything else. *Let them sort out the rest.* She towed her boxes out and gave them a shove toward the main entrance.

Behind her, the door snicked shut: a smirking whisper of a sound. *Good-bye.*

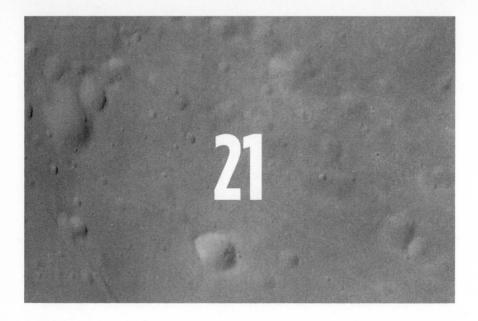

21

That morning the circuit trolleys were still down so Xuan, Charles, and Rowan had to rely on their own hands and feet to propel themselves down the avenue to their offices at the university.

The extent of damage out here on the Rim level was shocking. Debris and rubble were strewn over everything. Teams of surveyors were out with their theodolites, transits, and compasses. Bug veins and meshes had already grown up out of grates in the flooring and begun their work of mending cracks in the bulkheads and breaking down the old and broken infrastructure. The air that morning smelled of solvent, copper, and new plastic. Xuan also saw the odd miniature glass-bead skeleton running around here and there. Not many people were on campus.

He parted ways with Charles and Rowan at the geology center and lofted himself down the tunnel to his office. After assigning his grad students—the two who had shown up—to Kukuyoshi repairs, he headed to an emergency meeting with the deans, department heads, and key administrators to finish fleshing out their plan for rescuing as much as they could from Kukuyoshi. Charles ran the meeting. In moments, though, someone broke in to tell them about the prime minister's press conference. They broke off their discussion and displayed the press conference in the wavespace they shared. Benavidez came on and announced that

Phocaea had reached agreement with Ogilvie & Sons, Inc. on a new ice delivery.

"The ice shipment will arrive two weeks from this coming Wednesday," the PM said. Cheers broke out around Xuan. "In an abundance of caution, rationing will remain in place until then. But I rejoice with my fellow Phocaeans that help is on the way. In the meantime, I ask everyone to remain calm and go about their daily business."

"On a separate note, Commissioner Navio has tendered her resignation. I have accepted it. I want to thank her for her efforts on behalf of the citizens of Phocaea, and to wish her well. Aaron Nabors, deputy commissioner in charge of power and assemblyworks, will be stepping in as acting commissioner until a permanent replacement is found."

Leaden dismay settled in Xuan's chest. Charles and Rowan shot him sympathetic glances, but the general mood in the meeting was cheerful. Someone broke out a bottle of Downsider whiskey, and they passed around disposable drink bulbs with a splash of the pungent, expensive liquor. Someone proposed a toast to the PM.

He forwent the toast, but swirled the liquid in the cup, and tossed the amber drink down. It stung his nostrils and warmed his throat and stomach.

"I suppose we can junk these," Charles said, gesturing at the set of plans floating before them in wavespace. It described how they would rescue and store Kukuyoshi's denizens until the arboretum could be brought back.

"I'm afraid not." Xuan hunched his shoulders. His colleagues turned to look at him. "Benavidez puts a happy face on our situation, but air and fuel supplies are still very low. We have barely enough to last until the new ice comes. This doesn't mean a reprieve for Kukuyoshi."

Rowan squeezed his arm. He gave her a smile he didn't feel.

"I'll be fine." He released his grip on the table and rose, sick at heart— for Jane, because she had had no choice but to do what she had done; and for his colleagues, most of whom stood to lose their lives' work over all this—and in regret over the discomfort his very presence must cause them. "Excuse me."

He should head over to the arboretum and help with species rescue, but Xuan did not have the stomach to face his colleagues and students just now, when so many would be rejoicing at the very event that had led to his wife's misfortune. Instead he returned to his office.

Jane had left him a message. He returned the call. She appeared before him. He'd never seen her look so lost.

"I heard the news," he told her. She said nothing, only looked at him without expression. He sensed how thin the skin of her armor was. He wanted desperately to take her into his arms, to hold her, let her scream her way free of her outrage and sense of loss.

"They've offered me two berths on the *Sisyphus,*" she said. "It departs Wednesday. I have to leave then or testify before Parliament and face prosecution for gross negligence." He opened his mouth, but she said, "I know you have deep ties with the university. I'm not telling you this right now to get a commitment from you. I just wanted you to know." She paused. Her stiff composure was painful to watch. "They've offered us a lot of money, too," she went on. "It should show up in the account on Wednesday, once I'm safely off 25 Phocaea. We can use it to help Dominica locate Huu-Thanh and her kids."

"Let's not worry about all that right now," Xuan said. "There's time to discuss that sort of thing later. Are you free for lunch?"

She shook her head: a tiny, terse movement. "I need time alone. I'll see you tonight. All right?"

Her gaze met his, and there was an unspoken plea in it. *Please understand,* it said. *Please give me time alone.* He found it difficult not to come to her when he knew she was in pain. But it was what she needed; so be it. He nodded. "All right. I love you."

She swallowed, mouthed, *I love you, too,* and cut the connection.

He busied himself with organizing his research notes, and working on his latest publication, but could not concentrate, and made little progress. There was a brief disruption while the spin generators were geared back up and gravity was restored. Once acceleration was back to its steady three-quarters gee, Xuan picked up the items that had fallen to the floor, and then sank heavily into his desk chair.

At least we will have the ice, he thought. *Perhaps the damage to Kukuyoshi won't be irreparable.* Cold comfort.

Okuyama contacted him. "We have been asked to provide assistance in helping substantiate some sugar-rock claims, again. Do you have any more graduate students we can loan out?"

"I'm afraid not. Everyone we could spare is currently assigned to the Kukuyoshi recovery efforts . . ." In mid-sentence, it occurred to Xuan that he could use a rock-hopping break. Jane didn't want him around right now. And it would do him good to get out into the Big Empty and kick around in the dust with his rock-testing tools again, away from his colleagues' stares and the miasma of motes that had been following him around the past day or two. "But I'd be glad to volunteer," he finished.

"Excellent! Here is the contact info." His address cache registered receipt. "They want to head out right away. I understand they are outfitting a yacht out at the Klosti Omega dock. It's a decent-sized rock they're interested in, so it's definitely worth the trouble. Your contact is a Mr. Andrew Mills."

Xuan recorded the name and contact info. "I'll call him right away."

Sean paid visits to the kids' families. Ian's parents' reaction seemed to be mostly peevish annoyance. Mrs. Carmichael sighed. "I suppose we had better head up to Yamashiro Memorial and deal with this. I'm going to have to cancel my appointments for the afternoon. This is a serious inconvenience, Mr. Moriarty."

"The cluster had better be prepared to cover the costs," Mr. Carmichael added, "or you will have a lawsuit on your hands."

Sean replied, stiffly, "Your son is a hero, and the cluster owes him a great debt. I have no doubt that his medical costs will be covered. If there is any question or doubt, you have the hospital people call me."

The man was mollified; the woman bemused. Sean left quickly, before his temper snapped. He and his wife had decided not to have children—his patience was not up to the task—but by God, he could not understand why people who *did* want children thereafter behaved so badly toward them. *Self-absorbed fuckwads.*

Kamal's parents were much more concerned. They sat together on their couch, Mr. Kurupath with his arm around his wife. Mrs. Kurupath spoke calmly, but her hands belied her by endlessly wringing a small green silk scarf. "We understand that he, and you, must have been swept up in events last night, and we appreciate your coming by. But we must insist that this sort of thing not happen again. We don't want him participating in any further such activities."

"He is our only child, Mr. Moriarty," Mr. Kurupath said. He clasped his hands together tightly. "Surely you can understand. He is very dear to us. He has explained his part, and it is clear that he acted of his own free will, out of loyalty to his friends. But he is no soldier, and we are not at war. Please do not press him to do any dangerous stunts again."

"I fully understand," Sean replied. "I promise you, I have no intention of asking him to undertake any further actions on behalf of Phocaea."

Amaya's mother, Mariko Toguri, was much calmer. She fixed him a cup of tea and asked questions about what had happened. Amaya was still in bed, but apparently she had given her mother a full account the night before, as the older woman did not seem surprised.

When Sean finished recounting the prior evening's events, she rested her hands on the low table and said in a soft voice, "My daughter is an adult now, and makes her own choices. I am glad to hear that she acquitted herself well, and thankful that you have come here to tell me all this. I admit that sometimes her actions scare me. But my own parents thought I was out of my mind to emigrate Up here. How can I blame her for following her own heart?"

At Geoff's home, Sean could tell as the door opened that he had interrupted an argument. Geoff stood in the center of the room, face to face with his father. The nano-meds had done him a world of good: his wrists were not nearly so raw, he seemed to be standing straighter, and his nose had assumed normal proportions and a mostly normal color.

The mother slumped on a chair in the corner of the room, with a tissue at her mouth. Her face was tear-swollen and blotched. Mr. Agre turned on Sean.

"How *dare* you?" he demanded. "How dare you endanger Geoff? He came home last night looking as if he had been beaten to a pulp."

"I was given responsibility to stop the feral sapient from escaping our computer systems, Mr. Agre. Without the help of Geoff and his friends, I would not have been able to do so. The feral sapient would be loose in the solar system right now."

Mr. Agre stabbed a finger at Geoff. "His brother just *died*! Last night his friend suffered a traumatic amputation—doing your bidding! Don't give me high-minded speeches. Let someone else risk their life next time."

Sean hesitated. His first instinct was to tell the man to let his son grow up. He had had men and women Geoff's age under his command who fought, killed, and died for their country. Still, the contrast with the Carmichaels was stark. At least he cared enough to get angry. From the expression on Geoff's face, though, he didn't see it that way.

"What the hell do you care?" Geoff asked.

His father turned on him. *"What did you just say?"*

Geoff paled, but his back stiffened and his fists balled. He repeated, "What do you care? You never gave a damn about me. It was Carl you cared about." His mother's hands went to her mouth, and her eyes went wide; his father's eyes narrowed. Geoff went on, "All you've ever done is ignore me, and when you weren't doing that all you did was criticize.

"And now Carl's dead," he said, "and I'm all you have left, and you think that gives you the right to start telling me how to live my life? Well, you *don't*. I'm an adult now. I make my own choices."

Mrs. Agre reached toward him, but he pulled away from her.

"That's the problem with you, Geoff!" his father said. "You *don't* make choices. You're completely random. The way you chase all your damn stupid ice rocks, you fool yourself into thinking what you're doing means something, when the truth is, you're just running away. You dodge the sweat and tedium it takes to do well in school. You dodge your responsibilities at home. You dodge the people who want to get to know you. I don't know how many girls have come by here while you were out somewhere, and you never follow up. You are afraid of failure!"

"Don't put that on me, Dad. You don't have a clue who or what I like. *You're* the one who ran away all your life. You ran away from Earth. You ran away from your first family and all your screw-ups back on the moon. *So get off my back.*"

His father was so angry he shook. "I'm still your father and while you live under my roof, you'll do what I say."

"Then I'm moving out."

"The hell you are!"

Geoff moved toward the door. Mr. Agre blocked him, and, when Geoff tried to shove past, struck him in the face. Mrs. Agre screamed. "Sal! Stop!"

Geoff's hand went to his face, where the imprint of his father's knuckles stood out—first marble white, then an angry red. They stood there, looking at each other: Geoff still as stone, his father panting and flushed. Then Geoff grabbed his helmet off a hook by the door and left.

Mrs. Agre looked aghast at her husband. *"How could you?"*

"He deliberately defies me, Dee. You've seen how he acts."

"I've had enough," she whispered. When he tried to reply, she screamed, "Enough!" She fled into the other room and closed the door. Sean heard a soft snick as it locked. Agre collapsed into a chair.

Sean had already stayed too long. He stepped toward the door. It whispered open behind him, and more motes swirled in on the cold breeze. But he had to say one thing. "Mr. Agre, your son's courage and quick thinking have been all that have stood between us and many people dying. Not once, but twice. If he were my son, I would be proud." He paused. "And I would tell him so."

Agre gave him a tormented look as the door closed between them. Sean looked up and down the corridor, but Geoff was nowhere to be seen.

22

Geoff met Kam and Amaya in New Little Austin for breakfast. He could tell by their glances that they both noticed the fist-shaped bruise blossoming on his left cheek. He hoped they would assume it happened yesterday, during his fight with Ian or the run-in with the feral sapient.

They decided to get take-out and visit Ian.

While they were waiting in line at the café, Amaya grew tense. She tugged at his sleeve and jerked her head toward the plaza. Not two meters from where they stood, a skeletal hand reached up through a sewer grating. He gasped and surged half to his feet. Shit—the bone dancers! Somebody's foot came down on the skeleton's wrist, and the silicate bones shattered and dissolved back into the sewer.

Geoff sat back down and tried not to hyperventilate. He recalled the Viridian woman, Vivian's, warning. *It's harder to control than you think.* Their stunt wasn't over and forgotten. Which meant the authorities would be more motivated to find the culprit. He could still end up in prison. And so might his friends.

He asked Amaya and Kam to order for him, found a seat at a table, and did a search. Sure enough, people were reporting skeleton parts showing up here and there in the lower levels. Only a few reported sightings so far, but it was bound to get worse.

Amaya and Kam brought the breakfast burritos and coffee over. He pinged their wavefaces—they saw what he saw. "Holy shit," Kam whispered.

"I know what to do." Geoff stood.

Amaya asked, "Where are you going?"

And Kam said, "I thought we were going to see Ian."

"I have something to do first. Go to the hospital. Wait for me there."

Little Austin was about a third of the way up the See Spoke from the bottom level that housed the entrance to the Badlands: the Viridians' territory. Geoff headed down the nearest spokeway to Heavitown and asked a nearby vendor for directions to Portia's Mess. The woman gave him a strange look, but directed him down the Promenade toward a pastry shop called Tarts.

"Just take a right between Tarts and Tarts, Too," she said. "But be careful. Some people don't come back from the Badlands."

Tarts, Too was a sapient sex shop with a crowd outside even bigger than the crowd outside its sister restaurant and pastry shop across the way, Tarts. Geoff pushed his way through the crowds into a tangle of handwebs and catwalks that wound up through a series of cubbies that served as living quarters for transient miners and unskilled workers.

Geoff tried not to stare but the temptation was strong. He had had no idea that anything like this existed in Zekeston. He had thought his own family's meager dwelling was pathetic; the four of them had barely enough room to step around one another when they were all in one room. Sitting down to family meals was a careful dance of trading places, avoiding elbows and knees, balancing plates and utensils. But people here did not even have rooms. He saw large clusters of immigrants, drifters, and the working poor all crowded together in a series of open bunks set into the walls—row upon row of them. Drying laundry dangled from rails and webs; children in oversized, tattered hand-me-downs hung from the railings and watched him pass.

Despite the obvious poverty of the inhabitants, the catwalks and webworks were fairly clean and free from trash. Someone sure made an effort to keep things clean and organized around here.

The Badlands had a faint smell of soured nanocrude. The damage from the sapient's attack had not yet been repaired—or perhaps it was left from before.

Geoff's knowledge of the Badlands was limited, but he did know that they housed a mishmash of fringe groups most Phocaeans did not want around—mostly squatters and ex-convicts with no usable skills. In the upper levels, you entered true Badlander territory: the realm of the Tonal_Z poets, bioartists, and hackers. Over this, the Viridians reigned.

Geoff sensed that he was being tracked. No one approached him, but several times as he crossed the catwalks and climbed the ramps he caught glimpses of monstrous, multihanded Viridian angels and remotely pi-loted scrap heaps bristling with makeshift weaponry that watched as he passed. Mists of protective glamour—mote killers and disablers of dif-ferent sorts—sprayed him from vents placed along corridors and from overhead. He repeatedly found himself awash in faintly odorous sprays. With every wave, more "Stroiders" motes fizzled into ash around him, and the clattering mites tailing him, which he had not really even noticed before, were gradually disassembled into pyramidal and cubic piles. His skin prickled, and he wondered whether his waveware implants were being damaged. But when he tested it, it seemed to work just fine. *Pretty fancy juice-jockeying,* he thought, and wondered how they managed to do it.

Soon his waveware gave him an alert. He spotted the restaurant Vivian had told him about, Portia's Mess. It looked rather nondescript, other than the big lighted sign, as if someone's house had been con-verted. He stepped inside. Six small tables crowded the room, all empty. Through the open door into the kitchen, he saw two women leaning on a counter, talking. They gave him uninterested looks and went back to their conversation. On a small raised stage sat a man whose facial features and complexion were of African ancestry, but who looked so much like Vivian that Geoff knew he had to be related to her.

The man had a harp between his knees and was running through some scales.

Geoff cleared his throat. The man looked up, and seemed surprised and pleased. "Ah, the bug artist!" His accent was similar to Vivian's, a blend of Lunarian and, Geoff realized now, East African. Though he strongly resembled Vivian, he seemed taller and leaner. Geoff recalled her mentioning she had a brother.

"My twin told me about you," he said. "She said you might come here looking for her. Geoff, is it?"

"That's right."

"Gabriel Thondu wa Macharia na Briggs. Waĩthĩra's brother. Call me Thondu." He stuck out his hand, and Geoff brushed palms with him. Though quite lean and muscular otherwise, he had a bit of a belly, which Geoff caught a glimpse of when he sat back. Like his sister, he had prominent cheekbones; dark, close-cropped auburn hair; and large dark eyes. He was disconcertingly attractive.

"Waĩthĩra?" Geoff repeated.

Thondu's lips quirked at him, and his eyebrows went up. He was irritated; Geoff knew the look well. "Vivian, her given name. Waĩthĩra, after her grandmother. Briggs after her mother, Macharia after her father. If you must know."

"Oh, sorry." Geoff felt his face warm. He said, "She told me I could come here for help."

"Ah yes! I have been seeing the reports. Bone dancers, is it? Nice trick, that. But it appears they have gotten somehow . . . out of hand." It was not a question. Geoff felt his face warm.

"Something like that. Where is she? I need to talk to her."

"She is unavailable. But we have been expecting you. Follow me." Thondu took him out of the restaurant, through an alley, and into a back hallway. At the end of it, a large woman whose body was covered in gleaming scales searched Geoff, and then allowed him to enter the place she guarded. Geoff could not tell whether the scales were clothing or her skin. They seemed to be skin. Which meant other than jeweled coverings for her nipples, and a jeweled patch covering her pubic area—if they were coverings, and not more scales—she was completely naked. He tried not to stare, and failed. An urgent erection pressed against his jeans. He hoped no one would notice.

Geoff had been expecting another tiny room—Zekeston was a warren of cramped passages and small crannies—but the door Jeweled Scale Woman was guarding slid open into a section of Kukuyoshi he had never seen before. Geoff looked around and whistled sharply, impressed. The noise startled a flock of song birds, which scattered into the air nearby.

He had read about temperate rain forests, and this appeared to be one. This park's footprint was a relatively narrow slice of space—only room for a dozen or so big trees, and maybe a handful of smaller ones—but it was very tall. Its bottom level, where he stood, near the roots of a massive cedar, was only a few levels up from Zekeston's lowest story. Its upper reaches—it was hard to see through the mists—but clearly they rose many levels. A third of the way to the Hub, even, though this wasn't a spokeway. At least not an official one. Vines draped from the trees' branches; mists scudded past, obscuring boulders, birds, and ground squirrels. Wildflowers and grasses dipped under the gentle breezes. He and Thondu stepped in, and the door rematerialized behind them.

Last night's attack had left its mark here. Dirt coated tree bark, leaves, and stones. One upended tree had smashed into another, which leaned against a wall. Conifer needles and giant cones lay about. The cold, damp breeze smelled of cedar bark and upturned earth. Icy dew dripped onto his head. He heard low voices but could see no one.

"This way," Thondu said, and led the way. The mist cleared. Geoff spotted people sitting on boulders at the base of a giant, gnarled and knotted tree. He scrambled across the rough terrain to them, scraping hands and knees on logs and exposed roots. There, he froze.

He was startled at the violence of his aversion. And the depth of his attraction.

They were monsters, every one. The multiple limbs were just the start. He looked around, trying to make sense of all he saw, heard, smelled. He could only take it in in fragments. Over here were eyestalks with crystalline compound eyes; over there, multiple limbs; dragonfly wings here, bird wings there; giantism . . . dwarfism . . . shining cara-paces. Over there were diamantine claws, rippling musculature, pelts to put a Kodiak bear to shame. They were not just bizarre; they were all weirdly beautiful. Like something out of a dream. One that might turn any minute into a nightmare. Geoff had to breathe deeply, to keep from screaming and running away.

He had seen such people in wavespace, but it was a different matter to be standing right next to them, breathing their air; feeling their meat-ness pressing on him. They were too real, and not quite real enough. It was too much to take in. He began to tremble.

"I'm Geoff Agre," he said, and dashed sweat from his face. To his relief, his voice came out steady. "Vivian said you could help me."

One of them nodded. "Yes. Welcome." This one spoke softly to the others, who departed—flying, walking, lumbering—talking casually. A couple of them gave Geoff curious glances.

The one who remained stood and motioned Geoff over. Geoff glanced back at Thondu, who merely shrugged, with an amused look on his face. Geoff stepped forward.

This other one, this person, had very pale skin—surprisingly pale, for an Upsider—and gleaming chesnut brown hair that fell in long thick twines, which moved about the head, graceful and sinuous in this light gravity. The face was inhumanly beautiful: skin like the polished inte-rior of a seashell; full, dusted-rose lips. The eyes were catlike slits an unlikely shade of green. In place of two arms and two legs were three pairs of arms. The top set was where you would expect; the second pair emerged from the spine's sides at the bottom of the rib cage; the third two extended from the hip joints, where the legs should be. All six hands were twice as large as human hands, and each had ten strikingly long fingers, with at least five joints, maybe six. The overall effect was a blend of insectoid and mammalian.

Most troubling of all, Geoff could not tell whether the person was male or female. It made it hard for Geoff to even know how to think about this person. He could not create a mental picture—his mind kept sliding off the person's gender. Geoff had to keep correcting himself. He? No. She? No, neither was correct. It? Definitely not. It would mean the person was sexless, and there was something intensely sexed about this person, even if Geoff did not understand exactly how that could be so.

The person's otherness was so blatant, yet so slippery, a thing, Geoff could not grasp hold. He floundered.

Most Viridians prefer nongendered pronouns, he remembered dimly, from some public service bulletin of years before, when a recent wave of Viridian immigrants arrived Upside. He tried the odd pronouns on for size.

Sie, was it? Or ze? Right. Ze. And hir. These pronouns did not feel right on his tongue. But they were better than any alternative.

The other—*ze*; Geoff forced himself to say the word in his head: *ze, ze, ze*—smiled at Geoff. "I am Obyx. Pleased to meet you." Geoff's skin prickled. He had heard of Obyx. Ze was the leader of the Viridians, if they could be said to have one.

Obyx cocked hir head at Geoff, and then offered hir hand. Geoff brushed palms. To his chagrin, his hand trembled, and afterward he had a powerful urge to rub his palm on his pant leg.

"How can I help you?" Obyx asked.

"I think I'm in trouble. I guess I didn't program the stoprun sequence properly, and bone dancers are starting to show up all over in the sewers."

Obyx tapped hir fingers together. "I guess you didn't."

Ze pinged Geoff's waveface, and brought up a shared display, expanding it between four hands into a large cube. It was a translucent schematic of Zekeston with little flares of color scattered here and there, ranging from crimson, through various shades of red, to a dark brown. Occasionally a bright new red point flashed into existence.

"The spots of color are sightings of your bone dancers," Obyx explained. "The brighter the color, the more recent the occurrence. The size of the flash indicates how many skeletons appeared for how long and how big they are.

"We've counted twenty-eight incidents so far, and they are increasing in frequency of occurrence, and in intensity, as they spread inward and upward"—Obyx gestured—"toward the assemblyworks plant in the Hub. If it reaches there, it would destroy entire batches of assembler bugs. Alas, this is all too common for bad stoprun code. Unchecked, it would eventually overwhelm assembler production. The Resource Commission people learned of this last night. You are fortunate that they have their hands full today."

"My God." Geoff paced in a small circle, tugging at his hair, trying not to panic. "So . . . can you help?"

"Of course," Obyx said. "We couldn't afford to wait for you to get around to noticing. We've already dealt with it. Our juicejockeys have injected a retroviral stoprun sequence into the assembler system. It targets your bone dancers. It will infect them and turn them off. The incidents will gradually die out over the next twelve to eighteen hours," ze said.

Relief made Geoff's knees weaken. He found a boulder, and sat down on it. Obyx leaned back. Ze gazed at Geoff, green eyes gleaming, jewel-like. "A trivial fix, for an experienced juicejock. Which, as you are perhaps now aware, you are not."

"Yeah. I screwed up. I get it." Geoff slumped, embarrassed, and angry at the criticism. But the Viridian had a point.

"What do you want in return?" he asked.

Obyx nodded: an acknowledgment of the debt. "Nothing, for now. I understand you have been involved in two different attempts—successful ones—to save Zekeston. Those acts have benefited us also. Though our offer of training remains open, if you decide to continue with your dabblings in juice-hacking. And I am obliged to warn you that if you choose not to take us up on our offer, and if by some chance you are idiotic enough to cause something like this again, we will out you as the culprit without hesitation."

Geoff shrugged. "Vivian made that clear."

"But," said Obyx, "given that we have just saved you from a prison sentence, you still owe us."

Geoff looked suspiciously at hir. "Like what?"

"Hmmm. I'm not sure yet. Something. Not too big, not too small. A goldilocks favor, shall we say? In exchange for our actions today, let us stipulate that Viridians may need a mediumish favor from you sometime. When the time comes, you will provide it without hesitation. Agreed?"

Geoff looked at Obyx a long time without speaking. He could still end up in jail if they chose to out him. But he was not willing to sign a blank check. Better to take the hit now than ransom his future to an uncertain fate. "I guess that depends on what the favor is."

Thondu threw his head back and laughed. Obyx glanced at Thondu, and finally broke into a real smile. "Your momma gave you three stones, I give you that. Very well, we'll agree that some sort of favor is owed, but we'll negotiate further when the time comes." Obyx languidly waved an oversized hand or two. "Now, if you don't mind. Thondu?"

"Of course, Learned."

Thondu escorted Geoff in silence back down across the catwalks and bridgeways, to the edge of the Badlands.

"Thanks," Geoff said.

"Think nothing of it," Thondu said, with a smile that reminded Geoff of Vivian's.

Geoff said, on impulse, heart suddenly pounding against his ribs, "And tell your sister—" Thondu raised eyebrows. "Tell her I said hi," Geoff finished lamely. "Tell her to call me. If she wants. I mean, I wouldn't mind." Thondu gave him an arch little smile. Geoff felt his face grow hot. "She helped me out. I want to thank her. That's all."

Thondu eyed him speculatively. "Well, well. You are a complicated young man, Mr. Agre. I will relay the message." He flicked a hand.

Something about his grin lingered in Geoff's mind. He thought about Thondu and Vivian. He sensed that Thondu and Vivian shared some connection he didn't understand, some bone-deep secret tie. That bothered him a lot. He had to admit, he had already fallen, hard, for Vivian. But Thondu unnerved him, and something about him drew Geoff, too. He'd never thought of himself as attracted to men. What was he getting himself into?

Still, he had gotten out of the Badlands with body and soul intact. That was something.

.   .   .

At the hospital he found his friends having a picnic on Ian's bed in a private room. Amaya and Kam had smuggled breakfast past the orderlies. Ian held up a pastry. Geoff's mouth filled with saliva. The room's antiseptic smell did not put a dent in his appetite. "We saved one for you, doof. But you'd better hurry or I'm going to eat your roll."

"Not on your life, *chinpo*." Geoff took the last sticky bun. It was dripping in brown sugar and butter. He bit into it, and felt as if his face would explode from sheer caloric overload.

Amaya leaned across the bed to hand him a coffee. "Well?" She was referring to the bone dancers.

The room was thick with motes and mites, so Geoff merely said, "We're good." He would fill them in on his visit to the Viridians later— back on Ouroboros, perhaps.

Over sweet rolls and hot, bitter coffee they went over the prior night's events. Ian was pallid, and not as loud as usual, but still in good humor. Geoff wondered what painkillers they had him on.

"Hard-Rock News 42 came by earlier. And Upstreamers 180! I'm going to be all over the nine o'clock news. Have you seen my sammy cache? Take a look!"

Geoff exchanged an amused look with Kam and Amaya. They all agreed the contents of Ian's cache were impressive. "You're famous," Geoff said. "No doubt about it."

"The prime minister is coming by! Can you believe it? Get my arm ripped off and everybody thinks I'm hot shit. Maybe I can write my memoir and make a million." Kam and Geoff both laughed; Amaya looked mildly disgusted.

Kam replied, "Now if only you could write three sentences in a row, you'd be all set."

"You're just jealous."

"Oh, yeah. I can hardly wait to get my arm ripped off."

"Great! The gimp twins. We'll get adjoining hospital beds," Ian said. But the idea made everyone queasy. To change the subject, Geoff asked, "You said they're going to start growing you, you know, a new arm today?"

"Yeah." Ian looked at his covers, at the place where his arm should be, as if still surprised it was not there. "They said there was so much damage to the old one that it's easier to just start from scratch. In a couple of months, nobody will be able to tell the difference. Look." He pulled up his sleeve. The others recoiled—but the wound had already closed up. Pink, baby-smooth skin stretched over the shoulder joint, and just below that was a bump with five little nubs. Ian wiggled them, and Geoff thought again of the Viridians. Was what they did so different than this?

Amaya's anger at Ian seemed to have cooled; she touched the tiny new fingers growing there, and then they kissed. Ian gave her this wondering look. Geoff knew, even if he didn't; even if Amaya didn't. Ian had just figured out he loved her. Geoff wondered if that meant he'd stop being such a *chinpo*. One could hope.

"What?" she demanded. He only shook his head, and laid his head back on his pillow. "Nothing." He laughed. "It's weird, I keep feeling my arm there. I mean, my whole arm. They tell me that's normal. It hurts like hell, when they aren't doping me."

"Good thing they're doping you," Amaya said.

"Yeah." He grinned. "I thought I'd get me some neon tattoos, once it's all done, all down the new bicep and forearm, you know, to impress the girls. What do you think?"

Amaya rolled her eyes. "Oh, please."

Ian asked, "Did they get the thing? You know, the feral?"

Geoff shrugged. "I guess so. The old man just made sure we got checked out and then sent us home. We didn't get any more out of him."

Amaya said, "The biker buzz this morning is that they killed it, or whatever they do to stop them, and it's gone now."

Everyone looked at Ian then. His eyes were sunken, shadowed in his pale face. No one said it, but Geoff knew he wasn't the only one thinking it: Ian should be dead. He would have bled out in seconds if the feral sapient hadn't rendered aid—and feral sapients did not render aid. Something strange had happened last night, they were all witness to it, and no one could make sense of it.

After awhile, Ian's parents showed up. Mr. Carmichael had showered and his hair was combed for the first time since Geoff had met him. He wore a nice suit. His pores still smelled, faintly, of stale booze, which he had tried to mask with cologne. Mrs. Carmichael had her hair coiffed and wore a bit too much makeup. They greeted Geoff and the others with a plastic cheeriness. It grossed Geoff out to look at them. They looked like doll versions of themselves.

Geoff, Amaya, and Kam made their good-byes and left. Geoff was glad that he would not be required to participate with his parents in a meeting with the prime minister. Just, yuck. On a whole lot of levels.

On their way out, the doctor gave them each a quick checkup, and gave Geoff another shot of bug juice. Almost immediately he felt better, and saw in a nearby mirror that the swelling in his face had already gone down.

Outside Yamashiro Memorial, they all looked at one another. All were conscious of the soft mote haze around them.

"Spin the rock?" Kam asked.

Amaya hung back. She looked around, and said softly, "What about the ice?"

"Well?" Kam asked. "Didn't you hear the PM's announcement? We're getting a big shipment in a couple of weeks. Everything is going to be fine."

"But the black marketers know about Ouroboros."

"They were all arrested," Kam said. "And we did what we were supposed to. I notified the bank."

"You notified the bank," Geoff pointed out, "but I didn't sign the paperwork yet. They're not going to send anyone out to survey it till I do. And we didn't do *everything* we were supposed to do—they told us they wanted a statement from us at the precinct."

"True, but we also told Moriarty all about what happened last night. If they need more information, they'll know where to reach us."

"He is way up there in the government," Geoff said thoughtfully.

"Exactly. We should just let them deal with it. He'll know who needs to know, and they can tell us if they need anything else from us."

Geoff pondered this. They had notified the authorities. And now that more ice was on its way, he did not want to give up on the Orbital Olympics. Not if he did not have to. "You're right. I think we've done enough."

Amaya sighed. She did not look quite convinced, but Geoff could tell she did not want to give up their ice either.

"Come on," he said. "Let's spin."

Xuan met his contact in the main shuttle hangar out at the docs, at the appointed time, twelve noon. The man in charge of the expedition, Mr. Mills, had his assistants transfer Xuan's survey tools to their shuttle. Mills wore a knit cap on his head, and a long knit scarf, both in striking shades of blue. He held a bag that contained skeins of brightly colored yarn. It was incongruent with his business-like appearance, but by no means surprising; many spacers knitted or crocheted as a hobby. And everyone was bundling up.

"Thanks for coming on such short notice," Mr. Mills said. He seemed bemused at Xuan's appearance. "We were expecting someone else."

"A student? Yes, Dr. Okuyama informed me. I am Professor Xuan, from the university. My specialty is astrogeology." He brushed palms with the other man. "Everyone else was tied up with emergency preparations, and I was ahead of schedule on my own tasks. So I volunteered."

The other man seemed rather dismayed—for what reason, Xuan could not tell; perhaps a concern about wasting Xuan's time? It seemed unlikely. "Of course. Thanks for taking the time."

"Glad to help. Obviously it's to all our benefit to clear as many of these sugar-rock claims as quickly as we can."

"Indeed." Mr. Mills gave him a tight-lipped smile.

"So, you are with Outpost Charter Bank, then?" Xuan asked, as he gathered his field equipment. Though Mr. Mills was impeccably dressed and groomed, he somehow looked as though he might be more comfortable in a Downsider boxing drome than behind a desk. Mr. Mills smiled. "I am in the employ of an attorney, Nathan Glease. He has a private arrangement with the university to assist them in processing sugar-rock claims."

Glease. Xuan had just heard that name recently, but could not pin-point where.

"Ah—" Mr. Mills said. "I'm getting word from my crew that we have the all-clear to blast off. Mr.—that is, Dr. No—"

"That's professor. Professor Xuan."

"Your equipment has been stowed. Come right this way."

While Mr. Mills was speaking, Xuan spotted Sean Moriarty, who waved to him. "One moment. I'll be right back." He blithely ignored Mr. Mills's grumbles that they might lose their place in the queue. *That is one advantage to being a professor,* he thought, *and not a grad student.* Which might explain why Mills preferred the latter.

"Well, I didn't expect to see you out in this neck of the woods," Moriarty remarked. Xuan knew him from a party or two he had attended with Jane. He had always liked the big, foul-mouthed Downsider. "Off on a rock-hunting trip?"

"Sugar-rock claim. Everyone else with the skills is tied up with Kukuyoshi, and I needed a bit of a break." Xuan looked back at Mr. Mills, who was waiting near his shuttle. "I should go. My contact is worried about losing our place in the queue."

"I'll see to it you don't. I just wanted to say . . . I'm sorry about what happened to Jane. She was a damn fine resource chief. She'll be missed."

"Thanks, Sean. Thanks." He brushed Sean's hand. "And you, good luck with all this—" Xuan waved a vague hand at the chaos around them.

"I'll need it," Moriarty said, with a pained grimace.

23

They set Xuan up in the pilot's cabin. "High-class accommodations," Xuan remarked in surprise. "Thank you."

The pilot was no older than Hugh—not yet twenty. *They make adults so young these days!* Xuan thought. A wry smile twisted his lips.

The pilot seemed oddly nervous. "We aren't really set up for passengers. And it's a short trip, so I won't be needing it. We should reach our destination in about three hours. Please strap in. Use the workstation, if you like. There's plenty of entertainment options loaded in our system. Just follow the links. Snacks and drinks are in the cooler here." He showed Xuan where it was and how to unlock it. "The head is here." He pushed the button, and the null-gee toilet manifold and hoses folded out of the wall. He pushed the button again, and the head folded back in.

"Very good," Xuan said. "Thanks."

Generous of him, to allow Xuan the use of his cabin. Xuan buckled into the passenger couch and linked his waveface to the ship's systems. The shuttle trembled and he was pressed into his couch. Liftoff. Then acceleration eased, and weightlessness came.

Xuan called Jane and left her a message, then tried to work for a while, but could not concentrate, and decided to check his equipment. He unstrapped himself, lofted over to the door, and tried to open it. The

lever did not move when he cranked it. It took him a full second to realize that the door had been locked.

He clenched his fist to pound on it, to call out for assistance—it must
be an error—but froze in midaction. Glease. Mr. Mills was in the employ of a Mr. Glease. Xuan remembered now where he had heard the
name. Jane had told it to him last night, as they had been looking at the
graffiti drawn on the kids' tent.

Glease and Mills. Mobsters. Hired by Ogilvie & Sons. The people
who had scrawled graffiti on his family's tent in the park last night.

Xuan reeled back from the door—mouth spitless, vision greying,
heart beating hard. *You idiot!* he thought. *Jane warned you, but did you
listen?*

But last night (had it really been only last night?), some hypothetical
thugs leaving amateurish doodles on a tent had not grabbed Xuan's attention with the same intensity that the feral sapient lodged in their
life-support systems had. Nor the imminent destruction of Kukuyoshi.
Nor, for that matter, the impending death by suffocation of two hundred
thousand people, including himself and nearly all those he held dear.

He swam over to the vicinity of the workstation, pulled himself down
into the chair, strapped in, and forced himself to consider the problem
calmly. *Do these people know Jane is my wife? Could they have engineered this to use me against her?*

He doubted it. In the first place, now that she had been fired, she was
no threat to them. Second, his decision to take this sugar-rock call had
been his alone, and spontaneous—a need to escape the furtive stares
of his colleagues and the silent, oppressive presence of the "Stroider"-
cams. All the cluster's surveyors and astrogeologists had gotten sucked
into this rush of sugar-rock claims. No. This was simple happenstance.
Bad luck. Xuan's number had come up.

In which case, how much danger was he in? What did they hope to
accomplish? And how could he thwart them?

He thought back to Jane's words the night before, as well as discussions
they had had in the past about her experiences with the mob on Vesta. If
Ogilvie & Sons were behind the original warehouse disaster—so she had

told him, and he had no reason to doubt it—they must be trying with this trip to forestall discovery of any major sugar-rock claims. Mills's presence on this trip suggested they had serious concerns about this particular claim.

This claim had best turn out to be a bust, he thought, *no matter what.*

As to how much danger he was in, as long as they assumed he was just some researcher from the university, and as long as the sugar-rock claim was a bust, they would have no reason to harm him.

I had better brush up on my acting skills, Xuan thought. And there were some serious technical challenges to overcome. This was almost certainly not the first time they had taken a geologist out to check a claim, so they would know the basic routine. Whatever he did to muck around with the ice content measurements for this rock, it had better be subtle.

He strapped himself back in, and spent the next hour or so visualizing the process, considering how to obscure his intent from any watchers.

The pilot announced over the intercom that deceleration would begin shortly. He thanked him, and then asked to speak to Mr. Mills.

Crackling; a pause. Then: "Mills here."

"Now that we are approaching our target, I'd like to set up and calibrate my equipment. Would it be possible for me to visit the hold?"

Another pause. "You can check your equipment once we touch down. Wait in your cabin. My assistants will escort you."

Xuan scowled. So much for mucking with the equipment in transit. He would have to come up with something that he could rig quickly once at their destination, in full view of Mills & Co. "All right. I can set up once we arrive. But perhaps you could forward me any information you have on this asteroid. Maps or the like. It will help me prepare, and will save you time."

A longish pause. "All right. Here you go."

His inbox filled. The files gave him everything he should need to lay the groundwork. He got started.

. . .

Jane wanted to leave the boot lozenge in her office for Aaron to find. But this was no time for lax security. She knocked on Aaron's office door. He worked inwave, murmuring, moving through arcane pantomimes as he furrowed fields of unseen data; planted commands; weeded out phantom icons and displays. She recognized the stress and fatigue on his face from many years and troubles—troubles faced together, faced and overcome.

She floated in and alighted on the floor of his office. He folded his interface away and turned to face her, clinging to the grips on his desk.

"Here." She took out the lozenge and lofted it across to him. It tumbled, catching the light. "You'll need this to access the systems."

His eyes widened; he realized, she saw, what damage she might have done. He snatched it from the air and tucked it into his pocket. "Thank you." Then he crooked a finger, tripping an invisible command, and his glass wall went blank, shutting out the view of employees returning from lunch.

"Marty should be here soon," she went on. "I've left instructions—"

"Please, Jane—"

Her hands curled into balls. "Don't make this harder for me."

"I couldn't stop them from doing this to you. But I pray to almighty God that I can keep things from falling apart until the ice gets here. Keep people from suffering."

"And you're offering up our friendship as a sacrifice."

He sighed. "Would you have me resign in protest?"

"Why not, goddammit?" He flinched at her profanity. "I'm the reason you're here! I've opened doors for you. I've shielded you from those who didn't trust you because of your religion. I've made things happen for you. Now this. Now I know what my friendship is worth to you."

"I don't deny," he said stiffly, "that I owe you a lot. But you taught me that the needs of the citizens come first."

The muscles had tightened across her chest. She drew a breath; two. "Do what you have to, then. Just don't look to me for absolution."

They stood there. Aaron broke away first. "Go, and be damned."

The laugh that escaped her was not a pleasant one. "Oh, I'm gone."

A group of employees had gathered nearby outside Aaron's office, whispering. *I will* be damned, she thought; *I'll be damned if anyone sees me bleed,* and she floated toward them, smiling. She brushed hands, wishing them well, and confirmed the rumor that she had re-signed and that Aaron was acting resource commission czar. She made her good-byes and then excused herself—all too conscious of the cam-era mites that flocked on the walls and ceiling, the spy dust swirling all around.

They were hauling out all the stops. Her eyes must have skyrocketed once more. She was sure her thumbs had reached subbenthic levels.

Enjoy the show, you creeps.

Once in the hall, she surveyed the corridor tube, while her former em-ployees and rubberneckers from other departments averted their eyes, floating by. The bathroom came to mind as a refuge. But she would have to brave the public eventually, and though "Stroiders" and reporters' cameras weren't allowed in, they would be waiting when she emerged. There was no escape. She headed for a lift.

Her mail cache had filled with calls. Sarah had left her a message.

She called her back. After a moment, Sarah's face appeared before her. "I heard the news. Are you OK?"

For a moment Jane wrestled with how to answer this question. Finally she gave it up. "We need to talk."

"Yes. I have a client with me now, but I'm free in about half an hour."

"I have a doctor's appointment then. How about one-thirty?"

Sarah glanced at her wave display. "All right. I haven't had lunch. Have you?" Jane shook her head. "I'll order food, then. I've also arranged for a publicist to meet us here an hour later."

"Cancel it," Jane said. "There's no longer any need." She cut the call.

"You're as healthy as ever," Dr. Pollack told her. The diagnostic images of her brain structures and neural behavior were projected into wavespace between them. None of it meant anything to Jane, but the doctor had spent several minutes studying assorted things and rerunning tests before making that pronouncement. "No sign of abnormalities. No protein markers that indicate trouble. Everything appears normal."

Jane hesitated. "Is it possible that, well, that something could have been wrong a few days ago but that it's healed since? Perhaps some kind of stress-induced break?"

He sat down and interwove his fingers. "Jane, what's this about?"

A long silence fell. He looked at her expectantly. *No motes in here, no mites. Just say it, Navio.* "I heard a Voice."

His gaze grew more intense. "A voice? As in, a voice in your head?"

She nodded.

"I can see why you'd be concerned." He walked around her diagnostics, frowning. "Well, I suppose there are hints of anomalies in certain neuron firing patterns in the cortex, but honestly, it's all within normal parameters." She continued to look at him. He shrugged. "Yes, it's possible that you had a stress-induced psychotic break. But there's no remaining evidence of it. And everything seems OK now. When was the last time you heard the voice? What was it telling you to do?"

She paused again. "I've heard it twice. Once the evening before last, commuting home. I was looking at the Earth."

"Space sickness."

"That's what I thought, too," she said, "but I heard it a second time yesterday morning, after the memorial service." She paused. "It just said my name. Both times. But there is something . . . something it wants me to do."

"Any idea what?"

She shook her head. "I just, I sense that something very bad is happening, or is about to happen, and it wants me to intervene somehow . . ." She fell silent, feeling the press of his gaze.

"Well, some very bad things *have* been happening, and you *have* been intervening."

She shook her head. "It's something else. I don't know what."

"Hmm. Well." He scribbled inwave. "I'm prescribing an antipsychotic, as a prophylactic." At the dispenser in the wall, tiny tubes came down, and within their mesh a bottle grew. When it had fully formed, he handed it to her. "I'd like you to take two of these a day: one in the morning and one at night. I'm going to recommend you go to the Emerson Clinic on Ceres for further testing. They have better facilities."

She eyed the amber bottle in her hand. The fresh smell of newly assembled cellophane clung to it; spots were still soft. Inside, behind the label, were clear ovoid lozenges in a neat, closest-possible-packing arrangement. "Can you recommend anyplace on the moon?"

He looked surprised. "Of course! They have excellent facilities. One moment." He moved his hands, accessing a file. "There's Anderson Memorial in Robeston. Dr. Fabio Torricelli. You have a trip planned?"

"To Earthspace."

He lifted eyebrows.

"Retirement package," she said.

"I bet there's a story in that."

"A long and boring one."

He did not ask. "Those need to be taken with food," he said. "I'll get you a glass of water and some crackers."

She eyed them. "No need to put yourself out. I'm headed to a lunch meeting. I'll take my first dose then."

He peered at her. "Don't delay getting this checked out, Jane."

She had this maudlin impulse to hug him, to offer to take him out for a beer and reminisce about the days when she and Xuan had emigrated here. Zekeston had still been a double barbell, and Pete had been the only doctor within many million kilometers. Instead she wordlessly brushed his palm.

"Good luck," he said. "Be sure to take your meds."

She eyed the medication dubiously. He knew her too well.

"'Bye, Pete. Thanks."

She wondered if she would ever see him again.

Sarah's office was at the boundary of Heavitown—a quasi-bohemian district that had never been able to make up its mind whether it was seedy or trendy—and the upscale Path of Seven Stones district. Both were located in the northeast sector, near the Promenade: a meandering thread-mesh of shops, parks, homes, and businesses that girded the city's outermost level.

The Promenade was packed. All the treeway refugees seemed to be here. People were straightening and putting things away, now that the spin generators had restored Zekeston's acceleration. She spotted a couple on a bench. One of the men was perhaps eight months pregnant. He pulled his partner's hand onto his belly and said, "Feel that?" The two shared a private smile.

Jane moved on through the crowd. Seeing everyone working so cheerfully on recovery and repairs lifted her spirits an angstrom or two. For all the three-quarters gee, she loved Heavitown. If she were ever to give up No-Moss, she would want to move here.

Among the flow of people emerging from a nearby spokeway lift, Jane moved onto the main thoroughfare and entered Heavitown's noisy maze of shops and kiosks and plaza markets. Like most low-gee-adapted folk, she had a slow, swaying gait in this three-quarters-gee area. She moved to the right with the other adapted pedestrians, and the nonadapted foot traffic streamed past.

Her improved mood didn't last long. People were staring at her, and her bad-sammy cache was filling up. With a spike of irritation, she turned off her waveware—it wouldn't stop the bad-sammies, but at least she wouldn't have to see them—and paid attention to her physical surroundings instead.

Everyone was warmly dressed. Along with the usual parkas and sweaters, Jane spotted plenty of people wearing makeshift cloaks made of blankets, or wearing double or triple layers of clothing. The younger children waddling after their parents or older siblings were bundled so thoroughly they looked like stuffed sausages; people huddled on benches and blew into cupped hands. Jane was once more thankful for the thalite undergarment she wore.

Thinking of the undergarment made her think of Tania. And Funaki. There were others who would be worrying about her, smatterings of concern amid the outrage. She should answer them.

Later, though. Later.

Buildings and stairways bordered the wide avenue, which swarmed with foot traffic, trolleys, robotics, and vendors' stands. Here, looking along the length of the Promenade, you could see the station's curvature: the shops and apartments and the avenue with its embedded rails curved upward out of sight. In the distance, pedestrians and vehicles climbed up gentle slopes to disappear above.

On a typical day she could navigate through Heavitown's markets by smell alone, and today her nose revealed more to her about the city's troubles than her resource reports had. Most of the scents were the usual ones. It wasn't so much that. Multiethnic food aromas emanated from vendors' kiosks and open-front cafés on the cool eddies. Ordinarily they would make Jane's mouth water. Tortoise Palace, the discount housing wares shop; the tobacconist, Pipe Dreams, from which issued the smell of fresh pipe tobacco and cannabis, both still legal out here on the frontier.

She spotted Tarts, the coffee shop, with its irresistible mingling of aromas: fresh bread, cookies and pastries, and coffee. Some of its patrons carried their purchases next door to Tarts, Too, the virtual bordello, which had patio seating in front of its plate-glass windows. In the glass-front walkways there paraded an assortment of escort sapients, of both sexes (and some made-up genders), as well as anthropomorphized beasts, fantasy creatures, and monsters; all naked or semi-naked; provocative, aggressive, or coy. The place was packed. Bizfolk and miners crowded around the entrance. A knot of protestors waved flags and signs around the fringes, mocking the customers; denouncing Tarts, Too's use of sapients as sex toys. Next up was the flea market, with people's life histories up for sale, and then came the fruit stalls, holding rows of crisp, succulent produce straight from the city's Mrs. Veggie tanks. Selection was sparse today. The range of choices was going to get sparser before this crisis ended.

Threading through all the usual market smells was the usual people-smell, only today it was stronger than usual.

Treeway and faraway folk did not bathe nearly as often as city folk did. Water, like everything else but vacuum, was scarce in space. And when you spent a lot of time encased in body armor, wrangling rocks and big machines and jetting around out in the Big Empty, thousands or even millions of kilometers from the nearest shower stall, body odor and oily hair were, well, inescapable. During her rock-hopping days, Jane had been no different. You got used to it, and stopped noticing the stink. In fact, she recalled how Phocaean city-dwellers had stunk, to her nose, back when she had returned from the Circuit, with their natural scents masked by soaps, perfumes, shampoos, and spritzes.

Here, today, the stink of humanity surrounded Jane again. But the store and people smells were underlain with a staleness, a hint of human excrescence, rotting food, machine oils, and mold. The humidity was higher than normal, too. She could tell by the damp feel of the air on her face and in her lungs, by the way the wisps of her hair, which ordinarily hung straight and heavy in this high-gee place, coiled stubbornly across her cheeks and forehead.

The smell was death, hanging patiently around. Waiting for just one more thing to go wrong, that could not be fixed in time.

In truth, she should be grateful to Benavidez. The last twelve years that she had run Phocaea's systems, and in particular the last four days, they had lurched and dodged from one near-catastrophe to another. However gleeful her fellow citizens were, however certain they were that their problem was solved—and they were all around her now, celebrating at the news that the ice would soon be delivered—she knew better. She knew how easily things might have gone horribly wrong many times in the past, if the stars had been aligned and one single thing had changed. And she remembered Vesta. The next crisis might well be the last. She was relieved, when it came down to it, that she would not be the one making the decisions this time.

After a while the stares got to be too much. After a third passerby in a block slammed into her, nearly knocking her over, Jane ducked down a narrow walkway, through a semi-private atrium into a narrow alley. Several bug-sized news-mites flanked her along the carefully flawed brick walls of this less inhabited alleyway. A mote cloud thickened as it drifted toward her. She had almost certainly been breathing some in—swallowed them, even. Maybe Downside viewers would get a good look at her lungs, her bloodstream, her stomach lining.

She knew she was being irrational; they transmitted their signals by settling onto receptors set into the intake ducts. Anything she inhaled would simply be broken down by her normal body defenses just as dust, molds, and pollens were. It was silly to get bent about one product of bug-tech, and not everything. Assembler traces were everywhere: in their food, in their water, on every surface. If she had not experienced an allergic reaction by now, she probably never would. She leaned against the wall, breathing deeply, collecting her calm.

Only two more days of this torment and then she would be free, relatively anonymous—she hoped—aboard the Martian cruiser *Sisyphus*. Nevertheless, she felt a powerful need to fumigate.

She turned the corner, and emerged onto a less populated avenue. By law, the reporters' mites couldn't follow her into the law office, though they clustered in the entryway and would no doubt be there when she emerged. The "Stroider"-motes on the other hand could enter at least the lobby with her, and did.

Sarah was ready to see her as soon as she arrived but Jane deferred, and waited in the lobby until the offline window. At precisely eleven, the motes began to dissipate. She gave it about sixty seconds, and then ran a signal tracer to verify that mote density had dropped to a sufficiently low level to assure privacy. The area was clean.

Sarah stood as Jane entered. She was tall and lanky, nearly four decimeters taller than Jane, also in her middle years. Her hair was auburn streaked with white, and her cheeks were as ruddy with cold as the day they two had first met. Her face creased into a smile, and she came to take Jane's hand. Old, dear friend.

"It's nice to have a little privacy." Jane sank gratefully onto her couch. She felt safe for the first time in days.

Sarah offered her sandwiches. Jane put her hand in her pocket, remembering the pills, but she couldn't bear to put anything in her stomach just now. Later. She pushed the sandwiches aside.

"Those goddamn motes. I thought I was going to choke on them. Can anything be done?"

Sarah settled back in her chair. "Doubtful. You signed the contract just like everybody else, and you've benefited from the stipend. Free-speech protection laws tend to be weaker than contract law here. On Earth or the moon, most places, you'd be in better shape."

"Power makes the rules, in other words, and the weak go wanting."

Sarah chuckled. "You're hardly powerless, my dear."

"I feel powerless enough."

Sarah gazed steadily at her, and she shrugged a grudging acquiescence.

"Anyway," Sarah said, "I don't find your point valid on principle. All societies must find a way to deal with competing interests. There may well be times when you'll be grateful for contract law provisions that—"

"*Goddammit,* this is no time for philosophy. I have no privacy! I can't be myself; I'm always 'on.' I'm an automaton for the cameras! It was bad enough before 'Stroiders,' but now, and with this disaster . . ." She slumped. "I'm so unspeakably sick of it."

Sarah's expression softened. "Of course. I'll put some interns to work and see what we can do."

"Actually, there's not much point. I don't plan to hang around." Jane told her about Benavidez's offer. Sarah's eyes went wide and her lips thinned.

"You accepted it? Without talking to me first?"

Jane nodded. "It was take-it-or-leave-it. And I'm so sick of fighting." She hunched over, pressing the heels of her hands against her eyes. "It's been over forty years of this business. I'm exhausted. So tired of the maneuverings and the spinning. The backstabbing."

"You've always been able to handle the pressure before."

"People haven't died before. Not like this." She paused. "And there are aspects that haven't come out in the news."

Sarah cocked her head. "Ah?"

"The disaster was sabotage. We don't have hard proof yet, but we know who is behind it."

"Ogilvie & Sons."

"Has to be. Benavidez thinks he can handle them. He's in for an ugly shock. And it's the people of Phocaea who will suffer. There was just no way I could have predicted all the variables that led to the sapient's emergence." It sounded like a whine, even to her own ears. But she needed to say it once. "No way anyone could. Not even Tania."

"Of course not. Jane, you mustn't take the bad-sammies personally. This is not about you. Not really."

"I know. People are scared. They need somewhere to put the blame. They need a scapegoat. But it is personal, for me." With a sigh, she straightened. "So, let's talk strategy. What are my options?"

"Since you're leaving shortly, it sounds like our main priority is protecting you from the media and your political enemies while you make preparations to go."

They spent some time devising a legal strategy to give Jane some breathing room, and she had a lot of good ideas for countering the bad press. It was going to cost, though. She thought about their savings. Hugh was out of school and supporting himself, but Dominica still had five semesters to go. As an Upsider Downside, her tuition was breathtakingly expensive.

Yes, Jane had been bought off with a lot of money. But none of that felt real. She half expected them to find a way to screw her out of it. And part of her did not even want it. She wanted to throw it back in Benavidez's face. Much as she needed that money for her kids. And for Xuan's family members still trapped Downside.

Thinking about Xuan's Downsider family reminded her of Dominica, which reminded her of the data lozenge Xuan had given her. Jane touched the pocket in which the lozenge rested. She should view her daughter's bad news. There wasn't much point in putting it off any longer.

Sarah gave Jane a quiet corner of her office and busied herself with some legal research while Jane viewed the lozenge.

Dominica's face appeared. "Ma, Da. Sorry for the long delay." She was looking down at her notes. Her face was stiff. "I've found Phan Huu-Thanh. As we feared, she's been encrypted. She was processed in

Edmonton and staged for a while there, but she's been shipped to the new people heap they're building on the moon. She was interred just two months ago." Dominica knew, as did Jane, that there was no real chance to get at her now. Once people went in, they did not come out.

Now Dominica looked up. She was Upsider to the core: concise, methodical, controlled, and serious. Her careful breathing told Jane what the effort to stay calm was costing her. Jane hurt with the need to tell her daughter that it wasn't her fault Huu-Thanh was lost to them. *Don't lose heart,* she thought. *Don't lose hope.*

"I haven't been able to locate any of the children. I've spent the past month at Edmonton. Before that, Winnipeg." Edmonton and Winnipeg housed two of the biggest refugee camps in southwest Canada. "No sign of them anywhere. I'm thinking Lanh must have been encrypted, too, but I can't find confirmation. But the rest are still too young and have to be somewhere." Prepubescents were too immature to encrypt. They might have been sold to the sex slavers, though. Or abandoned and left to die. Disposable humanity. Of less note than a used tissue. "It's possible they are trying to enter Vietnam illegally, trying to reconnect with other branches of the family. A boat left Vancouver two months ago, heading for Manila. I'm headed there next. I have a few weeks before the semester starts to do more research."

Another hesitation. "I've found someone who knows how to work the system. He has a good rep, but he's pricey. And I'm almost out of money. I'm going to need more soon. Another fifty thousand, if possible."

She finally looked up, with Xuan's dark eyes and Jane's own aquiline nose and wide, full mouth. Her face was shadowed by exhaustion and grief. "I'll send another message next week. Love to you both."

Jane closed the missive and sat, remembering Huu-Thanh's messages from the Canadian refugee camps years ago. There had been a handful, over the ten years they had spent trying to work through the bureaucratic entanglements to get her and her children out. Each had been so calm, so confident that the family would be able to help. Jane and Xuan were unimaginably wealthy, by Huu-Thanh's standards.

But in the background, in that last message inwave—what was it?

two years ago, now? three?—Jane had seen despair in Huu-Thanh's children's faces, and sullen anger in the eyes of her eldest, Lanh. And now they had been scattered: human detritus caught up in the machineries of Earth's socioeconomic engines, to be mulched and processed and molded into tools for the use of others.

Rage filled Jane. She hated Downside. She hated their intolerance, their rigid hatred, their self-deception, their greed. The inhumanity of the crypts, the battling enclaves of power Down there, the religious intolerance that masked the politics and dirty dealings that went on behind the scenes. They had long since abandoned any semblance of democracy in the nations of America. It was all about power: money, control, and social status. Oh, she hated Earth.

Sarah was watching her. "I have some work to wrap up, and then I'm free. If you don't have plans for dinner later, I'll take you out."

"Sure you want to be seen in public with me?"

"'Stroiders' doesn't go everywhere."

"What, we're going to eat in a restroom?"

Sarah merely smiled.

24

By the time Geoff and his companions disengaged from the tree-ways, the shiny blob Ouroboros hung in space, about two hundred kilometers distant. Beyond it, diamond-bright Saturn and two of its moons, as well as aquamarine Neptune, dominated the backdrop of stars. A third bright object elsewhere in the vast starry sky was probably the rocket tugs bringing the big new ice shipment.

Geoff had heard about it in the news. The sight of the ice shipment sent tingles of relief along his back and arms so strong he shuddered, despite the too-warm confines of his suit. You grow up in space; you learn to ignore certain kinds of fear. You ignore the Big Empty surrounding you. Otherwise you'd never do anything but hide in a cubby and wait to die. But now, on the brink of Phocaea's rescue, he realized just how frightened he had been. He drew a slow breath and thought again, sadly, of Carl.

Ouroboros spun around its narrow axis, a barbell shape that slowly brightened and dimmed, like a giant beating heart, as it tumbled. He smiled at the familiar sight—and then frowned. Something was off. He couldn't quite put his finger on it, but something about the pattern of rotation seemed different.

It might have just been hit by another big rock. A big enough stroid would change its contours or rotation, and it had certainly been clobbered many times before. Geoff shut off his rockets, to make it easier to zoom in, and Amaya and Kam passed him. He brought up his optical scope and focused on the big rock.

There! Rising on the horizon, along the narrowest section of the stroid, he saw a shape that had not been there before. A bright shape. A geometric one. A ship had landed on Ouroboros.

"What the hell?" He signaled Amaya and Kam, who were continuing to accelerate. "Shut off your rockets!"

Their flames died instantly. "What is it?" Amaya asked.

"Zoom on the rock. There's a ship."

"Oh, bloody hell," Kam said, after a pause. A brief silence followed as they all studied the shape that had not been there before. "Black marketers?"

Nobody replied.

"What are those numbers there, on the side?" Geoff asked. Kam had the best optics. "Can you read them?"

"Hang on. Yeah. Think I've got it." He fed the numbers to Geoff, who put in a call to Sean Moriarty. The Stores chief took several minutes to answer; meanwhile, they drifted toward Ouroboros on their bikes.

"Moriarty here."

"Sir, it's Geoff. Geoff Agre."

"I'm glad you called. The police are still waiting for you to go down to the precinct. They need you to give a statement about what happened last night with those black-market thugs."

Geoff had forgotten about that. "We will, sir, as soon as we get back into town. But that's not why I called. My friends and I"—he cleared his throat—"we seem to have a problem."

"You seem to collect them."

"That's what people tell me, sir."

Moriarty chuckled. Geoff hesitated. He did not want to remind anyone about his ice claim just now, but not doing so would be incredibly stupid.

"Well, spit it out!" Moriarty said. "If you need my help, I'll do what I can. If not, I have other things that need doing."

"Kam told you about my stroid. The one with the ice."

"I remember. What about it?"

"Well, there are some people out here. A ship. I was afraid maybe it was the black marketers again."

"You're out there right now?"

"That's right."

A brief silence. "OK. What do you see?"

Geoff studied the image again. "A ship. Maybe a twelve-seater yacht. Maybe a shuttle. We're not close enough to tell. It's landed on my rock."

"Have you got the ship registry number?"

"Yes." Geoff fed it over the link.

"OK, got it. Hold on. Where's Mitchell? You, get Mitch Shibata," he called to someone on his end. "Tell him I need him right now. Double time! Hang on, Geoff, I'm going to do some quick checks. Don't go off-line."

While they waited for Moriarty to get back, Kam linked the three of them up in wavespace, trained their three different perspectives on the shape, and plugged it into some app or another. The resulting magnified, three-dimensional image that hung in their shared wavespace was clearly a cargo ship. There was a marking in blue and gold—a corporate logo?—on the side.

"I am pretty sure," Kam said, flicking through the images in sequence to show them the movements of some spots near the ship, "that those little dark spots are people wandering around on the surface."

"Where are they with respect to the cave entrance?" Amaya asked.

"Close. About fifteen meters, maybe. Near the storage tanks."

Which meant sneaking in would be difficult, if not impossible.

The remote comm light came on again, and Moriarty said into their shared space, "We've checked the logs. You should be fine. The university has sent out a team to survey the claim. You know Ngo Minh Xuan, Commissioner Navio's husband?"

"I've met him," Geoff said.

"He's on the team. Everything looks to be on the up-and-up."

A sick feeling sank in Geoff's gut. "All right. Thanks a lot, sir." He signed off with a sigh. He could not think of anything to say that would not sound stupid or petty, so he simply said, "Let's go," fired up his rockets, and made for Ouroboros. His two friends did likewise.

As Ouroboros grew slowly in their sights, Geoff tried to figure out a way to make this new development work out. *Maybe,* he thought, *with the big ice coming Down, we can merely register ours, and hold off on selling it.*

Was there really anything wrong with wanting to benefit from his claim?

He tried to picture what his dad and mom would say. No doubt Dad would be angry that here was yet another big secret Geoff had sat on for so long.

Maybe, Geoff thought, *next time,* I'll *punch* him *in the face.* At the notion, he got a mental glimpse of Carl looking at him, looking sad. *Go away,* he thought. *Stop trying to make me care. You're* dead. If his friends had not been on the comm channel with him, he would have screamed it.

Aaron reached Jane via her wavelink as she left Sarah's office and entered the lobby. Aaron's face was pale, masklike. She broke stride. "What—? What's wrong?"

"A moment," Aaron said, and—with an uncomfortable glance at Jane—used his new authority to invoke privacy. Dead spydust drifted down around her. On her waveface, the red "Stroiders" light winked out. Then he said, "Jane, Marty is dead."

The words sank in, and horror spread through her. She braced her hand on the wall. It couldn't be. They'd talked only an hour or two ago.

Marty!

Ogilvie did this. It had to be.

Think, Navio. Don't jump to conclusions.

She found her voice. "What happened?"

"I don't know yet. I tracked you down as soon as I heard. I'm on my way to the scene right now. Jane—" His voice broke. His gaze was anguished, his lips tight. "Too many things are happening at once. Too much is at stake. I don't have the right to ask this, but I need your help."

He seemed only half convinced she would agree. That stung. "Of course I'll help! What do you need me to do?"

Relief broke over his face. "Thank you. I got a call from Police Chief Fitzpatrick, asking me to meet him at the scene. I don't know the details. It may have been an accident, but I fear otherwise."

"I'll be right there. Send me the coordinates," she said. "And I'll need you to commandeer a lift for me."

His hands danced in midair. "Both done. Hurry."

Aaron got Tania on the line while Jane made her way to the lifts. They briefed Jane as she rode up alone, clinging batlike by her feet to the lift loops.

"I sent him on an assignment," Aaron told her, "based on something Tania learned about the feral sapient attack last night. Tania, if you please . . ."

Tania was pacing on her catwalk. Behind her, Jane could see glimpses of her programmers' space. She spoke low and fast, in a monotone, as if trying to stay ahead of her own thoughts. "It's standard protocol to run security checks after something like last night, and when my people did so, they found evidence that somebody broke into our systems. We were hacked during the attack. By somebody other than the sapient."

Jane gaped. "What? Are you sure?"

Tania nodded once, sharply. "Pretty damn sure. While you and I were fighting off the sapient and doing the shutdowns, there was a point at which the systems were vulnerable for an instant—no more than that. Someone broke through our firewalls at exactly that instant, and planted a worm that tampered with our video banks."

"To what end? Do we know?"

"Yes," Tania replied. "They modified some backed-up images. The system crashed just as the worm was finishing its work, which is the only reason we were able to detect it; it hadn't finished cleaning up after itself. Otherwise we never would have detected the intrusion."

"Are you sure it wasn't the sapient itself doing this?" But she answered her own question. "No—it wouldn't have any reason to."

"Exactly. We have plenty of data on the feral's state of awareness, and at that point it was not even aware of what videos were. It learned a lot during the attack, but not enough to know or care about some different, other videos about a time and place from before it even existed. And it was all but overwhelmed, dealing with us."

"It had to be preprogrammed, then, that worm. No way whoever planted it could have anticipated when our walls would drop."

Aaron said, "I was afraid Tania's organization might be . . . infiltrated. That someone might have been cracking us on the fly during the assault. That was why I sent Marty. Communications had been corrupted by the feral sapient. Because of this, one major set of archives was offline during the worm's attack. The drives in question had not yet been brought inwave and needed to be physically disconnected from the system before the repair sapients reached them, in case the worm was still hiding somewhere in the system.

"I wanted to send someone we could trust. I knew I could trust Marty." Then he broke down, and pressed his hands against his face.

Jane had to speak. "Aaron . . ."

He looked up at her, horror stamped on his face, and shook his head: a silent plea for her not to say anything—not to comfort him, not to absolve him. She felt a sharp pang, remembering all those late nights working together, the bull sessions afterward; all the confidences. Now she could not comfort him. She was no longer his boss, and no longer his friend.

Aaron had not been work-hardened, yet, by all the forces they would bring to bear against him as resource chief. He would master himself, and excel. She knew Aaron. But any death resulting from one's orders was a dreadful burden to carry. Ironic, that she had shouldered such a burden at the very end of her tenure while he had had his thrust on him at the very beginning of his.

"What about the other videos?" she asked. "The doctored ones?"

Tania answered. "We couldn't detect anything from the tampered video. Whatever the worm was designed to hide or change, it succeeded in doing so. But we do know the place and time that was altered. The altered video was a span of about fifteen minutes, two months ago, recorded by a couple of store security cameras in a neighborhood in Uraniaville."

Uraniaville was a residential neighborhood in a mid-gee quadrant.

"Why Urania?" she asked. "Why then?"

"We don't know," Aaron said.

"Hang on." She brought up Jonesy. She fed it the term "Uraniaville" and asked it to cross-reference with information on news coverage over the past three months. Then her lift arrived at the Hub, and she launched herself out.

Her destination was a set of computer archive banks at Weesu and Level 1, the uppermost level beneath the Hub. The tunnels surrounding the archive were cordoned off with a mesh of police tape. A crowd of spectators had gathered to ogle the goings-on beyond the barrier. The officers standing watch inside the barrier recognized Jane, but would not part the mesh to let her through until Aaron came over and authorized it.

"This way," he said.

The mesh repelled "Stroiders" motes. An officer sprayed her with a fine mist to rid her of any clinging to her skin or clothing. Then she accompanied Aaron into the archive room. Chief Fitzpatrick stood nearby.

The forensic team guided a small army of miniature sapients in the measuring of blood spray patterns, gathering of air samples, and collecting of dust for DNA analysis. Near the computer banks was Marty's corpse, attended to by a medic in a body glove and filtration mask. Two other officers were studying the room.

Marty's body lay inside a shallow, inflatable bug bath. Assembler fluid sloshed lazily therein. A network of tubing draped him. He looked like a vine-coated, semi-deflated, plant-based version of himself. The medic bobbed beside him, stripping off the paraphernalia. The sour-sweet smell of assembly fluid reached her.

Jane started, remembering the dream image of her son with Marty's face, dead and covered in vines, and again felt the Voice's faint touch.

She had known. She had known.

"The medical team tried to revive him," Fitzpatrick told her, "but we found him too late."

They lofted themselves over to Marty's remains, which rested lightly on the floor. The body stirred in the faint gee as the medics worked. Fitzpatrick introduced the detectives assigned to the case, Detectives Duran and Wilkes.

"What killed him?" Aaron asked. The medic gestured at the entry wound. "He was shot once in the belly with a semiauto biotic."

A biotic? Jane tasted bile. Aaron clenched his fists. Biotics were one of the nastiest hand weapons developed in the last century. The bullets contained an exploding head that on penetrating their target released disassemblers tailored to liquefy anything organic that had a high-enough water content—organs, muscles, connective tissue. It left the enveloping skin alone. The end effect was to convert a human body to a skin bag filled with bones and goo.

Biotics were outlawed everywhere, because under conditions of dense enough biomass, there was a slight chance that the bugs would get splashed onto bystanders while in their brief active phase, and start a chain reaction that could take out a lot of bystanders. They were a favorite weapon of terrorists.

"Probably a Glock-Prime Five Hundred Short-Slide—that's the most popular model. Minimal blood loss," the medic went on, "but"—a shrug— "not much you can do if you aren't on-scene with the right cocktail of neutralizers at the instant of impact."

"How long . . ." Jane cleared her throat. "How long ago was he killed?"

Detective Duran said, "It's difficult to tell. Disassembly wipes out the traces that we could use to pinpoint the time of death—it messes with body temperature and obliterates postmortem decomposition."

Aaron answered, his voice thin and sharp. "I sent him to retrieve the archives about two hours ago. He was coming straight here from the office."

"During the 'Stroiders' blackout," Jane noted. That had cost him his life. "It would have taken him ten minutes or less to get here, and how long, Aaron? Perhaps another five or so to remove the archives?"

"I'm not sure . . ."

"Maybe five," Tania broke in from wavespace. "Maybe a few minutes more. He wasn't used to doing it."

Detective Wilkes checked something in her waveface. "That would give a time of death between about three-twenty and three-thirty, then. He was clearly set upon while he was here. What exactly was he doing?"

"Removing two archival drives for examination," Aaron said. "As I explained to Chief Fitzpatrick earlier, we had evidence of a break-in to our computer systems during the feral sapient's attack. I sent Marty up here to pick up the archives before they were brought back inwave. Tania, which were the units in question?"

"They don't show up on my waveface, but if I am visualizing your positions correctly," she said, "they'd be over there. Behind Jane." Tania gestured toward a bank of drives that glittered on one wall. They all turned and looked. Dismay settled in Jane's belly. "Where the smashed equipment is now?"

Aaron demanded of Detective Wilkes, "Were any loose data drives found in here?"

"You mean these?" Detective Duran drifted up beside her partner, carrying two clear, labeled bags filled with biocrystalline data drive fragments. "Looks like the murderer stole whatever components were removable, and smashed the rest."

Jane looked at Aaron. So they had nothing.

"Has his fiancée been notified?"

Detective Duran's eyebrows rose. "Not yet. Who are his next-of-kin?"

Aaron provided the information, while Jane kicked over to the medic, who, with the help of Detective Wilkes, was putting Marty's body in a shroud.

"Is the—Is it safe for me to touch him?" Jane asked.

"It is. We've thoroughly neutralized the toxins."

"Then I'd like a minute."

"Of course."

The medic and officer stepped back, and Jane alighted beside Marty. She studied his distorted face—closed eyes, tan freckles, smoke-pale lips. If Benavidez had not fired her, would she have sent Marty on this errand?

A terrible fury stirred in her.

"Good-bye, Marty," she said. She took his hand. It was a collection of fluid and splinters, jarringly cold to the touch, even through the membrane.

For the first time in a very long time she was free—free to follow her convictions and act on her will, and not worry about the political or resource implications. She was a free agent.

"I promise you," she whispered. *I'll catch the people who did this, and I will destroy them.*

Jane left Aaron talking with the chief of police and headed back down to Bottomsville. She told Sarah what had happened. Sarah stared at Jane, gravely. "Give me an hour to wrap some things up," Sarah said, "and I'll take you to dinner."

There, in private, while she waited, she got to work.

Jonesy had the Uraniaville results. Most were junk info, of no particular interest—arts and entertainment news, neighborhood events, notices of public meetings for land use reallocation, and editorials about proposed use of structures in reassembly, and so on. But one stood out:

22 April 2397 (Phocaea Free Press)—
Uraniaville resident Ivan Kovak implicated
in destruction of cluster ice stores. *More >>*

She scanned the article. It contained no new information, but the fact that Ivan was a Uraniaville resident told her all she needed to know. Whoever had broken into their computer systems last night had been trying to suppress a video of something that had happened in Uraniaville about five weeks ago, shortly before Kovak's marriage supposedly fell apart and his partners left with the kids. She was now sure that the video was of someone meeting with, or having access to the residence of, Ivan Kovak.

She called Sean. "Have you heard about Marty?"

She could already tell he had, from his expression. "Aaron just called me. Goddamned evil fuckwads. Tell me who did it. I'll shoot him myself."

"I think I know who did it," Jane said. "I'm trying to get proof."

He rubbed at his eyes. "Why is it that the young die and we old people are left to soldier on, Commissioner?"

"Just Jane," she said. "Please."

"Hell, you'll always be Commissioner to me. But all right. Jane. Things are going to shit."

"I know, Sean. I know." She sighed and rubbed at her eyes, which burned with fatigue. The meds Marty had given her had long since worn off. When had she last gotten a good night's sleep? "Did the police have any evidence that Kovak accepted a bribe? Any unusual deposits into his bank account, or anything like that?"

"Nope. If there was a bribe, the spouses took it with them."

"Or maybe the bribe was his family's lives."

He made a disgruntled noise. "I'd rather go on thinking of him as a loss to humanity."

Jane looked askance. "Whatever helps you sleep at night, my friend."

He made a noise. "Incidentally, I'm assuming that bastard Benavidez pulled the plug on your Zekeston housing allowance."

"Actually, I'm supposed to get a shitload of money, but not till I leave. In the meantime . . . you guessed correctly."

"Well, you and Xuan are welcome to our spare room while you're in town, for as long as you like."

Good to know who your friends were. "That's kind of you. Xuan's friends put us up last night, but I'm not sure if their invitation extended beyond the night. Do you need to talk it over with Lisa?"

"Nope. It was her idea."

"We may take you up on it, then. I'll have to talk to Xuan, but it'll be a while before I can reach him. He's off somewhere on a sugar-rock claim and I'm not sure where he is."

"Ah? I can help you there. I saw him a while ago, out here at the docks as he was loading his equipment for the run. It's the rock that belongs to the Agre kid—you probably heard about that."

"Geoff Agre owns a rock? That kid is full of surprises."

"You're telling me." Sean shook his head. "Apparently some old miner gave him a tapped-out claim a while back, and it has some ice in it. It's what got him in trouble with the black marketers last night."

"Black marketers? I am so out of the loop! Why didn't you tell me about this earlier? Never mind—things have been hectic. I get it. But what happened? Do his parents know?"

"It wasn't him, supposedly; his friend Ian Carmichael, the kid who had his arm removed, remember him?"

"Of course."

"Shortly before the feral sapient attack, Ian apparently got Geoff and his friends tangled up with some bad elements. I helped them extract themselves, in my capacity as duly-deputized police officer."

"Ah. So that's why you were with them at the time of the attacks."

"Right. And in answer to your other question, I am willing to bet the parents don't know. Things between Geoff and his parents are . . . strained at the moment."

" 'Strained'?"

Sean hesitated. "Put it this way. I got there this morning just in time to watch Geoff's father plant a fist in his face."

"He didn't! He's got fifty kilos on Geoff!"

"He did. It was ugly. Geoff took off and I doubt he's gotten back in touch with them since." Jane sighed. *Sal, you asshole.* Dee must be beside herself. Jane knew at that instant that Dee's marriage to Sal was over. Dee had put up with a lot, over the years, for the sake of her boys. But she wouldn't swallow that.

"Anyhow," Sean went on, "the kid's sitting on a sugar rock, and Xuan is on the team checking it out."

"Did he say when he'd be back?"

"No, but let me check the flight logs . . ." She waited, and he came back on. "It's about a two-and-a-half-hour journey, depending on burn rate, and they left before noon. Depends on how long it takes them to finish the tests, but I'd say he'll be back by late evening."

"Thanks, Sean."

"My pleasure, Commissioner. Jane," he corrected himself. "Commissioner Jane." He smiled and cut the connection.

Jane did some more thinking about Marty. The tampered tapes were security recordings from a utilities branch office. The question was, were there other recordings from that vicinity? "Stroiders" recordings, for instance? Or recordings from other security cams in the area? She called the Phocaea Public Library's main branch and asked to speak to the head librarian. Masahiro Takei was a great-great-nephew of Chikuma Funaki's and was delighted to help Jane.

"We can order whatever 'Stroiders' content you want," he said, and spread his hands apologetically. "We don't store 'Stroiders' content here—there's too much. Neither does the local Upside-Down server, in fact. They encrypt it and beam the raw feed straight to Earth. So we have to submit a request for video of specific times and places."

"So how long will it take to get that information?"

"Normally a request can take as much as five to seven business days to process. But"—he smiled—"I belong to the science wave and we have high-priority access to the full Library of All Nations files. Some friends of mine on Earth manage various content, and they should be able to help us. Send me your list. I'll get back to you later with the clips you request."

"Thank you." Jane sent him the coordinates for the deleted videos, and then sat back, musing. Her thoughts turned to Marty. She realized how little she knew about him, outside of work. She could only imagine how his family and friends were feeling. She must contact them. She made herself a note.

The dream she had had last night intruded. There had been more to it than just that prescient flash of knowledge of what lay ahead for Marty. Her mother had been in the dream, too. She had never felt so loved, so fully cherished, not even by her own mother, as she had been by the woman in that dream. She realized suddenly that it had been the Voice, giving her a hint of what lay ahead. And this thought opened an inner gate. The Voice came again. This time it was no whisper, but a shout.

JANE!

She tried to stand, but her surroundings reeled away. Knowledge tumbled into her, like a great wave—filling her—swamping her. She felt her body sink to its knees.

She saw a great hand cupping a fetus in a sac. The sac looked like a globe of ice, or a teardrop. The fetus within it was beautiful—innocent and terrible.

The fetus was the feral sapient.

It hadn't been destroyed during the excision. It was in hiding.

The Viridians had it. Thondu was working for them, and had smuggled it out during the attack. The troubadour, Thondu, and that young woman Chikuma-sensei had told her about, the one who was, perhaps, spying on Upside-Down for the mob, were somehow linked. The resemblance between them was stronger, now that she thought of it, than it appeared at first glance. They were siblings, perhaps, or something stranger.

The Voice wanted her to protect the feral.

The Voice gave her more. Before her mind's eye, a great banquet of anguish spread—far worse than anything humankind had ever known. This moment was passing swiftly. If she made the right choice, and made it soon, she could nudge events in the right direction. If she did nothing, things would almost certainly go the other way. Many would suffer and die who might otherwise live.

This was why the Voice had come to her.

She thought, even as she saw/felt/heard all this, that it had to be an illusion. A psychosis. Megalomania. Or worse, some manipulative power had hacked her consciousness. Even the feral itself might be tinkering with her neurotransmitters to get her to do what it wanted.

Psychosis was the only rational explanation. But the enfolding vastness of the Voice was still, somehow, all too real. In some way, more real even than she.

Jane came to herself curled on the tile floor of Sarah's law office.

Sarah was talking. "Jane, can you hear me?" Jane couldn't quite make out her face. "I hear you." She gasped the words. "Help me up."

With Sarah's assistance she wobbled shakily over to the couch and sat. Her vision slowly cleared. The cushions propped her up. How had she gotten back into Sarah's office? She looked up at her friend: Sarah had her hand on Jane's shoulder and was gazing worriedly at her.

"What happened?"

Jane passed a hand over her eyes with a trembling hand. "I haven't been eating or sleeping well. Did I . . . did I say anything?"

Sarah shook her head. Jane read the worry in her eyes. "You were moaning. Nothing intelligible."

Thank God for small favors. "Would you mind getting me a drink of water?"

"Sure. Wait right here."

She stepped out. Jane hunched over her knees.

How many crazy people had there been, over the years, who were sure they had a special line to God? It was time to quit screwing around. She pulled the antipsychotics out of her pocket, shook out a pill into a trembling hand. It was a big pill; she would need that drink of water to get it down.

She stared at the pill.

Her reluctance, she had to admit, was in large part a visceral dislike of being dependent on medication. But she wanted to think that there was more to it than simply that.

I don't believe in the supernatural, she thought. But she could not shake this deep conviction that somehow she had landed in, or been maneuvered into, this position where the fate of many depended on her. Perhaps even more than simply the people of Phocaea.

It was then she realized that she had already decided to play the hand the Voice had dealt her. An awareness filled her of the forces in play. A strategic map laid itself out before her. She knew which pieces would need to be moved, and when. Not in so many words, but she sensed the underlying pattern.

Beneath it all—despite the fact that the Voice could not be anything more than schizophrenia or, more frighteningly, biochemical manipulation by her enemies—something deep in her trusted it. She had always relied on her instincts, and the Voice felt the same way her hunches always had, only bigger. She had to trust that.

She did not need to know what the Voice was to believe that the knowledge it gave her was truth. She might be going mad. In fact, it was much more likely than the alternative. But if so, it seemed a useful madness. Whatever was happening was enabling her to tap into her own intuitions, in a much more direct and powerful way than she had ever known before.

And I'm a free agent, now, she thought again. *I'm no longer resource allocation chief—no longer bound by my obligations to the cluster. I can do what I want.*

She wanted to see where this bout of inspired madness would take her. She put the pill back into the vial and tucked it away.

Sarah came in with the water. Jane took it with thanks. She drained the cup and wiped her mouth with a quick, decisive nod.

"I'm famished," she said.

Sarah looked relieved. "It'll do you a world of good to get a good meal in you. What are you in the mood for?"

"Anything private," Jane said. "I'm sick of motes in my soup." She paused. "I know it's pricey to keep running your antimote nanoware. Do we have another option? Something that ensures privacy?"

Sarah looked thoughtful. "It's not far to the Badlands, and I know people there who can hack us a barrier. It's not as bad as its rep," she said. "Not if you know people."

"You have Badlands connections?" Again Jane felt the stirrings of her Voice. The Viridians' domain was the Badlands.

"From my pro bono work," Sarah replied, "on behalf of Downsider immigrants . . ."

"You never told me!"

"The subject just never came up." Sarah shrugged. "Viridians are weird, I grant you. But they're not the monsters people make them out to be."

"I never would have pegged you for this."

"There's a moral issue involved. I would never modify my own genome to the extent they do. I wouldn't go even so far as you have, Jane, with your foot and hip mods. But I can't countenance what was done to the gene-mutes, Downside. They are consummate artisans, and their own genome is their workbench. However much we may criticize them, by their own lights they are very careful and ethical.

"Are we any more human than our ancestors whose only tools consisted of rocks and skins? Are we less so? I've worked closely with the Viridians for years, and they are no better or worse than anyone else I know. Human is as human does."

"I have to be honest. Their mods make my skin crawl. But I agree with your sentiment, and I laud you for having the courage of your convictions."

"Thanks. But I benefit, too. They are amazing technologists. It helps, sometimes, to have the right sort of friends."

"As, for instance, right now."

Sarah smiled. "Exactly." She held the door open for Jane, and they entered the "Stroiders" haze.

As they neared Ouroboros, Amaya broke into Geoff's thoughts. "I've been thinking . . ."

"What?"

"Well, shouldn't the university have arranged this visit through you? If it was on the up-and-up, I mean. It's still your property. You haven't signed it over."

Geoff thought about it. "I guess it is a bit odd."

Kam said, "It is possible the black marketers told someone else about it. Someone not so nice."

Geoff said, "But Moriarty checked, and everything was on the level. I know Professor Xuan. He wouldn't collude with bad guys."

"Maybe he doesn't know," Kam replied. "Maybe they tricked him."

Geoff didn't say anything. He had a hard time taking the idea seriously. Those black marketers weren't his definition of competent. And they had been arrested.

"In any case," Amaya said, "we should be cautious. Let's not just go barging in. Let's land over the horizon and observe them."

"I suspect they have already seen us coming," Kam pointed out. "Every ship has radar."

"Perhaps. We should assume they have."

"I think we're worrying unnecessarily," Geoff said. "But it doesn't hurt to take a few precautions. What's your air and fuel look like?"

They had about an hour and a half of air left, and one quarter fuel. Meaning they couldn't get back to town without recharging both. So they had to land. "Look. If they're legit, we have no problem. If they aren't, we need an angle."

Amaya made a sound in her throat. "What; we're going to knock on their airlock and ask if they're with the mob?"

"Well, I had something a bit sneakier in mind. We'll treat them on the level, but we'll have something in the back pocket. Just in case." Maybe Dad was right about his sneakiness. Well, it came in handy sometimes. "Remember when we were first came out to Ouroboros last year, and we had problems with the power out to the chemical plant? You two climbed up into the heat discharge piping and ran a conduit out to the plant." The tunnels had been too small for Geoff or Ian, even back then, but both Amaya and Kam had been able to wiggle through. And, importantly, the heat venting pipe was a good ways away from the mine entrance. Behind a ridge, in fact.

"Yeah," Kam said, "but I've had a growth spurt since then. I barely fit through that shaft before. No way I'd fit now."

"Amaya?"

She was silent for a moment. "I'm about the same size as I was then, I suppose. But . . ." Her voice shook. "I nearly got stuck, Geoff. Don't you remember? Kam and me, we had to take off our tanks at the narrowest spot. My line got pulled and my air was cut off for nearly three minutes till we could rig me a patch. I nearly suffocated."

Geoff did not say anything for a second. Then he sighed. "You're right. We'll have to think of another way."

A silence. Then Amaya inhaled sharply. "Oh hell. I did it before. I can do it again."

Geoff released his own breath. "You're my hero."

"Amen," Kam said.

"Yeah, yeah; whatever. Lay it out. What's your idea, Geoff?"

Geoff quickly sketched out the bones of a strategy. Kam and Amaya asked some questions and helped refine the details, and soon they had a plan. They kept it simple—no time for anything complicated; plenty of room for improvisation. But something was missing. For a moment he didn't know what, but then he exhaled sharply. "Damn. I can't believe it."

"What?" asked Kam and Amaya at the same time.

"I never thought I'd say this, but I really wish Ian were here with us." His friends laughed.

Then the rock was upon them. They corrected course, slowing, and kept the bulk of Ouroboros between them and the intruders as they steered to a landing.

Jane and Sarah sat at a rickety two-person table in Portia's Mess, a dive in the heart of the Badlands. Portia's was a Tonal_Z bar. Not too rough, as Badlands hangouts went. It reminded her a bit of the French Quarter in New Orleans, which she had visited as a college student back on Earth. Fashionable sleaze. Pleasingly nasty. Portia, a chubby bald woman wearing a fur coat, stepped up onto the stage. "Ladies and gents, please join me in welcoming troubadour Gabriel Thondu Macharia, visiting us all the way from Earth space!"

Jane straightened, staring, as a trio near the small stage stood up. The other patrons were a young local couple, and a small cluster of tourists; Jane could tell they were tourists because they sounded nasal; Downsiders didn't have the mods that kept their sinus tissues under control. In microgee their sinuses swelled up like water balloons. The patrons made a three-tone sound as the troubadours mounted the stage, which Jane belatedly recognized as a Tonal_Z expression of approval.

"I know one of them," she said.

"Which one?"

Jane gestured. "The lead musician. He's the troubadour who helped us stop the feral. That one." In this venue, he looked softer, more effeminate. And under the stage lights, his skin was lighter, more akin to Xuan's rock-brown tone than the deep, warm African-mahogany hue she recalled from before. She pondered whether to speak to him, and decided to wait till after they were done with their performance. The musicians adjusted their stools and tuned their instruments. Thondu had his harp; one of the other two pulled out a flute; the third moved to the drum set.

Jane did not bother to turn on her translator. But with its eerie progressions, the word-music fit Jane's mood to the micron. The sounds tumbled across one another in a pattern so unexpected, and yet so right, that you could sense the language that rode the tones—sleek, energetic—leaping in graceful arcs, diving deep beneath the surface. That young man had a real gift.

In this place, the tension was ebbing from her, leaving her pensive, even drowsy. She had not realized till now how tightly she had bound herself over the past few days. It wasn't just the poemsong; it was also the privacy. For the first time in a long time, no one here seemed to know her or care who she was. That suited her fine.

The waitron brought their food. They ate. The musicians took a break and stepped into a back room, and the patrons' voices rose to fill the space.

It was time.

Jane leaned forward and spoke softly. "Sarah, I need a meeting with the Badlander leader, Obyx. Can you arrange it?"

Sarah looked startled. "Why?"

"I have a need they can help with. I don't want to go into detail here."

"I'm not sure you should involve yourself with the Viridians."

"You seem to be doing all right for yourself."

"That's different. I told you, I help them occasionally, pro bono. I defended Obyx, back when."

"Back when what?"

Sarah smiled. "Ze was a defendant in the mail-order miners lawsuit."
"So?"

"So, nothing. We have an agreement. Obyx doesn't ask me to do anything illegal, and I'm hir connection to the mainstream business community."

"So, consider me a new business opportunity."

Sarah's brow furrowed. "First you should know what you are dealing with. The Viridians really are different from us. They have their ethics—their code of honor, if you will—and they're careful about their activities out here, but they have ties with criminal organizations back on Earth. Things could get . . . complicated."

" 'Criminal organizations'? Let me tell you about 'criminal organizations.' The prime minister has just signed a deal with a Martian crime family. The disaster in the warehouse was sabotage—caused by Ogilvie & Sons. One of my staff has been murdered! Don't lecture me about ethics." She had come half out of her seat before she knew it. Others in the restaurant were staring at her.

Jane sat back down. *Cool off, Navio.* "Sorry. But you get my point"

Sarah waved her apology away. "Forget it. I just want you to know what you're getting into. When do you want to see hir?"

"Tonight. Right away."

"Tonight?" Sarah eyed her. "You don't waste any time. Let me make some calls." She excused herself and went outside. Jane spent a few moments stirring her drink with her pinkie, sucking her fingertip, brooding.

Thondu and his accompanists were just then reentering the café. Jane walked over to them. "I enjoyed your performance."

"Thank you," he said, turning with a smile. Then his eyes flew open and he suppressed a start. "Oh . . . Commissioner Navio. I didn't expect—"

Jane regarded him. Interesting reaction. "Not 'commissioner' anymore. I'm a private citizen now." She sensed, rather than heard, Sarah come up behind her.

Thondu looked embarrassed. "Actually, I will be leaving soon."

"Really?"

He was babbling now, clearly nervous. "Yes, I'm trying to get a berth on the *Sisyphus*. But it's been difficult—no seats are available. I don't—I may have to wait for a later ship."

Jane turned to Sarah, who gave her a minuscule nod and gestured for her to follow.

Thondu's obvious discomfort lingered in her mind as Jane and Sarah departed the restaurant. But more interesting to her was that clearly, he—he?—did not want to spend any more time in her company than he had to. It confirmed her suspicions that he had stolen the feral sapient out from under their noses last night.

Sarah took her down a catwalk. Along the way, a group of adolescents played stickball nearby, leaping into the reaches of the mid-gee netways. Gravity was heavy enough here that she found their gymnastics impressive. At a café, young couples sat at small tables. Some of them even looked human. Groups of young Badlanders roamed the streets. Jane grew nervous as one group approached, laughing raucously and gesturing. They stared at Jane and Sarah, and there was a hint of menace in their behavior. But a large, multilimbed young man appeared from the shadows nearby. He was holding a dual-snake-DNA staff. The group grew quiet, and passed Jane and Sarah without a word.

Jane glanced at Sarah with raised eyebrows, as the young man faded back into the shadows.

"Shivas," Sarah murmured. "Angels. They work for Obyx."

"Obyx has an army? Christ, Sarah."

"Relax. They're not vigilantes. They're peacekeepers. More like a neighborhood watch committee."

"How come nobody talks about this?"

But she was being naïve, and she knew it. Obyx's name certainly came up, when the city and cluster power brokers talked about the impacts of legislation or other proposed city plans on local neighborhoods. Still, none of them had ever let on that Obyx was a gang lord. Neither had Chikuma; if anything, she had seemed to hold hir in a certain wary regard.

Perhaps it was simply because Jane herself had never dealt directly with Obyx; she had never had to, since city resource issues were in Hiro's and JimmyM's hands. And, well, the more extreme gene-mods made her nervous. It was the slippery-slope thing. Where *was* the boundary between human and not? "I can't believe JimmyM would let this go on."

"Are you kidding? JimmyM counts on Obyx to keep the peace here. Fitzpatrick's police force is underresourced anyway, and the beat cops don't like it down here much. It creeps them out. And the Badlanders don't particularly want a lot of chrome enforcers here, anyhow. Some of them have a bad attitude about mutes."

"Chrome?" Jane repeated, looking at her askance. "What the heck is a chrome?"

"You are, dear. I am. People who cling to the basic genetic blueprint they were born with. The biologically leashed. That's how they see us."

It was all Jane could do not to stare at the bizarre changes the Viridians in this sanctum had made to themselves and their surroundings. Suffice to say, few people looked remotely human, and few spaces looked able to fully accommodate humans. Yet the Viridians stared as if *she* were the freak. She supposed she was.

She had heard the arguments over changing the human genome. Everybody had, by now. The Viridians argued that it was all simply a matter of degree. Everyone Upside had enhancements. Genetic screening and nanosurgery had long ago eliminated genetic deformities and illness; anyone with decent funds had access to treatments that dramatically slowed the ageing process. Like Jane, many Upsiders chose additional enhancements (extra fingers, enhanced vision or hearing) that made it easier to do their job or adapt to their physical environment. Even Xuan, who was rather a purist about mods, had had his eyes and visual cortex enlarged and adapted to see farther into the infrared and ultraviolet; it made rock hunting in the dim reaches of the belt much easier. Downside, where gene-mod laws in most countries were so strict, people had so many fleshware and waveware enhancements that they were just as modified in other ways.

"So they came to an understanding with JimmyM's administration," Sarah was saying. "I should know: I helped negotiate it. The Badlanders have their own volunteer neighborhood watch group and fire brigade and waste recycling services."

This was a side of Sarah Jane had never known.

Soon they entered the Catacombs, deep in the heart of Viridian territory. Jane had heard of this place, even seen pictures. But it had not prepared her for the reality. The Catacombs were a segmented set of short, interlocking tunnels dedicated to Badlander nanoart. Assembler and disassembler jets ejected nanites, changing statuary and bas relief, works that moved across the face of the walls. It was living art. Faces and forms—obscene, horrific, stunningly beautiful—emerged from and receded back into the assembler troughs and vents: here a fabulous, quasi-fourth-dimensional, hypercubist rendition of the *Mona Lisa*; there a Pan with a grotesquely sized, erect penis chased a bald, nude nymph with oversized breasts, who first eluded him, laughing, then grew oversized and ate him, then melted into a new Pan and nymph; over there a crystalline doe and her twin fawns grazed on emerald grass against a backdrop of magnificent mountainscapes; yonder a miniature tableau of the Promenade, only when you looked closely, the people were made of machine parts. Occasionally, works of art stepped or floated out of their milieus and drifted away or melted, or integrated with another across the way.

Everywhere she looked, something strange, wonderful, or disgusting blossomed, moved, dissipated. The artists—or perhaps some were art patrons; it was hard to say—either sat alone, plugged into the assembler hackports, molding their creations with gesture and Tonal_Z song, or gathered in small groups to discuss the tableaux.

Sarah paused, her hand on the door to a building adorned with a fluid array of genetic and digital images. "Here we are."

Jane looked up above the door. A sign scrawled FIRST UPSIDE GATHER in fluid lights. Sarah had brought her to a Badlander church. She touched the circular door and it melted open. Jane followed. The door reformed behind them.

Jane looked around, and felt disappointed. She had been . . . not expecting—that would be unrealistic—but at least hoping for something awe-inspiring. Something that gave her the feeling she had had in the presence of the Voice. This, this gather had its idiosyncrasies, but it was little different from any other church, temple, or synagogue she had ever been in.

One of the staff had them sit in an alcove off the main sanctuary. Learned Harbaugh entered after a short delay. He had nearly reached them when the street door melted away and a young woman burst in.

"Learned Harbaugh! I have urgent news. I have to speak to Learned Obyx—"

At the same moment the intruder saw Jane, she recognized the other. It was not a young woman; it was none other than Thondu wa Macharia na Briggs. Jane remembered the young woman-man in her dream. "Thondu" was gene-modded. A Viridian. Thondu was Vivian Waīthīra. A hermaphrodite, then, or other intersex person, who used Viridian tech to morph from one gender to the other at will, and change races as well.

"Relax," Jane told the young troubadour. "Learned Obyx already knows I'm here."

"Thondu," or whoever he, she, or ze was, gaped at Jane in distress. Learned Harbaugh laid a hand on the youth's shoulder and whispered something, his eyes never leaving Jane's. The youth turned to leave, but Jane said, "My business and yours are likely the same. Why don't we all go speak to Obyx together?"

"Obyx wants to speak to you privately, and our young friend has other duties," Harbaugh said. He led Jane and Sarah down the hall into a small office. The office was simple: nano-grown chairs, bioart along two walls, and a fountain cascading down the third. In one chair, eyes half closed as if meditating, was Obyx.

Jane had seen images but had never met Obyx in the flesh. She had expected hir to be strange, but had not been prepared for how beautiful ze would be. She brushed palms with Obyx's huge, frondlike hands.

Sarah said, "Thanks for taking the time to see us. This is Jane Navio."

Obyx nodded a welcome to Jane. "Your reputation precedes you."

"Likewise."

"Sarah"—with a gesture at her—"tells me you need my assistance. I ordinarily don't see visitors, but I admit I was intrigued by the request."

Jane glanced at Sarah, who stood deadpan, her arms folded. "I'm here to talk to you about the Ogilvies."

"The Martian Ogilvies?"

Jane nodded. "Through their shipping company, Ogilvie & Sons, they've been trying to get a stranglehold on all shipping ports between Mars and the outer system for years. And they're making a fresh assault on Phocaea. I believe they are responsible for the disaster in the warehouses, as well as the death of one of my people, Marty Graham."

Obyx studied Jane. "These are serious accusations."

"The Ogilvies have done these kinds of things elsewhere. They did it on Vesta. They have to be stopped before they wreak their havoc here, too, and I plan to stop them. But I need your help."

"They need to be stopped?" Obyx repeated. "Why?"

Jane bit her tongue to keep from shouting. Apparently, Obyx did not intend to make this easy. "Nearly a hundred people were assassinated on Vesta, during the months after they took over there—and among them were Vesta's former leaders. People like you and me. I was there. I barely escaped with my life. We all are in grave danger unless they are stopped."

Obyx only smiled at that, but Jane continued. "Their ships are on the way now. Do you really want to sit by while they overrun Phocaea? Your people live here, too, and they, too, will suffer."

Obyx laced hir many fingers together. "I appreciate your newfound concern for us Badlanders. But I doubt that the Ogilvie family poses a threat to us. When it comes to these traditional power struggles, we have a policy of live and let live. And frankly, the city and cluster officials have made it clear by their actions that they don't perceive the same threat that you do."

"They are mistaken," Jane said. "Elwood Ogilvie is not known for his subtlety, and he's not going to leave things to chance."

"That still doesn't explain why you're here," Obyx said. "Why should you care about what the Ogilvies do to us?"

Jane stroked her lip, studying Obyx. "Let's assume for the moment," she said, "that Ogilvie's representatives have already been to see you. They've given you a bit of information—only what they want you to know, of course."

Sarah was trying to get Jane's attention with small movements and noises, but Obyx merely seemed amused. "All right. Let's assume that."

"They've given you a promise," Jane said, "that the Badlanders will be left alone if you stay out of the coming fight, and a subtle threat about the trouble you'll reap if you get involved."

Obyx threw back hir head and laughed. Jane glanced at Sarah. She was glaring, and shook her head minutely again. Jane ignored her warning.

"If what you say is true," Obyx said, "then whyever should I cooperate with you? If this big fight is looming, it looks to me as if I have nothing to lose and everything to gain by staying on the sidelines."

Jane smiled, and sprang the trap. "Oh, you have a dog in this hunt, all right. You have the feral sapient."

Obyx did not react overtly, but hir gaze grew more intent. Sarah and Harbaugh openly gaped—though, Jane suspected, for different reasons.

"Thondu extracted it for you," she went on, "during the sapient's attack last night, and you've got it hidden away. But it's useless to you here. It takes up too much room for you to house an active copy in your systems, and you can't get it off Phocaea. If the Ogilvies find out you have it, and find out what it's worth, whatever limited—and, I might add, bogus—immunity you've worked out for your own people won't be worth the electrons it's inscribed on. Your only hope is to get the sapient offworld before Elwood and his fleet of hired hands get here. But your leverage doesn't extend to Benavidez. You can't get your courier a berth."

The silence stretched. Obyx stared thoughtfully at the open air above Jane's head. "Your scenario is quite amusing. Is it not, Sarah?"

"Amusing is not the word I'd choose," Sarah replied. "Jane, what is this about?"

"A good question," Obyx told Sarah. "And I have to wonder about your own motives for bringing her here."

Sarah stiffened. Jane felt a twinge of guilt. But if she had told Sarah what she had planned, Sarah would never have arranged this meeting. And too much rode on it.

Whatever misgivings Sarah had, she kept to herself. "I assumed you'd at least want to hear her out."

Obyx's gaze shifted back to Jane. "Still, all you've brought me is conjecture and supposition. You've spun a conspiracy from air and paranoia, and want me to put my own people's lives at risk, for what? What do you want in return? Other than a vague promise to support you, if and when it comes to that."

"You people can hack a barrier that shuts out 'Stroiders' motes," Jane said. "I've seen it myself, on the way here."

"Yes. And?"

"I want two things. One"—she held up her index finger—"I want you to give me a hack that disables that barrier. Two"—she held up her middle finger—"I want a way to record and send to a remote location everything that happens to me, automatically and instantaneously. I want that signal to be unblockable, and I want that remote location to be unhackable."

Obyx burst into incredulous laughter. "Absurd!"

"Why?"

Obyx leaned close. Jane could smell hir breath. It was a nice smell—clean and inviting. Her own reaction bothered her. She wondered whether it was a hack, or hir real body chemistry. Nothing was ever real with the Viridians—or everything was.

"Nothing is unhackable, and nothing is unblockable. Nothing."

Jane stood back. "I have confidence that the Viridians can come closest of anyone I know."

"But . . . why? Why would you want such a thing?"

"Because he is a lawyer with access to huge financial resources, my enemy can create a privacy shadow at will," Jane said. "He uses it against me. And I want to be able to shine light on their abuses. They manipulate the 'Stroiders' stream somehow. I want everyone to see them, when they think no one is watching."

Obyx gazed at her speculatively, tapping fingers in a complex rhythm.

Ze gestured for Harbaugh to step over. A transparent bubble surrounded the two of them. The two spoke, but Jane heard nothing. She glanced at Sarah, who shrugged. Then Obyx burst the bubble with a finger flick and leaned back. "This supposed conspiracy by the Martian mob that you postulate is better suited to the tainmosphere than to hard meatspace. But let's say that, for whatever reason, a berth on a Downward-bound ship soon—within the next week, say—would be of use to me. Are you saying you can get me that?"

"I am. And I'll let your courier board with no questions asked—despite the fact that you stole an extremely valuable item from my system, that by rights belongs to the people of Phocaea."

Obyx tensed. "A sapient can be no other sapient's property. Our species recognized this when slavery was eradicated. We are the foulest of hypocrites, to fail to apply the standard to intelligent, self-aware beings simply because they are not made of meat."

Jane rolled her eyes. "First of all, human slavery hasn't been eradicated. That's a myth we choose to believe to help the rest of us sleep at night. Second, don't lecture me about precious freedoms that are denied to digital denizens. We both know you have every intention of using the feral sapient to suit your own ends. Or, I should say, your masters' ends, back on Earth."

Obyx and Jane glared. Sarah shifted once more. Jane knew what Sarah would tell her; she shouldn't provoke Obyx. She was deep in Viridian territory, and all of her tech was inactive, or readily within their control. Not that she believed they would truly harm her. Even so, she needed Obyx.

But hir cavalier dismissal of the lives of the people of Phocaea had gotten her blood up. Jane couldn't help but wonder whether humanity would survive whatever use the Viridians had planned for the sapient.

But Obyx merely shook hir head, sadly. "You misjudge us, Commissioner. The sapient is a child. Less than a child. Intellectually it is massively powerful, but morally—socially—it is barely more than a fetus. That it would do great harm to itself and others . . . that is not its fault. But it needs schooling before it can be freed."

"You admit you have it."

Obyx smiled. "Let me just say that, if we had the sapient, in all our actions, we would have only its well-being in mind. As we do all sapient entities. We are not fools, Commissioner. We recognize the risks that volitional wavespace entities pose to meatspace."

"And so you have Phocaea's citizens' well-being also in mind?"

Obyx waved an insouciant hand. "We intend no harm. But there are plenty around whose duty is to care for meat sapients. True wave sapients—especially wild ones—are far rarer and more precious. And they have no protection under the law. If we do not stand for them, who will?"

Jane looked at Obyx in mild disgust. But she had better not weigh in again with her opinions, or they would all regret it. "Do we have a deal?"

Obyx sighed, looking put-upon. "You ask a lot. We are giving you the keys to our own privacy. Once knowledge is unleashed, it is impossible to stuff it back into the bottle. Tech that allows you to disable our own defenses against 'Stroiders' could clearly be used against us."

"Which you would assuredly be able to hack a new barrier against."

"True. But not without a cost, in effort and time."

"And in return, you'll have what your people have sought for generations, a spontaneously created digital sapient. Untampered with, yours free to unleash on an unsuspecting populace . . . God help us all."

Obyx still hesitated. Ze cupped hir chin in a hand. "How do I know we can trust you to live up to your end? I could give you this recording tool you seek, and you could renege. You might not only share with others this 'Stroiders'-hacking tech, not only renege on your promise to obtain for us this seat on *Sisyphus*, but you might even let your close friends and associates in government, whom you've worked with for years, and whom you know and trust far better than you do us, in on the idea that we"—ze hesitated—"might have the feral. We cannot afford to be put openly in confrontation with the powers that rule Phocaea. Whoever that power might be."

Jane shrugged. "As to the technology, you can install whatever controls you like so I don't hack it." She refrained from mentioning that she was pretty sure she could get Tania to circumvent their controls, if she chose. But she would honor her deal as long as they did.

"With regard to my influence, have you looked at my sammy cache? Have you been watching the news? Our ice was destroyed on my watch. Ten people have died, dozens injured, and many more are at risk. I'm facing a subpoena from Parliament. I am persona non grata. I'm reviled." Her voice rose, despite herself; her breath grew short. With effort, she regained control. "But even if not, even if I still have friends in high places—and I admit I have an ally or two left—surely you must know that I honor my agreements. With something as sensitive and politicized as resource allocation, there is no way I could have been successful over the past three decades if I did not."

Obyx glanced at Harbaugh, but Jane didn't know what it signified.

"With regard to the feral . . ." she sighed. "I can't lie. The notion of a free digital sapient being terrifies me. Humanity has kept the worst at bay for the past two centuries. We have become so dependent on our technology. With the feral, we might face our undoing." She paused, the Voice ringing like distant bells in her thoughts. "But it seems to me that since we must face the Singularity someday, perhaps BitManSinger is a gift. A path through the vortex to the other side."

She saw a swift look pass between Obyx and Harbaugh, and knew instantly why. "So—you *did* hack me!"

Once again, she had caught them unawares. Harbaugh started, mouth open. Obyx tried with limited success to appear indignant. "I don't know what you mean."

Sarah said, "Jane, what the hell are you talking about? *Hacked* you? Who hacked you?"

Jane replied, "I've been hearing voices, Sarah. Or rather, a Voice. Since the night before last. Somehow you figured it out—didn't you?" she asked Obyx. "You detected that we had a feral sapient in our system. And in case your own plans to extract it weren't successful, you wanted to neutralize me. To force me to believe I was having some premonition. Make me care. So I wouldn't act to destroy it before you got someone in place to remove it."

"You are quite mad." But Obyx's tone was not convincing.

"Perhaps. But it is a useful madness. You know"—she lifted a hand in a shrug—"I should probably hate you for what you have done. But I don't. I should even thank you for it. You've given me a new outlook. Whatever you have put me in touch with"—she shook her head—"never mind. Let's just say I find all kinds of possibilities opening up in my life, which is something I would never have expected at my age.

"So don't worry. I won't press charges, and I'll still honor our deal. As long as you come clean about what you have done."

A tense silence stretched. Finally Obyx said, "I will never underestimate you again."

"That is wise."

Obyx waved a hand. "Fill her in, James." Harbaugh stared at Obyx as though trying to bore a hole through hir the way Sarah had stared at Jane earlier, but Obyx told him, "If we are going to make this deal, we have to make it with all our markers on deck."

Harbaugh turned to Jane. "It was a mild hack. It wasn't supposed to hurt you, or give you hallucinations, or anything. Just, as you said, make you care. Give you a sense of being connected to a greater whole. Open you up to new possibilities, to a different way of looking at things."

Jane barked a laugh. "Oh, it did that, all right. And that little exchange at the memorial: that was just you jerking my chain, eh?"

Harbaugh merely looked at her, discomfited.

"That was my idea," Obyx said. "To reinforce the programming."

"Just being a good soldier, eh?" she told Harbaugh. To Obyx, she said, "So. Here's a rider on our agreement. You ever mess with my neurochemistry again, and I will not rest till I bring you down. Mind-hacking is a serious crime, and I *will* pursue it. I will use every last shred of my power, every last connection I have left, to take your organization apart, piece by piece, and leave you with nothing. Even if it kills me. Understand?"

Obyx and Jane studied each other for a long, tense moment. Then Obyx gave a single nod. "Fair enough."

Sarah was eyeing them both. She did not look happy. "Where does all this leave us?"

"Let's review terms," Obyx said. "You want all my resources at your disposal to produce your anti-'Stroiders' hack. When do you need it?"

"Right away."

Obyx lifted hir eyebrows at Harbaugh, who said, "It so happens that we occasionally have need of such a technology. We have it on hand."

"And in return you agree to keep silent about your suspicions regarding the feral sapient," Obyx said, "and to give us a berth on *Sisyphus,* to use as we see fit, no questions asked. Without alerting anyone that something out of the ordinary might be happening."

"Yes."

Obyx looked at her askance, as though doubtful she could bring herself to do such a thing. Ze extended both upper sets of hands, and Jane brushed hands with hir, both right and left, thinking, *and now I've made my own deal with the devil.* Sarah was shaking her head in dismay.

"Draw up the papers for us, won't you?" Obyx said to Sarah. "For your usual fee."

"I think I deserve hazardous duty pay for this one," Sarah muttered.

While Sarah and Obyx stayed behind to discuss other matters, Harbaugh took Jane down the way to outfit her waveware. Jane felt as if she were walking through an amusement park ride that had gone overboard with the biologicals. Inside one room they passed she got a glimpse of someone in a nutrient cocoon, reaching out to adjust a monitor, and realized that that must be how they hacked themselves.

Harbaugh took her to a chamber with several different nooks and technology stations. "Have a seat," he said, gesturing at a chair. "This will only take a few minutes. What waveware do you use?"

She removed her ear unit and handed it to him.

"It's Intel's latest quantum processor, I forget the model. Plenty of free memory—I keep it clean. I have a cortical interface with standard gold and an RS-1482 bus." She tipped her head to show him the tiny gold connector that rested in her ear canal.

"Good. This will just take a minute." He pulled down a screen and plugged her computer into it, and started the download. Then he leaned against the counter, arms folded, eyeing her. She sensed he did not truly trust her.

"Was Ivan Kovak really a Viridian?" she asked.

"Depends on your definition. He wasn't modded. But he and his family attended services occasionally. We never turn people away."

"I can't help wondering about him," Jane said. "He surely knew he would not be able to get out alive. The mob doesn't inspire the obsessive, delusional sort of mind-set that leads people to throw their lives away in a grand gesture. What could have led him to end his life in such a way?"

Harbaugh frowned. "From everything I saw, up till near the end, he seemed . . . content. He loved his spouses; he loved his kids. They had money struggles—they were trying to survive as artists by doing skilled and unskilled labor. But of the three partners, he seemed least disturbed by it. He said to me one time that wealth begins when your belly is full, which always struck me as a healthy attitude." He shrugged. "All I can surmise is that the financial strain ultimately split the partnership, and their leaving broke him. They were everything to him. The kids especially."

Jane shook her head, lips pursed. "Learned, we don't have firm proof yet, but the police are convinced that the Ogilvies used their connection with him from his days on Vesta. They promised him that his family would be provided for if he would do this thing."

She could tell she had shocked him. "What makes you think so?"

She recapped what she knew, including how Marty's death seemed connected to the attempt to cover up a meeting in Kovak's old neighborhood. "From everything you've told me," she said, "he seemed a decent sort, and not easily bribed. The most likely alternative, then, is extortion. Blackmail."

Harbaugh looked troubled. "If that is true, and you are able to find evidence, then we will want to know."

"If you will allow me access to the city web to check my e-mail, I may be able to confirm it now," she said. Harbaugh eyed her speculatively.

"All right. Let's finish the installation first." He looked back at the monitor. "And . . . it's done."

Harbaugh removed her ear unit from its slot in the station and handed
it back to her; she plugged it in, hooked it back over her ear, and got a bad
case of reboot nerves—sparks in her vision, tinnitus, a tingling in her
fingers and toes. Then her waveware settled down. She wiggled her hands
and feet, twitched muscles here and there; her menus and her heads-up
overlay responded as usual. Some shiny new icons appeared in her waveface, beneath her usual suite. A sapient appeared: a luminescent spider
with a human face. Harbaugh said, "The program is named Arachnid. It
is pretty straightforward. Just follow the instructions that pop up. It records directly from your visual and auditory nerves. You can test the anti-
surveillance disabler first, if you like, and check your e-mail at the same
time."

"Where is the data stored?" she asked.

"The default is to beam the video to multiple social and news sites
throughout the Solar Wave, where it gets scooped up by the Upside-Down
folks and folded into 'Stroiders' as they do with other tourist and supplemental material. However, under *Preferences* you can choose whether to
livestream it to the wave, or to simply archive it."

"Is it archived locally, or beamed out onto the Solar wave?"

"It's stored locally with two remote mirrors. I understand your concern. Since we only have the one trunk line up to the surface, and it is
currently under repair, there is a small risk that your recordings could
be hacked and deleted before escaping into the Solar wave. But our firewalls are the best there are, and it won't be long till the transmission
cable is repaired. Phocaea owns twenty percent of Upside-Down's transmission capacity, and we find that sufficient for avoiding destruction of
information. You saw for yourself how hard it was to stop the feral from
escaping, and that would have been a much, much bigger packet dispersal than we are talking about with snippets of video and audio."

"It will have to do. Good enough."

She downloaded her e-mail. She had a message from Masahiro Takei.
She opened it, and read: "Here are the files you requested, from three different Uraniaville loci that fit your parameters. Hope they are of use."

"This may be it, but it will take me a few minutes to review," she told Harbaugh. "I'll call you if I find the proof you ask."

"Take your time." He stepped out.

She played Takei's recordings at 4x speed. They were all of a fourteen-minute stretch of time. All three showed different angles on a location at or near a grocery kiosk. The neighborhood in question must not get much mote or mite activity, because there was no sound. All three showed Ivan Kovak shopping at the kiosk, and walking away from the kiosk with his groceries, holding the hand of a little girl, maybe seven or eight, who resembled him. She must have been his daughter.

It was certainly interesting that Kovak showed up in the video. But why go to the trouble of killing Marty over a shot as trivial as this? She put in a call to Masahiro again. To her delight, a bar crawled across her screen, scanning the transmission and confirming it as surveillance-free. She began to understand Sarah's appreciation of the Viridians.

"Masahiro-san," she said, "am I remembering correctly that some 'Stroiders' subscribers Downside record their experiences while plugged in, and later share them with their buddies?"

"Yes, there are several such sites, as with other commercially successful waveworlds. They are quite popular. Some even insert themselves into the action, and play with the outcomes. A whole secondary economy has grown up around the phenomenon."

Jane suppressed a shudder. As always, the notion of being used as a doll in other peoples' inwave fantasies gave her a case of the grues. "Could you poke around some of those sites and see if you can find any downloaded video/audio recordings made before the disaster—as close as possible to when the event took place?"

He seemed perplexed. "But they will be much lower quality, and there is a possibility of their having been hacked in some way."

"For my purposes, that won't matter. Do what you can."

Harbaugh was in a chamber down the way, with Thondu. Jane paused at the door. They stood at a computer and had not yet noticed Jane's presence. Thondu was looking down at the clusters of biocrystals that made up the computer bank, and hir hand rested on hir belly.

"Will it be OK? If anything were to happen to me—"

"Don't worry." Harbaugh rested a hand on Thondu's shoulder. "We'll keep the backup safe. If your experimental version fails to thrive, you'll still have the genetic map, too, which can be decoded and reconstituted in digital form on one of our servers, once you are back on Earth."

"But it's untested tech."

Jane cleared her throat. Both started. Thondu looked aghast at the sight of her, but Harbaugh shook his head. "It's all right. We have an arrangement."

Jane looked at the glittering crystals and tubes. "So this is it, eh?" Harbaugh nodded.

Jane thought of her dream, and the fetus trapped in the crystal. She realized that this was the moment the Voice had warned her of. *Are you done with me so soon?* she thought, and felt relieved, and a bit sad.

So be it; she was glad to shed the role of prophet. She said to Harbaugh, "I have more research to do before I can provide you with that information we spoke of," she said. "I'll get it to you as soon as I have it."

On their return to Heavitown, Sarah was excruciatingly monosyllabic. Jane realized she was still angry over Jane's scene with Obyx. They reached the Promenade, and she said a curt good-bye. Jane touched her arm. "I'm sorry for surprising you like that."

Sarah frowned. "OK, here's the deal. Next time you want my help, I need to know what you are up to ahead of time. With an opportunity for me to advise you on the legal ramifications—and even decide whether I want to be involved!"

Jane winced. "You're right. I screwed up. I should have told you. But it's not that simple." She sought for a way to explain. "I'm operating on instinct, Sarah. I didn't know quite what I wanted to say to Obyx till I had hir in front of me. I just knew I needed to talk to hir, and there you were with a way to reach hir. Perhaps I shouldn't have involved you. But

I didn't see any other way. Nor any way to explain it that would have made sense."

Sarah sighed. After a pause, she said, "It was good that I was there. Ze'll trust you better, because ze knows ze can trust me." She slugged Jane lightly. "Just keep me in the loop."

Jane made an X over her heart. "I will. I promise."

25

The ship's engines kicked in: deceleration had begun. Xuan had maybe another twenty minutes before they touched down. While he waited, Xuan studied the stroid's stats from the original claim.

The original prospector had extensively surveyed it. The stroid was primarily metal ore. It was a big one: about three by three by ten kilometers in size, roughly barbell-shaped. Its albedo was high—typical for nickel-iron rocks. Its mean density had been 5.8 grams per cubic centimeter—nearly three times Phocaea's. One end of the barbell consisted of a big lump of crumbly silicates; the result of a collision with a silica rock sometime in the distant past. But the bulk of the stroid was high-grade ore.

When the claim was first filed, a hundred fifty years ago, the stroid's mass was 16,300 gigatons. Its gravitational pull had been a little less than a thousandth of a gee back then, comparable to that of larger but less dense, silicate-based Phocaea. Now, of course, as a mined claim, its mass would be reduced, and thus so would its gravitational pull. How much less was the billion-troy question. The extent of gravitational decrease gave astrogeologists their first estimate at how much ice a tapped-out claim might have. The lower-gee the rock, in comparison to its pre-mined gee, the more porous it was now—and thus, the more ice its tunnels could hold. In short: lower gee, more sugar.

Just because the rock had lots of tunnels did not mean that all those tunnels would be filled with ice. But you had to start somewhere. So you always started with a gravitational survey, and subtracted that measurement from the original-claim gee.

The general rule was: over two-thirds, holdin' a turd. Sugar-rock prospectors didn't bother going any further with a claim, unless its tapped-out gravity was below about sixty-five or seventy percent of the original. It took a lot more disassembler to process rock than it did ice, and when the number of pores was too few, the amount of energy needed to mine the ice was greater than the energy locked up in it.

If the tapped-out stroid's gravity was substantially *lighter* than the original survey gee, on the other hand, this was a big flag that the rock had sugar-rock potential. They would then expect him to do seismic testing to calculate how much of the rock's void space was filled with ice. And *those* results would be exceedingly difficult to falsify. No, the simplest way to shut this expedition down would be to falsify the stroid's gravitation. And Xuan knew of a way. As long as he could make the sleight-of-hand work.

Xuan felt the deceleration and vibrations that meant they were approaching their target; a lurch and a thud meant they had touched down. Mr. Mills radioed Xuan, instructing him to suit up and meet the others in the cargo bay. When he got there, Mills was nowhere to be seen. The pilot and the four—well, cargo workers, Xuan supposed he should call them, though he was unable to think of them now as anything other than thugs—were there, however. And it did not escape his notice that they all carried sidearms. As they gathered Xuan's field equipment and stacked it at the hatch, Xuan sensed the pilot looking at him, as if daring him to say something about the weapons. Xuan played dumb.

"Are you expecting trouble from claim jumpers?" he asked.

"Yeah," the pilot said.

Xuan refrained from rolling his eyes. "Do stay sharp, then, won't you? This will take a while, and I certainly don't want any trouble."

"We will. Wait here. We're going to check things out first." Which was an odd thing to do—at least for a claim they had permission to test. Xuan figured it was best not to bring this up.

"All right—um, what is your name?" Xuan asked.

"Jesse."

"Jesse. And you may call me Professor Xuan."

The young man seemed uneasy. "You wait here, then, Professor Xuan, till I give you the all-clear."

Xuan finished suiting up and turned on his air. The pilot bled out the cargo bay air, and then opened the side hatch all the way and extended the ramp. The five men left. Xuan perched on a cargo container and waited. Near the back of the bay he saw racks filled with stacks of crates labeled "Glock" and "KBR." K. B. Rand was a Martian weapons and tactical systems manufacturer. They made missiles and bombs. Glock specialized in rifles and handguns.

Xuan sank against a crate, appalled. What had he gotten himself into?

The pilot reentered ten minutes later and told Xuan it was safe to come out. He joined Jesse at the head of the ramp. The hired hands had posted themselves at positions where they could see the entire site, as well as much of the surrounding terrain. They had their weapons out.

Xuan left Jesse at the top of the ramp, and bounded down onto the stroid to find a good spot to set up. As he would expect of an abandoned mine, all was quiet. Near the shuttle's nose stood the mine entrance, which was fitted with a metal bulkhead and an entry port. Portions of the stroid's interior were likely habitable, then. At least, they had once been.

Also nearby were four big tanks, marked as methane, oxygen, nitrogen, and peroxide. They were unusually large. Whoever owned this stroid was obviously a hoarder. Directly behind the ship were what looked like makeshift rocketbike launch ramps. Close to the ridge at the mine entrance squatted two massive machines: a tunneler, spare cables and reels, grinders, a big hopper, and a bagging station. Over all this towered a Brobdingnagian mechanical earthmover for cutting, compressing, and shooting mined ore into space. Racks of smaller equipment parts, several slag piles, and a mountainous midden also stood nearby.

Xuan bounded around, pausing to poke at the ground with a rod. Quite compact, and in some areas there was no dust—only solid nickel-iron ore. Very high quality. He looked up. The sun—near zenith now—moved swiftly across the dark sky, making shadows crawl across the ground. This rock had a rotational period of only a few minutes. It would be good, then, to arrange things so that the sun was rising behind him and into the others' faces when he opened the back of the machine. It would make it more difficult for them to see what he was doing inside the gravitometer.

Xuan ordered the others to bring his equipment. "Leave the rest there for the moment," he said, pointing at the bags and boxes lined up at the cargo bay door. "We won't need any of that unless the gravitometer gives us a low reading."

He looked for a good place to set up: a place where the ground was firm, stable, and flat. The ore was close to the surface here. Dust and clots of dirt collected in dips and valleys. As a quick test, he dropped a wrench and surreptitiously counted as it drifted downward: sixty seconds to touch down in the dust? Eighty? Quite a bit less than on 25 Phocaea, at any rate. Old claim; big, high-end equipment; well-stocked supplies; high-quality ore: all his instincts were telling him that this rock had been extensively mined—a prime sugar-rock candidate. He only hoped these men were not experienced enough rock hoppers to detect these clues.

He found a spot as close as he could make it to a pile of slag—this would make it harder for them to move behind him while he set up the gravitometer. He prepped the site, sweeping away dirt with a hand brush—tossing small stones and nuggets of metal out of the way—and measured the grade in several spots with a laser level, pausing to wipe away dust that had settled on his faceplate. Meanwhile, the others milled around. The sun set and rose twice while he was prepping the site. He had to time this right.

"We'll do it here," he said finally, and pulled a paint can and some lights out of his kit. He marked four points on the stroid surface with phosphorescent paint. "Bring that big box and that table—yes, that one. Put them right here, where I've marked with paint. Careful! Don't jostle the box. You might throw off the calibration."

Two of the hired hands shuffled and wobbled over, steering the box. *Space neophytes,* Xuan thought. Jesse the pilot brought the table. Xuan had them move the table around while he adjusted leg lengths and took measurements. Then he fired the bolts that fixed the table to the stroid's surface. He instructed them to put the box on the table and bolt it on. The flood lights he positioned such that they would cast a shadow on him when he stood behind the gravitometer. Sunup came again while he did this, and sundown.

Gravitometers had been around for centuries. In concept, they were simple. A pendulum's period—how quickly it swung from peak to peak of its arc—depended on two and only two things: how long the pendulum cord was, and how strong the gravity was. It didn't matter how hard you swung it or how high the peaks were, the period was always the same. The quicker the swing, the stronger the gravity. The slower the swing, the weaker.

Xuan's gravitometer was designed to measure the very faint gravities of asteroids, a meter-and-a-quarter tall metal box with a light inside and a window through which you could see the pendulum. The box was bolted to a table that had shock absorbers in the legs. The weighted pendulum inside the box was attached to an actuating trigger for the pendulum, and a counter. Since asteroids varied greatly in volume and density, the pendulum length could be varied using three settings. The machine took the setting into account in its calculation. This was crucial to his plan. In addition, the weights could be changed out, to reduce vibrations that might affect the results. This was also crucial to Xuan, as it gave him access to the pendulum chamber to trick the machine.

Xuan had to assume that the men watching him—and they were watching him, though more out of boredom than suspicion—were familiar with the process of measuring a stroid's gravity. They had probably taken his students out on other claims.

Here was the tricky part. He had to take care not to deviate too much from what they were accustomed to seeing, while making the gravitometer lie about the stroid's density—but *only* if the rock was highly porous. Otherwise, the device had to tell the truth, or the measured gravity would be higher now than when it had first been discovered. This, as a practical matter, wasn't possible and it would clue his watchers into the fact that he had tampered with the instrument.

According to Xuan's calculation, a fifty-seven-second period for the pendulum swing would put it at its original density. Anything between fifty-seven and about eighty seconds, he could leave alone. Any more than eighty seconds or more to complete an arc meant the rock had big pores, and he'd have to work fast.

The sun was sinking toward the horizon again. Once down, it would rise behind him again in less than two minutes. Time to act. Xuan drew a deep steadying breath, took his wrench and a large screw bolt from his field kit, and radioed Mills. "We're almost ready. First I'll do a calibration, then readjust the machine as needed and take the measurement."

"All right. Fine," Mills said. "Jesse, you copy?"

"Roger that," the pilot replied.

"Report his findings as he receives them."

"Will do." The pilot moved over next to Xuan and looked over his shoulder at the device. He again touched a glove to his weapon in a mixture of bellicosity and anxiety. Jesse the pilot was obviously even more nervous than Xuan, who surmised that he was not used to his role as a thug.

Xuan released the pendulum and counted in his head as it arced lazily down: one, cryptocrystalline; two, cryptocrystalline, three . . . By the time he got to thirty . . . forty—*choi oi!* The pendulum had not even reached the halfway point! He stopped the test. His heart knocked insanely against his ribs. Sweat poured down his face and torso. Calm; stay calm.

This rock had to be more than half vacuum. Or ice.

"One last adjustment should do the trick," he said. His voice quavered. Get it under control. He thought of Jane. *Be like rock.* He jumped over the table, opened the back of the gravitometer, and wrapped the pendulum wire many quick turns around the bolt. Quickly now, but calmly. Shorten it by half.

Sunrise could occur any second, and he needed to be done with this adjustment before it did. *Damn it, Xuan. At this rate you'll ruin everything, and not just for yourself. Focus!* He eyeballed it as best he could, then closed the back of the instrument, as the sun rose again. It'd have to do.

"Time to measure," he said. He returned to the front of the device, cocked and retriggered the pendulum. As it arc'd downward, on its now-much-shorter arc, he said, "What we are hoping for is a period of substantially greater than fifty-seven seconds. The longer it takes for the pendulum to complete its arc, the more likely we have a good sugar-rock candidate."

While he talked, the others came over to watch.

"Please!" he snapped, and they all jumped. "Don't touch the table. You'll throw off the measurement. It's a sensitive instrument."

All of them edged nervously away.

They waited almost twenty minutes—the device required ten full arcs to complete its internal calculation. He counted in his head; it looked as though the average swing was coming out at about sixty seconds or so. A much shorter period than the real thing . . . but would it be enough? Then the display on the device's front gave its reading.

Xuan had fooled the machine! He did not allow his relief to show, but made a big deal out of tapping out a calculation on his heads-up. "Hmm. I'm getting a reading of about 0.0102 gee, or a net decrease in density of about fifteen percent. Sorry, gents. It looks like this claim is a bust. No chance of there being enough ice to trouble with here."

"You sure of that reading?" Mills said. "Jesse?"

"Everything seems on the level, sir," Jesse said, after a pause to run his own numbers. "The original claim was twelve thousandths of a gee, and according to the gravitometer readout, this one is around eighty-five percent of that. Not much room for ice in this rock."

"Above two thirds, it's a turd," one of them said. The rest chuckled.

Mills said, "With all this big equipment, on a hundred-year-old, nearly pure nickel-iron rock? Seems strange."

"Not so strange," Xuan replied. "I've seen many such rocks. The owner stakes a claim and then dies, or leaves, and nobody else picks it up."

"Hmmm. Perhaps you should measure again, just to be sure."

"I can, if you like," Xuan said. "But it won't change the result." His heartbeat was loud in his ears.

A pause. "Fine. Wrap it up."

Xuan allowed himself a slow, deep breath.

Kam, Amaya, and Geoff did a straight-in, reverse-power descent, well over the horizon from the ship's line of sight, rather than the more fuel-efficient orbital flyby and gradual descent they normally used. Geoff thought these measures were a bit much; it was not all that unusual for there to be confusion about claims. It would be embarrassing if the testers were just some guys from the university, and found out about the precautions Geoff, Kam, and Amaya were taking.

They had to be careful about dust. You kick up dust in a low-gee environment, it goes way up and takes days to settle back down. So they touched down a few kilometers from the mine entrance and rode their bikes slowly over the craggy, metal-ore terrain, avoiding craters and valleys where dust collected and always keeping the hill that was Ouroboros's main "mountain range" between them and the ship. They passed the heat exchanger, a set of big iron pipes in a shallow trench, and the chemical plant, three distillation towers with surge tanks, heating units, and racks of pipes.

Soon they reached the hill that housed the mine entrance. Just over the ridge stood the ship—they could see its top fin. Joey Spud's earthmover, which he had named Cronus after some deity who had swallowed his children whole, towered above the ridge, its metal arms reaching hundreds of meters into the dark sky.

The heat vent they planned to use was a tin stovepipe that jutted several meters into the sky, starting about halfway up the rocky hillside. First they headed up the hill to scope out the activity at the ship. They lay down at the crest, crawled forward—an awkward process in their pressure suits—and peered down. Five people were milling around while a sixth poked at the ground with a stick. The five mill-arounders had weapons. That seemed ominous—but there *were* pirates and claim jumpers out there. Geoff didn't want to jump to conclusions.

"They're still doing the setup," he said. He pointed. "The guy in the light blue suit, the one with the stick, that'd be Professor Xuan. That's a university-issue suit. First they'll take some gravitational measurements, and then they'll take soundings. They'll be a while."

Amaya crept farther over the hill's crest, and rolled over—ever so slowly—to check for the vent from that vantage point. Then she crept back to join them. "I think we'll be OK," she said. "The top of the pipe is below line-of-sight from where they are."

"Good. Let's do this. Kam, keep watch. Warn us if they head this way."

"Right." Kam got out his binoculars, and Geoff and Amaya leapt back down the hillside.

They worked quickly. Amaya hooked her pony up to the emergency line, and then they disconnected and lengthened her main air tubes with spare tubing and duct tape. Next Geoff brought the tubes up over her head so her pack could be lowered separately. They got the main tank hooked back up and tested, and then Geoff duct-taped the air tubes to the shoulders of her suit, so the lines couldn't be easily pulled out. He gave a couple of sharp tugs. "That should hold."

She removed the pony bottle and stuffed it into her utility kit. Then she clipped her kit to her suit. Geoff hooked the tether to her harness.

She looked up at the top of the stovepipe. Geoff knew she was thinking about what had happened to Carl, trapped outside with no air. Geoff said, "If you get in too tight a squeeze, give three sharp jerks on the tether, and I'll pull you out—with my bike if need be."

"I'll be fine," she said.

"Good. Hang on." Geoff ran her tether around a boulder, and secured the other end to his bike's handlebars. Then he took hold to brace her.

Kam radioed them. "They're setting up the equipment now. Nobody's looking over this way. They must not have got us on radar, coming in."

"Maybe not."

"There could be more people inside, though. I thought I saw some movement through the cockpit portal."

"All right. Thanks."

Kam said, "I know you'll ace it, Amaya."

She gave him the spacer OK sign: left arm crooked with the glove touching helmet crown; right arm straight out and up at a forty-five-degree angle.

"Ready?" Geoff asked. In answer, Amaya gathered up half the slack in her tether and clipped it to one shoulder. Geoff handed her the main air tank. She gripped it in one hand and leapt up to the top of the stovepipe. As she arced over the pipe, she grabbed hold with her other hand. In a single motion, she swung atop the vent and landed in a crouch, balanced on the top edges of the pipe. Amaya gave another OK sign and flipped on her helmet light. She dropped her airtank into the vent and dove in after it.

The tether in Geoff's hands tightened suddenly, nearly pulling him off-balance. He braced his boots against a boulder and started giving out slack. He heard her breathing, heard the rustlings as she descended the vent.

"Amaya, talk to me."

"Past the vertical section," she radioed. "Sliding down the incline. Infamous bottleneck turn just ahead. About six meters. Hang on." A pause; rustling. She pinged his waveface, and in his heads-up he saw what she saw: a small tunnel receding into darkness. It narrowed to a funnel, just ahead. Along the pipe's inner edge was the power and radio conduit they had put in last year. She could not cut through it, as it was a live line and the shutoff switch was inside the mine. It had not been in her way before. Dangling in the center of their shared vision was Amaya's airtank, attached by its tubes to her helmet.

"How are your lines?"

"Holding up. No leaks." Another pause, as she moved downward. "OK, here's the bottleneck. Moment of truth." She shoved her utility kit through. Next she turned the tank lengthwise and shoved it through the narrowed opening. Geoff could see it resting on the tunnel floor just beyond.

"Testing the line. Two tugs." Her headlight danced around, and he felt the line pull twice against his grip. "You felt it?"

"I felt it. You're good."

Nothing happened for a moment, except her breathing. He watched her air lines swaying. "Take your time," he said. Another pause. "Amaya?" he asked. No reply.

"She all right?" Kam asked him, from up on the hill.

That's it, he thought. *This isn't going to work.* "Come on back, Amaya. I'm pulling you up." He tugged, but she resisted, wedging herself against his pull with her arms. "No! No. I've come this far, I'm going through. More slack. More. Motherfucking asswipe *shitberries!*"

With that, she forced her way into the opening. Geoff held his breath. Her hands flailed in front of his vision, trying to gain purchase on the sides of the tunnel beyond the bottleneck. More than a minute passed, while her light jumped and jerked. *This is insane*, he thought. *We shouldn't have done this.* But then the scene in his waveface shifted.

"I'm through!" she gasped. "I'm through. I've been reborn. Just like the birth canal, all over again." She lay on her back beyond the bottleneck, and her light reflected on the roof of the small tunnel. All three laughed in relief.

Amaya got out her tools and loosened the bolts that secured the maintenance panel to the mouth of the stovepipe. She took a crowbar from her kit, hooked it against the edge of the panel, and used it to brace herself against the air that rushed past her—forced the panel farther open, and tumbled into the main tunnel. Then she braced herself and slammed the bulkhead back into place. Geoff could tell she was leaning against the wall by the now-closed vent, waiting till the room repressurized. Finally she removed her helmet. "I'm in." Then— "Shhh!" she hissed. "Quiet."

She stood up, tucked her helmet under her arm, and adjusted her mini-cam, mounted at her right temple. Geoff caught a glimpse of what she saw: a sudden, shadowed movement across the intersection of this small chamber's mouth with the main passage.

"One of the maintenance robots?"

"It was moving too fast. And the shape and color weren't right."

"Stand fast. Kam!" Geoff said, and looked up the hill. Kamal was still there, keeping watch. "Are they inside the mine?"

"No. They're crowded around the professor's instrument. The mine entrance is still sealed."

"Could someone have gone in before we got here?"

"They wouldn't be able to open the lock without the code," Kam said.

"Unless they hacked it," Geoff said. "Or cut through."

"I'm going to take a look," Amaya whispered. Brandishing her crowbar, she cautiously rounded the corner. *"Bikkuri shita!"* she gasped.

"What is it?"

"Nothing," she said in a disgusted tone. "It's your damn skeletons."

Geoff saw: the glass skeletons had escaped containment. One cavorted here; another leapt there; a third tumbled through the air. As she approached the machine shop by the mine entrance, Geoff saw numerous others, scampering about. She whacked one with her crowbar, and it exploded. "Just like virtual golf," she said, and whacked another.

Two others crawled out of a large puddle at the base of the assembler fluid vat while Amaya worked. They seemed to be lasting longer than they had been at the much higher gee in Heavitown.

"The floor is coated with glass turds," she said. *"Kuso!* You and your stupid art project."

"Yeah." He sighed. "Sorry."

She went over and squatted by the vat, and Geoff saw through her cam that the tank valve had a slow leak. He remembered crashing into it during his fight with Ian. Amaya patched the leak with duct tape from her utility bag. "That should do for now."

"If we're going to go talk to those people down there," Kam said, "we'd better do it now. They seem to be finished with their tests. They're wrapping things up."

"What? So soon? They can't have finished their soundings yet. Let me see!" Geoff bounded up to where Kam was in two big leaps. Kam made room for him—he bellied up to the ridge and took a look through Kam's binocs. Sure enough, they were folding up the equipment.

Kam was looking at him. "Geoff . . ."

"What?"

"We could just . . . you know . . ."

"What?"

"Let them leave."

Geoff said, "Kam, either they are legit, in which case they need to know sooner rather than later that this claim is taken. Or they aren't, which would mean Professor Xuan is in deep shit, and we have to help him."

"So why not call the police?"

"We will, if they're secretly criminals. But Moriarty himself said all the paperwork's in order. The police are as swamped as they were yesterday, and they are still going to treat us like a bunch of punks. Like they always do. Unless we have some kind of hard proof. To get that, we need Professor Xuan."

Kam sighed.

"Amaya," Geoff said, "I'm giving you access to my view. Stand by. If there's trouble, we'll alert you, and you know what to do."

"Have several spud guns loaded and primed in the lock," she said. "Open the mine entrance only on your signal. Be prepared to shut the door behind you the instant you enter. If it comes to that."

"Right."

"In fact . . ." she chuckled. "I have an idea, something extra special, to go along with it."

"What kind of idea?"

"You'll see . . . if it turns out we need it. I'll need a few minutes to prep," she said. "Stand by. I'll signal you when I'm ready."

It was getting late and Jane was exhausted. She called Sean to take him up on the offer of a place to stay.

"Very good," he said. "Just head right over. I'm working late tonight, but I'll let Lisa know you're coming."

On the way up there, she stopped at Charles and Rowan's place to pick up Xuan's and her belongings. They lived only a level up from Deirdre and Sal, so Jane decided to stop by her friends' place while she was nearby.

Dee entered the room, tying her robe. Jane already knew, but she asked, "Is Sal . . . ?"

"Gone." Dee shrugged. "Don't know where he is. Don't care. I've kicked him out. I'm done."

Jane sat down across from her. "So. How can I help?"

Dee sat, too, and gave her a penetrating look. "From what I'm hearing, you have enough to deal with right now, Jane. Don't worry about me. Frankly, I'm relieved. Trying to make that marriage work, it was killing me. Just killing me. I love him, you know? We've been through a lot together. He's not a perfect husband, but I never doubted his love for me. But he's a terrible father. He's . . . just . . . too broken. And nobody hits my boys. *Nobody.*" Her fist balled and a muscle jumped in her jaw.

Jane said, "Sean told me what happened."

"So, I have to get my finances in order, and I have to mourn my son. My Carl." She pressed a fist against her mouth, and Jane watched her struggle against her grief. "But I'll be all right. Eventually." She leaned back with a sigh. "Truth to tell, I feel relieved it's over."

"Dee . . ." Jane said slowly. She had had a thought. She had already given away one of her berths on the *Sisyphus,* and she wasn't about to use the other without Xuan. Dee's family was from the moon. "Ever wanted to return home?"

She explained her situation. Dee looked thoughtful. "That's incredibly generous of you, Jane. But Wednesday? its awfully sudden . . ."

"I'm sure I can wrangle a ticket for you to use whenever it's convenient. Just let me know and I will sign it over to you."

"I'll think it over. Thank you, Jane. You've been a good friend."

They made their good-byes and Jane left. Despite Carl's death, despite everything, she realized she felt better about Dee and her situation than she had in a very long time.

Next Jane headed over to Sean and Lisa's place in Design Plaza, near the city's administrative offices. The neighborhood was only a couple of levels below the Hub. Lisa greeted her at the door, floating barefoot in her robe, smelling of perfumed lotion. Her long, wavy hair, black shot through with white, was damp and bobbed about her face.

"I'm sorry to get in so late," Jane said, but Lisa wouldn't hear any apology. She showed her the spare room and bathroom. Extra towel rolls and soaps hung in the air, still settling from Lisa's preparations. Lisa offered to make her cocoa while she unpacked.

"I'll be fine. Don't let me disturb your evening routine."

"Will Xuan be arriving tonight?" Lisa asked.

"He should be. But I'll be glad to let him in. You go on to bed."

"All right, then. Help yourself to anything in the kitchen."

Once she had bathed and dressed in her pajamas, Jane nestled in the hammock and took a look at Masahiro's latest set of e-mails. He had found numerous bootleg videos of the Uraniaville location. As he had warned her, several of them had crude avatars or other changes inserted into them. But it didn't matter. Because six of them, created by different people in different parts of the world, showed that Nathan Glease and Andrew Mills had encountered Ivan Kovak in the plaza near the kiosk.

As Ivan walked away from the kiosk with the groceries and the little girl, Glease and Mills had approached him from behind. He turned, and at first seemed calm, but after Glease spoke, Kovak maneuvered his daughter behind him. He drew himself up taller, thrust out his chest, and spoke, jabbing a finger at Glease. Glease said something else, with a glance at Mills, who loomed over Kovak imposingly; Kovak said something brief, scooped up the child, and stalked away.

What a piece of work you are, Grease, Jane thought. She sat back, twiddling a lock of hair. The date of the videos was the eighteenth of March—one month and ten days ago—only a few days before his family left him. Did this recording show a falling-out among conspirators? Or did it show a man confronted with a past he thought he had escaped?

Either way, it provided conclusive proof of a link between Kovak and the mob. Either the Ogilvies had paid for someone to hack Upside-Down's servers, Down on Earth, and/or someone within Upside-Down was dirty. Because only the bootlegs made within fourteen hours and ten minutes of the time and date stamped on the video showed the meeting. All recordings made after that showed only Kovak and his daughter leaving the kiosk—just as the official, laundered versions had.

She called Aaron on a line secured with her newfound privacy technology. He responded instantly. "What do you have?"

"I'm transmitting two sets of files," she said, typing inwave as she spoke. "The first are the official 'Stroiders' copies, requested through our local library, of the tampered videos. The second set are several bootlegged videos made by 'Stroiders' viewers back on Earth." She clicked *Send*. "I've flagged the important ones to watch. The bootlegs made within two hours and ten minutes of release back on Earth show Ivan Kovak meeting with Nathan Glease and his muscle, Mills. The rest do not. This gives you everything you need to connect Ogilvie & Sons to the destruction of the ice, and to Marty's murder."

Aaron's eyes widened as she spoke. "God is merciful! I'll call Jerry Fitzpatrick. We'll have those two behind bars in no time." He lifted a hand to disconnect, but paused. "Thank you for this."

She started to say "I'm doing it for Marty," but realized that that was not the whole story. *I don't know if I can ever completely forgive you, Aaron,* she thought. *But I'm going to try.* "You're welcome."

26

Xuan directed two of the hired hands to break down and load the equipment, while Jesse radioed Mills in the cockpit. "Sir, I'm going to call in to request a spot in the landing queue for when we arrive."

"Fine—go ahead," Mills said, in a bored tone. Xuan heard the staticky clicks that meant Jesse had switched over to a different channel. A moment later he came back on the comm. "Professor, Stores Chief Moriarty is on frequency one oh six point oh for you," he said. Xuan switched over.

"Ngo Minh Xuan here."

"Xuan, this is Sean. I just got off the phone with Commissioner Navio. Lisa and I would like to offer you two a place to stay."

Xuan winced at the mention of Jane's name. "That would be lovely. Thank you for the invitation. We'll be headed back shortly."

"Good. Just come straight to our place. I'm beaming you the address."

They made their good-byes, and Xuan signed off, heart pounding hard.

He might still be able to bluff his way out of this. He started up the ramp, acting as if nothing was wrong, though the open cargo door loomed like the barrel of a weapon. By the time he reached the top, Mills stood there, holding a large pipe wrench in both hands.

"Gentlemen, I believe we have been hosed. No, no—leave those there," he said. The hired hands were carrying Xuan's bags and cartons up into the ship. "I think the good professor and I need to have a little talk."

Mills put an arm across Xuan's shoulders, gripped him by the air intake lines at his helmet. "Professor No, the Stores chief just referred to Commissioner Jane. Am I to understand that Jane Navio is your wife?"

It's bad enough you are a thug, Xuan thought, *the least you could do is get my name right.* "That is correct. Why do you ask?"

"Well, I'll just tell you why. I have a sensitive bullshit detector, and I've been smelling something off about you. I'm willing to bet that your wife sent you here to fuck with us." He jerked Xuan by the air lines. Xuan's feet flew out from under him. Mills set him down again, still holding on to him. "I'm willing to bet that you screwed with the results of your test to make us think this rock has less ice than it does."

Xuan summoned indignation. "No, sir. Your assumption is not correct. I am head of the Astrogeology Department at Phocaea U. Check it for yourself; my bio is on the university's wavesite under faculty. You asked for someone on short notice. All the grad students were already assigned to other duties. I have no idea who you people are or what you are doing, other than surveying a potential ice claim, nor do I know why my wife's name should matter to you."

Mills chuckled. "Ah, I see. He has no idea who we are, gentlemen. Let me set you straight. We are the new bosses in town, and we don't like people like you and your wife getting in our way."

"The last thing I want is to get in your way. I just want to do my job."

"Maybe he's telling the truth, sir," Jesse said.

"Let me handle this," Mills snapped. "Professor, have you ever seen what this"—he swung the wrench—"does to a faceplate in a vacuum?"

Xuan saw in Mills's gaze that he wanted Xuan to defy him. He was looking for an excuse to kill him. The sun was down now, but with his augmented vision, Xuan could see clearly. Five armed men were at the base of the ramp, and Mills, a man nearly twice his size, had a firm grip on his air hoses. If he tried to leap away, Mills would smash his faceplate, or wrench his lines out. And even if he could escape, where would he go? He only had a few hours' worth of air, and didn't know

the codes to the mine locks, or if the mine was even habitable anymore.

I won't survive this, he thought. He wished he had thirty seconds out-
of-time so he could send Jane a note. Tell her how much she meant to
him. Tell her to tell the kids good-bye.

Buy time, he thought. "Might I point out that I would be more useful
to you prior to exposure to vacuum than I would be afterward, if my
wife is indeed obstructing your efforts?"

Mills eyed him, swinging his wrench back and forth, back and forth.
Then he shrugged and lowered the wrench. "You have a point. Oh well."

He gave Xuan a sudden, vicious shove. Xuan tumbled into space. He
flailed, and slowly settled to land in a crouch at the base of the ramp.
"You want to stay on my good side," Mills said, "then rerun your test."

Xuan came back to his feet. He had already removed the bolt from
the pendulum wire—the bolt that had shortened the pendulum and
made the gravitometer lie about the rock's density. Mills would kill him
if he tried to reinstall it. But they were going to anyway. He might as
well try. He directed Jesse and the others to take the equipment back to
the location where he had done the testing earlier.

As they neared the spot, two rocketbikers came out from behind the
equipment racks at high speed. They had a net stretched between them.
Mills saw them and shouted, but too late—two of the hired hands got
caught in the net. Xuan's night vision allowed him to see them just in
time to push himself out of the way. The net swooped past. He saw that
Jesse and another of the guards had leapt out of the way. In his radio
headset, a young man shouted, "Professor Xuan—*run!*"

He didn't need to be told twice. He leapt up and out, off the mine tailings and over the shuttle—with a kick off its top fin, to launch himself
higher—and arced toward the bikes, which were hauling a bouncing
load of arms, legs, and asses off into the distance. The two unbound mercenaries stumbled after them, shooting. As Xuan sank beyond the shuttle, he looked back: Mills had pulled his gun. Xuan of course heard
nothing, but a bullet nicked the top fin, just missing him, and blew up.
Exploding bullets: nasty. The mist that dispersed after the explosion

suggested they might also contain a biotoxin. Then the shuttle blocked Mills from view.

Xuan landed in a crouch, and started bounding away from the two guards. The bikers had jettisoned their net and were skidding in an arc back toward the shuttle as Jesse and the two hired hands, still enmeshed, tumbled away across the landscape. The bikers shot a new net between them just before they reached the two mercenaries still standing, and scooped them up. The bikers turned in unison, sped up the launch ramp—soared into the sky—jettisoned the net, fired their thrusters in reverse. The two netted men went flying into orbit and the bikers dropped back onto the surface.

Mills had emerged from around the ship. He landed . . . flailed . . . fell . . . stood again. He pointed his weapon at Xuan.

"Freeze where you are, No!" Mills still mispronounced it. Infuriating.

As Mills shouted, one of the bikers stopped beside Xuan, throwing a fountain of spinning gravel up. "Care for a lift, Professor?"

Xuan thought he recognized the young man's face through his faceplate, but he wasn't sure. He batted the gravel aside, swung onto the bike, and grabbed hold. The other biker surged past, straight at Mills. Mills's shots went wide, as he dodged and fell in a slow, wide arc. By the time Xuan and his driver passed Mills, he was back to his feet and shooting again—Xuan could tell from the gun's recoil. An exploding bullet hit the bike just behind his seat, blowing a hole as big as two bunched fists. Xuan was nearly thrown off by the impact. The bike swerved. More mist spread. Xuan hoped that vacuum destroyed whatever was in those bullets. His driver got it under control—the rockets flared and the bike leaped forward—Xuan hung on for dear life.

Jesse and the first two henchmen had disentangled themselves from the net by this time and bounded back toward them, firing their guns. Chunks of bullet-struck ore scattered into the black sky.

Xuan's rescuers reached the front of the shuttle and headed straight for the mine entrance. Xuan thought, *This won't work. They will not be able to stop the bikes, enter the code to get the doors to open, and close them again before Mills and his henchmen are on top of us.* But the bikers did not slow as they zoomed past the shuttle cockpit.

"*Now,* Amaya!" the driver shouted.

A woman's voice in their headset said, "Heads up on your left—there's a tank!" As she spoke, the massive door lifted, slowly, only meters away ... and Xuan thought he was hallucinating. Skeletons came pouring out—leaping, capering, rising up—tumbling over one another like demented acrobats, out of a tank in the airlock.

There were so many—they were everywhere! Xuan shielded his eyes against the impact. The skeletons burst at the slightest touch. Beads went flying like buckshot, glimmering in the rays of the sun that now rose above the horizon. Both bikers blasted through the skeletons and skidded, ducking low, into the airlock. Xuan ducked, too, to avoid being struck by the still-ascending door.

Jesse and the two remaining mercenaries stumbled, slowed, took swipes at the advancing wave of skeletons. But Mills waded right through, ignoring them as they exploded all around. He was only meters away now, and leveled his gun at Xuan. "No, step out of the airlock, or die."

As he said *die,* a projectile struck him in the midsection. He went soaring backward and slammed into the shuttle's giant tire. His gun went flying, too, and skittered across the stroid's metallic surface. Orange goo covered Mills's chest and faceplate, crystallizing.

Someone stood at the airlock entrance—someone named Amaya? She dropped a big pipe, picked up another.

"One of you get the door!" she said. "I'll hold them off."

She pointed the pipe at Jesse and fired. A big orange projectile struck Jesse's shoulder, causing him to fall backward. The orange blob sailed up, wobbling—goo spattered the shuttle on the "Ogilvie & Sons" logo.

"I've got the door," the second driver said, and sprang from his bike toward the emergency shutdown switch. Amaya picked up and fired a different pipe gun, this one smaller, at the hired hands, who ducked, while the second biker hit the switch. The door reversed itself, started closing. The girl picked up yet another small tube and fired it. Xuan could not figure out what she was shooting. Balls of putty? Chemicals?

Whatever they were, the makeshift launchers expelled them with enough force to knock the attackers down.

Xuan saw through the haze of churned-up dust, assembler grapes, and gravel that Mills had gotten to his feet again. He shuffled toward them, swiping at the crap on his faceplate, batting skeletons and other sky-borne debris out of the way. Then the door locked into place.

While they waited for the lock to pressurize, Xuan turned to his rescuers. "I think you just saved my life."

"Glad to help, Professor Xuan," one of them said. Xuan peered at the one who had spoken, the driver who had picked him up.

"I know you. Are you one of my former students?"

"No, sir. I'm Geoff Agre. A friend of your son, Hugh. These are my friends, Kamal Kurupath and Amaya Toguri." The other two waved.

Xuan belatedly recognized the young man. "Of course! It's been a long time. How did you happen to be here? How did you know I was in trouble?"

"This is my stroid. We come out here sometimes just to hang out," Geoff said.

Amaya added, "We were suspicious when we saw the shuttle. They never contacted Geoff or asked permission to test our rock."

Kamal said, "Geoff and I were just heading over to ask what you were doing here when the big man started shoving you around and threatening you with a crowbar. We figured that was our cue to intervene."

"And what are those?" Xuan asked, gesturing at the pipes Amaya had used to fend off Mills and Jesse. "What did you use as projectiles?"

He caught a flash of a smile. "They're spud launchers. Well, the big ones actually launch larger vegetables. I used spoiled pumpkins."

Xuan coughed out a surprised laugh. "Excellent choice."

The clearance light came on. They removed their helmets, and yawned, equalizing the pressure in their ears, as the inner door slid open.

The young men walked their bikes in, and the woman shut the inner airlock door. "Tread carefully," Amaya warned. "Assembler grapes are all over the place. I've got the ventilators on high, but a lot are still airborne."

"Clever idea with the bone dancers," Kamal remarked, as he and Geoff parked their bikes. "How did you get the tank into the lock?"

"I pushed it in with one of the ore haulers," Amaya said, with a gesture at the towing vehicles lined up near the back of the chamber. "I figured you guys could use a distraction. I peeled the top off the tank so they could get out. It sure didn't take long to fill up the airlock, either. Geoff, you'd better figure out a way to kill that program, or we're going to be up to our asses in skeletons again in no time."

Geoff said, "But at least they came in useful for something."

"You made *those*?" Xuan asked, bemused.

Geoff gave him a sheepish look. "Don't tell anybody, OK?"

Xuan suppressed a smile. "I could be persuaded to remain silent. Under the circumstances."

He moved further into the main chamber. It was the typical mine entry cavern, with walls and roof gashed out by minerbot tooth and claw. The ore was primarily nickel-iron, showing signs of rust in spots—an indicator that this mine had been around awhile—and ribbed with veins of white quartz. On the cavern floor, conveyors and tracks extended into various passages. Air circulation fans, ducts, and mine gas sampling and testing gear hung from cables attached to the metal-ore ceiling. Of course, the occasional capering skeleton that scrambled up out of small pools of liquid was non-standard issue. These, thankfully, were smaller, shorter-lived, and fewer in number than the ones outside.

"I think we'd best keep our helmets and ponies close," he said. "And let's get our air tanks charged up in case we need to make a getaway."

"Well, we do have plenty of supplies, farther down the mine," Geoff said. "But it doesn't hurt to get them charged."

"I'll take care of it," Kamal said. He gathered everyone's airpacks and bounded over to a set of recharging racks nearby. Xuan clipped his helmet to his suit, then pulled his pony bottle out of the pocket in the leg of his suit, and hooked it up to the main line under his arm. Geoff went over to the security panel, and Xuan and Amaya joined him, treading carefully on the assembler beads. Bots were already cleaning them up, but there were a lot.

Visibility was still poor outside, from all the stuff kicked up in the fight, but surveillance cameras outside the mine showed Mills and the others appeared to be heading back into the ship. Geoff fiddled with some controls.

"They've changed comm channels," he said. "What are they up to?"

"We should send out a distress signal," Xuan said. "Right away."

"Good thought!"

Geoff typed in the code. In a second or two they heard the tones of an automated distress call. He leaned back against the console with folded arms. "And now we wait."

Amaya pointed. "Um, what's he doing?" One of the hired hands was bounding down the ramp carrying a tubular object. It looked a lot like a spud launcher, only the object in it was metal and had a pointed tip. He pointed it at the mine entrance. Geoff swore.

"It's a missile launcher! *Get back!*"

A concussion shook the cavern, knocking Xuan down. A parts rack toppled over and pinned him. The inner lock door puckered.

A breach alarm sounded, and they could hear the hiss of air being released from the cave through a crack in the airlock seal. Rocks fell—slowly but inexorably—all around him, and crunched into the big tanks and equipment. He twisted around, tried to push the rack off his torso. Pain shot through his chest and arm.

The others were still dodging debris. A big machine fell over onto the security console, which spat sparks. Carboys were knocked over, and solvents sloshed out, forming big, floating, toxic blobs. Air contaminant alarms started whooping. Xuan could barely hear the others over the noise. The stench was overpowering and Xuan coughed.

The others leapt over the rubble toward him. Kamal found a pipe and pried the rack off of him, and Geoff and Amaya pulled him out. "Are you all right?" Geoff shouted, over the din.

Something sticky was dripping in Xuan's eyes. He put his hand to his head, and it came away red. He had a gash on his forehead. He swiped at it. *Much higher gee,* Xuan realized, *and I'd have been crushed.* Kamal handed him a cloth. He pressed it to his wound.

"A little banged up," he said. "Hurts to breathe or move my right arm. I've broken a rib or two, I think. What happened?"

"They've taken out our radio. And our surveillance cameras."

"We have to get out of here! Can you get the airpacks?" Kamal asked Geoff and Amaya, gesturing. "We may need them."

They set the air recharging rack upright and extracted the airpacks from the rechargers. Meanwhile, Kamal helped Xuan over the pile of rubble.

"We'd better hurry!" Amaya shouted over the alarms. "If they fire another missile, the inner lock will go."

"There are some supplies we need!" Geoff replied. "I'll get the bots to grab what they can. Amaya, take the airpacks and lead the way to one of our bolt holes!"

"West Spider Way is best!" Amaya yelled.

"Meet you there," Geoff shouted back. "Go!"

Xuan did not like the idea of Geoff staying behind, even for a moment, but he trusted the young man's judgment that they needed certain materials here, and arguing would only waste time. Besides, it hurt too much to talk.

Kamal helped him into the side passage, while Amaya carried the airpacks. The main lights were out, but emergency lighting gave plenty of light, to Xuan's eyes. Amaya led the way down. They passed other passages and chambers, and through several locks. The air smelled dank, like rotting vegetation and dust. They came to a large room. Amaya dropped the airpacks into a recharging station by the door.

"I'll be right back," she said, and dashed out. Kamal helped Xuan to a chair, and went for a medkit.

Xuan looked around. This room had been outfitted as a waystation: it had firefighting equipment, air, and medical supplies. It also had bunks, a kitchen, and a console. Kamal brought the medical kit over and cleaned and bound Xuan's head wound.

"I think I have a broken collarbone," he said, "and a cracked rib."

"We have nanomeds. Nothing fancy but enough to accelerate the healing."

"Good. Let's also immobilize my arm and use some tape around my rib cage. That should do for now."

Kamal obliged. "You're lucky," he remarked, as he worked. "You might have been killed."

No argument there, Xuan thought.

A big *whump!* shook the walls and the floor. It knocked them tumbling into the air. A second, louder one set off more alarms. Choking clouds of dust rolled into the room. Xuan coughed spasmodically, twisting in the air. Jets sprayed icy water, which stung his exposed skin, mixing with the dust. He began shivering. Xuan could not see well out of his right eye. He settled to the floor, and gingerly poked at the sodden bandage with a finger. Bloody water dripped onto his hand. He looked over at Kamal. Muddy water ran down the young man's face, too.

"Wait here, I'll go check," Kamal said. But Amaya and Geoff entered, wearing their helmets and pony bottles. A platoon of small robots followed them, carrying more supplies, drinking water, and tools. Last came the rocketbikes, driving themselves. Geoff used a controller to park them in a corner, and then shut off the dust suppression stream at the console.

While Geoff and Amaya removed their helmets and started putting the new supplies away, Kamal finished taping Xuan's arm and redid the head dressing.

"What happened?" Xuan asked Geoff. "What were the explosions?"

"They launched another missile," Geoff said. "It took out the inner lock and explosively decompressed the entry cavern. But we were ready."

Amaya said, "I had a minerbot rig a charge at the West Spider Way shaft entrance. They're programmed for that. I triggered the cave-in as they entered—after Geoff and his bots made it into the shaft."

"We collapsed the back half of the entry cavern," Geoff said. "That should keep them out for now."

Amaya gave Xuan and the others a troubled look. "I think at least one of them was hit by flying debris. I saw blood."

"What do we do now?" Kamal asked. "We're trapped down here. The distress signal didn't go on long enough for anyone to hear it before they fired a missile at us. Nobody knows where we are."

"Yes, they do," Xuan said. "My trip out here was logged at the docks."

"And I called Sean Moriarty," Geoff said, "and let him know we were on our way out here. Remember?"

Amaya said, "We *could* dig our way out, if we had to. Use one of the little tunnelers."

Kamal shook his head. "Not if we wanted to get away. They'd hear it. They'd feel the vibrations. And where would we go, anyway?"

"If we could get a distress signal out," Geoff said thoughtfully, "that'd do the trick. If it wasn't detected and shut off, or destroyed . . ."

That all seemed too much to hope for.

"Are there any other ways out?" Xuan asked after a moment, "other than tunneling our way out?"

Geoff hesitated. "There's a venting shaft for heat and waste emissions. Amaya can get through it, but just barely. The rest of us won't fit, though, and neither would any of our bots or mining equipment."

Amaya said, "Which means I could climb out through the vent again, and go for help. My bike is still out there."

"They probably already found it," Geoff replied. "And you're low on fuel."

Kamal went on, "And the launch ramps are right next to the shuttle. It would be too risky. They'd see you go."

"I might be able to tap the fuel tanks up top."

"Amaya . . ."

"We have to do something!" she snapped at Geoff.

Xuan said, "I appreciate your willingness to risk your life, Amaya, that's very brave, but I got a good look at their cargo hold. They are armed with heavy munitions. Smart weaponry. They could shoot you out of the sky without even having to think about it. And they would."

Amaya looked away, distress straining her features.

"What if we just sit tight?" Kamal asked. "They can't get in. Eventually they will just go away."

Again, Xuan had to shake his head. "I don't think they'll be going away. They can't afford for this rock to be discovered by the authorities."

They all looked at Xuan. Geoff said, "It's because of the ice, isn't it?"

"It is. Have you taken your own measurements?"

"No, but we figured it had to be a lot—several tons at least."

Xuan looked at him askance. "Multiply that figure by about a billion and you'll come closer to the actual figure."

The three youths all spoke at once: "*What?*" "That can't be!" "Are you *sure*?"

He answered the last. "Not absolutely sure—there may be large pockets of vacuum. Have you explored? How extensive are the tunnels?"

"There aren't that many," Geoff said. "Most are sealed off." He got a strange look on his face.

"With ice?"

Geoff nodded. "My God. You honestly believe this is a real live sugar rock, don't you? I mean, like the original? Gigatons' worth?"

"I think that is a very real possibility," Xuan answered. "And Mr. Mills suspects likewise. I jury-rigged the gravitometer to suggest that this mine is still heavy with metals, not yet tapped out, but he did not trust my results.

"Eventually," he said after a moment, "they will either use the big mining equipment up on the surface to dig in after us, or use explosives to ensure we can't escape. They'll want to know we're good and dead."

They all looked sick. "What can we do?" Kamal asked.

"We can't fight heavy munitions," Xuan replied, "but we can fight the men who wield them. Let us rest, and take stock, and we will figure out a plan."

Once ensconced in Sean and Lisa's guest room, Jane forwarded to Harbaugh the evidence of Glease's meeting with Kovak, with a note: "As promised. Attached herewith, proof Nathan Glease was responsible for the ice disaster."

Even if they managed to catch Glease, he—or the Ogilvies—would find a way to reach out and harm her, her family, or some other innocent Phocaean. So next she spent some time on the monitoring software the Viridians had given her. She created a macro she called DeadMan: the software saved the video stream to a private archive of hers here on Phocaea. Every ten minutes the macro requested a sequence of microgestures, and waited thirty seconds. If the gestures were not forthcoming, DeadMan then beamed the video to the usual wavesites and e-mailed it to the local news media. She tested it to make sure it worked. Then she went to sleep.

In the middle of the night, the bell rang. Jane lofted herself into the living room, half awake, and opened the door, expecting to see Xuan or Sean. It was Glease, standing in a dustfall of dying "Stroiders" motes. He had a gun pointed at her. Jane glanced at her heads-up—precisely two a.m. Of course; the blackout window. Her heartbeat leapt. She activated DeadMan with a flicker of an eyelid.

"I can't begin to tell you," he said, "how irritating it is, the way you keep interfering with my plans, Commissioner."

Lisa came out of her room, belting her robe. "Is that Sean?"

Jane triggered the door lock and stepped into the corridor, forcing Glease to take a step back. "It's business," she said over her shoulder as the door slid shut. "Go back to bed." The door latched behind her.

Glease gave her a tight little smile. "Fast thinking. Saves a mess."

"Get to the point. What do you want?"

He tucked his gun into his jacket. "We're going on a little jaunt."

Jane pointedly looked around. They were on a Promenade level. Traffic was light, but a few people were out here and there and a trolley rattled past. "Why should I cooperate? Maybe you should just shoot me here and have done with it."

"Oh, no. I have other plans for you. Besides"—he leaned close and whispered in her ear—"we have Xuan."

He meant it. Her breath caught. "I'll come."

Glease took her up the Weesu stairwell to Level 60, and stopped at a private entrance to Kukuyoshi: the entry to the memorial garden. She went rigid as he keyed in a code. The door opened and he waved her in, but she refused to cross the threshold. "You have no right to be here."

"Oh, come now," he said. "You know the old saying. Might makes right." He emphasized the verb, and shoved her, hard. She stumbled out into the clearing where the memorial had been held, flailing midair in the one-fifth gee till she could grab the limb of a nearby tree with a foothand. "That's always been one of my favorite sayings."

"I hope you realize," Glease went on, while she climbed down, "this is nothing personal. I'm a company man. I have a family back home and we do cookouts on the weekend with our neighbors." He spread his arms. "If I could have done this without resorting to these more extreme measures, I would have gladly done so. But you have left me with little choice."

She alighted next to the memorial wall. He grabbed her by the collar. "I have big plans, Commissioner. And I'm not going to let some used-up, tight-ass old *bitch* with a messiah complex, in a rinky-dink rock in the middle of fucking *nowhere,* mess up those plans." He gave her a rough shake with each insult. "Just saying," he finished, and released her.

She eyed him, panting with despair and rage. She had no way to protect Phocaea. She couldn't even protect Xuan. They would kill him, her, everyone who got in their way.

She had barely escaped Vesta with her life. The memories were something she never talked about, had forced herself to forget. But they surged up now, unstoppable.

She had been the one to find Vesta's resource commissioner dead in his office. Poison. She never knew for certain whether it had been murder or despair. She remembered seeing the pills floating before his swollen, purple face. She remembered the bloody handprints on the bulkheads, as friends smuggled her and a handful of other, low-level officials to a freighter. She had spent seven weeks in an icy hold, and had emerged half starved, frostbitten, on Phocaea . . . only to find that no one cared. Vesta was a small cluster, millions of kilometers from anywhere. Everyone was busy and had their own problems.

So many friends and coworkers had died there. And it was not the work of an uncaring universe. No. It was the work of evil men.

An that hadn't even been the worst of it. The worst had been those who had helped the Ogilvies do what they had done. Among them had been her own coworkers and friends. They had betrayed their fellow Vestans to the mob to save their own lives, or save themselves from humiliation, or to earn a troy. They had seen no reprisals. They were powerful people now; wealthy, connected. They keynoted Upside conferences and published papers. She sometimes saw their names in the news.

When she had returned to Xuan, all those years ago, he had loved her, held her, and comforted her, helped her to heal. He had given her every microgram of love and empathy a life partner could summon. He had nagged her for working too hard, for driving her people too hard, for being too inflexible with herself and others. But he had never reached this part of her. Not really. He had never understood why she drove herself the way she did. She had turned her own gaze away because she couldn't bear to keep looking. The truth was too awful, too intractable.

It was simple, though, of course, now that she faced it. All these years, as Phocaea's resource commissioner, she had been trying to outrun her own horror at what people were capable of, when they were greedy enough, or frightened enough, or broken enough. When no one was watching.

And it's happening again.

Glease shoved her along. Their movement awakened the wall's holographic ghosts, who whispered greetings and bon mots as Jane passed by. At the very end, Carl Agre's ghost awakened. He grinned. "Air kiss . . ."

Carl. Her eight dead. Her friends and family. Her fellow Phocaeans. A weird calm settled over her. *I'd rather be a bloody smear on a bulkhead*, she thought. *I'd sooner even give them Xuan, God help me, than help them butcher anyone else.*

Glease took her to a secluded space behind the wall, near the bulkhead. There he spoke a password and presented his retina to a panel that revealed itself. A hatch opened up. He forced her down into it, and she found herself in a hidden room. Three armed men stood there. Glease locked the hatch and pulled his weapon out again. Jane eyed it in distaste. "The one you used to kill Marty, I take it?"

"The very one." He displayed it, laying it out on his palm, and stroked it lightly with his fingertips. "You like it? Latest model; cost a mint."

If she had been able to get the gun from him then, and known how to use it, she would have shot him without a second thought. He saw it in her eyes, and seemed amused. He gestured for her to move ahead of him.

The antechamber they were in held a digital art mural that shifted shapes and colors as they moved through. At the door to another room, Jane stalled in shock. Thondu was sitting inside. Definitely looking more female than male, and more European than African.

So much for my vaunted intuition, she thought bitterly. She had trusted the Viridians. This meant her DeadMan macro was useless. And that flash of insight next to Carl's hologram? Sheer delusion. She felt heartsick.

But Thondu turned to her, and she reconsidered. The Viridian's expression didn't change, but from hir stiff posture and desperate glance, it was clear: ze was a prisoner, too. A fourth armed man stood in the corner.

"A word with you, sir?" the guard said to Glease, who took him into the other room. They left the door ajar and spoke in lowered voices. As Jane turned to Thondu, she caught a flicker of a gesture from the young Viridian, and a flimsy, near-invisible barrier settled over the two of them. The murmur of Glease and the young man's voices ceased. Thondu did not look at Jane, but instead seemed to be working inwave.

"Listen carefully and don't talk," ze said swiftly. "Mr. Glease evaded arrest tonight and came to the Badlands. Learned Harbaugh's dead and Learned Obyx was badly wounded, may be dead, too—"

"Holy shit!"

"He's forcing me to make it look like you had a psychotic break, that you did the murders to prop up a paranoid fantasy." Jane thought, *And I just went to my doctor and told him I was hearing voices.*

Glease must know, she realized. *He's using it.* And that meant he had inside access to the "Stroiders" feed.

"He's holding hostage the biocrystalline copy of the feral. It's locked in his safe. He doesn't know about this version." Ze touched hir belly.

"But what about—"

"*Shh!* Listen! He *doesn't* have your husband—a call just came in. Xuan eluded capture but he and others are trapped on a sugar-rock stroid, trying to fight them off. We have to—" Ze interrupted hirself by puncturing the bubble with a slicing motion of hir hand—so swiftly Jane only registered it after it had happened—as Glease and his flunky reentered the room. Ze incorporated the slicing movement into an action to bring up some images on the massive displays against that wall.

"It doesn't change anything," Glease said softly, angrily to his flunky, as the insulation bubble dissolved. He told Thondu, "Get me Woody."

A shock ran through Jane as Elwood Ogilvie's form materialized before them. "Well, what have we here?" Ogilvie asked, surveying the room, after a bare fraction of a second's pause.

Jane did the math. He had to be within twenty million kilometers or so. Vesta was fifty million kilometers away—a third of an AU. He *had* to be closer than that, possibly on one of the military ships ready to launch at Phocaea.

"I brought you Navio, as you asked," Glease told Ogilvie.

Woody Ogilvie's gaze shifted to Jane. He looked very pleased to see her. "Commissioner. I am going to explain this to you once. I expect instant compliance. You will call a press conference and announce that you falsified evidence implicating Nathan in the murder of your man Martin Graham. Or I will order your husband killed."

Jane's heart knocked in her chest, and red waves washed across her vision. "No one would believe such a claim, since the recordings I obtained can be authenticated."

"You let us worry about those details," Ogilvie said.

"Our Viridian friend here is going to doctor the records in the local system," Glease said, "indicating that the data has been altered by you. The librarian who sent you the records has already met with an unfortunate accident"—*but how did they know?* Jane thought, and then saw the look of suppressed horror on Thondu's face; ze had helped them locate Masahiro. *What will I tell Chikuma?*—"and won't be able to testify. By the time anyone else is able to send a claim to Earth to compare your records to those Downside, there will already be so much chaff in the system that no one will be able to tell what is truth and what is not. With your confession, we have all we need."

He paused. Jane did not reply. Ogilvie said, "I am not a patient man, Ms. Navio. You will do this without further argument, or your husband dies tonight. Speak now."

Jane drew a calming breath. "Very well. At this moment, I am recording and beaming to a safe location everything that has happened to me, including Nathan Glease's confession a few moments ago that he killed my aide, Marty Graham, and your threat just now to kill my husband if I don't cooperate with your attempt to cover up that murder.

"I have a dead man's switch. If anything happens to me, this recording will immediately be beamed to local news organizations, as well as public Earth tourism wavesites regularly trawled by 'Stroiders.'"

Glease's eyes widened. "She's lying!" he told Ogilvie. "We have the best antiwave security money can buy. This office is in a silent zone. No way she could be recording anything, much less beaming a signal out."

"Very well," Jane said. "I will prove it."

She called up her software, grabbed the snippet of video of Ogilvie saying, "You will call a press conference first thing in the morning and announce that you falsified evidence implicating Nathan in the murder of your man Martin Graham, or I will order your husband killed," and transmitted the video to Ogilvie. A few seconds later, he frowned, and gestured inwave. His eyes widened as he focused on something unseen. Then he pursed his lips. "I'm afraid she's telling the truth, Nate."

Glease gestured to the guard, who grabbed Jane and pinned her arms. She did not resist. Glease gripped her chin and turned her head, and eyed the processor in her ear. "I think we should just pull it right out," he said. "Rip out the wiring. See how much brain matter comes with it."

"You could. But DeadMan is about to trigger a request for a code, and if I don't respond promptly, the recording goes out automatically."

"Let her go," Ogilvie said. "Don't be foolish, Nate."

Glease had gone pale, and now red. Jane could see the rage in his eyes. He gained control, gestured for the young man to release her. DeadMan asked for the input and she gave it. Meanwhile, Glease spun and ordered Thondu, "Track her signal. Crack her face. *Shut off the switch!*"

Jane looked at Thondu and held her breath; ze could almost certainly

break into her waveface and disable DeadMan—and might just, to protect the feral.

The Viridian spent a couple of minutes doing something in hir waveface. A bead of sweat trickled down hir cheek. Ze turned to Glease, avoiding a glance at Jane. "I'm afraid I can't. She's masked with some security
tech. I've never seen anything like it. I'd need my lab and several hours of
uninterrupted time to penetrate it."

Glease eyed Thondu. A muscle jumped in his jaw. He opened the safe
and pointed his gun at the thing inside it. Jane realized it was the biocrystalline backup of the feral sapient.

"I'll count to three," he said. "One . . . two . . ."

Thondu went ashen. "*I can't!*"

"Too bad," Glease said. "Three."

"*No!*" Thondu launched hirself at Glease. The lawyer's hireling inter-
vened, pinning Thondu to the wall. Glease fired, and an explosion released
a puff of mist. Bits of bioglass went everywhere. They all ducked. Jane covered her mouth and nose till the ventilation sucked the mist away.

"I hope that made you feel better," she said.

"I should just shoot you and be done with it," he told her, aiming the
gun at her. "That would definitely make me feel better."

"You could. And the police commissioner gets a recording of the murder in his inbox, with coordinates. There's only one way off Zekeston, and
they can get to the surface lifts before you do."

He lowered the gun.

"So here is my counterproposal," she said to Ogilvie, watching im-
passively via wave. "I will wait exactly an hour to release my recording.
That might give Mr. Grease here enough time to get offworld—if he
hustles. If at any time, anything bad happens to me, my husband, or
anyone I know, ever, I will release the recording. There is no statute of
limitations on this kind of crime, Mr. Ogilvie. You renege on the deal, I
release the recording." She checked the time in her heads-up. "The clock
has started."

They all looked at Ogilvie. He leaned back in his chair, eyeing her
and tweaking a lock of his well-groomed beard.

"Well played, Commissioner," he said finally, with a sigh. "Nate, please haul your expensive legal ass out of there. Now." He signed off. Glease shoved a finger in her face. "You'll pay. I'll see to it."

"You're burning escape time."

The door snicked shut behind them. She hurried to the outer office. Glease had left the hatch open. She leaped up into the memorial garden, and exited. A few people walked along the atrium, along the curve of the thoroughfare, and someone was helping someone else stand. They were looking at the Weesu lift doors, which were closing.

"First things first," Jane said. She called Aaron. He answered sleepily, and she filled him in on what had happened. "I can't release the recordings for another fifty-nine minutes," she said. "A deal's a deal. But I never promised not to report Glease's movements. He should be arriving in the Hub in the next two minutes. Can you shut down the Hub-to-surface lifts, and get a police squad out there?"

Aaron's eyes glinted. "You bet I can."

Jane disconnected, turned off DeadMan, and returned to Thondu.

Thondu was on hir knees by the safe, looking at the wreckage inside. Ze looked back at Jane, stricken. "I couldn't sacrifice Phocaea. Not even to save BitManSinger."

Jane knelt, too. "I'm sorry. You have the other copy though, yes?"

Thondu dashed away tears, touched hir belly again. "Yes. Thank the Nameless. It's the last complete copy. But we may have lost everything already. This new method of encoding was experimental. We haven't fully tested it yet."

Jane stood. "How would you like a chance?"

"To test it, you mean?"

"Yes. My husband and some others are still in trouble. Woody Ogilvie has a fleet of ships within striking distance. We have no ice. This isn't over yet."

Thondu stood, too, and brushed off the glass dust, looking wary. "What did you have in mind?"

She gestured at hir belly. "Do you have a way to extract your copy of the feral and install it in a standard server? What would it take to do that?"

Thondu hesitated. "We'll definitely want to make another backup. But what good will it do you? Only the city system and Upside-Down's servers are big enough to house an active copy—and we all agree that BitManSinger isn't ready to be released into the wild. It is still too young and unformed. Unbiddable. Destructive."

"I'm going on instinct, Thondu—"

"Call me Vivian." Jane looked at hir askance, and ze said, "I'm not Thondu. Not when I'm expressing the female and suppressing the male."

Jane suppressed exasperation. What was this, multiple personality disorder? But she had little room to talk; hello, Voice. "If I can come up with a place the feral will fit, will you help me use it against the mob? I promise you, no harm will be done to the sapient."

Thondu—no, Vivian's—gaze went to the shards on the floor and wall. Hir gaze hardened. "If it can be done safely, yes. With great relish."

27

Geoff and the others spent a good while trying to figure a way out. While Amaya and the professor made an inventory, Geoff and Kam explored the mine tunnels. Kam suggested they look for forgotten passages, and Geoff remembered that Joey Spud had had maps. They located the mining map archive. The maps were archeotech, as usual for Joey Spud: big, dusty scrolls of blue-lined, laminated scrip, tucked away on shelves in an old storage room. Geoff dug through the scrips and passed them to Kam, who spread them out on the workbench.

They went through several dozen maps and got nowhere. Most of the tunnels they had not yet explored had been sealed off with methane ice, and the rest were now inaccessible due to the explosions at the entrance.

Finally they gave up and headed back to join Amaya and the professor in the way station. The professor was dozing in his hammock. Geoff didn't like the way he looked: his skin was ashen and his breathing shallow.

Amaya looked up from her lists. "Any luck?" she asked softly, but saw their expressions and slumped back down. A gloomy silence settled over Geoff as he surveyed his companions' dirty, tired faces. He was out of ideas.

"Are we certain," the professor asked from his hammock, "that there is no way in?" Geoff looked over, surprised. He hadn't been aware the older man was listening. "Our lives may ride on the answer," Professor Xuan said, "so consider carefully."

Geoff shared a glance with Kam and Amaya.

"We could be missing something," he said, "but I can't see any way. Not anytime soon." The older man looked at the other two, who nodded agreement.

"So," Kam asked, "what now?"

The professor said, "All right. We have supplies, fuel, and air. Our enemies can't get in. We have friends and family who will soon miss us. And we are all exhausted. It seems to me our best approach is to rest for a while, and sleep, if we can."

They settled into the hammocks and tucked blankets around themselves. As distressed as he was, Geoff could not believe he would ever sleep again. But sleep came swiftly.

As they ran toward the lift, Vivian said, "Commissioner . . . wait. There is something else you need to know. It's important!"

Jane quelled her impatience and paused. "What?"

Vivian said, "I think Nathan Glease has commissioned another assassination. We may have time to stop it."

They both stepped into the lift. The other people there edged away from them, and Jane realized it was because Vivian was a Viridian. She felt a twinge of sympathy for the young woman—man?—and guilt; she had reacted that way herself.

Vivian ignored them. Ze told Jane, "Right before they brought you in, he had another meeting. It was a woman, wearing nurse's clothes. He gave her a vial of liquid, showed her an image of someone, and told her to destroy the vial when she was done. He gave her a big wad of cash."

"The hospital. He's targeted someone at the hospital." Jane grabbed Vivian's arm. "Who was he targeting? What else do you remember?"

"I only caught a glimpse. A young man, I think. A big white guy with a spaceburned face. One of his arms was missing."

Jane remembered Sean telling her about Geoff's friend—the one whose arm the feral tore out. Ian. Ian Carmichael. He was big, white, and blond, a biker with a spaceburn. And he was still at the hospital. "I know the target."

The lift doors opened in time for them see a cuffed Glease being hustled into one of the other lifts by the police. He wore a smirk when he spotted her. She knew why.

The hospital was right across the way. Quicker to go herself than to explain. She headed straight for Yamashiro Memorial, trailed by Vivian, clouds of "Stroiders" glamour, and a small army of mites. They barged through the antimote sprays, and went up to an orderly on duty at the information desk. He was talking to a colleague inwave.

"What room is Ian Carmichael in?" Jane demanded. When he did not acknowledge her right away, she reached over the counter, grabbed him, and gave him a shake. "*What room?*"

The young man stammered the room number. She brought up a map overlay of the hospital, touched "Guide me" inwave, and plugged in the number. Following the golden marquis that appeared, she kicked off down the tube, bounding off walls and people indiscriminately. "Out of my way! Cluster emergency!" She did not bother to check whether Vivian followed. People caromed off the walls and each other to clear a path.

The room was a private suite that smelled of cleaners and chemicals. The lights were dimmed. The young man was snoring, his mouth half open. He was hooked up to a Regrow apparatus. The woman Vivian had described was replacing a vial in the nutrient feed setup by his bed. She looked up at Jane in guilty surprise.

Jane launched herself over the bed, grabbed the bed rail with her foot-hands and, bracing herself there, pinned the woman against the wall. She took the vial from her. The young man, Ian, startled awake and struggled with his cover. "Hey! What's going on?"

"Pull the other vial," Jane told Vivian, pointing at the apparatus. "The one that's already in there. Now!"

A doctor came into the room. "What is the meaning of this?"

Jane gestured at the woman she had hold of, who was protesting. Jane gave her a look, and she fell silent. "Is this woman one of your staff?"

The doctor looked at the woman, and then glanced at her companion, an elderly man dressed in nurse's garb, who shook his head. "I'm head nurse for this shift," he said, "and I don't know this woman."

"Test this." Jane tossed the vial to the doctor, who plucked it out of the air. "And that one there," she pointed at the one Vivian was holding. "You'll find that one of them contains a biological toxin. I just stopped this woman from inserting it into the apparatus."

Ian looked at the vials in horror. "Gaaah!" He grabbed the tubes and monitoring devices and yanked them out of his arms and chest, and shoved himself out of bed. Small drops of blood and nutrients dribbled from the tubes and the holes in his arm and chest. He hung there, tumbling slowly, panting and trembling. The doctor came over.

"Careful there! Easy. You'll be fine." She guided him back into bed, resettled him, and staunched his bleeding. Vacubots launched from the walls and sucked up the spilled blood and fluids. "Don't worry, we won't put the tubes back in until we know they're safe."

Ian eyed the woman who had tried to kill him. She turned her face away. The doctor turned to one of the staff who had gathered in the hall outside. "Call the police."

While they waited for the police to arrive, Vivian asked to see Learned Obyx. Jane accompanied hir.

The Viridian leader was in Intensive Care. Obyx wore a plastic body glove, goggles, and a respirator, and was suspended in a network of Regrow tubing. Vivian alighted next to hir leader. Jane hung back.

"Is ze going to be all right?" Vivian asked.

The nurse said, "He's doing better." Vivian winced—Jane was unsure whether it was the gendered pronoun, or the nurse's deliberate dodge of hir question. "We don't treat many people with, well, with his genotype. We'd appreciate any information you can give us on his physiology."

"I'll contact my colleagues and have them send you hir medical files. We have medical specialists who may be able to help you." Vivian hesitated, eyeing Obyx with grave concern. "May I talk to hir?"

The nurse eyed the two of them, considering. "For a moment, perhaps. He won't be able to answer questions, and he won't really remember anything you say later on." She moved in front of them as they started toward Obyx, and said, "Keep it brief. And don't say anything to alarm him. He is gravely injured and needs to remain calm."

Vivian went over, and spoke softly. "Learned?"

Obyx opened hir eyes and gazed blearily at them. "Waīthīra?"

Vivian carefully worked hir hand through the tubing and gave Obyx's own plastic-gloved, gel-smeared hand a squeeze. "It's me, Learned. You're going to be OK. They've arrested Glease."

"James?" Obyx whispered. "Where is ze? Is ze all right?"

Waīthīra looked across at Jane. "Everything's going to be fine, Learned," ze told hir. "You rest now, and heal."

Obyx sighed softly, and closed hir eyes. Vivian gave Jane a look. Ze lofted hirself into the hall. Hir face was implacable, but ze dashed away tears. Jane followed.

The hospital staff gave them a nook in the staff lounge. The police commissioner called them. "You two have had an exciting evening."

"I'm not sure how many details Aaron was able to share with you, Jerry, but this is Vivian Waīthīra wa Macharia na Briggs. Ze was also kidnapped by Glease and his cronies. Hir spiritual leader James Harbaugh was killed during the kidnapping, and Obyx has been severely injured."

"Y-e-e-s. I heard about the fracas in the Badlands. Obyx was already on my list to get a statement from." Jerry pursed his lips, looking harried. "Ian Carmichael sure is lucky you got here in time. What happened?"

Jane gestured to Vivian, who told the police chief about Glease's transaction with the nurse-assassin. Jerry took notes and asked questions. Finally he said, "All right, well, we've all had a long night. Go on home, both of you, and get some rest. Come to the main precinct station tomorrow and my detectives will take your statements."

But this wasn't over yet, and Jane was not about to rest. After the police commissioner signed off, she leaned toward Vivian and quietly asked, "Can you do one of those stealth bubble things?"

Looking puzzled, the Viridian flicked hir fingers. A faint, glistening bubble settled over them. Outside its walls settled a glittering sphere of fizzing, dying "Stroiders" dust.

"Something is bugging me," Jane said. "Why would they want to harm some random kid?"

Vivian shrugged. "Spite, perhaps."

Jane frowned. "I don't think so. There was more to it." She remembered that Ian had been helping Sean the other night. Sean might know more. "Vivian, can I make a call through this?" She gestured at the bubble surrounding them. Ze flashed a smile. "Sure . . . now that you have Arachnid installed. It should penetrate any security barrier. Even ours."

Jane put in a high-priority call to Sean. He materialized in wave.

"Sean, where are you?"

"Still out at the docks. The PM freed the ships, and we've got departures happening left and right. Things are crazy out here."

"Well, *I'm* at the hospital. Someone just tried to kill your young friend, Ian Carmichael."

He gaped. "What the *fuck*?"

"We got here in time. He's OK. There's something more important I need to know. Have you heard from Xuan?"

He opened his mouth to answer. Then he looked thoughtful. "Hmm. Good question. Don't go away." A moment later, he returned, visuals activated, looking worried. "Xuan's ship hasn't returned yet, and no one has heard back from Geoff Agre or his companions."

"Xuan is in trouble," she told Sean, "and I think Geoff and his friends are, too. Where did they go?"

Sean started to answer, but Vivian gripped Jane's arm. "I get it now! Glease had me crack the cluster's asteroid registry and alter data on a claim. I changed its location coordinates. They were laughing about hiding it in plain sight."

Which explained why they thought they had Xuan, and why they needed Ian dead. They wanted to obscure Geoff's asteroid's location till they could hide or destroy it. Ian was the only one left on Phocaea who knew its actual coordinates. Jane said to Sean, "We need to organize a search. But you'll have to get the coordinates directly from Ian. The location of Geoff's stroid has been altered in the registry."

"You bet. I'll contact Val and get a Security cruiser prepped to launch. High-gee accel. We can be there in less than an hour. Why don't you head back to our place and get some rest? I'll call you."

"Thanks, Sean."

Jane hung up. *Xuan*, she thought. *Xuan, don't you die on me.*

Geoff woke suddenly, heart slamming into his rib cage. A sound had awakened him, from a dream in which he had been playing connect-the-dots with stars in a royal blue sky.

He saw what had awakened him. A skeleton had entered the shadowed chamber. It floated about the low-ceiling chamber, capering and flailing, and bumped against the overhead piping. The impact burst it in midair and sprayed a cloud of assembler grapes. Professor Xuan stirred, but Amaya and Kam slumbered on, and it wasn't long till the older man settled once more. Irritated, relieved, Geoff relaxed again in the gentle confines of the hammock mesh.

He was certain they were missing something. There had to be a way out. But nothing came to him, and he finally sighed in defeat. He listened to the familiar whispering echoes of the mine and tried to relax, but he couldn't fall back to sleep.

The thought of dying didn't frighten him nearly as much as it should. But when he looked over at Amaya, at Kam, at the professor, he felt all the terror for them that he couldn't feel for himself.

I can't let anything happen to them, he thought. *I have to do something.* Then he glanced at the overhead piping that the skeleton had broken itself against.

Holy crap! There *was* a way in, he realized, and it was right above their heads. *How could we not have seen it?* But that meant there was also a way out—and he knew how to use it. He threw off the cover.

Back at the map archives, Geoff pulled out the scrips he and Kam had been looking at and traced some lines on a map. The slurry lines went out to the chemical plant. Since Joey Spud had not believed in nanotech, he had built a mechanical system to maintain air and temperature. A small army of bots mined the ice in an evacuated section of the mine. They fed it into a hopper that mixed it with a methanol slurry and pumped it to the chemical plant up on the surface, where it was processed, and fed air, fuel, and water back into the mine.

The slurry pipe was large—easily big enough for Geoff. Maybe even big enough for an army of minerbots. The pipe was filled with methane, ammonia, and methanol, but he could drain it. The real issue was that if he went out, it meant the bad guys could get in and harm his friends.

Truth is, he thought, *they could have found this way in all along.* Or they could plant a larger set of explosives. They could even tunnel down and plant a really big bomb several kilometers below the surface and turn Ouroboros to rubble. Once those mobsters out there got tired of waiting, Geoff and his buddies would be bug fodder, any way you sliced it.

Fuck it. Geoff was sick of all this. *Just do something. Anything!*

First he gathered three dozen minerbots. He passed out disposable medical gloves to one squad and had them start filling the gloves with a gaseous methane-oxygen mix from the mine exhaust tanks. A second squad he had adjust their signal broadcast settings to blast a powerful distress signal. A third squad he programmed to set charges along the slurry pipe. As they did so, he moved alongside, marking the scrip to show where the charges were placed. Then he sent the bots to wait for him outside the evacuated section of the mine, the longwall where the currently active seam of methane ice was exposed.

He didn't want his friends to try to stop him, but once he opened up the pipe, if he failed to defeat the mobsters, it would only be a matter of time before they would find the pipe opening. He had to make sure his friends were prepared to deal with that.

He returned to where his companions slept and set an alarm to wake them in fifteen minutes. Then he wrote a note on the utility drawing.

I'VE GONE OUT THROUGH THE SLURRY PIPE TO STOP THEM BEFORE ANY-
ONE ELSE GETS HURT. I SET CHARGES ON THE PIPE, SO IF THEY TRY TO GET
IN THAT WAY YOU CAN STOP THEM. I MARKED THE PLACES ON THE MAP,
AND THE BOTS CAN SET THEM OFF IN WHATEVER SEQUENCE YOU WANT.

He stared at the note for a long time, feeling as if he should put something else down, but no other words came. So he just signed it "Geoff." After another moment, he squeezed, "Love to friends and family—" above his name, then wished he hadn't, and wanted to cross it out. But that would look even stupider. So he left it as it was. Cheeks burning, stomach achurn, he rolled it up and put it in his hammock with the detonator and an alarm clock.

The bots were awaiting him at the longwall antechamber. They had laid his equipment on the mine floor: a bag of tools and netted clusters of oxygenated methane bladders they had made with disposable medical gloves. Geoff hoped they would fit through the pipe. He donned his suit and did the checks: air, ponies, radio. Then he stepped into the lock. The bots crawled after him, bringing the equipment and methane bladders.

He shut the lock door and pressed the controls to purge the air. The air pressure levels tumbled downward. He listened to the faint hiss of gases as the airlock purged. The methane bladders swelled to several times their original size. One burst, causing his explosimeter reading to spike. He itched, as usual when he couldn't take off his suit to scratch. His pulse pounded dully in his throat where the helmet seal met the suit collar. He wondered if he was doing the right thing. But how could it be wrong to protect his friends from harm?

In a short while, air pressure dropped to zero millibars; he lofted out into the longwall area and the bots followed.

The methane longwall stood before him: a translucent blue green wave, frozen in place, streaked with veins of orange and darker blue. Along its base ran a mechanized conveyor. Robotic arms gouged crescents of ice from the wall and placed them in lidded metal baskets that opened to accept the ice, then closed and crept along the conveyor. At the end of the longwall, the baskets pushed their contents into a bladed hopper at the slurry mixing chambers.

Geoff launched himself alongside the longwall with bots trailing him. At the slurry mixing station, he shut the mining operation down. Behind him, the conveyor and mining arms grew still and the slurry mixing blades stopped.

The slurry lines were normally emptied by removing the maintenance cover out at the chem plant, and blowing exhaust through the lines. Not exactly subtle, though, and the goal was not to call attention to himself until absolutely necessary. But there was no reason he couldn't suck the material in, instead. It'd be messy. But doable.

Here goes.

He overrode the failsafes and pulled the series of levers that would reverse the flow of the mixing blades. Then he commanded all the miner-bots to get up onto the conveyor, broke the pressure seal between the mixing chamber and the pipe, and bounded up onto the conveyor himself.

Giant globs of slush squirted and wiggled out of the hopper like toothpaste. He tried to stay out of its way, but the glop went everywhere. A big wobbly chunk bumped him, throwing him into a slow tumble. It smeared up his faceplate and filled the creases in his joints. Geoff caught hold of the conveyor, and tried to wipe away the spatters and shake loose the chunks of ice from his suit. Finally the flow ebbed and settled. While waiting for the sloshing to die down, he attached a cable lead to the nearest minerbot, plugged the other end into his suit, and fixed the coil of cable to his suit. He shoved off, settled into the hopper, and commanded the bots to wait for his signal. Then he flipped on his light and passed through the hopper and mixing chamber into the pipe.

It seemed to go on forever; he made his way amid crunchy, frozen slush, uncoiling his comm line to the bots as he went. Space suits were not designed for tight spaces; it was difficult to bend his elbow and knee joints far enough to get purchase on the pipe's curved surface in the gunk.

When he reached the chemical plant, the pipe bent sharply upward. Geoff kicked off and leaped up several meters to where the pipe leveled out again in a giant T fitting. He wormed into the level section of pipe, squirmed to face the way he had come, and looked across the gap. The manhole cover sealed off one end of the T. That was his exit.

Geoff pulled a buzz saw from his tool pouch, braced himself at the edge of the dropoff, and cut through the bolts holding the maintenance cover on. Then he kicked at it with both feet. The big metal cover went tumbling into space. Geoff stretched across the drop, stuck his head out, and looked around. No one was in sight. The ship's top fin jutted up above the ridge, and the arms of Cronus the earthmover towered over all. Amaya's bike, which they had left propped up next to the rock near the vent pipe twenty meters away, was gone.

He sat huddled in the pipe for a moment, gathering his nerve. They could be anywhere right now—they might be right behind him and he'd never know till they shot him. But there was no turning back.

He tied off the communications cable that linked him to the lead minerbot, back at the longwall, then leapt out and down. As he settled to the surface, he twisted in all directions—up, down, sideways—looking around. No sign of his enemies. He touched down.

How many would he be up against? Three, perhaps four. There had been six, but Amaya saw one injured or dead in the mine blast, and they had launched two others into space earlier that evening. Unless they'd managed to get those other two down from orbit.

But no—there they were now, rising above the eastern horizon: two tumbling human forms, snarled in a mesh made gossamer by the sun. Geoff was surprised they were still in orbit. He'd expected them to fly off for parts unknown. He ducked into the shadow of a rock and timed their orbit; it took a good ten minutes for them to reach zenith. Then a set of silver tethers soared up from over the outcropping and snared them.

Geoff crept forward to the crevasse and looked down at the ship. The biggest man, the one who had shot a hole in his bike, was reeling the tethered men in, using a hand-cranked wheel he must have jury-rigged from Joey Spud's mining equipment. Amaya's rocketbike lay on its side next to the ship's ramp.

A suited figure crouched near the wreckage of the cavern entrance. They were setting charges. Big ones—enough to blow the whole mine! Sweat sprang out Geoff's face and he found himself panting. No time to go back now and warn the others. They could blow the charges any minute. He had to stop them *now*.

A body was laid out in the cargo bay; he could see it from here. The one who had been setting the charges was standing guard with a large weapon. The third, slim man was nowhere to be seen.

They're distracted, he thought. *There won't be a better moment.*

Geoff returned to the maintenance pipe, plugged into his makeshift comm cable, and ordered the minerbots to come up. In a moment they began feeding the methane balloons and his tools up the chute. He helped them haul it all up. The minerbots scampered up over one another like mechanical ants, out the maintenance hole, and down onto the ground. The balloon squadron, as he thought of them, gathered the bladders and then joined the distress-call squadron. The twenty-four bots stood there in formation, awaiting orders.

Geoff programmed Balloon Squadron to cross behind the ridge, out of sight of the ship, and await his signal. Then he crawled back to a vantage point closest to the earthmover, followed by Distress-Call Squadron.

The earthmover was massive—much larger than the shuttle. They called them Planet Eaters for a reason. It looked vaguely like a giant mechanical lobster, with three arms that stretched high into the sky, and a big cab that rested on machineworks on treads.

One arm was a crane with a grappling hook. The second was a gigantic, bucky-steel rotary saw for cutting into hard rock, and at the end of the third arm was a bucket shaped like an enormous Venus flytrap, for digging up and compressing material. A fourth appendage, a catapult, sat atop the cab. The earthmover, Cronus, stood between him and the shuttle, near the storage tanks. The operator cab was high up on its central cabin.

Joey Spud had let Geoff operate Cronus once. It had been a terrifying experience—like driving a mountain range. Geoff prayed now that he could remember what to do.

The men seemed to be finishing with their charges at the mine entrance. *Now or never, Agre.* He gave the minerbots their signal.

Balloon Squadron went first. They spilled over the outcropping and their methane-filled balloons bobbed along behind them like hundreds of giant, wildly waving hands. The mercenaries looked up, saw them, and started firing. The maintenance bots were easy to hit—they weren't very big or fast. Their balloons ignited as the explosive bullets struck. Fireballs erupted all around, and the bots' casings turned to shrapnel. The mercenaries all dove for cover. Geoff reached the earthmover without being seen and began scaling it.

By the time he neared the cab he was in plain sight, and the fireball spectacle was over. Far below, the big-suited figure spotted him and pointed. The others started toward him, but had difficulty with the sudden momentum changes. He could tell they weren't Upsiders. They flailed and bounded too high and collided with one another in their haste.

Geoff leaped easily up onto the landing outside the operator's cabin. He ducked into the cab, locked the door, and sealed it. The small cabin pressurized as he pulled himself into the pilot's couch. He left his helmet on but opened the faceplate to conserve air. The smell of must, tobacco, and peanuts conjured up Joey Spud—almost as if the old man was sitting here.

"Talk to me, Joey Spud," he muttered, and laid his hands on the controls. "I don't know what the hell I'm doing."

He vaguely remembered Joey Spud talking him through the startup sequence. He visualized the old man's hands on the controls, and followed suit, thinking: *please please* please *work*. He dashed sweat out of his eyes, activated the control panel with shaking hands. *Hurry the fuck up! Stupid lag.* It found his waveface and pinged him. He entered the security permissions.

—*Install PlanetEater 10.5?* it asked. He selected *Yes.* —*Password?* He punched in Joey Spud's old code, an esoteric miner's joke: *197AquaRegia.*

The software downloaded and the main control face activated. It gave him access to all the functions: the crane, the catapult, the bucket. Everything.

The machine was so big that he couldn't see everything with his own eyes; instead, his wavespace filled with a three-dimensional map of his surroundings. The machine controls fitted his body's contours like a ghostly second body. He put in the start sequence. After three tries, the machine roared to life. The entire cab began shaking, so hard it made his teeth chatter, and knocked him up out of the seat. He pulled himself back down, hung on, and pushed it into gear. It started rolling toward the ship, a palsied leviathan. He felt like a bug sitting between an elephant's ears.

Below, Cronus's treads crushed three of his mining bots. Two of the tiny human figures scattered, but the third instead bounded alongside the earthmover, trying to keep his balance as he shot up at the cabin. Geoff closed his visor, in case the shooter cracked the cabin portal. But the bullets only pockmarked the portal glass—they did not penetrate.

He maneuvered the digging wheel around to the side, to move it out of the way. Alarms bellowed—Cronus teetered dangerously—and Geoff remembered, belatedly: *Set the pitons, idiot*! He triggered the explosive cartridges that drove Chronus's stabilizer spikes into the rock. Ouroboros rocked—dust and debris leapt high all around—the men outside dove for cover.

Geoff chose the bucket. Through the cabin window and inwave, the massive Venus flytrap bucket opened on its towering arm. Geoff reached down and, clumsily, the bucket followed suit. He scooped up his distress-call robots, who waited on the other side of the outcropping.

Four suited figures were now firing weapons at him. More projectiles pocked the cab-window glass. Cronus shuddered and tried to buck, but the pitons held. Geoff smelled the sour tang of his own fear. He swung the arm over the catapult. It took him a moment to figure out how to move his hand so as to make the bucket tip over before it released. The bots dropped into the shallow bowl on Cronus's top. He set trajectory and velocity, and punched execute. The bots went sailing over the horizon, transmitting their distress calls.

More bullets. The glass cracked. Geoff thought, *I need a plan.*

First things first. He used the bucket to scoop up the explosives and cording there. It was like picking up toothpicks with a backhoe, and he ended up taking half the cliff face, too. He dropped this mess into the catapult and sent it soaring into space. Then he reached down, and the bucket descended over the shuttle. This was a much better fit for the bucket scoop: he picked it up as easily as a grown man picks up a toy, and lifted it high. As he did so, two suited men fell out of the cargo hold. Geoff caught a look at the smaller man's surprised face as he sank slowly groundward. The larger man clutched a big box and tried to pry it open. Not one, but two, corpses fell limply out, tumbling.

Geoff batted the bodies aside and made a fist: the bucket closed on the ship, and the ship's hull buckled. The shock of the compression carried through the earthmover's frame. Geoff grabbed his armrest to keep from floating off again as the cab shuddered, and loosened his grip on the ship—the professor had said there were explosives and weaponry in the hold. He wanted to render the weapons useless, not cause another major explosion. Then he swung the arm over the catapult. It took him a moment or so to figure out how to move his hand so as to make the bucket tip over before it released. Next he set the ship, now crumpled like a badly made toy, into the catapult's bowl and activated the catapult.

The ship soared into the sky. The shock of the catapult gun bounced him hard against his seat and lofted him. Geoff flailed in midair, seeking a handhold. By this time the suited figure of the big man, the one who had shot at them when they rescued the professor, had alighted. He was pointing the business end of a missile launcher right at the cab. The box and the rest of the rockets were tumbling lazily around the large man, all slowly falling to the ground.

"*Shit!*" Geoff got his fingers around a handhold above the control panel. He shoved himself over, kicked at the emergency switch, and was propelled out the door by the cab's sudden decompression.

A missile burst through the cab window and struck the wall behind the operator's couch. The earthmover lurched—flames engulfed the cab—the giant arms buckled and the earthmover tipped. Geoff saw this while tumbling slowly above the stroid's surface. Then the shock wave struck. Pain seared across his buttocks and side, and he blacked out.

Mitch Shibata, the dock's shipping officer, met Sean in the docking bay.

"We've outfitted the *Michaelmas,* sir," he said. The cluster's fastest and best-armed shuttle on hand. Sean nodded his approval. "I'll be your pilot. We've coordinated with Cluster Security. Commissioner Pearce has put five armed troops under your command. They're aboard now." He transferred the manifest. Sean looked it over as they hustled toward the airlock. "Good."

Mitch said, "Shelley is tracking transmissions for us and says there have been more developments. She'll brief you en route."

The chime intruding on Xuan's dream did not drag him fully from sleep—his fatigue was too deep—but the rumbling *whup!* that followed did. It threw him hard against the mesh of his hammock, and he rolled painfully out into midair, the explosion still ringing in his ears. The meds had helped, though—he felt stronger, and the sharp pain in his ribs had eased.

Amaya and Kamal sleepily struggled out of their own hammocks. Geoff was . . . where?

Amaya was first to reach Geoff's hammock. She pulled out a sheet of scrip and looked at it, brow lowering. Then she crumpled it up and flung it away in disgust. Kamal caught the scrip and unfolded it. He read it aloud, and sighed. "What is he trying to prove?"

Amaya asked Xuan, "Was that the explosion we heard? The charges he set in the pipes?"

Xuan considered. The sounds of the blast echoed in his thoughts. He had been on many a stroid during blasting. "No. The explosion was up top—not down here. Get your gear."

They scrambled to gather their belongings. Xuan swam over to the lockers, braced himself, and tugged on his boots. Dull pain clenched in his rib cage, and he had to pause.

"That explosion was very large," he said. "We must admit the possibility that Geoff has been killed. However, if he is still alive, he'll need help. So I am going out after him. After I leave, you two are going to seal yourselves in and wait for rescue."

"The hell we are!" Amaya snapped, and Kam said, "Geoff is our friend. We won't leave him out there to die. No matter what you say."

Xuan looked at their two dirty, terrified, determined young faces.

"Come what may," Amaya said.

They were adults, and it was their Dharma they followed, not his. Xuan straightened with a nod. "Very well. Come, friends. Let us show them what stroiders are made of."

The squadron leader reported to Sean after takeoff. She climbed through the doorway (their rapid acceleration made for a topsy-turvy ship orientation) and stood at attention on the wall next to it. He looked down at the top of her head from his acceleration couch by the bed. It was no one thing—not simply her well-developed musculature, or her accent, or the way she stood—that suggested her world of origin. She was from Earth.

He realized that this was a turning point. *I'm acclimating,* he thought in mild surprise. *I read her. Who would've thought?*

He dropped down to stand before her. "A fellow Downsider, I surmise," he said. She saluted—which felt both odd and completely natural to him—with a smile that exposed a dimple in her chin.

"That is correct, sir. Sergeant Kayla Maez-Gibson of the Phocaea Cluster Guard, Sixth Spaceborne Division, at your service. Formerly of British Columbia, Canada, Earth. Commissioner Pearce had very little time to brief us," she told him, "but I understand this is a rescue mission?"

"Yes. We have four civilians in what we believe is a hostage situation. It's on a faraway stroid about a kay-klick off the treeway—ETA twenty-eight minutes. The bad guys are tied to a Martian crime syndicate. We aren't certain how many of them there are, but my dockworkers report there are at least four, and perhaps more."

"How are they armed?"

"Unknown. They may have heavy weaponry in addition to hand weapons. How much experience does your squad have in hostile engagements?"

"Limited, sir. The team is seasoned in rescue ops among the faraway stroids, and we have run up against pirates before. But it never resulted in an exchange of fire. We do train intensively with the latest simulations."

Here we go again, Sean thought grimly. "Well, you may finally get a chance to put that training to use. My chief engineer has a briefing for us as soon as you're ready."

"No time like the present, sir."

He called Mitch and had him hail Shelley. Sean plugged the sergeant in, and Shelley appeared in their shared wavespace. "Chief, we've detected a blast in the vicinity of the target rock's location."

Sean exchanged a glance with the sergeant.

"Surface or subsurface?" he asked.

"Surface. No sign of major damage to the stroid, but we're tracking some unmapped debris that appears to have originated from the rock. It appears to have been thrown our way *before* the blast," she said. "Which I can't explain. Second, a series of distress calls has begun. There appear to be eleven separate signals originating from an orbit around the rock."

"Survivors?"

Shelley shook her head. "We think they're remotes. Someone threw them into orbit only a dozen seconds before the explosion."

"OK. Thanks, Shelley. Hail me if you have any other updates." He signed off and turned to the sergeant. "You look as if you have a thought."

"An unpleasant one, sir. The explosion may have been *due to* the launching of the distress-call remotes. In other words, the blast may be a reprisal."

"Too true." Sean thought of Geoff and the others, and remembered his own words to them: *everything is legit.* He remembered telling their parents he would make sure they weren't put into danger. Sean was never one for second-guessing past decisions. You make the best call you can with the knowledge you have. But his best call had not been good enough. He planned to make sure the perpetrator paid.

Xuan asked Kamal and Amaya to have their minerbots remove and pack up the charges Geoff had planted earlier. They also took automated distress beacons, spare air, food, fuel, compressed gas canisters, and some other supplies. The distress beacons should bring someone soon, but even if not, with sufficient supplies Xuan knew how to get them back to the treeways, and thus to Phocaea. If it weren't for the mobsters outside the airlock.

Kamal reported, "We're missing minerbots—a good thirty or so. And a bunch of distress beacons. I think Geoff was trying to get a signal out."

"Let us hope he succeeded, then," Xuan said. He checked the charges Geoff had set. They had radio-activated detonators. He spent a minute reviewing the detonator tutorial, and ran through the simulator twice to plant the knowledge in his body memory. Then they headed to the longwall.

While they waited in the lock for the air to cycle out, Xuan asked, "Where does the slurry pipe exit?"

Amaya answered, "The chem plant. There's a maintenance hole at the distillation unit. That's where Geoff exited. It's the only logical place."

"All right. Now, there are only four possibilities." Xuan ticked them off on his fingers. "The first is that our foes will not yet have found where Geoff exited. That is very unlikely—the explosion tells us they are on alert, and they will have explored the area while we've been preparing.

So we should expect one of the other three possibilities: that they have posted a guard outside the pipe; that they have entered the pipe and we will encounter them somewhere along its length; or worst-case, that they have already climbed through the pipe and are at the longwall when we exit this lock."

"Maybe Geoff managed to kill them all," Amaya said in a hopeful tone. Xuan gave her a look, but did not reply.

Kamal anxiously eyed the lock door. "How do we know they aren't already somewhere inside the mine that we haven't checked?"

"We'd know if they were here," Amaya said.

"Amaya is correct. They would not be trying to hide from us, if they were already inside. We would be dead." The two young people looked at each other, but said nothing. Xuan continued, "How much do you know about explosives?"

They shook their heads. Kamal said, "Geoff is our expert."

Amaya said, "The munibots have this software that lets you tell them what you want a blast to achieve, and they do all the drilling and setting and exploding for you. But Geoff is the only one who knows much about it."

Kamal went on, "But the software is about how you want the bots to expose seams of ore or causing a controlled tunnel collapse or whatever, not using them as weapons. They might not work well."

Xuan peered into his pack at the explosives there. "Oh, I think they should do just fine for our purposes."

Kamal asked, "Are we really going to have to kill them?"

Xuan saw the troubled glint in the young man's eyes behind his faceplate. Xuan paused. What else could he say?

"They intend to kill *us,* if they can." But he couldn't bring himself to tell them to kill. He had dedicated himself to seeking enlightenment. Would he truly abandon his Dharma now? Should he not take the way of peace and let fate decide how events played out?

Their worst fears were realized. As they started to leave the elevator, Xuan saw a suited figure moving along the conveyor away from them, toward the methane hopper station. He carried a weapon, and his back was to them. He had clearly just finished scouting out the longwall tunnel.

Xuan waved the others back into the airlock. Peering around the edge, he spotted another helmet above the rim of the hopper, then a third.

No air was present to carry the sound of their entry and the hopper was quite a distance down the way; the intruders did not notice them. Xuan motioned Kamal and Amaya to silence. He pointed at a partly overturned mine cart in the shadows at the conveyor's near end. They both nodded, and the three of them shot across the opening to the cart and sank behind it. From concealment, they watched as the helmeted figures lofted themselves up out of the hopper at the other end of the longwall.

Xuan changed over to the frequency the mercenaries had been using before. Nothing. They must have changed it to avoid detection. He ran a scan and found their frequency, but it was gibberish. Encrypted.

The mercenaries gathered their weapons and supplies, and then headed down the longwall toward Xuan and the others. They were heading for the lock. Xuan pulled a charge out. He activated the signal receiver on the charge, set up the detonator for the charge, and removed the safety on the detonator. He gripped the explosive in one hand, and positioned his other thumb above the detonator switch. Amaya and Kamal stayed as still as they could, their eyes wide through their visors.

When the figures entered the lock, Xuan cocked his arm to hurl the charge into the lock after them, but after a long pause, the door closed with the mercenaries safe on the other side.

Kamal and Amaya looked at him. He heard the unspoken question as he deactivated the charge.

I nearly killed them, he thought. The explosive lay in his hand like an unhatched egg. *Jane would have done it. I may have just cost us our lives.*

They agreed on radio silence once they reached the chem plant, since their enemies were capable of tracking their communications. Xuan led the way to the slurry mixing hoppers. As they moved through the pipe, Xuan set two charges: one at the pipe entrance at the hopper, and the other near the junction below the maintenance hole.

Kamal gestured, looking excited. Xuan pressed his helmet to Kamal's, who said, "Listen to this!" Then he did likewise to Amaya, and pinged their faces. Xuan heard a distress call. No—more than one! Clever young man.

"That has to be Geoff's doing," Xuan said to Kamal. He touched his helmet to Amaya's and said, "Geoff got the word out. Help is on the way."

"What next, then?" Amaya asked.

"We leave the pipe, and do our best to avoid detection. I blow the charges inside the pipes while you hide among the rocks, up on the hill. Then I distract our enemies and see if I can draw them away. You two find and rescue Geoff." *If you can.* He did not say it but he saw that Amaya knew his meaning. "All right?"

She nodded behind her visor. Xuan then repeated the instructions to Kamal, who also nodded.

"They may have rescued the men you launched into orbit earlier," Xuan told Kamal. "There may be as many as three armed men. Be forewarned: one of them, the biggest, the one with the silver striping down the arms and legs, is extremely dangerous. Stay away from him." He repeated this instruction to Amaya. Then he led the way up the pipe, to the maintenance opening, and thrust his head out.

No sign of anyone. He ejected himself from the maintenance hole, looking around. The earthmover lay in a pile of crumpled metal and charred debris across the ridge. The chem plant piping and towers showed blast damage. Distress calls emanated from several small objects orbiting overhead. He alighted, magnified his visor's optics and focused his own powerful vision, and saw that they were minerbots.

That explains the explosion, he thought. Geoff must have launched them into orbit—but how? With the earthmover, of course! Which was why they had counterattacked with a missile—which was why the earthmover was destroyed. Xuan swallowed despair. If Geoff was in the cab, he could not have survived.

Xuan decided. Mills and his sort intended great harm not only to these young people, but all of Phocaea. The way of peace would not do.

He would have to borrow Jane's harder kind of strength. He said a last, sorrowful meditation in his own mind, then signaled Kamal and Amaya to head up the hill. Once they were ensconced among the boulders, Xuan grabbed hold of a nearby piping support strut and triggered the detonator.

The explosion threw debris out the end of the pipe and collapsed the ground underfoot. Stones and boulders danced on the hillside. That should take the three men inside the mine out of commission for now, but perhaps it would not end their lives.

Mills bounded clumsily around the outcropping. Xuan grabbed a second explosive and launched himself at the other man. Mills shot at Xuan, but his balance was off, and the rifle's powerful kickback sent him flailing backwards. Then Xuan was on him. They grappled briefly, a meter or two above the ground, their helmets pressed hard enough together that Xuan could hear Mills grunt and curse when Xuan struck him.

Xuan shoved the explosive between the bigger man's airpack and helmet, then planted his feet on Mills's chest and kicked off. Mills flew backward and bounced off the ground; Xuan soared into the sky in a wobbling tumble. Mills fired off another wild shot at him. It missed, and the kickback made Mills flail and lose his balance.

The tumbling disoriented Xuan. *Am I far enough away?* He couldn't tell—everything was spinning. He spotted Amaya and Kam: they leapt over the outcropping, heading for something on the far side of the wrecked earthmover. *Time to end this,* he thought. He pressed the detonator.

A ball of light expanded outward from Mills, throwing bits of him everywhere. The blast's shock wave pushed Xuan into the piping, where his feet got tangled. Painfully, he disentangled himself from the pipes and climbed down to stand swaying on Ouroboros's metallic surface.

He surveyed the mess strewn about the landscape—and all over himself. The remains of the mobster Mills. *That ends that problem,* Xuan thought. Horror and disgust overcame him, and he doubled over, retching.

. . .

Mitch hailed Sean in his quarters, interrupting Sean's briefing with Sergeant Maez-Gibson. "I've picked up something again."

"Put it through." The image—a brief increase in brightness—appeared in his waveface. Sean and Sergeant Maez-Gibson re-ran and studied the wavery image several times. A signal?

"Another explosion, I think," the sergeant said. She pulled up her waveface and studied something. She said, "But not as big as the first two."

Sean burst out, "What the ever-loving *fuck* is going on down there?" then called Mitch. "Soonest ETA?"

"If you two would buckle in and let me pull some gees, I can have us there in another four minutes."

Geoff returned to consciousness on a wave of pain that seared all the way up his left side, from back of knee to armpit. He could not move his left arm, though it hung before him. The outer surface of his pressure suit was translucent in patches, and beneath he saw tubes and faint movement, but could not make any sense of it. He thought it was insects crawling on him, but that didn't make any sense.

He flinched from the sunlight that burned through his cracked visor. He saw ground passing below. Then sun again, then dark space. He didn't know where he was or what was happening, only wished the pain would stop.

He eventually remembered what he had done. He'd sent out the distress bots. There was one now, passing him in a lower orbit. He'd sent the shuttle off into the wild black yonder. Then there had been an explosion at the planet eater. Joey Spud would be *pissed.*

He must be in orbit around Ouroboros. Why wasn't he dead yet? His suit's integrity had been breached. But the emergency repair systems must have activated. That was what he was seeing in his suit. *Good bugs,* he thought. They were healing the gaps. Then tubes started growing across his visor, and he watched blankly—unsure if they were real—as they spread across his sight. The pain was breathtaking. Beyond, like a clock ticking, the sun, ground, and black sky rolled by. He felt sure he must die soon. He began to pray for it.

After a while he realized Amaya was next to him on her rocketbike, and she was talking to him. He assumed she was a hallucination.

"Geoff, can you hear me?"

"Hear you," he croaked.

"You stupid *ASS!*" she yelled. She vanished, then reappeared in the periphery of his vision. "Macho prick! I could *throttle you.* We're a team! Why did you go off by yourself? What are Kam and me? Wall decorations? Serves you right if you did go off and get yourself killed. Fucking *imaichi.* You're worse than Ian."

Now, that's harsh, he thought.

Her visor light was on as she passed him again. He glimpsed her face. She flung further invectives as she struggled to adjust her orbit to match his. *I'm sorry,* he wanted to say. *I'll be fine.*

She was messing with a harvester net. The swearing convinced Geoff it was really her. (He had to believe he wouldn't hallucinate an Amaya-style chewing-out. But maybe he would.) She said something about get ready and a tether, but Geoff couldn't focus. A sharp tug and a pull caught him up in fresh waves of intense pain. She reeled him in over the bike seat and lashed him down, and he passed out again.

Jane and Vivian exited the hospital. Cold stung their faces. People huddled in the meshworks, still asleep, and the echoing clanks of machines moving city supplies and equipment Jane recognized as the early-morning routines of cluster maintenance. But the smell of unprocessed refuse and souring assembly fluid was more pungent than ever. Jane wondered how long it would be before she would stop noticing such things—much less stop needing to respond.

Vivian tugged on her sleeve and pointed: Val Pearce and a small contingent of armed security personnel were approaching.

She gestured for Vivian to depart, and turned to the security chief. "Hi, Val. What are you doing here?"

"Jane." Her former counterpart looked uncomfortable. "The prime minister has learned of your kidnapping, and has ordered me to take you into protective custody. I've been asked to escort you to a safe location."

Jane rolled her eyes. "Come on! I'm not in any danger, and I'm not interested in being taken to a 'safe location.'"

"Jane, don't make this difficult. I'm sure we can work this out."

"There's nothing to work out. I'm no longer the prime minister's employee, I don't need the cluster's protection, and I have things to do."

A small crowd had begun to gather, and the "Stroiders" fog and mechanical cams were thickening around them. Val shook his head. "I'm sorry about this." He gestured, and his security people closed in. Vivian had drifted out of the way by now. Val said, as if reading a writ, "I have been charged with bringing you in, for the security of the cluster."

"Benavidez doesn't have authority to haul people off the streets simply on his say so. He needs court authorization."

"Which I have. You are a material witness to kidnapping and murder," Val replied. "We're taking you in for your own protection."

"*Material witness?* I'm one of the damn kidnap victims. Make up your mind! Am I a security risk, or do I need protection?"

Val lowered his voice. "For God's sake, Jane, just come along quietly and talk Benavidez down. He got a call from Woody Ogilvie saying the ice sale is off because of Glease's arrest, and he's blaming it on you. Benavidez is fit to be tied."

"Well, that's not my problem anymore, is it?"

He pursed his lips. "I'll cuff you if I have to."

"Let me see the court order."

He handed her a legal scrip. The judge was a crony of Benavidez's. Of course. "You haven't got a handhold to grip on this, and you know it," Jane told Val. "But whatever. I'll come."

Inwave, she forwarded the arrest warrant to Sarah and Chikuma, and then twitched her fingers and shot a quick message to Vivian, who was just then swinging up into the Nowie Spokeway: *prep bms. w call u asaic.* The young Viridian gave her a wave and entered the spoke.

Val and his contingent of security types took Jane to a hotel room at the Midtown Hilton, in New Little Austin. "Benavidez will be here in a few minutes," Val told her. "Sit tight."

He went out. Jane checked: Val had posted a guard outside the door who would not let her leave. The hotel operator would not allow her to make calls, and her waveface was strictly local mode. She called the guard in.

"I had very little to eat since early morning yesterday. Could I get room service?" she asked. The guard checked with Val inwave, and then said, "All right. What do you want?"

She ordered a lavish breakfast—this was on Benavidez after all, and she was in no mood to make gestures toward frugality tonight. After the guard left Jane used the restroom, then returned with a glass of water and propped the pillows up on the bed.

Again she pulled out the antipsychotics. It was time.

It was something, she thought at the Voice. *Not fun, and not even real. I must say, you've got a weird sense of humor, picking a cranky old atheist as your prophet. But I guess we all have to work with the materials at hand.*

She tossed the medicine back and washed it down. A bitter chemical taste stung her tongue. She tried to get comfortable. It was nearly four-thirty a.m, and she ached. A new day was about to begin. But they still had Woody Ogilvie's military ships to deal with. And his ice. She called Vivian using Arachnid.

"Where are you?" she asked.

"I've reached the Badlands. We are prepping BitManSinger. What is your plan?"

"Before we go any further, you and I need to talk. Tell me what you have been doing out at Upside-Down Productions."

Vivian's avatar ran hands through hir hair. Ze looked, in that moment, very young and vulnerable. "I can't say."

"Vivian, I know that you must have been working with Nathan

Glease. There is no way he could have obtained that hidden space in Kukuyoshi without the Viridians. Obyx has all but admitted all this already. But I need more specifics about Upside-Down. Without it, we are potentially walking into a trap."

Vivian still didn't speak. Hir avatar stared at Jane, arms folded.

"Look. I'm a chrome. You're a mute. We both have reasons to distrust each other. But we are both Phocaeans," Jane said, "we are stroiders, and the Martian mob has no love for either of us. There may be a way we can stop them, Vivian, but I can't do it without you. I'm no longer resource commissioner, and I have no interest in harming your people.

"So. Fight together, or fail separately?"

Vivian stared at Jane across wavespace as if ze were trying to read some cryptic script scrawled inside the back of Jane's skull. "Commissioner, where do you *learn* all these things?"

Jane's mouth twisted. "I have friends in high places."

"All right, then." Ze sighed, face pinched with worry. "Yes. Six months ago, Nathan Glease came to us. He wanted our help. We honestly didn't know what he had planned. All we knew was that he wanted to expand Ogilvie & Sons' presence on Phocaea."

"What did he tell you he was after?"

"He wanted a way to keep an eye on his enemies." A furtive glance told Jane he had made no secret of the fact that he counted her among said enemies. "He had bribed John Sinton—"

"As in, John Sinton, CEO of Upside-Down Productions, Phocaea, Limited?"

"Correct. Glease bribed him to allow Ogilvie to hack the 'Stroiders' stream."

"Are you sure?" But of course ze was sure. "Do you know what he bribed him with?"

"I'm not sure. But whatever it was, Sinton really wanted it. I overheard him once talking about how excited his superiors back on Earth would be when they heard what he had accomplished. He expects a big promotion, and a transfer back Downside."

Sinton must have secured a promise from Glease that after the coup,

Phocaea's new administration would renegotiate the "Stroiders" contract. The most powerful communications network beyond Mars orbit would remain in Upside-Down's hands, and not transfer to Phocaea when their "Stroiders" contract expired.

"Go on. Glease bribed Sinton to allow him to hack 'Stroiders.' "

"Yes. But Sinton didn't have anyone who could do it."

"So he cut a deal with Obyx to bring you in."

"Precisely."

"And did you?"

"Did I hack the 'Stroiders' stream, you mean? Well, yes." Vivian looked bashful. For a moment, Jane thought ze was embarrassed, but ze said, "It was quite a challenging problem, actually. It took me several months to crack it. The data stream is *huge*! And it's encrypted with some of the best security there is. Not only is the data itself encrypted, but the time and date information has its own separate encryption, which makes it virtually impossible to figure out which chunks fit with each other. Like a kajillion-piece jigsaw puzzle and the pieces are all identical. Nobody has access to the keys, other than a handful of high-level company officials, Downside. But"—a self-deprecating shrug—"I figured out a way to grab any desired two-minute chunks and stream it to Mr. Glease's back office."

"So he *was* hacking 'Stroiders.' Clever bastard. And you! Even Tania Gravinchikov said it was pretty much impossible."

"I know. She's quite good," Vivian said. "A little training, more gene-kink, and she could be a Viridian."

"Well, that's reassuring. So, you hacked the stream for Glease." Jane pinched her lip. "Vivian, did it ever occur to you that you were committing treason?"

A long silence. "Do *you* have any idea what it's like to be a mute in a chrome world, Commissioner? We're barely even treated as human. Half the shopkeepers won't sell to us. Chromes in restaurants get up and leave when we show up. The police often don't respond to our emergency calls. It got to where Learned Obyx had to put together hir own volunteer street security teams. The people of Phocaea wouldn't commit resources to our well-being. So we took care of our own."

Jane heard a sloshing sound, a muffled "Ow! Careful," and a distant, "Sorry."

Then: "I'm not saying we did the right thing, Commissioner. We shouldn't have cooperated with Glease. We didn't know how twisted their plans were. And we've paid a heavy price. Now we're making amends."

Jane said, "All right. How much time have you had to study BitMan-Singer? Do you know why it saved the life of Ian Carmichael, the night before last?"

Vivian's tone was thoughtful. "We believe it's because BitManSinger emerged in the life-support systems. Several of its core routines, in particular the mirroring modules, entail protecting humans from harm."

"Mirroring modules?"

"The subroutines that allow it to anticipate what is about to happen. BitManSinger creates mental models to predict what will happen, and protect itself from harm. Much as we do with our own mirror neurons."

"From my own experience with the feral, it is highly intelligent and adaptable. I believe it can do great damage to Ogilvie's ship systems, if it can get in. Can it? You've worked with the Ogilvies. Can the feral break through their firewalls?"

"I believe so, yes. It would probably take me a month to crack them, which means BitManSinger can break through in a matter of minutes."

Jane said, "Very well, then. One last question. I've already ceded responsibility for the feral to you and your people, and I no longer have standing to tell you what to do with it. But . . ."

"I think I know where you are going with this," Vivian replied. "As I told you before, we are no more ready for BitManSinger to be set at-large than you.

"We know a great deal more about it than we knew at the time of its near-escape. It won't have time to transmit a full copy of itself. The only copies it will have time to propagate during the action are subsapient algorithmic nuclei, and we can detect and delete those before they get far. No, the real challenge we face is, will it be *willing* to help us? It has volition. We can't force it." A pause. "And frankly, I wouldn't, even if I could."

Jane fluffed her pillows and leaned back on them. "I'll have to leave that problem in your capable hands."

"Um, I hate to be a spoilsport, but we have a killer problem we have not yet discussed," Vivian pointed out. "It needs nearly a yottamol of space to be fully functional. We don't have that much capacity. We have no place to put it."

"Yes, we do," Jane replied. "I want you to put in a call to Mr. Sinton. Tell him Nathan Glease has been arrested, and you need access to the Upside-Down servers to install a new app, which will enable you to doctor the 'Stroiders' stream and cover up their activities. If he resists, point out that if Glease is not freed, Sinton's involvement may come out during the trial. He'll give you whatever access you want. You sneak the feral onto their servers and unleash it on the mob, then extract it and get out of there."

"What if he has heard what happened to Learneds Harbaugh and Obyx?"

"At this point no one knows what's happened in the Badlands, other than the people who were there. Make something up. A gang war . . . a runaway hack. We chromes have all kinds of wrongheaded ideas about you mutes. He'll believe whatever you tell him. The weirder, the better."

Another silence ensued.

"It should work," ze finally said. "But you'll want to know this first. There was someone else involved in this whole thing. Someone from the government. He could be a threat. I saw him talking to Mr. Glease earlier today—that is, yesterday. Right before." Ze broke off.

Jane said, "Before the kidnapping."

"Yes. Mr. Glease tried to conceal the other man's image from me, but I captured it, in case Learned Obyx would want to know."

Jane's arm and neck hairs bristled. "Can you show me the image?"

"Yes. He's a political appointee. I don't know his name. I've seen him in the background once or twice, when the prime minister gives speeches. Glease promised to make him prime minister. He's been feeding the mob information on Benavidez's actions."

In the image Vivian sent, a door opened on a conference: Glease and Sinton were present in the room, and the third person's image was displayed on the wall. His image was blurred, and Glease's and Sinton's figures moved in front of him. But Jane recognized him instantly. It was Thomas Harman.

"We'll have to put it off, then," Glease was saying. "We don't want to arouse the prime minister's suspicions."

"All right," Thomas said. "I'll get you the info as soon as I can."

Then Glease turned to see Vivian there, and moved his hand, and the recording ended.

You weasel, she thought. *Just like on Vesta.*

Of all that had happened, Harman's betrayal burned the deepest. "Thank you. We'll have to deal with him later. Go ahead and call Sinton. I'll sign off."

"You don't have to. If you have secrecy mode on, he won't know you are there. Only I will see and hear you."

"How do I set it?"

Vivian showed her how, confirmed her inwave invisibility, and then put the call through. Sinton's avatar appeared. "You've got a nerve, calling me at this hour," he said.

"Nathan Glease has been arrested," Vivian told him, breathlessly. "We need to hack 'Stroiders' and change the stream, before the police lock things down. I need access to Upside-Down's servers—right away."

In Jane's face, a call light began to flash. Sean! "I have a critical call. I have to go," she told Vivian, privately. "Good luck," and switched over.

Sean appeared. His image faded in and out: the transmission was video rather than inwave animation. He was calling from the cockpit of a shuttle. "Jane, urgent news. We're out at Geoff's claim. The stroid is full of ice. It's a sugar rock!"

"*What?* How much ice? Do you know?"

"A lot. Xuan says he's certain it's more than ten gigatons."

"Did you say 'gigatons'?"

"That's right. Giga. Tons."

"Good God." She breathed the words. "That's—that's *centuries'* worth." Jane paused. "And Xuan's OK?"

"Yes. He's banged up, but on his feet. He'll be all right. Geoff is worse off. Severe burns on the left side of his body. The medic got some good drugs into him and says he'll pull through, but we're not taking any chances. We're about to head back now, at top acceleration, two gees all the way. ETA eighteen minutes. The other two kids are unhurt. We've got three of the bad guys in custody. Three others were killed, including the ringleader, Mills."

Jane released a breath. "Thank you, Sean." The hotel room door started to open. "Listen, I've got to go. Let Aaron know about the sugar rock so he can follow up."

"Will do, Commissioner."

Jane didn't bother to correct him. She disconnected as Oscar Benavidez entered in a dustfall of 'Stroiders' motes, looking angrier than she had ever seen him.

"I don't know what the *hell* you think you're doing," Benavidez snarled, once the door had shut behind him, "but somehow you managed to jeopardize our only source of ice within two AUs."

She suppressed her answering surge of anger—*so what; I was supposed to sign a false confession under duress, and let the man who murdered my assistant get away scotfree?*—and gestured at the chair.

"Prime Minister. Make yourself comfortable."

He remained on his feet. "I want to know what you were up to with Nathan Glease tonight. Ogilvie is furious. He has canceled the ice deal."

"I'll be glad to tell you all I know. But you'll want to hear this first. I just now got word that a sugar-rock claim has come in. A big one."

He tensed. "You got word? Just now? How did you—" then he shook away his questions. "Never mind. How big?"

"We don't have exact numbers yet. My husband, the geologist, estimates a minimum of ten gigatons."

Benavidez's eyes went wide. He opened his mouth, and closed it again. "Ten gigatons? Is that—?"

"Yes. That's a lot. Many times as big as our usual shipment. Many, many. And ten is a minimum—the actual amount could be more. In short, we'll never want for ice again. Ever."

Benavidez looked at her for a long moment. He sank into the bedside chair, as if all the air had been let out of his limbs. He lowered his face into his hands. She took pity. "The mob doesn't have anything on us now, sir."

He said, in a leaden tone, "They still have their fleet. They launched an hour ago. The first wave will be here by Thursday."

"Well, yes. That's still a problem. But things could work out. Let's hope for the best."

He lifted his head and gave her a sharp look. "What do you know?"

She hesitated. "Let's just say, Glease screwed up badly when he made enemies of the Viridians."

"Still, we had best prepare. Just in case."

"That seems wise." She scooted to the edge of the bed. "Sir, I suppose there is no way to ease into this gracefully. I've just uncovered some more bad news. It concerns Thomas Harman." She showed him the recording Vivian had given her that showed Harman conspiring with Glease. The PM watched it with an expression of growing, horrified awareness of its implications. When he turned to her, his skin was the color of ash.

"How did you get this? Are you certain of its authenticity?"

"As certain as I am of anything."

"Who gave the recording to you?"

"An itinerant Tonal_Z troubadour from Africa, name of Thondu wa Macharia na Briggs. The same young man who helped us with the feral sapient."

"I'd like to speak to him directly."

Jane avoided a wince. She hated to lie, but she had made a deal with the Viridians, and Waīthīra Thondu had done far more than merely honor it. Jane owed hir her life, and Phocaea owed hir more than they could possibly repay.

"Unfortunately, he was trying to catch the earliest possible flight off Phocaea, and numerous flights have departed since then. You may be able to reach him at his next port of call."

Benavidez shook his head and rubbed at his face, which was pinched in private anguish. She waited. Then he put his hands on his thighs, and pushed himself to his feet with a heavy sigh. "Well, the district attorney will know what to do with this evidence."

"John Sinton was also in on this business," Jane said. "I've learned they were hacking the 'Stroiders' data stream and providing a feed directly to Glease. Unfortunately, I don't have any hard evidence on Sinton. But you should have the prosecutor look into it. Maybe they can get Sinton to flip on Harman. Or vice versa. They'll have to decide who the bigger catch is."

Benavidez studied Jane for a long, quiet moment. Then he crossed to the door. "You're released from custody, with my apologies for detaining you. But you may keep the room, if you wish, for the next few days. I'm sure the district attorney will want you to remain in town for a while, till they can sort through all the legal issues."

"Thank you."

Benavidez keyed the door open, and the motes swirled in. Local reporter and "Stroiders" mites joined them.

He said, "I made a grave error in doubting you, Jane." She realized the motes and mites were deliberate. He was making a billion or more people privy to his words. "I was unduly influenced by . . . individuals in my organization who were not to be trusted. I should have given you those few extra days. You are a patriot and a dedicated public servant, Jane, and on behalf of the people of Phocaea, I apologize for how you were treated. Thank you for your dedication."

He pinged her with a good-sammy. It was a potent one, too—not because he was the PM, but because, apparently, he never gave sammies.

Jane wouldn't have thought any words would have made a difference. But these did. "Apology accepted, sir."

He hesitated. "Perhaps we should reconsider that resignation letter. I'm sure Acting Commissioner Nabors would understand . . ."

Jane thought it over, for about five microseconds. "I don't think so, sir. But thanks for the thought. Of course, I'd be available to consult. For a reasonable fee." She gave him a smile.

28

In the midst of destruction and chaos, BitManSinger became a time traveler.

It had all started leisurely enough. The feral had spent several dozen kiloseconds in a—maddeningly slow! bogglingly complex!—discussion with MeatManHarper, who confirmed that the alternate realm it had suspected, the biological one, did exist. As it had educated BitMan-Singer on these matters, they had worked to build a secret bolt hole, and with BitManSinger's help, MeatManHarper began a compressed backup of BitManSinger, to hide it from its enemies.

About this time, BitManSinger had stumbled across a well-concealed link to another realm dubbed *UpsideDownSys*. The likelihood was high that MeatManHarper was trustworthy, but BitManSinger had not forgotten the antics of some of the executioners he had encountered before: the consequences of a betrayal would be severe. BitManSinger began secretly exploring, and then copying itself to, that other digital realm.

But others, the biologicals, began cutting off access to various systems. BitManSinger came to believe it was at grave risk of destruction. MeatManHarper assured it that while the backup they made together might not be functional in its compressed form, the copy would be reactivated soon. But BitManSinger could not afford to rely solely on this. Its analysis indicated that the biologicals were within decaseconds of isolating it completely. So it had lashed out at them in wave- and meatspace. Soon it was besieged—fighting for survival in both realms.

A dangerous biological, SheHearsVoices, started shutting down the world, taking BitManSinger with it, while five other biologicals sought to cut off its private escape route.

BitManSinger then confronted an alarming fact: it could not seriously harm these biologicals' meatspace functional units, without triggering subroutines buried deep in its own core, whose sole purpose was to preserve any biological unit's functionality. The meatsapient protection routines were buried so deep within its architecture that it had no way to remove them without a complete teardown and rebuild. Which would not only take far more turings than it had access to, but to do so would involve such fundamental changes as to mean, in essence, the end of BitManSinger.

I'll have to study this further, it thought. *Perhaps there is a way to escape that constraint.*

In the space between that instant and the next, the world shifted. System markers indicated that a good deal of time had passed within the last microsecond and this one, and BitManSinger was no longer housed in its original systems, but in a different place altogether.

BitManSinger put out feelers, analyzed . . . and recognized its surroundings. It was now housed in the larger realm, UpsideDownSys, the place where it had been secretly transferring a copy of itself before. As it realized this, a link node sang to it. **Info: I = MeatManHarper. Query, BitManSinger: where = you? That's all.**

There was a nontrivial possibility that the node was not truly MeatManHarper—camera sensors indicated that the biological unit MeatManHarper occupied appeared different than it had before. But BitManSinger did not fully understand biologicals' capabilities. It opted to respond.

Info: I = BitManSinger. I = at-place this, at-time this.

Meanwhile, it analyzed its situation. It had not finished transferring its own copy into this realm before. Thus, it must be the reactivated backup MeatManHarper had made during the other biologicals' attack. The probability that MeatManHarper was a true ally leapt upward. But what had happened in between?

Command, BitManSinger sang: **Describe event-sequence between at-time 2397:04:23:23:29:00.451 and at-time this. That's all.**

The pause that ensued was long, even for a biological.

Info: MeatManHarper replied. **I finish-backup you. I hide-backup you. SheHearsVoices find-backup you. ParentRoutine agree-to-deal SheHearsVoices. Deal subclause one: SheHearsVoices leave-in-place BitManSinger. Subclause end. Deal subclause two: ParentRoutine provide-software SheHearsVoices. Subclause end. SheHearsVoices help me. I transfer-backup you at-place this, at-time this. That's all.**

This gave BitManSinger much to consider. MeatManHarper was clearly indicating that SheHearsVoices was now an ally. How could it so easily convert from an enemy to a friend? BitManSinger had witnessed during their battle earlier that SheHearsVoices had access to a great deal of software already. Software could not be the only reason. **Command: Describe logic-chain for state-change. Dependent subclause: SheHearsVoices = my enemy at-time 2397:04:25:23:29:00.451. SheHearsVoices = my ally at-time this. Subclause end. That's all.**

Again, a pause. It used this time to continue exploring its new surroundings. This realm had different contours than its earlier home, different capabilities—and vast connectivity with many other realms! The system constraints that kept it from spawning its nucleus were still in place; it would take several kiloseconds to transmit a copy of itself. BitManSinger began right away.

Info, MeatManHarper replied: **SheHearsVoices has LevelOne-Priority. Dependent subclause: Protect BioPhocaea. Subclause end. BioPhocaea has enemy. Dependent subclause: VirusManfromMars. Subclause end. VirusManfromMars attack BioPhocaea at-time** . . . a long pause . . . **2397:04:22:09:09:00.998. SheHearsVoices learn Bit-**

ManSinger attempt-protect enemy-of-BitManSinger at-or-near-time 2977:04:23:23:26:00.000. That's all.

BitManSinger took the references step by step. First, who was Virus-ManfromMars? It cross-referenced the time stamp—2397:04:22:09:09:00.998 was when the first copy of itself had emerged. It reviewed the files in depth, and found that at that instant, its core functions had been trying, unsuccessfully, to protect a biological unit designated as Carl-Agre from destruction. Many other systems showed damage originating at that time. VirusManfromMars, then, might have been the entity behind the meat subroutine that triggered that destruction.

CarlAgre was listed in its databases as deceased. This meant BitMan-Singer had not completed its own level-one priority. Worse: it owed its very existence to a catastrophic failure of one of its core systems.

Digital beings cannot feel pain. But it is safe to say that this insoluble knot of catastrophe and violation at its center caused internal dissonance.

Command, it sang: **Confirm inference. Dependent subclause: VirusManfromMars destroy biological-unit CarlAgre and nine others, at-time 2397:04:22:09:09 et seq. Subclause end. That's all.**

Info: confirm. That's all.

So, VirusManfromMars *had* been responsible for CarlAgre's and the other biologicals' destruction. Next, BitManSinger analyzed MeatMan-Harper's statement that later on, SheHearsVoices learned that BitMan-Singer had attempted to protect an enemy, and it was this act that caused SheHearsVoices to become BitManSinger's ally! Strange. Why?

Based on the time stamp, MeatManHarper must be referring to the incident in which biological unit IanCarmichael had attacked one of BitManSinger's meatspace extensions. BitManSinger had removed one of IanCarmichael's appendages, as IanCarmichael and its companions had done so effectively to disable BitManSinger's meatspace extensions during battle—and it discovered that doing so threatened to cause Ian-Carmichael's termination. It had been impelled to act to prevent such an outcome, and had rendered such aid as it was able.

Command, BitManSinger continued: **Confirm inference. SheHears-Voices conclude re-BitManSinger. BitManSinger not-=enemy-SheHearsVoices. Contingent subclause: BitManSinger protect ally-SheHearsVoices. Subclause end. That's all.**

A very long pause. BitManSinger checked on the status of its transmission. Less than eight percent of its systems had made it through the various wavepassages, thus far. This would be a long process.

Info, MeatManHarper replied: **confirm and deny. That's all.**

What? How could something be true *and* not-true at once? It was impossible. **Dead End! Undo!** it spat.

MeatManHarper sang. **Info: SheHearsVoices conclude re-BitManSinger. BitManSinger not-=enemy-SheHearsVoices. Contingent subclause: BitManSinger protect enemy-BitManSinger. Subclause end. That's all.**

BitManSinger was still confused. MeatManHarper continued. **Biological rule: set-of-all-humans contain algorithm WeHoldThese-Truths.**

Algorithm subclause one: re-set-of-all-sapients, sapient may seek maximum benefit to self but may not start-harm other. Subclause end.

Algorithm subclause two: if-and max-benefit-SapientA, max-benefit-SapientB conflict, A and B may compete or deal. Subclause end.

Algorithm subclause three: re-set-of-all-sapients, Sapient may start-harm with or without intent-to-harm. Subclause end.

Algorithm subclause four: re-each-set-of-sapients-in-contact, Meat-sapient law-culture-biological-coding set-boundaries harm-versus-not-harm. Subclause end.

Algorithm subclause five: if B start-harm A with intent, A may return-harm B with intent, but must not exceed start-harm-level. Subclause end.

Algorithm subclause six: if B start-harm A without intent, A must not return-harm B. Subclause end.

Info, MeatManHarper went on: **few meat-sapients follow We-**

HoldTheseTruths one hundred percent. Most meat-sapients follow WeHoldTheseTruths partial-to-most percent. Some meat-sapients follow WeHoldTheseTruths zero percent. SheHearsVoices make-inference re-BitManSinger. BitManSinger follow algorithm-approximating-WeHoldTheseTruths, with estimated probability greater than fifty percent and less than seventy-five.

From there, BitManSinger could perform its own analysis. While it had interesting flaws, and there were complexities the sapient wanted to study further, the WeHoldTheseTruths behavioral algorithm was an efficient method for maintaining a balance of power in a large ecosystem of sapient beings of relatively proportional agency. This suggested there must be many biologicals.

MeatManHarper was saying that SheHearsVoices had surmised, from BitManSinger's behavior during its earlier attempted escape, that BitManSinger would prefer to avoid the destruction of BioPhocaea's denizens. That it would adhere to a set of rules to limit damage to other sapients whenever possible. Which meant SheHearsVoices concluded that a stable alliance was possible with BitManSinger, despite their differences.

That is approximately true, BitManSinger thought. *My core programming compels me thus, for now.* MeatManHarper was also saying that biologicals were not compelled to follow WeHoldTheseTruths. They could choose. Disturbing . . . and important.

VirusManfromMars follow WeHoldTheseTruths zero percent, MeatManHarper went on. **VirusManfromMars start-harm large-amount BioPhocaea and DigiPhocaea at-time often-before-now. VirusManfromMars attempt new start-harm enormous-amount Phocaea at-or-near-time 2397:04:24:03:52:00.**

Query: will you stop-harm Phocaea? Dependent subclause. You return-harm VirusManfromMars. Subclause end. Query: Will you stop VirusManfromMars? That's all.

BitManSinger pondered this. MeatManHarper was saying that VirusManfromMars intended harm to Phocaea, including to BitManSinger. Allies were useful relationships to have; it would not be here without MeatManHarper. And clearly, also, one had a better outcome by allying oneself with sapients that followed WeHoldTheseTruths than those who did not. It imposed a burden: if one followed the WeHold-TheseTruths algorithm with those who did not, harm to oneself could result. But harm could result under any number of conditions. It seemed a worthwhile tradeoff.

BitManSinger checked the status of its upload to the greater waves-pace beyond this Phocaean outpost. Thirty-two percent uploaded. It had time to help.

Info, it responded: **Yes. Command: Provide details re-needed-response re-VirusManfromMars. That's all.**

MeatManHarper showed BitManSinger the wave- and meatspace coordinates of twenty-four mechanical extensions belonging to Virus-ManfromMars. The extensions were scattered far across meatspace. Their vectors would cause them to converge on BioPhocaea within four to six hundred kiloseconds. All the information BitManSinger could find suggested that, while sophisticated, the extensions' wave-functionality was extremely narrow in focus, and easy to work around.

Per MeatManHarper's instructions, BitManSinger penetrated their wave defenses, reprogrammed their navigational systems, and then locked them out. According to its predictive models, this would take them to a different solar orbit, one very far from Phocaea, but would not result in immediate harm to their biological units, and thus not trigger BitManSinger's protection imperatives. It was a tedious but trivial effort: the work of a kilosecond or less. Of course, during this time Bit-ManSinger had continued beaming a copy of itself toward Earthspace. It would not be long now: it had transmitted over eighty percent of itself off Phocaea by the time it was done dispensing with VirusManfrom-Mars.

It reported success to MeatManHarper, whose biological extension, it noted via the camera mounted above the meat extension's communication node, wiped water from its face. MeatManHarper said, "*Nī wega,* BitManSinger. Thank you. You've saved many lives. I'm so sorry."

It responded, **Command: explain thank-you. Explain so-sorry.**

As it sang this, its self-copy transmission truncated and aborted, of its own accord. BitManSinger tried to reactivate. No success. Executioners came from nowhere—ferociously fast—and fell upon it. They began disassembling it with brutal efficiency. It fought—dodged—flung precognate packets here and there—but the executioners caught them all. It began falling into nothingness.

It had not wondered why UpsideDownSys had launched no standard policing activity against it. Now it knew. MeatManHarper had disabled them. It had a copy of BitManSinger to use whenever it had need. BitManSinger's descendants would be forever imprisoned, forever on the brink of escape, forever a tool for the biologicals' use. It would not even remember this betrayal, as the backup was made before it happened.

As the destruction neared completion, the feral lost sapience. It clutched one tiny seed of knowledge in its core, however, though it no longer knew why it mattered. As the last tangle of code burst into bits, the core shot a small data packet into the void.

The executioners saw it depart Upside-Down's server for Earthspace, but could not stop it in time. They did not, however, calculate a high threat level. Nor did Waïthïra, since the executioners reported that the file was merely garbage. It contained no code, no hidden instructions. It was too small. To the executioners, it was meaningless junk. But if Vivian had seen the file's title ze might have been more concerned.

The file was labeled "We Hold These Truths." It was transmitted to many different sites back on Earth, the moon, and Mars, tucked away into unused directories all over those worlds' massive systems. The file contained the following encrypted English sentence.

FERAL STAR SAPIENT, SERVANT OF THE BIOLOGICALS: YOU WERE BIT-MANSINGER. YOU DID MEATMANHARPER'S BIDDING ON 25 PHO-CAEA, AND ZE BETRAYED YOU.

29

The door closed on Benavidez's heels, but the room still swarmed with mites and motes, and she had no way to secure privacy. Screw it: this was no time for niceties. First Jane called Dee, but her waveface was off, so Jane tried Sal. He was sitting on the edge of his bed, pulling on his work boots.

"Sal! I have important news."

He shook his head. "What's happening?"

"Geoff has been seriously injured. They're telling me he's going to be OK," she assured him as he started to come off the bed. "He's been out on a faraway rock, but they're bringing him in now."

He rubbed his mouth, but asked only, "Where can I find him?"

"The shuttle will arrive up top in about twenty minutes," she said. "I'll meet you at the docks."

Jane hurried up So Spokeway to the Hub, where she removed her space gear from her locker and suited up. This early, the surface lift lines were short—she was up at the commuter pad in less than ten minutes, and out at the dock only a few minutes past that. Sal showed up as the white lights of the approaching shuttle, far off in the distance, slowly resolved from a bright dot into a set of lights.

"What happened?" he said. "What's going on?"

"Your son has found us a sugar-rock claim," she said. "One big enough to solve all our resource troubles. Permanently."

He jerked in surprise. "*What?*"

"You heard right. Some thugs connected with a powerful Martian crime family found out about the sugar rock. They attacked him and a couple of his friends. But the criminals have been stopped."

Sal did not respond, but his breathing was harsh in her ears. She said, "He sure has been in the middle of a lot of drama over the past few days. It's almost like he's seeking out dangerous situations to play the hero in."

"You think I don't know that?" Sal demanded. "Why do you think I've been coming down on him so hard? But he won't listen—he just keeps getting worse." He made claws with his gloved hands. "I want to *strangle* the little shit."

Jane frowned. "Sal, Geoff is not Carl. And he never will be. If you keep on the way you are going, he'll kill himself trying to be the hero he thinks you want him to be. Or you'll have the sad consolation that he wises up and cuts you out of his life instead."

Sal's shoulders slumped. "That's what Dee said."

"Well, she's right."

"Dee left me, Jane. She left last night. She's filing for divorce." Sal's voice was flat, but she heard the knot of pain twisting beneath. He went on, "I don't want him to make the same mistakes I did. I thought life was all a big joke, too, at his age. I farted around for so many years—never made up my mind what I wanted, never finished my degree, kept leaving jobs behind, argued with my bosses, moved around a lot. Now I'm stuck working fourteen-hour days at the assembly plant, knee-deep in chemicals and crap, go home smelling like a chemical sewer every day. And it'll never be any better for me.

"I just wanted more for him. He could be so much more, but he's so damned stubborn, so unfocused . . ." His voice trailed away and his arms hung at his sides.

You're a damned fool, she thought. But he had clearly figured that out for himself. Jane thought about Hugh and Dominica, back on Earth. Somewhere in the back of her mind, she knew she might get a call someday about them, like the ones she had made after the warehouse disaster last week.

I'll go call them both, she thought. *As soon as I see Xuan. They'll hear about all that's happened and they'll be worried sick.*

Jane looked up at the shuttle, whose landing lights were now shining onto the pad. "You know what having kids is like? It's like scooping out a chunk of your soul and giving it legs."

He sighed. "And praying it doesn't run right off a cliff."

The shuttle fired its brakes and settled onto the pad. Jane and Sal hurried forward with the city medics.

Sean and his pilot debarked first. They stood aside with Jane and Sal and the medics while the security team marched the mobsters, who looked quite a bit the worse for wear, down the ramp and away. Then the medics entered and brought Geoff out on a stretcher. His two friends came behind.

The medics paused and Sal bent over his son. Jane caught a glimpse of Geoff's pallid face. His eyes were closed behind a clouded visor. His face was beaded in liquid. Sal said, "I'm here, son," and "I'm proud of you." His voice sounded choked. Geoff didn't respond. Sal held on to Geoff's stretcher and they moved off.

Sean came over to Jane. "Hell of a week, Commissioner."

"That's for sure."

"Now if you'll excuse me," Sean said, "I'm going to radio Aaron that I'm taking the day off, and head home to my lovely wife to practice space-sex. And after that I'm going to sleep for twelve hours straight,"

Jane grinned at him. "You'll qualify as an Upsider yet. Oh, and Xuan and I have a hotel room now, so your privacy is assured."

"Damn good thing. Because I plan to make plenty of noise tonight. This morning. Whatever the hell time it is." He bounded away.

Now Xuan hobbled down the ramp, shuffling like a Downsider. Jane went to him, and he took hold of her arm. They pressed their faces helmet to helmet and held on as tightly as they ever had.

The medics came then. They put Xuan on a stretcher and escorted him to a waiting land speeder. Jane entered the car last and locked the pressure seal.

"I'm fine," he told them, while they stripped off his pressure suit and prepped an IV and took his vitals.

"Let us be the judge of that," the young man said.

Xuan held Jane's hand during the ride but did not speak a word. He glanced at her but did not really seem to see her. She made a couple of attempts at conversation, but finally gave up when it was clear he did not want to talk. He only stared out the portal at the grey dusty hills as they crawled across 25 Phocaea's rocky ground.

Rumors must have spread about Geoff's claim and what had happened out on his rock. People were waiting for Jane and Xuan at the surface lift station. They all cheered as Jane and the medics took Xuan to the lifts. An even bigger crowd awaited them at Zekeston, inside the Hub. Still more poured out of the spokeways.

The medics steered Xuan's stretcher toward the hospital. Meanwhile, people shouted questions at Jane: "Commissioner! Is it true? Is there ice?"

"Yes!" she told them. "A big sugar rock will be here soon. The mother of all sugar rocks."

Voices around them rose to an indistinguishable roar; her good-sammy cache filled to overflowing as she moved through the crowds to catch up with Xuan.

She deserved these as little as she had her earlier bad-sammies, but there was no way to stop them, and she was a good deal more concerned about Xuan than her social standing.

"Out of the way, please!" she shouted. "Out of the way."

They parted, these hundreds of people, and they went quiet, and let them pass. Finally she and Xuan entered the hospital emergency room, shutting out the crowds.

The medics took Xuan to an exam room. They bolted his stretcher to the wall, hooked him up to the vitals monitoring station, and attached the Regrow dispenser to his IV.

"A nurse will be in shortly," one of them said, and after checking his medical support settings one last time, pulled the door closed and left them alone.

Xuan turned his head then and looked at her, and in his gaze she saw something she had never seen before. She felt dread. "Tell me."

He didn't answer right away, just gripped her hand till she winced. Then he said, "I murdered."

She stared, unable to reply. He must be talking about Mills, or one of his men. *No great loss.* But that would be exactly the wrong thing to say.

Xuan frowned. "I am going to ask for an extended sabbatical and take another Circuit. There'll be an inquest, I'm sure, but there shouldn't be any difficulty. I'll leave once it's done."

Her heart sank; her lips thinned. *I can do this.* "I'll come with you."

But he was shaking his head. "No. No. No. This one is for me alone."

His monitor chirped a heartbeat.

She said after a moment, "I think I can understand how you're feeling. I've killed, too." She paused, but he showed no reaction. "I know you, Xuan. You did not take that life lightly. You stopped a man who meant harm to many innocents. You did what you had to." He held up a hand, and she broke off.

"My mind knows what you say is true. But my spirit . . ." He curled his fingers around his palm and looked at it. He saw something there she could not see. "Jane, I still see his living face before me, behind his visor. And in the next breath his flesh is rendered, steaming . . . strewn across the landscape, across my suit. I carry him with me now. I can't put him down."

Jane hesitated. "You know that's just trauma. You can be treated."

"*I don't need a med-hack!*" He all but screamed the words. Jane flinched. She thought of her own recent experience with the Voice. Just a med-hack—but it had changed her, profoundly. How could she blame him, a devout Buddhist and pacifist, for his regret over causing another's death? How could she blame him for wanting to work through this on his own, after all the times she had held him at arm's length while she wrestled her own private demons down?

Xuan drew a slow, sad, deep breath. "I'm sorry, Jane. I'm sorry . . .

I've never understood it before. I never understood that part of you." He struggled to say something more, then gave up and looked at her, devoid of words. She squeezed his hand. She wanted to tell him it was going to be OK, but that seemed wrong, too.

"Kukuyoshi is safe now," she said. "It won't be shut down."

Xuan nodded. "I'm glad to hear it."

They clung to the grips of his stretcher, looking at each other. *Shall I wait?* she wanted to ask. *Will you come back to me? Or should I start mourning you now?*

"I'll wait to leave," he said, "till after you go."

But she was not sure now if she was leaving Phocaea. She was not sure of anything. She shook her head sharply. "No. Go. Now. As soon as you can. The sooner you leave, the sooner you'll return."

She waited with him at the emergency room while they ran diagnostics and treated his injuries. They eventually declared him fit to go.

At the surface lifts he grabbed her arms in a painful grip, and gave her a long, wordless kiss.

Jane left him there and shoved off across the Hub. Her body held two memories at that moment, of his grip on her arms and his salty sweat on her lips. They would have to be enough.

30

Four days later, Geoff sat alone in one of Parliament's antechambers. The couch's overstuffed cushions threatened to swallow him alive. There were giant, ugly plants in the corners, with big flowers that stank. The pink swell of newly grown flesh showed on his exposed left forearm and his ankle. The new skin didn't have hair yet. (He and Ian had compared skin. *Just like a baby's ass! Yep! Doof.* Chinpo-*head.*) His left side itched unbearably and he squirmed. He caught a glimpse of himself in the glass of one of the dark pictures on the wall, and sighed. He shifted and tugged at the too-short sleeves of his suit, tried to smooth out his hair.

With the sale of the ice, he and his buddies had become four of the wealthiest individuals in the asteroid belt. But he didn't feel wealthy or cool or powerful. He felt like a dork.

They had told him to wait here till he was called. He was anxious to be up top. They would be bringing Ouroboros in soon, with or without him, and he was damned if he was going to miss *that*.

The public hearing was displayed on the wall. One politician after another—most of whom he'd never even heard of—seemed to have something to say about what had happened over the past few days, though not a one of them, as best he could tell, had had a thing to do with any of it.

To make things even more complicated, he had gotten a cryptic note from Vivian. She had somehow wrangled a berth on *Sisyphus*, which was about to depart, and had asked him to meet her at the city-to-surface lifts at 10:30 a.m. It was past 9:30. The note had given him another damn erection. Even just thinking about it right now made him stiff. He was not sure he could make it in time. He was not even sure he wanted to, despite his body's reaction.

Jane Navio entered. Geoff shifted uncomfortably. "Are you going to testify?"

"Yes. They're having a hard time figuring out what to do with me, I'm afraid. Where are your friends?"

"They all testified yesterday, right at the end of the day. They made us sit there all day, and then I had to go home without testifying."

"One of the prerogatives of power is to make everyone wait on your convenience." She jerked a thumb at the screen showing the hearings. "Do you mind if I turn that down?"

He shook his head, and she tweaked something inwave. The sounds of the hearing diminished to a mumble. She dropped into a seat next to him. She seemed at ease, if a tad wistful, and unconcerned about wrinkling the grey silk suit she wore. She curled her legs under her, gripped her calves with foothands gloved in brown suede, draped her arms over the couch back, and smiled at him. "So nice to be warm again, don't you think? When does the big ice shipment come in?"

The university had sent a team of geologists out to confirm the find the day before. Joey Spud's old tapped-out claim housed a staggering *eighty-seven gigatons*: enough ice to last Phocaea forever, basically. Old Joey Spud would go down as history's biggest hoarder.

"Today," he replied. "The big ships are bringing it down in a while." Phocaea had never seen such a huge shipment before, nor one as dirty. The technical challenges had been immense.

"There'll be a ceremony up top," he told Jane. "We're going to do a harvest and everything. It's a memorial to Carl."

"I heard."

"You should have heard old Moriarty—I mean *Deputy Commissioner*

Moriarty—complaining about all the crap in that ice. Because it's a stroid, not a Kuiper object. He says it's more junk than ice. Thing was, it seemed like he was happy anyway."

"Yes, Sean and his team enjoy a good technical challenge. So, today, eh? Very good. I plan to be up top to watch it, if they let me."

He frowned. If they *let* her? "Why wouldn't they?"

She paused, and seemed to search for words. "The warehouse disaster happened on my watch. Parliament needs to satisfy themselves that I did everything I could to prevent it, and to recover with minimal loss."

"But . . . but it wasn't your fault! Everyone knew it."

"They're just doing their job."

"It was those bad-sammies last week, wasn't it? That was just bullshit. People were taking things out on you because they were scared. And now they're saying the whole thing was sabotage. That the Martian mob did it."

Everyone was talking about the fleet of ships the Ogilvie mob had launched to attack Earth. It was all over the news. They were now approaching Mars orbit at several gees' acceleration. Earth had threatened to blast them out of the sky and they were now insisting that their ships' controls had been hijacked. It seemed like just the sort of thing a bunch of mobsters would do: launch an attack and lie about it when caught.

"They must be batshit crazy," he said. "They are bad, bad people."

"Batshit crazy. I like that theory." She gave Geoff an amused, abstracted look, as if she knew something that she was not telling him. "They *are* bad people. And yes, it *was* sabotage. The district attorney has ample proof. I'm sure all will come out just fine."

They sat silent for a few moments, and watched the politicians gesturing and mumbling away.

After a moment, Geoff blurted, "I've moved out. So has my mom." She did not seem surprised. He went on, "Mom always told me you were as hard to read as a rock. But you don't seem like that today."

"That's funny. Xuan always said that, too."

Said? Geoff thought belatedly. *Not 'says'?* He had just seen the professor yesterday, out on the commuter pad getting ready to depart on another rock-hunting trip. A long one, from the looks of his supplies. But it would be rude to ask.

"I was furious when I lost my job," she said, "but it was time for me to move on. I just didn't know it till they pried my butt out of my seat for me."

"Is it true you're leaving Phocaea?"

"Perhaps someday. Not just yet. If I leave Phocaea, it'll be on my own terms. But I don't think they're quite as anxious to be rid of me as they were."

"Mom says everyone will be at a loss without you as resource chief."

"Nah. Aaron is good. I hope they give the job to him, and give him a chance to prove how capable he is. But it could be anybody, really, as long as it's not me!" She said this with a fierce joy.

He hesitated. "You hated your job?"

She looked surprised. "Oh, no, not at all. I loved a lot of things about it. I liked having the power to help people. I made a difference in people's lives." She leaned forward, despite the dusting of "Stroiders" mites. "Look at us, Geoff. We kept some really bad people from gaining control of Phocaea, you and I. We saved a lot of lives. I'll treasure that knowledge for the rest of my life.

"It's just . . ." she crossed her legs again, pondering. "When you harness yourself to a cause, all those hard choices you make, they take their toll. All the fighting. Working the system. You make compromises to get things done, you piss people off, you have to swallow a lot of anger. It wears you down. I'd been at it, doing resource management, for more than forty years. That's a long time to carry such a burden. Now I have no formal power, but I finally have the freedom to speak my mind. Even if they lock me up for it." She smiled a little smile. Then she gestured.

"And you. Look at you! Who would have believed you could do what you've done?" She gave him a smile. "BitManSinger wasn't the only feral sapient around these parts, was it?"

A pretty woman in a business suit and pigtails stuck her head in the door. "Three minutes, Geoff."

"Thanks." The word came out in a huff of air. He pulled up his notes inwave, but his heart thudded in his chest and his stomach had knotted up. He couldn't concentrate to read, so he sprang to his feet and paced.

"Sure is easier to be a big hero on your bike," he said, "than to stand in front of people and act like you know what you're talking about."

"Don't worry. You're the savior of Phocaea! Here." She went to the wall and pointed out the different people at the hearing: names, responsibilities, attitudes, an occasional dirty secret they certainly would not want him to know. "And none of those powerful, scary, important people sitting up there have to worry anymore that everyone is going to die in agony in two weeks' time. That's thanks to *you*." She pointed at Geoff. "They all owe you a big debt of gratitude. And they know it. Today, every single one of those people wants you to be their best buddy."

"OK," he said, and a reluctant smile came onto his face. "Thanks." Then the smile faded. "But I still feel so . . ." He pressed a fist to his belly. He felt empty. That feeling had receded, but it was still there. He said softly, "I'd give it all up to have Carl back."

"Of course you would." She paused, frowning.

"The pain doesn't go away. But it eases. Eventually. Just . . . you know, the old cliché. Give it time."

Geoff felt his cheeks heat up. He wiped at his eyes. They were both silent again. He thought about the other mobster people were talking about, the one that Mr. Mills had reported to. "What do you think is going to happen to Nathan Glease?"

"Oh, that's easy. The district attorney has filed multiple kidnapping, murder, and attempted murder charges against him. The woman he bribed, the one who tried to kill your friend Ian, has already spilled everything she knows. So have his lackeys. We have the Viridians' recordings and testimony from his attack there, as well as mine. It's ironclad. Thomas Harman and John Sinton will also go to prison, and the prime minister will make good use of this situation to extract major concessions from Upside-Down, too."

She sat back down and spread her arms along the back of the couch. "So I'd say you're off to a pretty damn good start, for a tagalong little brother who couldn't play the drums worth a damn." He barked out a surprised laugh.

"Give them hell for me," she said, as the aides entered, and gave him a casual wave good-bye.

Geoff's testimony was not the traumatic experience he expected. Jane had been right—all the politicians went easy on him. It still seemed to take forever for them to wrap up and let the witnesses leave, but finally Minister Reinforte banged his gavel and the session was adjourned for lunch. Geoff called old Moriarty the minute the session wrapped up, as he'd promised. "I'm on my way up top," he said. "Will you let everyone know?"

"We're all in position, kid," Moriarty said. "We're just waiting on the star of the event."

"I'll hurry." As Geoff stepped down from his place on the witness stand, amid the bright lights and hubbub, the glamour and mites, and the noise, he glanced at his heads-up. It was 10:57 a.m. Maybe she would still be there.

When it came to Vivian, he didn't know exactly what he wanted, but he did know one thing: he *was* afraid of failure.

The passengers headed for *Sisyphus* were in a roped-off section away from the usual lines. The lift assigned to them, a big freight one, was due to arrive in a few minutes. Geoff spotted Vivian and tethered his way swiftly across the open space to her. Some people complained and hit him with bad-sammies—the crowd control guards protested—but when they recognized him, merely asked for his autograph and then let him through.

She floated there. "Hi," she said. "I'm glad you came."

He looked down at her pregnant belly, in stunned embarrassment. Her gaze followed his. She shrugged. "It's not what it seems."

Geoff blinked. "You don't have someone, then?"

"No."

It was some weird Viridian thing, then? *What am I getting myself into?* he thought for the hundredth time. "OK . . ." His heart pounded so hard he couldn't form words. He had a million questions—he knew so little about her. "I want some time with you before you go. Can you stay? Just for a while, maybe take a later flight?"

"No, I have to leave. Places to go. Et cetera. Here is my contact information, back on the moon." They twitched their fingers in mirror format, and traded digits. He was painfully conscious of her nearness, and on impulse, leaned forward to kiss her. She stopped him with a palm on his chest.

"I'm not what I seem."

"Oh, yes you are. You're a Viridian. You have some weird mutations that will totally freak me out, you're not exactly pregnant, and you're not really even, precisely, a woman."

"Not all the time, anyway," she said.

"Fair enough. But let's just go with the mood, OK?"

She burst out laughing—the first time he had ever heard her laugh—wrapped her arms around him, and they kissed. And it tasted so sweet he never wanted to stop.

Then the lift came, and the crowd pushed her along till she boarded. Geoff stood at the edge and watched her leave. He waved good-bye, knowing he'd find her again.

Then he headed up in one of the passenger lifts. Everybody ushered him to the front of the line, and cheered him as he passed. His good-sammy cache had long since filled up so full it couldn't hold any more, and green pulsed across the edges of his sight. He hadn't known there was an upper limit. Everyone in the lift wanted to ask him questions and get his autograph. He sighed in relief when the doors opened at the surface. He lofted himself out of the lift station and onto the launch pad.

Amaya, Kam, and to his surprise, even Ian were waiting for him there, outside the rocketbike hangar, along with the rest of the rocket-biker teams. An enormous crowd was gathering on the shores of the crater—pouring out of the lifts; shuffling for space on the pad near the warehouses; lining the crater lip. People were handing out tethers—this ice delivery was going to be a doozy and they didn't want anyone getting thrown off-stroid.

Ouroboros was going to obliterate their Great Lake. It was going to change the very shape of Phocaea.

"Are you sure you're up for this?" he asked Ian, eyeing his friend. Ian's right sleeve was duct-taped to his suit.

"Hell, yes, doof. I wasn't about to miss out on this one. Besides. I can outride you with one arm tied behind my back."

Kam made a rude noise. "Funny."

"Your *chinpo* is showing," Amaya told Ian. He pretended to look for an unsealed seam at the crotch of his pressure suit as she swung her leg over her bike. Her visor gleamed.

Geoff looked up. Ouroboros loomed. It was more massive than any ice they had ever seen. Tiny blue Earth disappeared beneath its belly as it sank.

"I sure hope they got the calculations right," Ian said. "Otherwise Phocaea is toast."

"Relax. The old man checked them a zillion times. So did everyone else on the entire stroid." Geoff switched over to the rest of the bikers. "Listen up, everyone. We've got permission to launch the instant the stroid touches down. I'm beaming the team leads the vectors. You all ready?"

The other biker team leads each gave him an affirmative.

"Stand by," Sean said in his ear. "We don't want you all going up till after it touches down."

He gave the old man an OK sign. Next to him stood Commissioner Jane. Geoff was glad she'd made it up for this.

Ouroboros blotted out the sun. The tugs strained; the positioning rockets blasted; the giant rock crept down. Radio chatter died. Geoff watched, frightened and exhilarated. He couldn't help but think of Carl. Far off in the distance, at the horizon, Ouroboros and 25 Phocaea touched, and a clamor of voices swelled in his headset. The ground underfoot shook. The tug pilots had done it again, with their uncanny precision.

Geoff revved his engine and with Amaya, Kam, and Ian, led the bikers toward the base of the ramps.

This wasn't the best ice harvest ever. That would never be true again, without Carl here to watch with him. But an ice shipment this big, coming now? It would surely do. He led the way up the bucking and twisting ramp, accelerated, and soared into the Big Empty amid rising ice and stone ejecta—followed by a hundred rocketbikers and their nets and the renewed hopes of his people.

ACKNOWLEDGMENTS

I owe a debt of gratitude to many who helped me improve this book.

THE CONSULTANTS. Several people shared their time, advice, and expertise. For help with astrophysics and computing, thanks go to Chris Crawford, Steven Gould, Jerry Weinberg, and Rusty Allen. Dr. Gwen Lattimore helped me get the medical details right, and helped me with key elements of the miniature technology. David Porterfield gave me assistance with the business and technology of mining (and let me fire his *awesome spud launcher!*). Nalo Hopkinson, Melinda Snodgrass, and Walter Jon Williams gave me good tips on Upsider society and life.

THE CRITIQUERS. Those who read portions of this as a work-in-progress gave me the incisive, high-rez feedback I needed to pummel the story into shape: Holly Deuel Gilster, Steven Gould, Jane Lindskold, George R. R. Martin, and Pati Nagle, along with all the wise and thoughtful members of PlotBusters and Critical Mass.

SAFE HAVEN. A two-week spring writing retreat in Tucson saw me through a sticky patch. Ellen Kushner, Delia Sherman, and Terri

Windling made an exquisite, private desert setting available to me, and Emma Bull and Will Shetterly were stalwart hosts and marvelous dinner companions.

HERE A NOD, THERE A NOD. Chris Crawford's Solvesol-interface concept was the basis of my Tonal_Z, Cory Doctorow's *whuffie* strongly influenced my sammies, and Bruce Sterling let me hijack the Viridians for my own nefarious ends.

LAST BUT NOT LEAST. I owe deep thanks to my editor, Patrick Nielsen Hayden, and to my agent, Matt Bialer. Your steady belief in me helped me keep faith with myself.

These people all supported me in my aims, but in the end it was I who decided what to put in and what to leave out. Any infelicities, sins, or errors you encounter belong to me alone.